Bridle Path
Press

THE GREEN REMAINS

Best wishes to
Case County Public Library

Marni Graff
28th May 2014

M. K. Graff

Bridle Path Press, LLC
8419 Stevenson Road
Baltimore, MD 21208

www.bridlepathpress.com

Direct orders to the above address.

Printed in the United States of America.
First edition.
ISBN 978-0-9852331-0-5

Library of Congress Control Number: 2012936162

Illustrations and design by Giordana Segneri.

Cover photographs © Kurt Drubbel/istockphoto.com and
© xyno6/istockphoto.com.

Bridle Path
Press

FOR SEAN

Friday's child is loving and giving ...

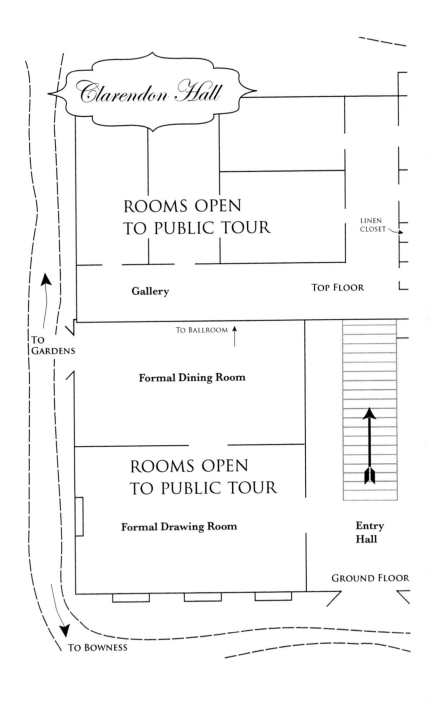

Clarendon Hall

ROOMS OPEN
TO PUBLIC TOUR

LINEN
CLOSET

Gallery

TOP FLOOR

TO
GARDENS

TO BALLROOM

Formal Dining Room

ROOMS OPEN
TO PUBLIC TOUR

Formal Drawing Room

Entry
Hall

GROUND FLOOR

TO BOWNESS

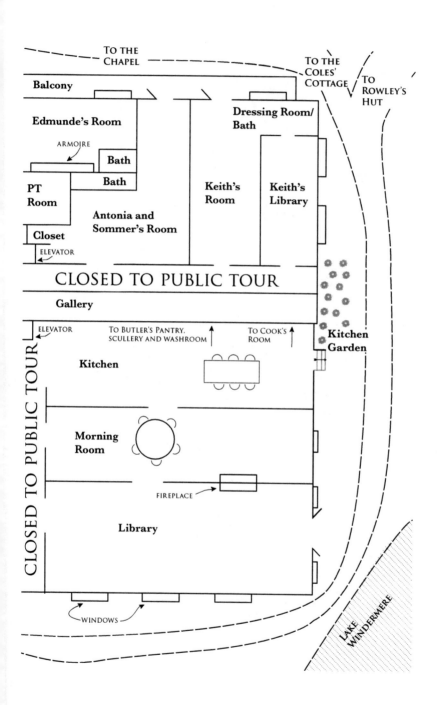

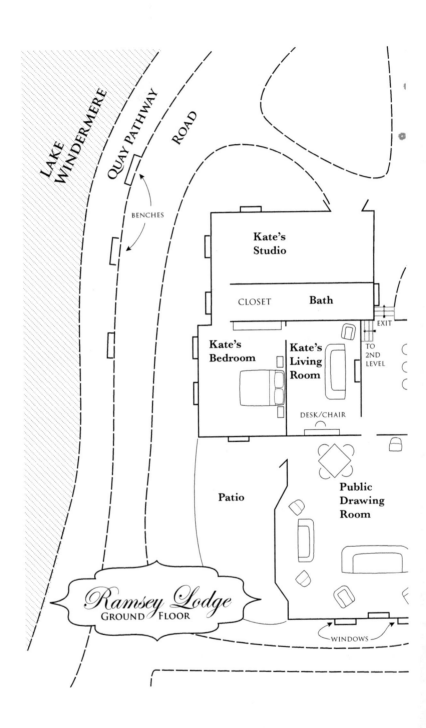

LAKE WINDERMERE

QUAY PATHWAY

ROAD

BENCHES

Kate's Studio

CLOSET   Bath

EXIT

Kate's Bedroom

Kate's Living Room

TO 2ND LEVEL

DESK/CHAIR

Patio

Public Drawing Room

Ramsey Lodge
GROUND FLOOR

WINDOWS

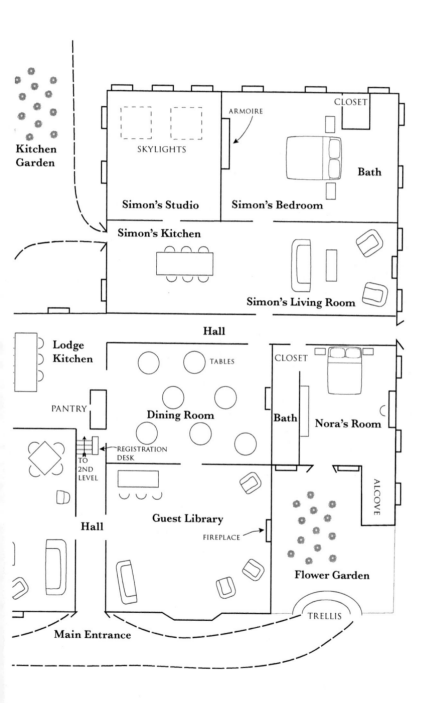

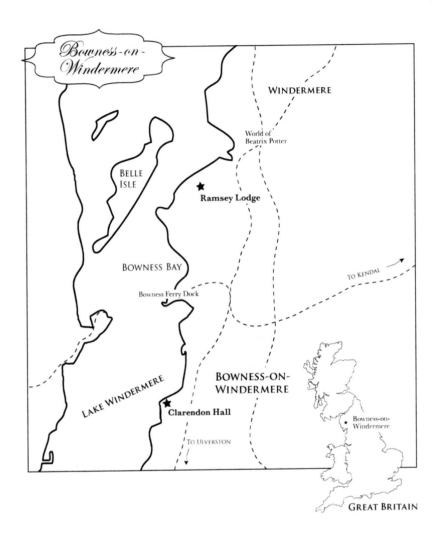

Bowness-on-Windermere

WINDERMERE

BELLE ISLE

World of Beatrix Potter

★ Ramsey Lodge

BOWNESS BAY

Bowness Ferry Dock

TO KENDAL

LAKE WINDERMERE

BOWNESS-ON-WINDERMERE

★ Clarendon Hall

TO ULVERSTON

Bowness-on-Windermere

GREAT BRITAIN

CAST OF CHARACTERS

in order of appearance

NORA TIERNEY — American writer

AGNES — cook at Ramsey Lodge

KATE RAMSEY — co-owner, Ramsey Lodge

SIMON RAMSEY — Kate's artist brother and co-owner, Ramsey Lodge; illustrator of Nora's children's books

VAL ROGAN — textile artist; Nora's best friend in Oxford

DETECTIVE INSPECTOR DECLAN BARNES — Senior Investigation Officer in Oxford, Thames Valley Police Criminal Investigation Department

KEITH CLARENDON — agent at Worth's Travel Agency; heir to the Clarendon estate

CLIVE JENKINS — Nora's former boss at *People and Places* magazine

DANIEL ROWLEY — handyman at Ramsey Lodge and at Clarendon Hall

DETECTIVE INSPECTOR IAN TRAVERS — Cumbria Constabulary Criminal Investigation Department; Kate's fiancé

DR. MILO FOREMAN —pathologist

COOK — Elsie Ewart, cook at Clarendon Hall

SOMMER CLARENDON — younger Clarendon brother; Keith's father

ANTONIA CLARENDON — Sommer's wife; Keith's mother

DETECTIVE CHIEF INSPECTOR WILLIAM CLARKE —
Cumbria Constabulary Criminal Investigation Department;
Ian's superior

ANNE REED — missing eighteen-year-old from Windermere

GILLIAN COLE — nurse at Clarendon Hall

DOC LATTIMORE — Bowness and Windermere general
practitioner

EDMUNDE CLARENDON — older Clarendon brother

MAEVE ADDAMS — assistant manager at Ramsey Lodge

JULIA BROOKES CLARENDON — Edmunde's deceased wife

TONY WARNER — writer for *People and Places* magazine;
Nora's former colleague

GLENN HACKNEY — Keith's colleague at Worth's Travel Agency

JACK HALSEY — Daniel Rowley's friend and drinking buddy

EDGAR WORTH — owner, Worth's Travel Agency

ROBBIE COLE — Gillian's son

DETECTIVE SERGEANT STEPHEN HIGGINS — Cumbria
Constabulary Criminal Investigation Department; on
Ian's team

JODIE HALSEY — Jack's daughter-in-law

ANDREW HALSEY JR. — Jack's grandson; Jodie's son

SALLY KINCAID — Agnes' substitute at Ramsey Lodge

BASIL NORTHRUP — local vicar serving Clarendon Chapel

THE GREEN REMAINS

"A mother's love for her child is like nothing else in the world. It knows no law, no pity, it dares all things and crushes down remorselessly all that stands in its path."
— Agatha Christie

CHAPTER ONE

*"... The lowest and vilest alleys in London do not present a
more dreadful record of sin than does the smiling and
beautiful countryside."*
— Sir Arthur Conan Doyle,
The Adventure of the Copper Beeches

Friday, 22nd October

8 AM

The vicar carefully cradled the infant in his left arm over the
open baptismal font, the child's long, ivory dress trailing down
the front of the priest's bright white cassock. He dipped the fingers of his right hand into the holy water, making the sign of the
cross on the sleeping child's head. "I baptize thee Ferdinand ... "

From her place at the front of the old church, Nora Tierney
broke into a cold sweat and opened her mouth to protest: "Not
the bull!" she tried to cry, but the words stuck in her throat.

The snick of the opening door roused Nora from her dream.
It was followed by a tiny chink as her tea was set down on the
nightstand. She heard the stealthy footsteps of Agnes leaving
and a second snick as the door shut behind her. Nora kept her
eyes closed, waiting for the scent of the tea to reach her and calm
her down from the dream that was not quite a nightmare.

Bergamot: her favorite today, Earl Grey. Thank goodness
Ferdinand was just a dream. She might write children's books,
and she certainly enjoyed the story about the young bull who
would rather smell flowers than be in a bullfight, but she'd never
choose that name for her son. This business about choosing her
baby's name was really taking its toll.

Nora sat up in bed and reached for her cup. As her pregnancy advanced, it was Agnes, Ramsey Lodge's cook, who had taken to bringing her tea each morning.

"You need a bit of a lie-in whilst you can; when that bairn gets born, you'll not be sleeping much, trust me on that," Agnes insisted in her soft Scottish burr. With her own son in Canada, Agnes was happy to fuss over Ramsey Lodge's American resident.

Nora stretched luxuriously in her four-poster bed and immediately felt the strong kick of her son as he woke, too. She placed a hand on her bulging side to feel the healthy thrust—surely a rugby player in there. It was a source of constant fascination for her that in mere weeks her child would be lying beside her in a cot, as cribs were called in England, instead of still inside her. She skipped over the part where he actually made his appearance, preferring not to raise her anxiety by dwelling on labor and delivery, or on facing parenting alone. That decision had been made. She'd become an expert at compartmentalizing and would face things as they occurred.

She planned her day as soft autumn light fell over her quilt. After a quick shower and breakfast, she would take her daily walk, then visit St. Martin's Church in Bowness-on-Windermere while her energy level was at its highest. She wanted to tour the historic church thoroughly, with an eye to gaining inspiration for the story line in one of her upcoming books. Nora imagined her troupe of fairies visiting the historic church. She could picture Cosmo, her cantankerous elf, falling into one of the organ's pipes. While she soaked up the atmosphere, she would photograph the ornately carved memorial plaques, set into the church walls that boasted flowery eighteenth- and nineteenth-century language. Her young readers would learn a bit of history while they read about the Belle Isle Fairies' latest escapade.

Nora sipped her tea, appreciative of how her adopted family took care of her. Only last night, Kate and Simon Ramsey had completed taking birthing classes with her. The siblings, alike in many ways but with distinct personalities, had gathered her up when Nora decided last March to keep this baby and raise it alone. They'd convinced her to move into Ramsey Lodge for at least a year. It made sense after she and Simon had signed a contract for a three-book deal. He'd charmingly illustrated the first, and they could continue their collaboration on the next two with ease. Besides, after taking a leave from her job to work for a few months with Simon, she'd grown genuinely fond of him and of his sister, Kate. In August, she formally resigned her Oxford job as a magazine editor, packed up her flat and moved to Bowness-on-Windermere, a bustling Cumbrian village on the shore of England's largest lake.

The truth was, she'd been glad to leave Oxford. After her decision to move to Cumbria, her last days there packing up had been fraught with anxiety and tension, as she found herself involved in a murder investigation. Her nosiness had caused a close brush with the murderer, but all had turned out well; she'd helped prove her best friend, Val Rogan, innocent of the murder of Val's lover, Bryn Wallace.

She'd also met Declan Barnes, the senior investigating officer on the case, who'd grudgingly come to appreciate her inquisitiveness after a rocky start. He remained in Oxford but was still in her thoughts; would he be a larger part of her life if she'd not left that city behind?

Nora shook off the tangled memories and reached for her glasses and the book of baby names she kept on her pine nightstand. Over the summer, she'd learned the sex of her child, making the female half of the book superfluous. The remaining pages were dog-eared, with notes in the margin. She wanted a name that would allow her son to fit in with their life in the United Kingdom but that wouldn't ignore his American roots. Her choice would saddle her boy for the rest of his life, as she'd realized when she read Alexander McCall Smith's series on the inhabitants of 44 Scotland Street. One vegan father had named his son Tofu, and Nora shuddered at the thought.

She flipped pages. Names from Shakespeare. Now this might do the trick. Casting her eye down the list, Nora discounted the antiquated names she would never choose, like Antigonus or Polonius. She read aloud, trying a few names on for their sound: Aaron, Abraham, Arthur, Bernardo ... " She flipped a few pages: "Malcolm, Oswald, Paris, Snuff—*Snuff*?"

Maybe not Shakespeare after all.

8:30 AM

It was Simon's turn to staff the front desk, leaving Nora to breakfast with Kate in the lodge's sunny dining room. Many of the guests ate and left for their activities as the two women finished eating. Nora put her fork down and sat back with a happy sigh.

"That should hold the two of us until lunch. This eating for two will be tough to stop once he's born," Nora said. "I'm so short I feel I'm beginning to waddle like a duck, one of my mother's favorite sayings." She ran her hand over her huge belly.

"Nonsense," Kate admonished. "You're carrying very well, no waddles in sight. But I've enjoyed watching your waistline expand all the same," she added with a grin.

"Says she of the tall, lean body," Nora said. She leaned over and placed her hand for a moment on top of Kate's, pleased they'd become close in the past months.

Kate squeezed Nora's hand. "We both enjoy having you around, and Agnes is beside herself with a baby on the way. Just think this all started because you won that contest Keith Clarendon drummed up."

"And because Simon agreed to take part—taking on an unknown writer can't have been an easy decision."

Kate shrugged. "He loves his landscape and portrait work, but he's always said he'd enjoy doing watercolor illustrations—so you see, you're really wish fulfillment for him. Probably in more ways than one, even if the two of you are in different places on a personal level."

Nora thought Kate's phrasing showed she was one of the fairest people Nora had ever known. She saw Kate glance at her brother, talking with a guest in the doorway. With his sandy hair and slight frame, he was a fairer version of his sister. "I just wish I could give him the commitment he wants from me, Kate." Simon's affection for her was heartwarming, and she didn't want to feel she was taking advantage of him. "It's just with this baby on the way, and after Paul's death—"

It was Kate's turn to pat Nora's hand. "Hush—I didn't mean to upset you. Of course you're in no position to make long-term plans right now. On some level, he knows that. Look, you never did tell me the story of how you found out you'd won the contest."

Nora gratefully let her change the subject. "I got a telegram at work from Worth's Travel Agency telling me to expect an important meeting the next afternoon. I lay awake half the night thinking I'd won the essay contest yet doubting it at the same time."

"So you weren't sure you'd won?"

"No, and Paul was locked away as usual in his lab. Our relationship was already on the rocks, and it was just a matter of time before one of us broke the engagement. By morning, I'd decided some bloody wanker was coming to give me a consolation prize of free bus passes for a month."

Kate laughed. "What happened the next day?"

"I was in my office when I heard this bustle from the reception area." Nora recalled the buzz on the intercom calling her to the lobby. She remembered her heels tapping smartly on the wood floor. "I expected to meet a pimply-faced young man who would give me a sheaf of coupons. Instead, I walked into a circle of camera flashes and noisy reporters. It must have been a slow news week. My jaw dropped when my boss, Mr. Jenkins, hurried over to introduce me to this very nice-looking young man with curly, dark hair. Keith was the ultimate marketer. He was wearing a well-cut suit and shiny leather brogues and was talking animatedly to one of the newsmen." Nora described the scent of Keith's cologne filling the air and the ensuing scene:

" ... That's spelled C-L-A-R-E-N-D-O-N." Keith turned to shake Nora's hand with a broad smile, hushing the crowd with his other.

"Who are all these people?" Nora hissed to Jenkins under her breath.

"Came in with the Clarendon lad," he whispered. "Be polite."

Keith extracted a glossy envelope from his suit pocket. "Miss Nora Tierney, it gives me great pleasure to present you with this prize package from the Worth Travel Agency. The grand prize for the essay describing an illustrated children's book includes working with famed Cumbrian artist Simon Ramsey during a three-week stay at Ramsey Lodge in the Lake District, right on the shore of Lake Windermere, the land of Wordsworth, Coleridge and Potter ... "

Kate laughed out loud. "I can see Keith droning on like that. He and Simon had huge disagreements about Keith's development scheme at town meetings. Our calm and patient Simon can get quite red in the face and even shout if he's worked up enough."

Nora raised an eyebrow. "I've never seen him like that."

Kate passed it off with a wave of her hand. "Tell me what happened when it sank in you'd really won."

Nora poured more tea into her mug. "Old Jenks presented me with an obnoxiously huge bouquet of flowers he'd had one of our writers, Tony Warner, run and buy when Keith appeared with his entourage. That didn't endear me to Tony, who abhorred me already for editing him, I might add." She pushed her plate away and moved her mug closer. "I thought Keith a little full of himself, but he was so earnest, with this idea of making Bowness an even bigger tourist area, if that's possible. I doubted right away his expensive tailoring had come from his salary at Worth's—he wore those clothes with the air of someone used to quality. At my congratulatory dinner that night, he explained he is the only child of the wealthy Clarendons. I'd never heard of them before, but I acted appropriately impressed."

"Oh, yes," Kate agreed. "The Clarendons have been a force in the village for centuries. We'll take a tour of Clarendon Hall one of these days."

"I'd like that," Nora said, picturing another site for her fairies to sully. "Keith seems a bit obsessed with his family name, but there's no doubt he feels strong ties to this land. He told me he's researching a book about the history of the family and their contributions to this area. I think he sees his name being added to that list in future books. I might like to use some of that research, and he said he would share, but I haven't taken him up on that yet."

"I had no idea he was writing a book," Kate said.

"It's one of the reasons he engineered the contest at Worth's. He sees it as the first step in promoting this edge of the lake as a creative hub for visiting artists, writers and photographers."

"*That's* the part Simon objects to," Kate said. "Keith envisions Bowness enticing wealthy visitors who are drawn to artsy areas. He assumes that with Simon as a center of attention, my brother should embrace the idea."

"Simon would hate that," Nora stated bluntly. "Maybe it's a good thing I haven't visited Keith yet. I wouldn't want to upset Simon. I didn't realize there was tension between them."

"Yes, and it doesn't help that I think Keith's idea would be good for lodge business." Kate looked at her watch. "Goodness, I've got to see what's left in the garden for dinner."

Nora pushed her chair back and stood. "And I've got a walk to take."

A few minutes later, long auburn hair clipped away from her face, Nora wound her way through the dining room, nodding to the waitresses readying the room for dinner. The lodge served breakfast to its customers daily, dinners to the public Thursday through Saturday and a Sunday brunch. The small staff bustled with efficiency under the watchful eye of Agnes and the Ramseys.

Nora looked for Darby, the siblings' Lakeland Terrier, who usually pranced up to join her on her walks. He must be in the kitchen, begging Agnes for scraps. Nora slipped out through the heavy lodge door and strode down the flagstone walk as briskly as her advanced pregnancy would allow. Crossing the road to the path that wound along the eastern shore of Lake Windermere, she rubbed her lower back. The ten-and-a-half mile lake stretched out to the north and south horizons, and the impossibly blue sky was filled with downy, white clouds. Directly across the lake, on the western shore, she could see peaks of stone houses breaking through the trees, often boasting elaborate matching boathouses or gazebos at the end of their docks. The trees lining the fell were lit with autumn colors of gold and reds; higher up, the firs remained green. Clusters of boats swayed at docks along both sides of the shore, accompanied by noisy personal watercrafts and quieter windsurfers. Lines of brightly colored canoes, kayaks and sculls waited to skim over the clear water.

Overhead, a squawking flock of Greylag geese broke the quiet. Nora recognized them from a guidebook that she'd almost memorized over the last few months. The geese whirled overhead. Nora had seen them bathing and roosting in the area's tarns and lakes. It had been windy last night, and now she wondered where they went in poor weather. Farther up the shore, the huge, white steamship *Swan* stood tethered to its dock, too early for the crew or for the strings of tourists who eventually would cram on board. Nora decided she would ask if Kate would take the cruise with her later this week, as the boat passed Belle Isle on its way up and back to Waterhead. That island in the middle of the lake was home to her imagined fairy family, and seeing it again from all sides would be stimulating and help in her story planning.

Across the road, the back door to Ramsey Lodge opened, and Nora slowed her steps. Darby darted out followed by Kate, with a basket slung over one willowy arm. Simon followed, and the siblings made their way down the remaining rows of their extensive vegetable garden, stopping at times to confer, making selections of squash and late greens that would appear on tonight's menu. Nora admired their energy and determination to keep the lodge running after their parents' deaths. Kate had been a set designer in London and now enjoyed decorating the lodge rooms according to different themes. She refinished most of the furniture and gathered objects that fit each room's motif. Simon continued painting in the studio in his part of the lodge. An Oxford gallery was the lucky recipient of most of his landscapes and portraits. Now, Nora thought, he had the additional pleasure of illustrating her books. Life had a way of presenting change when you least expected it, but these two seemed to roll with the punches. Resilient, she decided.

Nora turned back to the water and continued her walk, swinging her arms to loosen up. Kate had recently become engaged to a local detective, and Nora was excited for her friend. Simon, she knew, would be overjoyed if Nora would be willing to pledge herself to him in the same way. His affection stirred feelings that Nora found comforting at times and overwhelming at others. He was so creative and patient, very kind and understanding. Sometimes his perfection grated on her. She didn't understand her convoluted feelings toward him and wasn't ready to explore them.

Nora heard Kate's raised voice and looked back to see Simon playfully throw a carrot at her before returning to the lodge. Lately, Nora had sensed friction between the siblings—not open confrontation but more of a dissonance. Kate was in favor of expanding the lodge, but Simon feared expansion wouldn't allow time for his art. Just last night at dinner he'd pronounced: "I think you're going to see that all of these changes won't be necessary."

Nora wasn't on either side—she didn't have experience in their kind of business. As an only child, she'd often wished for the kind of companionship and understanding she thought a brother or sister would have provided, the comfortable relationship Kate and Simon usually enjoyed. She was confident they would work through this hitch. People can't agree on everything.

Nora drew in great gulps of fresh air—deep, cleansing breaths to expand her lungs. Her baby waved inside her, kicking during his own morning calisthenics. As she rounded the corner of Bowness Bay, her gaze flitted across the shallow water along the pebbly shore. Simon had explained that the lake dropped to well more than two hundred feet at its center, but here the water was clear, and Nora searched for small fish among the waving grasses at its edge. A few yards ahead, the tip of an overturned green scull caught her attention; it was wobbling up and down at the stony shore, disturbing its neatness.

As she came abreast of the scull, the next slopping wave nudged it higher onto the pebbly shingle. Without pausing, Nora left the path and reached out to pull on the scull's tip to keep it on shore. Someone would be looking for it later today. She was surprised when it barely budged, and she heaved harder, throwing her small frame into the effort. It must be filled with sand and water, she thought, and tugged harder. There was a sucking sound, and suddenly the scull slid up the bank, knocking Nora off balance and onto her knees on the damp sand. She was abruptly opposite the swollen, glassy-eyed face of a very dead man, partially covered in muck. He lay curled on his side, half-hidden by the scull. There was a greenish cast to his skin, mottled with gouges and missing pieces of flesh. His swollen, purple lips grinned grotesquely at her; one eye socket was empty. The distorted features shifted with the next wave.

Nora's stomach roiled, and her breakfast threatened to come back up. She sucked in air and gasped. Then she heard her own screams echoing across the water as she realized the dead man was someone she knew.

CHAPTER TWO

*"But surely the study of fingerprints and footprints, cigarette ash,
different kinds of mud and other clues that comprise the minute
observations of details—all these are of vital importance?"*
— Agatha Christie, *Murder on the Links*

9:20 AM

From his porch across the curve of Bowness Bay, hidden by a
stand of juniper bushes, Daniel Rowley watched the commotion
as a crowd gathered near a pregnant girl. She waddled like a
duck, and her screams had woken him far too soon.

He had reluctantly opened his eyes, then had felt the pressure
on his bladder and had swung his thick legs over the cot's edge
to land with a heavy thump on the bare wooden floor. There
was a chill in the room this morning, and he knew he must
have fallen into bed again without banking up the fire. A glance
down at his still-clothed body had confirmed this. He'd wiped
his grimy hands across his face and had staggered to the toilet,
ignoring the dull headache he'd come to expect.

The screams had stopped, and after splashing cold water on
his face, Daniel had toweled off with a corner of the torn bath-
robe he'd thrown over the bathroom door. He'd crept to the
rickety porch, careful to stay out of sight.

A police siren announced official business. A police car skid-
ded to a stop near the footpath. Thankfully, the constable turned
off the siren before running over to the screamer—that American
writer, Daniel realized, who'd been staying at the lodge. She sat
huddled on a bench between Kate and Simon Ramsey. Simon had
his arm around her, and all three were speaking to the officer.

Simon stood and walked the officer over to an upturned green scull. The policeman knelt, then came quickly upright and ran at a brisk trot back to his vehicle, speaking into a radio clipped to his shoulder. Simon stood with his hands on his hips for a moment, then returned to the bench.

Daniel enjoyed the way the blue-white-red light bar on top of the panda car reflected off the water's surface. Too bad his pal Jack Halsey wasn't here to see it. They would raise a toast to the whirling lights. That Jack, he was ready to raise a toast to anything at all. It was one of the reasons they got on so well.

Daniel chose kindling from a stack on the porch. Inside, he lit the fire, then set up his kettle on the two-ring hot plate for a good cuppa. He sloshed water into a huge mug and dropped in the tea. When it had steeped to a point dark enough for him, he poured three overflowing tablespoons of honey into it and carried the sweet brew back to the porch.

In his absence, a second official car had arrived, its beam chasing that of the first car across the lake's surface. Making his tea, Daniel had also missed seeing the blue-and-white crime scene tape being spread over a portion of the footpath, blocking access from either end. Two constables now stood watch along the path.

The Ramseys and the pregnant woman had disappeared, but Daniel knew more cars would arrive, soon to be followed by the SOCOs—Scene of Crime Officers—who would look like giant insects scouring the scene in their lint-free suits. It was amazing what you could learn from television these days. Minutes later, a police van pulled up, and a photographer gathered his equipment from the back. The uproar attracted villagers and tourists, all kept at bay by the tape and the constables on guard.

Daniel sipped his tea, and the liquid burned its way down his raw throat. He glanced at the sun and knew he had time before he had to be at Clarendon Hall. He balanced his chipped mug carefully on the porch railing and, heading back inside, inspected his three chairs. He chose the one with the sturdiest legs and dragged it out from the cottage to the porch. Placing it in his vantage point behind the screen of bushes, he settled back to enjoy the show.

CHAPTER THREE

"All that we see or seem is but a dream within a dream."
—Edgar Allen Poe, "A Dream Within a Dream"

9:45 AM

Nora sat in stunned silence at the pine table in Simon's kitchen. She flashed on the memory of Bryn Wallace's death in Oxford and shivered. A death like this would set the wheels of an investigation into motion and would engulf her. She *would* have to be the person who had found the dead man—and not just any man, either.

By the sink, Kate tapped her foot impatiently. She'd called her fiancé, Detective Inspector Ian Travers, and was waiting for him to pick up the phone at the main police station in Kendal. Grabbing a fluffy, loomed shawl from a peg near the door, she draped it over Nora's shoulders.

Nora roused herself to thank Kate. The scent of strong black tea was helping her maintain her grasp on reality in a surreal situation. She stared into the depths of the mug, forcing her mind from dwelling on the atrocity at the water's edge. As though he sensed the tense mood, Darby kept quiet watch at Nora's feet under the table. Her baby had waved an arm, so she felt reasonably confident the shock hadn't hurt the child.

"Ian, thank goodness. Something awful happened, and Nora"— Kate threw Nora a tense look as she listened. "Yes, she's right here with me. ... No, I won't. ... Nora and Simon both did. Ian, it's Keith Clarendon."

As they waited for Ian, Kate brought a mug of tea to the female police constable on duty outside the door, then poured her own and sat across from Nora.

"It's awful—all I can think of is our conversation at breakfast, and how enthusiastic Keith was about my winning the contest." Nora wrapped the shawl tighter around her shoulders.

"It *is* awful. Ian said you're to stay inside, away from the reporters milling around. Simon will keep them at bay," Kate explained.

"Thanks." Nora put her face in her hands. "I don't think I could handle reporters right now." She looked up with a wan smile. "It's odd because I used to be one and never realized how intrusive I might be." She shook her head, the reddish waves bouncing. Somewhere in the fuss her clip had come off, and long strands fell forward, partially covering her face.

"You have every right to be upset," Kate said. "Poor Keith. His family has already faced so much tragedy."

Kate didn't explain, and Nora was too upset to ask. She looked past the kitchen to the living area, with its cozy fireplace, at the far end of the large room. Two sets of French doors in the wall opposite her led to Simon's studio and to his bedroom suite. Her own suite was just across a wide hallway. Once it had belonged to the head housekeeper, who had lived at the lodge during the senior Ramseys' tenure. What had become a haven of comfort for her now appeared unfamiliar and strange.

She contemplated her cooling tea where she'd set it down. With her huge belly keeping her at a distance from the table, it felt like too much effort to lean that far over to sip it; she didn't think she had the strength in her hands to pick it up.

"I keep seeing Keith's face, at least what was left of it," she told Kate in a low voice. "I wonder if he committed suicide?

Why not try to get out of his scull, if it sprang a leak or started to sink? It doesn't make sense."

Kate shook her head. "I don't know, Nora. I hope Ian will sort it out quickly. He's very good at his job."

Nora sighed. "Now Keith will never finish his book. Instead he's out there, waiting for the coroner." A chill coursed through her body.

Kate looked up at the clock. "It's getting late. I have to talk to Agnes about the dinner menu. Do you mind staying here alone, or would you rather come with me?"

"No, you go ahead." Nora rested one hand lightly on her belly and remained rooted to the chair.

"Come on, Darby. Let's go see Agnes." The dog obediently followed Kate out through the pocket door.

The room was quiet. Nora could hear the clock tick. She couldn't hide any longer from the memories of the night her father drowned. She remembered how her mother's face, blotched and red from crying, had turned white when they'd been allowed into the emergency room cubicle to say goodbye. Then she recalled her father's body, cold and slack, his lively, hazel eyes dulled. Closing her own eyes, Nora willed the images back to the dark corner of her mind she rarely visited.

She couldn't sit there any longer; she carried her mug over to the sink, pouring out the cold tea. Eventually, she knew, the police would have to interview her. She looked out the window and saw the crowd that the flurry of activity had attracted, along with several news vans already parked along the road. At least they'd had the good grace to arrive after she was safely inside, and she wouldn't see her face on the evening news.

The constable at the door saw Nora standing by the window and brought in her own empty mug. She nodded toward the scene outside. "First thing of this kind we've had in the area in some time. How are you feeling?" She was a polite girl, with a neatly ironed uniform and hair carefully braided to stay out of her way during work.

"I don't know," Nora replied truthfully. "This feels like a dream, you know—so real it seems unreal."

The woman nodded thoughtfully as they watched the photographer packing up, then said, "I expect poor Keith would wish it were someone else's dream."

CHAPTER FOUR

*"'My dear Charles,' said the young man with the monocle, 'it doesn't
do for people, especially doctors, to go about "thinking" things. They
may get into frightful trouble.'"*
— Dorothy L. Sayers, *Unnatural Death*

10:20 AM

Detective Inspector Ian Travers from the Southern Base Command Unit unfolded his lanky frame from the car with practiced ease. He rambled over to Simon Ramsey, and the two men
shook hands.

"Nasty business, this," Ian said. "Not a nice way to start
your day."

Simon nodded. "Worse for Nora, finding him like that."

The two men approached a burly man standing by the scull,
jotting notes into a tiny leather notebook with his meaty left
hand. Ian was aware their movements were being watched by
a large gathering of onlookers and reporters, held back by the
police cordon.

Ian knew Dr. Milo Foreman would already have examined the
body *in situ* and dictated his initial findings into a voice recorder.
The medical examiner was known in town as a cheerful man who
enjoyed cooking and eating the results of his own efforts. His tiny
wife encouraged his exploits, daintily sampled his fare and then
cheerfully cleaned up after him. They ate out most weekends and
were regulars at Ramsey Lodge. Thankfully, the fat cigar Milo
favored did not make an appearance at the crime scene.

"What have we got, Milo?" Ian asked.

"You mean, what have *you* got, dear boy. I am only a vessel of knowledge for your labors, such as they might be. I interpret the body's clues, and it is *your* job to find the answers."

Milo liked his discourse, but Ian was inured to the pathologist's digressions. "Yes, but you always make my job so much easier." In reality, Milo was notoriously difficult to pin down on specifics until he'd completed his excruciatingly detailed postmortem.

The large man consulted his notebook. "You know it's the Clarendon boy, I presume?" At Ian's nod, he asked: "Parents informed?"

"The chief decided to visit them himself." Ian didn't envy his boss this part of the job.

"It's nice for them to hear it from someone they know, rather than the village pipeline." Milo turned a page. "To the job at hand. Cause of death, possible drowning, but not classic; can't say more until I get him on the table. Time of death? Hmm, maybe between 7 PM and 2 AM. Difficult to say as he's been in cold water. Can't say more—"

"Until you get him on the table, I know, Milo," Ian said. "When is that likely?"

"After the formal ID is done and I start my sauce, a nice Bolognese today. We don't have much on just now. Let's say I'll see you around 3 at the Westmorland, shall we?" Milo's eyes gleamed as though he was setting up a sherry party.

Here is a man who thoroughly enjoys his work, Ian thought not for the first time—and shuddered.

He and Simon left Milo and crossed the road to the lodge, dismissing the constable and using Simon's back door to enter the kitchen. They found Kate urging Nora to eat a piece of toast. Nora stopped with the toast in midair, halfway to her mouth, and slowly lowered the slice to her plate.

"You keep right on eating that, Missy," Simon instructed, sitting down next to her.

Kate rose to greet Ian. "Thank goodness you're here." He gave her a warm hug, and they sat down at the table. "Do you have any idea what happened to Keith?"

Ian saw Simon give Nora's shoulder a squeeze. She was pale, but she brushed the crumbs off her hand to shake Ian's, her green eyes studying him. Now that he was here in his official capacity, Ian could feel the tension in the room increase. He felt it in every investigation, and this would be no exception. It came with the job, but his copper's instincts told him this time the entire situation was going to be much worse.

"Not much to go on yet," he said. "I need to ask Nora a few questions. Perhaps you two should wait in another room while we talk."

"No, thank you, we're quite comfortable here." Simon draped his arm over the back of Nora's chair.

Ian hesitated and decided not to press the point. He brought out his notebook. "Nora, tell me exactly what happened this morning."

Nora described her walk, how she'd noticed the scull and pulled on it until she slid down next to it and found Keith's body.

Ian said, "And you pulled on it because … "

Nora shrugged. "Because it was there and it shouldn't have been."

"So in your months here you've become an expert on how the lakeside should be?" Ian asked with a smile. He was rewarded with a kick under the table from Kate.

Nora frowned. "There were no other sculls floating loose; all the other boats were neatly tied up. I thought I was saving it from floating away."

Ian nodded. "Okay, what happened then?" Beside him, Kate cleared her throat.

"I screamed when I recognized Keith," Nora replied, "and

then Simon and Kate were there. Simon called for help on his mobile, and Kate sat on the bench with me until the constable arrived. I've been waiting in here ever since." She tilted her head to one side. "Well, I did go into my room once to pee."

"And you'd known the deceased how long?" Ian asked.

Beside him, Kate snorted. "Honestly, Ian, stop being so damned officious. We all knew Keith, deceased or not, and you know that."

"Don't you and Simon have work to do?" Ian asked, giving Kate a studied look.

"Actually, Ian, I'm enjoying watching you play detective," Simon said.

Ian paused, then decided to let it go. He knew Simon doted on Nora; it was rational he'd be protective. He noticed her massage her temples. "Kate, could you get Nora some paracetamol?"

"I'm not surprised you have a headache, Nora," Kate said. She rose and threw Ian a warning look.

Ian heard her murmur "bloody ass" as she passed him. "Sorry, Nora, just doing my job. And I am sorry you had to find Keith like that."

Nora nodded. "I'm sorry you have to deal with this. You've known him so much longer than I have."

"I know Keith loved the lake," Ian said. "Almost every weekend, I'd see him in his scull at some point. His death will affect the entire community."

"What's the Clarendon family like?" Nora asked. "Keith told me he was researching their history for a book."

"I didn't know about any book," Ian said. "Clarendon Hall is that stone mansion farther down the shore, overlooking the lake. Both of his parents are still alive, but his father, Sommer, had a car accident around the time Keith was born. He's been an invalid ever since."

"That must be the tragedy Kate mentioned," Nora said. "Did he have any brothers or sisters?" she asked.

"Just an uncle, also an invalid. I guess the accident ended the possibility of more children."

"His mother must have had so much to deal with, taking care of his father and an infant," Nora speculated, cradling her belly.

Simon smiled at that. "I don't think caring for Sommer was ever a personal chore for Keith's mum. But Antonia's a nice lady—rather nervous, I might add." He stood up and stretched. "No, the Clarendons have enough of everything except good luck. I'll tell you their story later." He ran his hand through his hair, and Ian caught his eye. "Sorry about that remark before, Ian." He turned to Nora. "Ian's ready to throw me out of here, so I'll beat him to it and head for my studio. If he gets too rough, knock, and I'll rescue you."

CHAPTER FIVE

"Isabel lay on her bed in a fog of fatigue, too tired even to undress."
— May Sarton, *Faithful Are the Wounds*

II AM

Nora walked Ian to the kitchen door and watched him cross the road to speak to the constable guarding the scene. A shaft of sunlight highlighted his flaxen hair. His tone had been softer this time around, more like the Ian she'd come to know.

Kate had returned with her pills, then left immediately. After a few more questions, Ian had patted Nora on the back as he rose to leave, and Nora felt Kate's influence on him.

Agnes appeared in the doorway. "Give us a hug, hen." She smothered Nora to her ample breast, her clean lavender scent filling Nora's nose. Nora let herself sink into the embrace as close as her belly would allow. It felt good to be comforted. "I can't believe it. And you the one to find him like that." Agnes smoothed Nora's hair and kissed her brow.

"Thanks, Agnes. I'm fine, really. I still can't believe it was Keith."

Agnes clucked. "Kate's Ian will get it all sorted, just you watch."

When Agnes left, Nora glanced around the kitchen and cleared the table of her uneaten toast, wondering what she should do next. She approached Simon's studio door and had her hand raised to knock when she heard his voice and realized he was on the telephone.

" ... It won't be soon, but perhaps after the holidays I can get away ... " The sweet affection fell carelessly from his voice.

Embarrassed at overhearing his private conversation, Nora

quickly walked to her own room. She closed the door and leaned against it, pushing away a shred of guilt from eavesdropping. Who wouldn't? But whom was he hoping to visit in the spring? Months ago, when they were in Oxford, Simon had told her he loved her. Obviously, there was someone else to whom he had ties. She didn't know whether to be hurt or angry.

She sighed. She didn't have the right to either emotion. She was the one who kept Simon at arm's length after their one coupling earlier in the year, just before she'd found out she was pregnant. He maintained he was ready to help her parent her baby. He also insisted he understood her reticence to commit to a relationship, knowing she'd been engaged to the baby's father but on the verge of breaking it off when Paul had died in a plane accident.

Kicking her shoes off, Nora climbed up on the bed and sank back against the pillows, looking around the room that had become safe and familiar. On her right, a door led to a closet and her bathroom; opposite her bed, a set of French doors led to a private flower garden and flooded her room with natural light. Her desk was set up at the left side of the room, and the alcove beyond it, used by the housekeeper as a sitting room, would be the baby's nursery. At the back of her mind, neatly tucked away as a result of her usual survival mode, was the knowledge that living at Ramsey Lodge was a temporary matter.

What a jumbled mess she'd become. Her emotions careened and crashed into each other in spectacular disarray. Nora cradled her stomach and thought of how much she loved the child she carried but hadn't even met. She understood that Simon's willingness to be a part of the baby's life came from his love for her, but she questioned how much of that was real or was due to his romantic notions. At times, she thought she might kiss him or hug him spontaneously, but Declan Barnes' face would rear up, and she would back off. She seemed unable to forget the Oxford detective. But why was she thinking of any relationship except the one with her unborn baby? She felt huge, weighed down by a basketball she carried everywhere. Though everyone told her she was "carrying so well," Nora doubted she looked sexy to anyone. She certainly didn't feel sexy—just filled to the brim with emotions she couldn't sort.

Her thoughts turned to Keith's mother and father, who had just been told their only child was dead. She couldn't fathom what they must be feeling, and then she remembered Janet Wallace, Bryn's mother, who lost her daughter and was bravely soldiering on with her life, even as its very foundation had been destroyed.

Did she herself possess that kind of inner strength? Nora wondered. It was all very well to say you were going to be a good parent, but how did you know you would be one, despite the best intentions? You thought you'd done a decent job of it, as Janet Wallace had and as the Clarendons surely had, and then the life you had created was taken away from you in the space of a heartbeat. Sweat popped up on Nora's brow. It was a horrific and frightening thought. Would she ever relax again?

She couldn't keep her thoughts from circling back to Keith. How could she possibly be involved in another murder, if that's what this turned out to be? With a sigh, she sat back against the pillows. She'd not seen Bryn Wallace's body except posed in the mortuary. Keith's bloated, green face was right in front of her, no matter how hard she tried to forget it.

Nora shook herself and rolled on her side. Drawing up a quilt from the bottom of the bed, she covered herself and closed her eyes, focusing on her breathing. She'd never mastered meditating, but she knew breath control would relax her. Her last thought before she dropped off to nap was of her son, blissfully swimming in his watery cocoon, unaware that death had touched his mother yet again.

CHAPTER SIX

" ... Miss Winifred Grainger sat in the last of the lawn chairs
that had not yet been put away for the winter, holding in her
hand, which lay in the lap of her corduroy skirt, a
black-bordered announcement."
— Charles Jackson, *A Second-Hand Life*

11:10 AM

Cook checked the time on the large school clock that hung on the wall, just over the door to the butler's pantry, as she waited for the kettle to boil. The huge Aga stove never let her down, but today she'd been sluggish, and Cook was running ten minutes behind schedule for elevenses. Not that Sommer or Antonia Clarendon ever commented on such things. She was a regular part of their small family, preferring "Cook" to the usual address. It had the ring of a title to it, whereas "Mrs. Ewart" did not.

A knock at the kitchen door startled her just as she was taking the kettle off the hob, and she pushed it off center and left to answer the door. Her round face lit with a wide smile when she saw her visitor through the window and opened the door for him.

"Billy! What a nice surprise. Come in, come in." The large man wiped his feet carefully and entered her domain as she bustled toward the stove. Cook's chatter trailed away as she turned and saw the serious expression on her visitor's face. "I was just going to pour elevenses, and I can get us each a cup ... "

Detective Chief Inspector William Clarke didn't have many people in his life besides his wife who called him "Billy," but his mum and Cook were sisters. "I'm sorry, Aunt Elsie. I'm here on police business."

Cook's hand flew to her mouth. "Not your mum, Billy?" Her color drained, and he hastened to her side.

"No, no, Mum's fine, really. Sit down, Aunt Elsie." He helped her to one of the chairs lining the long table at one end of the kitchen. "It's about Keith. I didn't use the front door because of the tours, but it's really the Clarendons I've come to see."

"Oh, Billy, whatever's happened to the boy? I didn't see him this morning and thought he'd gone out early in that fast car of his—was he in an accident?"

DCI Clarke hesitated. "I really should talk to his parents first, but you're almost family to them, and it seems unfair to keep you hanging." He squeezed her hand. "I'm going to need you to be very strong for Miss Antonia, Auntie. Keith's dead."

Ten minutes later, the tea tray was loaded, and Cook had composed herself. With her nephew trailing behind, she pushed the teacart into the morning room. Sommer Clarendon sat in his motorized wheelchair next to the large window and perused the paper. His wife, Antonia, stood near the doorway in front of a glass étagère, rearranging a collection of Dresden porcelain figurines. The mail sat on a round table, where one place was left open for Sommer's wheelchair. It was a scene of quiet domesticity Cook knew would soon be ruined. Her breath caught a hitch she covered with a cough before she could sob.

"There you are, Cook, just as I was feeling thirsty. And William! How nice of you to drop in." Sommer seemed genuinely happy to see their visitor. "Come to visit your aunt? How's your mother faring?" The two men had served on more than one Southern Lakes community committee together.

"Quite well, Sommer. But I'm afraid I'm here on official business."

Antonia stepped to the table and sat down; Cook thought she was steeling herself. Sommer folded his newspaper. Cook held her breath as her nephew's eyes flicked between the two parents. She felt sorry for this part of his job; there was no good way to do it.

"I'm very sorry to tell you Keith drowned in the lake last night," he said. His pause allowed them to absorb his statement. Cook saw Antonia's astonishment.

"No! That's not possible." Antonia's hands flew to her mouth. "You must be mistaken."

"I'm sorry. I'm afraid there's no question it's Keith," the chief said.

Antonia stared at him a moment longer in the shocked silence. Then her chair scraped back, and she rushed from the room. A second later, her footsteps clattered up the main stairs.

Cook took out the hankie she'd stuffed in her apron pocket to stifle a fresh bout of tears. Sommer lost his color and looked away. She could see the muscles in his jaw working as he took in the news and fought his own tears.

"What happened?" Sommer finally asked.

Her nephew gave a succinct account of what was known at this point. Cook had to admire her nephew in his official capacity, composed even as they heard Antonia running back down the stairs. There were no more traces of the freckled lad he'd been. "I'm afraid someone will have to formally identify his body."

Sommer waved the thought away with a grimace and closed his eyes briefly. He hit the arms of his wheelchair in frustration. "I'll have Gillian drive me down shortly in the van. We need a little time—I have to be with Antonia first."

The chief nodded as Antonia burst into the room. "His bed's not been slept in."

Cook watched Antonia's eyes roam from face to face, not

wanting to accept the truth. The mother's face was white and her body trembled. Cook took Antonia's arm and led her to a chair at the table. "Let's sit, and I'll pour, shall I?" Her words felt thick in her throat.

Antonia woodenly allowed Cook to lead her to the table and push her into a chair, her eyes glazed over. Cook caught her nephew's eye and nodded, and he sat down next to Antonia in what he couldn't have known had been Keith's chair. Antonia flinched.

Sommer wheeled himself over to the place that was always left open for him. Cook poured tea for them all and left the cream and sugar on the table, trying not to cry openly, her heart hammering.

"Please sit down, Cook," Sommer said, gesturing to the last chair. He drew a ragged breath. "What happens now?" he asked the detective.

Before Clarke could answer, Antonia jerked upright and stood. "What happens now? Our lives are over, Sommer, that's what happens *now*." Cook rose, but before she could make her way around the table, Antonia had dashed to the set of glass shelves. Raising her arm, she swept it quickly across the shelves, one after another, sending her collection of Dresden figures to shatter noisily on the floor.

CHAPTER SEVEN

*"… now he was wide-awake in a world of cheerless realities,
persistent and inexorable."*
— H. G. Wells, *Brynhild*

2:15 PM

Ian settled his team on house-to-house enquiries of the residents of the cottages overlooking the portion of the lake where the scull had been found before he returned to the station house. He supervised the setup of the incident room at the Kendal Divisional Police Headquarters on Busher Walk, a fifteen-minute drive on the A591 from Bowness. He'd been notified that Sommer Clarendon had formally identified Keith's body. Looking at his watch, he saw he had a few minutes before he had to head for the postmortem.

He was reviewing reports at his desk when the call came from the Windermere station that a young girl had gone missing. Eighteen-year-old Anne Reed had not returned home Thursday evening after an outing with friends. Her physical description was faxed over, and he studied the page, committing her details to his short-term memory. "Brunette; 165 centimeters height; athletic, slim build; experienced hiker." Ian studied the color photograph. "Last seen wearing" would always remind him of Colin Dexter's Inspector Morse novel of that title, as he read through her specifics: jeans, Saucony trainers, a pricey teal anorak and a black suede backpack her anxious mother said she "refused to be parted from."

Additional information on the Windermere report indicated Anne was the eldest child of three; two younger siblings were fathered by a stepfather of five years with whom she seemed to get on. An excellent student, Anne was taking a gap year to decide on a major at college; she tutored and babysat for spending money and to save for her own car.

Anne Reed sounded like a nice kid. Ian hoped she hadn't decided to act out or run off, but he knew there was a great likelihood she would never be found. He sighed at the enormous pain the loss of a child must inflict, a terrible rent that could never heal, left to fester by the lack of knowledge of her whereabouts. But then he thought of the Clarendons and wasn't certain that knowing exactly what happened to Keith would help his parents with their grief. Ian stuffed the fax in a folder. One more child to worry about.

Ian worked hard and took great pride in being named a detective inspector, yet at times the inability to achieve a positive outcome haunted him. He remembered a case from the previous year, when a missing child had been found near a secluded tarn, dead from exposure to the elements. It had been difficult to reconcile that he could not always affect the outcome of a case, despite his team's best efforts. He remembered how shocked his older brother, Gordon, a successful realtor in Carlisle, had been when Ian had told the family he wanted to be a detective.

"What's it to be then, Ian? Deerstalker hat and pipe?" Gordon had roared with laughter. "And here I thought you just wanted to wear the plod uniform." Still, his parents had been puffed up when he made detective inspector, and Gordon's family had shown up for the celebration dinner. Ian knew his parents supported both their boys, but he also knew he would rise in their estimation when he produced a grandchild to match Gordie's twin girls.

Thinking of his nieces brought him full circle back to Kate and the children he hoped one day to have with her. He'd left

Ramsey Lodge without smoothing over her ruffled feathers, a situation he hoped to rectify shortly. He wouldn't let her annoyance get to him; he was doing the job he was paid to do, after all. But he also wouldn't let too much time go by without sorting things out with her—she was too important to him. When she calmed down, she might see she had overreacted and that this situation with Keith's death and Nora's involvement wasn't easy on him, either.

He looked down at the report on the missing Anne Reed, a new priority, as was Keith's death, an event that by its very nature would change his calm, well-ordered part of the world. Not just a life passing on from age or illness, but a young life, full of promise and unfulfilled ambition, and a member of the area's most prominent family to boot. He'd already checked the computers for any form Keith might have collected—nothing surfaced. A clean record, then. What else could his death be but an accident? Ian would be thorough in his investigation, as usual, but felt confident at this stage that nothing untoward was likely to surface.

Then why did he have this feeling of apprehension?

Ian shook his head. He really was getting ahead of himself; he didn't have enough information to answer his many questions. He jotted a list of interviews he would need his team to conduct, while part of his mind wondered how Kate was faring. She would learn that this job didn't allow for being pleasant to witnesses. Nor, most of the time, was his work fun—like now, when he had to attend Keith's postmortem.

3 PM

Milo's sauce was simmering nicely in a large Crock-Pot in his office when Ian arrived at the pathology department at Westmorland General Hospital in Kendal. The aroma of a rich, tomato-based pasta sauce with basil perfumed the anteroom, barely covering the thick scent of cigar smoke and autopsy room odors, as Ian made his way to the autopsy suite. He knew Milo would share his concoction with his colleagues, pouring rations into clean glass jars before taking his slow cooker home. Ian didn't know if he'd want to partake in a meal started anywhere near a pathology lab. He donned a paper suit and shoe protectors and entered the autopsy suite, where the other smells fell away and left him with the sharp scent of disinfectant overlaid with the cloying odors of death.

Keith Clarendon's body, with its greenish cast and purple mottling, lay waiting on the stainless steel table. Ian tried to distance himself emotionally from the man he'd known who had resembled this corpse. Milo started dictating into a microphone that hung from the ceiling before Ian got the menthol gel under his nose and snapped on a mask.

"The body is that of a well-developed, well-nourished Caucasian male, twenty-eight years of age."

Milo's assistant, a quiet man with incredibly small hands, snapped a tape measure open smartly and compared it to the markings that ran down the table's side. Milo consulted both marks and continued: "The body is 177.8 centimeters in length and weighs ... " Milo's voice droned on in the external examination.

It was the mask that bothered Ian most. He had never understood how doctors and nurses who worked in the operating theater could breathe their own stale, hot air, in and out, for hours at a time behind a paper wall. He didn't feel claustrophobic but was greatly relieved when he was able to drop the mask. Ian inhaled the menthol gel deeply. He was a firm believer in anything that helped to camouflage the repulsive, metallic scent of death.

The fluorescent glare of the overhead light obliterated shadows and left Keith's body a study in sharp, unnatural colors. Ian fixed his stance with his hands clasped behind his back and breathed shallowly. He had developed an art to active listening during autopsies: concentrating on Milo's receding hairline, he heard what the pathologist dictated without letting his gaze linger on the gaping body on the table. This allowed him to appear interested if Milo should look up. He knew the pathologist would draw his attention to anything pertinent, and he did when he opened the lungs.

"A dry drowning. See here?"

Ian nodded and glanced briefly at the bronchial tissue Milo held filleted for his inspection. He felt an expectation to contribute to the conversation. "Shouldn't there be water if he drowned?" His eyes drifted back to Milo's forehead as the man gave his assistant a piece of lung tissue to prepare slide samples.

"About fifteen percent of drownings are dry; no water in the lungs. You get a laryngeal spasm that closes the throat. This greenish skin is due to the blue-green algae he soaked in overnight, and those bites are from fish and other buggers that had a go at him, but see here—" Milo held out his right hand, and his assistant slapped a magnifying glass into it. Milo held up Keith's right hand for Ian's inspection.

Ian leaned in as Milo waved the glass around. "I would expect to see signs of a struggle if he'd truly drowned, broken nails or scratches from trying to get out of the scull if he'd capsized and tried to swim out from under it. But it's as if he just let the water do him in—there's nothing there at all, no effort on his part, and that's pointing me in another direction. There's extensive venous congestion on everything I've seen, and I expect to find dilated cardiac ventricles and myocardial hypoxia in the heart, a lack of oxygen to the cardiac tissue. I've seen this scenario before, in training." The man's eyes gleamed. "Have to run the toxicology, but I suspect sudden heart stoppage with respiratory arrest before the scull ever capsized, from an ingested agent—we'll rush the toxicology through to see what it might be. Let's take a look at the heart and then the stomach contents, shall we?"

Let's not, thought Ian, but he nodded solemnly instead.

Chapter Eight

"There is such a thing as hunger for more than food, and that
was the hunger I fed on."
— Robert Nathan, *Portrait of Jennie*

3:10 PM

Nora woke with a start. The afternoon light was casting shadows
from the arched trellis in the garden onto the floor. She was surprised she'd slept so long. She rolled on her side, pushed up to
get out of bed as gracefully as possible with her current bulk and
used the bathroom yet again. Pregnancy had pushed her navel
outward, and she wondered what her body would look like after
she delivered. At the very least, it would be nice to look down
and see her feet again. Nora splashed cold water on her face. After running a brush through her hair, she left her room.

The hall door to Simon's rooms was slid open, but the large
main room was empty, and his studio door was firmly closed.
Nora walked to his kitchen area, looking out the window over
the sink. Across the garden, blue-and-white police tape fluttered
in a light breeze. One panda car still stood at the edge of the
road. Most of the crowd had dispersed, although a few youths
hung around the perimeter in a cluster near the one remaining
news van, hoping to get their faces on the evening news. As
Nora watched, the van doors opened, and a man climbed out
and hoisted a video camera onto his shoulder.

There wasn't much left to see, but even as this thought crossed
her mind, the squad car door opened. Nora saw the constable
signal, pointing to the shore. There was a raucous squeal of air
brakes as a flat bed truck came into view and halted. The driver

jumped down, and Nora watched him spread a large, green tarp across the empty bed. Once the two men conferred, they pulled on gloves and headed down to the scull, where the officer attached a tag to one of its ribs. They carried it easily between them up the shore to the truck's bed, then wrapped the scull in the tarp and sealed it. The scull was secured to the flatbed using thick bungee cords, and a second tag was attached to the wrapped bundle. The constable signed the driver's clipboard, and the truck roared off.

It was strange being an observer to the scene. Nora turned away, the rumbling of the truck matched by her empty stomach. Simon's studio door remained closed. She wasn't about to eavesdrop twice in one day to determine if he was inside, so she wandered over to the fireplace at the opposite end of the room.

Nora scanned Simon's bookshelves on either side of the fireplace without absorbing any titles, trying to stop the pictures of Keith, alive and dead, in her brain. She gave the painting over the mantel a close inspection. It was a Carl Larsson print, with vivid colors of his Swedish homestead defining the pictured ornamented furniture. A blonde child with braids churned butter, while her younger sister tried to help. It spoke of domesticity and the comforts of childhood, and Nora felt a pang of hurt for her son, whose mother seemed to have Death sitting on her shoulder.

"Wonderful, isn't it?" Simon had crept up behind her, Darby by his side. "He's a big influence on my style."

Nora reached down to rub the terrier's ears. "My father used to say he wished modern writers could capture in a story as much as Larsson told in one picture," she said and casually moved away before Simon could put his hands on her shoulders.

"Agnes left some sandwiches, if you feel up to going over the proof," Simon said.

She watched him brush his sandy hair off his forehead in a familiar gesture as he said, "I'll get us milk."

"Sure," she said, sitting down at the table and watching him pour two glasses; he brought them over with a plate of sandwiches. Until today, she'd had a ravenous appetite and had carefully watched her weight. Now she hardly felt like eating, but she knew she had to keep nutrients coming for her growing baby. She picked up a sandwich and nibbled on it to keep Simon, the baby and her stomach quiet.

They sat across from each other and passed pages of Nora's first book back and forth. Their trip to Oxford the past summer had secured a contract with a publisher who specialized in children's literature, and *The Secret of Belle Isle* would hit the shelves in time for the holiday buying season.

That contract had been the highlight of a trip fraught with jeopardy and murder, and she flashed on scenes from that investigation: Janet Wallace being informed her daughter, Bryn, had been murdered; the anguish of her best friend being considered a serious suspect in Bryn's death; the moment the murderer had been revealed, placing Nora and the baby in peril; and always, the face of Declan Barnes, who came to mind whenever she thought of Oxford. Her son kicked hard, bringing Nora back to today and the work in front of her.

"I thought you were going to eat," Simon said, pointing to Nora's half-eaten sandwich.

Nora sipped her milk and studied the page in front of her. Simon's illustrations caught the different demeanors of the fairies who lived on Belle Isle in a round house, under the root of a huge, two hundred-year-old rowan tree. Head fairy Daria lived with the wise elf, Cosmo, and the strong gnome, Logan. The smaller fairies were named Dove, Sky and Tess. In this first book, Nora had Tess getting into trouble.

"I don't see any text errors or typos yet," she said as she inspected each page. The bits of sandwich she'd eaten sat heavily in her stomach, and she regretted eating them.

"I'm happy with the color transitions," Simon announced. "There's no bleeding, either. Nigel Rumley's printer is as good as he promised." He finished his sandwich and reached for another.

Nora couldn't help but smile. "Mr. Argyle himself," she said, referring to the eccentric publisher's penchant for colorful tartan socks.

When Simon rose to refill his glass, Nora held the rest of her sandwich under the table. Darby obliged by gobbling it up. "Simon, thanks for all your help this morning," she said to cover the dog's gulping noises.

"You're most welcome." He shut the refrigerator door. "I'm cutting you some slack today, but by tomorrow I hope your appetite will be back. Darby will get fat on your handouts and—" A brisk rap at the kitchen door stopped him.

When Simon opened it, Ian was on the doorstep. Nora noted the set of the detective's shoulders and his sober expression, but Simon seemed oblivious to Ian's mood.

"Hallo, Ian. Come to cart one of us off?" Simon clapped Ian on his back and pulled out a chair for him.

Ian remained standing. "I need to speak with Nora again. I've just come from the autopsy." The detective hesitated. "There was no water in Keith's lungs, what Milo called a dry drowning. He's running tox reports, but it seems Keith may have taken drugs to commit suicide." Stress lines trenched Ian's brow. "The other theory is that he was deliberately drugged to drown—and that makes this a case of murder."

Chapter Nine

"Blessed are they that mourn; for they shall be comforted."
— Saint Matthew (Matthew 5:4)

3:15 PM

"The beige stone building called Clarendon Hall was built by an early Clarendon landowner in the Tudor period. Although a massive fire destroyed parts of the interior, later generations of the family rebuilt it, using parts of the existing stone outer walls and retaining the massive fireplaces and the remaining linenfold paneling. This wide staircase splits the marble-floored entry hall, and our tour today will take in the rooms on the left side of the house: the formal drawing room, an elegant dining room that seats twenty and the ballroom with its musicians' gallery. I'll point out many interesting features and valued antiques. Balls and dinner parties were regularly held here, and Saint Margaret's Hospital still uses the facility for its annual charity gala ... "

The docent was a good one, and Sommer had regretted having to interrupt her talk earlier to cancel the tour. It couldn't be helped, and the woman's eyes widened when he'd discreetly explained his reasons. After speaking with the tour director, the guide hurriedly shepherded the surprised people through the dining room to exit a door on the far side of that room without pointing out any interesting features.

That had been right after DCI Clarke left. The hours from then until now had been some of the toughest he'd endured. Sommer waited while his nurse, Gillian Cole, opened the door to the private family library. All of the doorsills had been removed years ago after Sommer's accident, which allowed him to glide effortlessly from room to room in his wheelchair. He used his toggle switch to move past Gillian and manipulated himself next to his wife, who sat in her usual chair. Early on he'd christened the motorized chair "My Carriage," and the name had stuck as he continued to update the models.

Behind them, the window-filled wall let in the light his prized rare plants craved. Sommer checked his collection daily, misting some, snipping away at others, the flowers arranged on low, slatted shelves he could reach. Sommer raised rare orchids, South American lilies and several African species unseen in England. He had been the subject of several magazine articles and was known in Cumbria as an authority on rare plants. Other than doctor's appointments, the infrequent outings he and Antonia took were usually to area garden shows. It was one of the few activities he could enjoy with his incapacitation.

Today, he avoided his precious plants, his attention focused on his wife. As Gillian bent over and adjusted his lap rug, strings of her wiry grey and black hair fell over her bony shoulder. She squeezed his hand in comfort.

"Can I get either of you anything?" Gillian's voice was raspy but kind. She had been taking care of Sommer since just after his accident and was a fixture at Clarendon Hall.

Sommer glanced at his wife as he consulted his watch. Antonia sat woodenly in the exact middle of the chair, her back doing penance by not relaxing against the worn cushion. He looked into the earnest gaze of the nurse who had kept his body moving and healthy all these years.

"No, thank you, Gillian. But perhaps we could do with a sherry. Would you ask Cook to bring us the Croft?"

Gillian nodded and left the room, her flat nurse oxfords squishing on the wooden floor. The library was one of the rooms off limits to the public tours Sommer had been forced to initiate to make ends meet. After he'd suspended the rest of the day's tours, he'd also cancelled those set for the next week. It would be an added financial burden, but he didn't see how any of them could cope just now with groups of strangers clumping around their home. It was bad enough they only had the use of half of the family residence.

Sommer sighed and looked around the familiar room, eyes scanning books read and loved—not seeing the shabbiness of the room but only its tall windows and thick moldings. He soaked up the comfort the books usually provided him. Reading thrust him out of his wheelchair and into a different time or place, an essential solace.

Silence haunted the long room. A fire crackled in the grate, spreading its warmth, creating a circle of heat and golden light in the autumn afternoon. He had a sudden image of himself as a newlywed standing in front of this fireplace. His back had always been cooler than the front that faced the warmth. Nothing in those halcyon days had suggested or prepared him for the tragedies he and his wife would face, but they had managed to survive—until this unspeakable event.

After thirty-three years of marriage, he didn't know how to initiate a conversation with his wife. What was there to say that would soften the blow they'd had? Antonia's hazel eyes were red rimmed and dulled with anguish, her sweet mouth set in a grimace of pain. Her impeccable blonde curls, usually neat and close to her head, stood up wildly around her closed face, as though she had been pulling at her hair. A visceral tremor ran through him. She had aged ten years in a matter of hours.

After breaking her precious figurines, Antonia had rushed about, upstairs and down, crying in frantic waves of hysteria that had echoed throughout the stone halls. Unable to soothe her, Sommer had eventually allowed Gillian to take him upstairs for his whirlpool while Cook had taken over trying to calm Antonia. The elevator door in the kitchen had blunted the frenzied cries of his wife, the sound receding as the lift rose.

Gillian had set him in the bath and tactfully left him for a few minutes. He'd wept alone there, the warm water swirling over and around his withered legs. When he was spent, he'd firmed up his resolve for both of them. Gillian had driven him in his van to the mortuary for the formal identification. He was glad Antonia had been spared the sight of their son's distorted face.

Antonia finally met his look. He'd persuaded her to take one of the pills Doc Lattimore had left, and thankfully the sedative was taking hold. As her gaze softened, Sommer reached his calloused hand out to grasp hers and was shocked to feel its coolness in the warm room. He leaned over as far as the confines of his chair would allow and warmed first one of Antonia's hands and then the other between his own, rubbing them briskly.

"Blast this bloody chair. I want to sit with you and hold you and comfort you as best I can, my darling." Sommer looked down in disgust at his wasted legs, sensing movement as Antonia rose and cautiously, carefully arranged herself across his lap. She leaned against him, resting her head under his chin, and his shoulders had never felt stronger as he wrapped his arms protectively around her.

Sommer was continually surprised at how delicately Cook carried the small silver tray by its ornate handles, despite her rotund frame. She set the tray down carefully, sherry glasses clinking softly, on a barley twist side table that been his great-grandmother's. Sommer leafed through a poetry anthology, trying to find words for Keith's eventual funeral service. Antonia was back in her chair, paging through a photograph album, composed except for her blotched face and reddened eyes. She smoothed her hair down and motioned Cook over, pointing to one snapshot in particular.

"Look, Cook. Here's the day we went down to the pier, and Keith first swam in the lake without his water wings. Remember how proud he was?"

Cook raised her eyes from the picture of the sturdy boy waving to those gathered on the dock, ready to record his every move, and Sommer saw the question in her eyes. He dipped his head in confirmation that the sedative was working.

"Yes, a right fearless boy he is." Unable to use the past tense, Cook stifled a sob, then cleared her throat as Antonia looked into the distance, lost in the memory.

"I thought a bowl of thick soup tonight for supper, dear, unless you had other ideas," Sommer said.

Antonia continued her stare, caught up in the memory spurred by the photo.

Sommer continued. "That sounds just the ticket, doesn't it? Warm and filling, just what the doctor ordered. I don't think we'll want any heavy meals for the next few days. Use your judgment, Cook."

Cook brightened, evidently pleased at the opportunity Sommer gave her to help in a concrete way. She poured their sherry and, after refusing the glass Sommer offered her, bustled off to start the soup.

Sommer watched his wife replace the photo and flip to the next page. Sommer sipped his sherry and bent his head over *The Oxford Book of English Verse*, contemplating two things: how they would endure these next few days and what hell they had brought on themselves so many years ago.

CHAPTER TEN

"All my life I have had an awareness of other times and places."
— Jack London, *The Star Rover*

The lift let nurse Gillian Cole out at the center of the two upper wings of Clarendon Hall. The left wing, with its bedchambers still furnished as though Henry VIII slept there nightly, was used on the tours. On the right were Antonia and Sommer's suites, Keith's room and the playroom at the end of the hall that Keith had turned into his library. Edmunde Clarendon, Sommer's older brother, occupied a former guest suite, and Gillian headed there to check on him. The area just to the right of the central hallway was kitted out with the hydro tub and exercise equipment both brothers used.

As Gillian rounded the corner from the elevator, she stopped to gather a stack of fresh linens. Her routine today had been severely disrupted, and while she felt callous for thinking that, she was always honest in her own thoughts. The scent of cool, clean sheets never failed to steady her. She stuck her nose deeply into a pile and inhaled, then chose a washcloth and towel and carried them into Edmunde's room.

Gillian had always been slender, but lately her uniform hung from her shoulders as though her frame had diminished. Her skin had a pallor associated with a lack of sunshine, but over the years she'd grown used to being indoors most of the day. She was extremely proud of her nursing services to first one and then both of the Clarendon brothers.

The door banged as she opened it, startling the tall, broad

man dozing in a mechanical wheelchair. His left side faced the door, and for a moment Gillian felt a prick of longing as she surveyed the strong profile. Edmunde's dark hair swirled over his high forehead; white streaks like frosting lent him an elegant look from this angle. The hand that gripped the armrest appeared solid and strong.

As the nurse moved around the bed, the man's shriveled right side came into view. His mouth drooped grotesquely; a thread of spittle oozed from the gaping lip. His gnarled right hand curled around the rolled facecloth Gillian always left there to prevent further contractions or skin breakdown, a practice the physical therapist had taught her. The muscles on the entire right side of Edmunde's large frame displayed atrophy from the debilitating stroke that had reduced the once-powerful man to a monstrous mountain of rubbish. Gillian had learned early on to rein in her reaction to his appearance.

She opened the window to let the crisp autumn air rush into the chamber. "There now, let's get some of the fusty smell out of here. Antonia is calmer, and the timbers have stopped rattling."

Edmunde grunted an acknowledgment.

Gillian flipped the pillows that propped Edmunde's right side up when he sat in his chair. His motorized wheelchair had an attached table that covered his lap and kept him from sliding down to the floor. He could use his left arm when he wanted to, and she thought there was real progress with the strength in his left leg when the physiotherapist worked with him—when he felt like cooperating.

Gillian pried the facecloth out of the grip of Edmunde's right claw, wet it with warm water from the bathroom and then used it to wash inside the hand. Drying his palm and fingers carefully, Gillian rolled up the fresh cloth she'd brought in, powdered it with the cornstarch she kept in Edmunde's bedside table and adeptly reinserted it.

"You could do this yourself, you know. You do have a good side," she complained, but her smile softened the statement.

He grunted again, his aphasia nearly complete. She remembered the day he'd given up on speech therapy. She thought he would have thrown the therapist bodily out of the room if he'd been capable of it. After that, even though the therapist had still insisted on coming, Edmunde refused to make eye contact and sat mutely in his chair. Finally, the therapist got the message and terminated treatment. Now, Edmunde chose to communicate with nods and grumbles.

Edmunde pointed to a cabinet near the door and nodded, waiting for Gillian's response.

She considered his request. "I suppose a nip today is deserved." She took a pint bottle of his favorite Islay Lagavulin Malt and opened it. The pungent peat scent made her eyes tear as she poured him a dram. "I never could understand how you can drink this stuff," she pronounced, holding the glass out to him.

Edmunde took the glass in his good hand and held it near his nose. He sucked in a deep breath, eyes closed. Then he knocked back the entire dram at once, his face reddening as his eyes watered. He held out the glass for a refill of the single malt scotch.

"Enough," she said, rinsing the glass in his bathroom and stowing it away with the bottle. "You'll stink of it the rest of the day as it is."

Gillian combed Edmunde's hair off his face. She took a lemon-glycerin swab from a packet on the nightstand and ran it around the interior of Edmunde's mouth. "That should help with the fumes." She put her hands on nonexistent hips and considered him. "Want to sit near the window a bit? I love the light at this time of day." She moved him to the window, with its view of Clarendon Chapel. Behind it to the right, she could just make out the edge of the cottage she shared with her son.

When he was settled, she bent down to his eye level and spoke directly to him. His deep-brown eyes met hers, the right lid drooping over the iris, clouding the thoughts behind it. His left one stared back at her without blinking. Although she had no idea how much he absorbed, Gillian always spoke to him clearly.

"There will be questions, you know," she said. "Someone will come around, but they'll go away eventually. Now, do you want me to put the disc on? You were just getting to the good part yesterday."

Edmunde nodded, and Gillian hit play on his CD player. As she tidied his bed, the voice of Colin Buchanan narrating Reginald Hill's mystery *A Cure for All Diseases* filled the room.

CHAPTER ELEVEN

"The day started badly and then got worse."
— John Treherne, *The Trap*

3:45 PM

Nora sat silently at Simon's kitchen table, watching as Ian left, closing the door behind him. This time he had not objected to Simon's presence while he questioned her, reviewing all of her actions since she'd woken that morning. He pushed into the evening before, when Nora, Kate and Simon had eaten in the lodge dining room, then had watched a video together.

"*Sleepless in Seattle*," Simon explained. "Ladies' choice."

Nora described going to her room after the movie and settling in bed, reading her name book before falling asleep. Ian told her he'd probably have more questions after the toxicology results were in. He seemed apologetic as he left.

Simon stood at the sink, watching Ian walk away. "Why is he harping on you? You'd think you were a suspect. He bloody well knows you had nothing to do with this."

Nora shook her head. "Of course he does—but I found the body. Ian has to ask me the same questions he would of anyone. His every action will be scrutinized."

Especially, she thought but didn't say, given his close friendship with the Ramsey family. She noted Ian hadn't asked to speak with Kate.

Simon turned to face her as she rose from her chair to join him at the window. She knew he wanted to help her up, but months of getting to know her independent streak had taught him she'd ask for help if she wanted it. Fingers of dull sunlight hit her face, and she relished their warmth. Pushing her glasses back up her nose, Nora straightened her shoulders, causing her belly to protrude further. She flashed Simon a brief smile. "Thanks for staying with me."

He nodded, moving nearer, his deep-blue eyes searching hers for an invitation. She longed to lay her head against his chest and gather his heat. Fear of fulfilling her own needs but wrongly encouraging him held her back. The moment of silence stretched too long between them.

"Let's finish the proofing," Nora said. "Anything to keep Keith from my mind."

For more than an hour, they worked on the book. Nora scrutinized the text and checked to ensure that the fairies' expressions in Simon's illustrations were delightful rather than frightful for young readers. Simon used a magnifying glass to look for minute color errors in the illustrations. The light faded more, and sounds from the lodge kitchen indicated the prep work for the evening meal had begun.

Despite her nap, the strain of the day had caught up with Nora. Her arms and legs felt weighted down and heavy. Even the baby had been relentless in his kicking this afternoon. She and Simon had just closed the proof book when Simon's buzzer rang, and he slid open the pocket door between his suite and the hallway to reveal a young woman with shiny, brunette hair falling over one eye. Maeve Addams, the lodge's assistant manager, stood framed in the doorway, wearing a silky blouse and a short, plaid skirt that showed off her excellent legs. Nora didn't know why the woman aroused such negative feelings in her.

That was nonsense; of course she knew. Maeve made no secret of her attraction to Simon. Nora's dislike of Maeve had only intensified as her pregnancy advanced and was amplified by the fact that Nora had no clarity concerning her own feelings for the man and also had no right to be possessive of him.

Maeve held a clipboard in one hand. "Sorry to bother, guv, but there's a shortage on the paper goods, and I didn't want to let the shipper go until you straightened it out with him."

"No problem; we're finished here," Simon answered. "Please tell Agnes to have our table set for three tonight, would you? We're all going to take a break from work this evening."

Nora saw a flash of anger cross Maeve's pretty face that Simon, washing his hands at his kitchen sink, missed.

"Will do. You're the talk of the town, Nora, what with finding Keith's body and everything," Maeve said. She flashed Nora a dazzling smile.

Nora groped for a snappy comeback, but none came to mind. Instead, she found herself saying, "I think I'll have a rest before dinner," when she wasn't tired at all. She had a sudden need to be alone.

"Good idea. I'll knock on your door ten minutes before, shall I?" Simon said, drying his hands.

Nora resisted her impulse to hug him tightly in front of Maeve. "That will be great," she said and crossed the hall to her suite. Closing the door behind her, her mind in turmoil, she looked at the rumpled bed from her earlier nap. She hit the button on her CD player, and the sound of Johnny Hartman singing "I'll Never Smile Again" filled the room. Nora smirked at the choice of song, a perfect fit for her mood, and kicked off her shoes before stretching out on her bed. She drew the duvet from the foot of the bed over her and reached for her name book. Pregnancy tired her, but this was different. She wanted to run backward in time to a place where everything felt safe, and there were few surprises and even less choices to have to make. Who would understand how drained she felt?

Perhaps only someone who lived with murder as a frequent companion, someone like Declan Barnes.

CHAPTER TWELVE

"I had the story, bit by bit, from various people, and, as generally happens in such cases, each time it was a different story."
— Edith Wharton, *Ethan Frome*

8 PM

Friday evenings were a popular night at the lodge, and the dining room was full. Nora was grateful their table stood in one corner, where she could watch people coming and going. She hoped Maeve was wrong, that people were not talking about her. It was an odd and uncomfortable feeling, and she wondered if Maeve had been telling the truth or just trying to wind her up, as Val would say.

She watched Maeve move about the room, seating a few diners. Was that a smirk of derision on the woman's face when she caught Nora observing her? Nora speculated about Simon's awareness of Maeve's interest and wondered if he ever encouraged it. He'd been called over to a table to offer a wine recommendation, and as he stood talking to the guests, she saw Maeve undress him with her eyes. Bloody hell—she wished for a better mood.

When Simon returned, Kate took her seat, and the three of them lingered over dinner, a delectable prime rib of beef with Yorkshire pudding. Nora's stomach seemed finally to be relaxing, and she ate more than she'd anticipated. If only she could indulge in a glass of wine.

From time to time, Kate jumped up to greet a patron. Nora had seen how Simon and his sister were the heart of Ramsey Lodge, gracious to the people they knew, welcoming to those passing through or staying the night. The fireplace glowed in the elegant room, reflecting off the polished wide-plank floors. White table linens were a crisp oasis; the clink of glass and china against silver provided backdrop noise, accompanied by soft, piped-in classical music.

"All done?" Simon asked, his smile lighting up his face.

In this light, his eyes were a clear blue, and Nora felt a surge of attraction to him immediately followed by a rush of annoyance for his ability to confuse her. Sod off, Mr. Perfect. She quickly chastised herself. Totally wrong, Nora. It's not his fault you're heavily pregnant, have roiling hormones and found a dead body this morning. "Stuffed," she answered.

"It's Kate's turn to close down," he said. "Let's sit and talk."

She followed him to his rooms, accompanied by Darby, the little dog trotting beside her. Simon shut the door to his studio and locked his kitchen door. He set about competently lighting a fire. Nora sank into one of the overstuffed swivel chairs in Simon's sitting area and snuggled into the down cushion. She rotated the chair to watch as Simon rolled up his shirtsleeves. The blonde hair covering his forearms became visible in the light from the flames, and their lean muscles and tendons stood out. Nora's annoyance with Simon faded as the wood caught and filled the room with its comforting scent.

Without asking, Simon put on a kettle and bustled about his kitchen making proper tea. Nora swiveled again to watch him pour a healthy shot of brandy into his mug. He brought both mugs over and set them to cool on the glass-topped trunk that doubled as a coffee table.

Leaning over her, he lightly rubbed his hand over her belly and gave her a smile. "All right in there after today?"

"I think so. He was very active this afternoon." They sat together quietly as the flames grew, the colors deepening as yellow and orange gave way to streaks of blue.

"What were you working on today in your studio?" Nora asked. She was surprised when he hesitated. Did it have something to do with that phone call?

"A special project," he answered vaguely.

Nora stole a glance at Simon. He studiously avoided meeting her eye. Whatever it was, he clearly didn't want to talk about it. She chewed the inside of her cheek and decided it was in both of their interests to change the subject.

"You said you'd tell me about the Clarendons," she reminded him. "Tell me their story."

Simon slipped off his shoes and shoved aside a pile of art magazines to prop his long feet on the coffee table. Darby jumped up and settled on his lap, and he rubbed the dog's ears.

Nora slipped her own loafers off and grabbed her mug of tea. Her feet didn't reach the floor, so she curled them to one side and pushed a throw pillow under her baby bulge to support it. Comfortable, she settled back to hear the story.

"There are two brothers, the older Edmunde and the younger Sommer. Edmunde was a big man with a hearty laugh and what my mum delicately called 'a roving eye.' He could have had any woman he wanted, he was that charming, but the one he wanted was an actress he saw on stage in London. He was smitten and followed her all over Europe as the play toured, until he captured her heart. Julia was a beautiful woman who gave up her career to marry him and settle here. Everyone thought she would tire of Edmunde and miss her life in the theater, but she seemed to like being buried in these hills."

Simon was a natural storyteller. Nora closed her eyes and pictured the events as they unfolded.

"They lived at Clarendon Hall with Sommer and Antonia, who had already been married a few years without children. Antonia wanted children desperately and became depressed about it. But she and Julia became great friends, and they finally got pregnant around the same time. The family owned huge amounts of property at the time and had their fingers in several industries, including agriculture. They rented land to farmers and herders, while other tenants lived in cottages on their land. When they were happy, the town prospered from their generosity. Rumor had it they might even build a new school."

Simon paused to take a sip of his laced tea.

"Sommer was always interested in horticulture and was known for his gardens. Just before the babies were due, he took a trip north to a factory in Scotland, where prize seeds of his were being grown for hybrid perennials. On his way home, there was a terrible accident: A lorry pulled out of a rest stop and didn't see his black car coming over the top of a hill. It was a miracle he survived, but there were severe injuries to his spinal cord. The shock and strain put Antonia into labor, and while she was delivering, Julia went into labor, too."

Nora's eyes popped opened. "What happened?"

"Antonia delivered Keith, but Julia developed complications. She delivered a little girl, but she died a few hours later." Simon's voice softened. "Her baby was sickly, and Edmunde refused to see or hold her. He blamed the poor thing for Julia's death. I think the infant only lived a matter of hours and then she died, too."

"What a heartache for them all," Nora said. She placed a hand across her belly. A surge of affection for the child she carried rushed over her, and she closed her eyes. Please, she silently prayed, let my baby be born healthy.

"It was a bad time for the whole town. Everywhere, people mourned Julia and the baby, while they worried about Sommer and his accident. It took a long time for things to settle down. Baby Keith was a delight to everyone—but his uncle, Edmunde, became withdrawn. As the years passed, he took to drinking, and it spun out of control. He never got over Julia's death and became reclusive except for drunken forays and bouts of womanizing. About two years ago, he had a terrible stroke. One entire side of him is paralyzed, the rest weakened, and he's given up trying to speak."

"My God," Nora breathed. "It's like some kind of Greek tragedy."

"That it is, my girl." Simon stared deeply into the fire. A knock at the door had Darby sitting up. Kate pulled the door open and walked in, empty glass in hand.

"I've come for my spot of brandy, but I see you've started without me."

"I was just telling Nora the saga of the Clarendons." Simon rose and retrieved the brandy bottle, then poured Kate a shot.

Kate spread out on the couch, propping her head on the arm. "Quite a story, isn't it? I feel so badly for Antonia. She was devoted to Keith, and this will devastate her. I'll go and see her—Mum would have." She sipped her brandy. "By the way, that charter for breakfast tomorrow cancelled—they've gone to Hawkshead instead—so it should be quiet."

Simon nodded. "I'll be around if you'd like the day off until dinner."

Kate smiled at him with affection. "That would be lovely. Ian called, but I haven't returned his call yet. I'm still miffed at how he treated Nora this morning."

Nora rushed to reassure her, explaining how Ian's attitude had changed at their second meeting that afternoon. The last thing she wanted was to be a source of friction in the life of the happy couple. "Ian said the pathologist didn't find water in Keith's lungs. He thinks he might have been under the influence of some kind of drug," Nora said.

Kate sat up at the news. "Drugs? You mean suicide or murder? Either sounds so unlikely. Why would Keith kill himself—and who would want him dead?"

As Nora sipped her tea, she wondered the same thing. Her shock over finding Keith's body was wearing off, and her usual grit and determination were returning. Her reporter's instincts kicked in. Here was an opportunity for her to snoop and to get to the bottom of things, and while she was at it, she could try to identify the research that Keith had mentioned he would share with her. If she found the reason for Keith's death, it would clear the air between Kate and Ian, too. "Kate, when you visit Keith's mother, might I tag along? I feel like I should offer my condolences, especially since I knew him in Oxford, and I'm the one who found him. And maybe I can get a look at those books he offered me." She ignored Simon's throat clearing. It would be just like him to tell her not to get involved. There was more than a hint of mystery surrounding Keith's death, and she had perfectly good reasons to visit his home.

"I'd love the company, Nora. Let's go later in the morning, shall we?" Kate stretched out luxuriously. "I, for once, am sleeping in."

CHAPTER THIRTEEN

*"Every thing, saith Epictetus, hath two handles,
the one to be held by, the other not."*
— Robert Burton, *The Anatomy of Melancholy*

Daniel Rowley had almost finished in the lodge kitchen when Agnes sighed.

"These long days at the end of the week aren't good for my arthritis, but then staying home drives me crazy and doesn't pay the bills," she said, drying her hands on a towel.

Daniel grunted in acknowledgment as he tied the last garbage bag shut in preparation for taking it out to the commercial bins. He watched Agnes take one last look around.

"I like coming in mornings to a clean workspace, no doubt about it," she told him, wiping a rag across the stainless steel countertop and using it to dry out the clean sinks. She threw the wet rag into a laundry hamper, then paused and sniffed hard. "What's this, then?" She lifted the lid off a small bucket kept in the corner by the sinks.

He waited for her yell.

"Daniel! You've forgotten the compost bucket." She was on a tear now. "Jings! You can't remember anything. And I'll not tell you again, if you don't wash that greasy hair and beard, I'll not be having you in my kitchen tomorrow night."

He finally found his tongue. "Relax, it's on my list for tonight," he told her, scooping up the bucket.

"I know what's on your list on a Friday night, and a good washing won't be found at the pub. I mean what I'm saying, you minger." With that firm pronouncement, Agnes tied a red kerchief around her grey curls. She pulled on a bulky cardigan and headed out the kitchen door. "Mind you lock the door behind you."

"Bloody bitch," he muttered when he was certain Agnes was out of earshot. Dullard he might be, but he was lucky to have this scullery job and didn't intend to lose it. He emptied the bucket into the outside compost pile, then rinsed it with the garden hose and left it drying on the end of the counter.

Daniel stood at the head of the hall while counting slowly to a hundred on his fingers. Tiptoeing through the door and down the hallway to Simon's door, he paused outside, one ear pressed against it.

From inside came the murmur of voices. Daniel stole back across the hallway and entered the dining room. The tables were bare, the chairs placed upside-down on them, the floor swept clean. He crossed the darkened room by the light coming in from the main hall, and paused in the doorway. No movement came from either of the front rooms the guests used. The public had gone home, and the few lodgers were all upstairs in their rooms.

Avoiding a floorboard he knew from past experience contained a persistent creak, Daniel approached the registration desk and opened the third drawer on the left. Lifting out a metal box, he picked the lock and rummaged under the credit card slips. Avoiding the large bills, he stuffed a few pound notes and a handful of coins in his pocket, then relocked the box and replaced it, sliding the drawer closed.

When he returned to the kitchen, he turned out the lights and left the way the kitchen help should, by the back door, which he remembered to lock as he exited. He turned left, toward Jack Halsey and his other buddies waiting for him at The Scarlet Wench, where he was now prepared to enjoy himself on his employers.

9:25 PM

Nora basked in the warmth of the fire, listening to Kate and Simon talk about changing the Sunday lunch to a buffet in the future.

"We can save money yet offer locals a more varied menu by serving a buffet," Kate said. "If Keith's plans go ahead, and Clarendon Hall eventually opens as an art center, people wanting a change from their menu would get served at a buffet much faster. If we have more guests dropping in to eat, we need to keep them moving along."

Simon pushed for keeping their current waitress service. "I can see updating the menu, but we do that seasonally anyway. I don't want to encourage busloads of tourists to stream in here every Sunday, no matter what happens at the Hall. Besides, with Keith dead, who knows what will happen to those plans now?"

With her eyes closed, Nora thought Simon sounded petulant, a new note for him, and came off as not the best business owner. Did his artistic side chafe at having to run the lodge? Their chat seemed amiable enough, but what would happen when Kate married, eventually had children and was less available to share their chores? Nora shook herself out of her state. It wasn't her worry right now. She should go to bed or risk falling asleep in the comfortable chair by the fire.

Nora said goodnight and left, crossing to her door. She stopped abruptly when she heard a noise. For a moment, she had the eerie feeling she was not alone. A door latch clicked into place somewhere down the hall; then there was silence.

Nora swallowed and opened her door to the welcoming light next to her bed. She shut the door and calmed herself. Chiding herself for her foolishness, she felt her son waving. Could he be an Evan or a Rory? She put a hand on her belly to feel the movement, pushing back against him, and was rewarded with the responsive kick that never failed to thrill her. Then she thought of meeting Antonia Clarendon tomorrow and wondered if her pregnancy would upset the mother who'd just lost her son.

Still feeling uneasy, she walked over to look out the French doors to the front of the lodge property. She saw a large figure cross the road beyond the garden and hurry away, and a feeling of menace ran through her.

CHAPTER FOURTEEN

*"Whoever is spared personal pain must feel himself called upon to
help in diminishing the pain of others."*
— Albert Schweitzer, *Memoirs of Childhood and Youth*

Saturday, 23rd October

8:20 AM

Nora woke with the sense she'd been dreaming, but it faded as
she sat up. Surprisingly, she'd had no nightmares of Keith that
she remembered, and she resolved not to let the experience of
finding Keith haunt her.

She recalled the firelight etching shadows last night in the
planes of the Ramseys' faces before she'd left them in Simon's
sitting room. Nora envied them even their sparring, friendly as
it was, a warm playfulness between a brother and a sister who
respected and loved each other. She wondered if they ever had
knock-down, drag-out fights. She also wondered how different her life would have been if she'd had a sibling to share it.
Certainly, her guilt over her father's death would have been as-
suaged sooner if she'd had a sister or brother to turn to. Despite
her mother's efforts to encourage Nora's self-forgiveness, it had
taken her years to feel she wasn't the cause of her father's death.
He'd drowned while sailing alone after she'd turned down his
invitation to accompany him in favor of a date whose name she'd
long forgotten. She got out of bed, cradling her belly. The fact
that he'd not know this child was one of her deepest regrets.

Nora turned on the shower and heard a rumble as chairs were
put into position in the dining room. Agnes knocked, then came

in and left Nora's tea; Nora called out her thanks. Should she mention the noises she heard or the person she saw last night? No, Ramsey Lodge was more than a hundred years old, a haven for creaks and noises. What she thought was a door click could have been the roof settling. And the figure could have been anyone—and not necessarily connected with the lodge. In the daylight, last night's fears seemed more a reaction to the events of that day, reasonable as that was, and not anything concrete or reportable.

Nora took her time in the shower, remembering that Kate had said she wanted to sleep in. As she dressed, Nora caught the smell of frying bacon and realized she was hungry. She added a scarf to the same old denim skirt and tunic blouse she'd been wearing far too long. It had taken a while to find a maternity skirt with pockets, and she didn't want to spend money on a temporary wardrobe. Only a few weeks more, and she might contemplate getting back into her soft, washed-out jeans again.

She entered the dining room, nodding to the guests she passed on her way to the table. Simon waved to her from across the room, where he stood at the kitchen door conferring with Agnes.

It was close to 9 AM when Kate joined her. Nora ordered a full English breakfast from Maeve, who'd decided to wait on them herself. She seemed dour today, wearing a crisp, white blouse and black skirt, doing double duty as a waitress.

"Make that two, please. Did someone call in?" Kate asked.

"Daisy has a cold," Maeve answered, rolling her eyes to let them know what she thought of that excuse. She left to put in their order.

Her curtness surprised both women. "I wish that woman would learn to smile even if she's in a bad mood," Kate sighed as she stirred honey into her tea. "She can look like she's just lost her best friend."

"Maybe she has," Nora countered, wondering if Maeve had

been a friend of Keith's. Who knew if they'd dated before Maeve's crush on Simon? Both were single and good-looking; it wasn't too much of a stretch to imagine it.

"Perhaps you're right. We never do know what others carry around, do we? I should be nicer to her." Kate sipped her tea. "Ready to face the fortress later? I thought we'd walk to Clarendon Hall. It's only a quarter of a mile, but a portion is uphill."

Nora brightened at the thought. "I can use the exercise. I'll bring my camera, maybe get some shots of Belle Isle from up there." She remembered what she'd been thinking before falling asleep the night before. "Kate, do you think my pregnancy will be a problem for anyone at the Hall?"

"I really don't think so," Kate answered as Maeve appeared. "I believe they'll appreciate your regards." She paused as Maeve set their plates down. "Thank you, Maeve."

Not a blink from Maeve, who moved on to clear another table. So Maeve could be moody, Nora decided. Maybe that's why Simon resisted her—if he had. Time to find out.

"I wondered if Maeve and Keith dated and that's why she's upset today. Or even she and Simon?"

Kate smiled. "Not for her lack of trying again with Simon. I never saw her with Keith, but that doesn't mean it didn't happen."

Again? Nora nodded. "I didn't realize she and Simon had been an item."

Kate waved the thought away. "Eons ago, before he went to France. They had a few dates, but I got the impression she was too shallow for my dear brother."

That explained it—history that Maeve was trying to resurrect. Nora attacked her breakfast with relish, surprised at her hunger. When she was finished, she put her fork down with a sense of satisfaction.

"I think the young man and I have had our fill of breakfast

this morning. I'll just get some air before we take that walk. You take your time here."

They agreed to meet at 10:30, and Nora left the dining room, exiting the main lodge door. The fresh morning air was bracing. She looked at the lake across the road and hesitated. She turned away, passing instead through the curved trellis draped with vines that led to the flower garden just outside her own room. Empty. With a grateful sigh, she pulled out a chair and sat down. Her baby was quiet this morning, just an occasional flutter to remind her of his presence—as if her constant backache could let her forget. Most evenings, her feet and ankles were swollen, but Dr. Ling, her obstetrician in nearby Windermere, assured her this was normal.

Despite having ignored the lake, Nora thought of Keith and remembered clearly how his eyes had shone when he'd talked about the water he loved. Could he have chosen it deliberately as the place to spend his final moments, lulled to eternal sleep in its depths? But why would he have wanted to end his life? He seemed so positive, so filled with ideas for the future. If his death was at the hand of another, what had Keith done to provoke someone to kill him?

Even though she was blameless, Nora wasn't happy to be any part of Ian's investigation. She knew being involved in a murder inquiry cast widening circles, like the ripples of a mud puddle, contaminating and infecting everyone within its reach. Nora slipped her feet out of her loafers and wiggled her toes. She wouldn't be in the middle of another death investigation if she'd stayed at her job at the magazine, she thought ruefully.

Nora remembered her last day at work before leaving for the Lake District. She wrinkled her nose with distaste when she recalled the morning spent reading a truly awful piece of Tony Warner's on a new memorial being built for Princess Diana.

Nora thought the readers of *People and Places* wanted the poor, dead princess to rest in peace so many years after her death as much as she did, but the Third Floor insisted that one article per issue highlight some royal, and Nora had stopped fighting the Third Floor early on in favor of her weekly paycheck. Tony's stunted prose reflected the smugness he felt because a distant uncle was an earl. He also had the habit of coining new words he insisted were trendy, words Nora ruthlessly obliterated with her sharp, blue pencil. "Punkishness" would not be printed in any article edited by Nora Tierney.

At least she didn't have to deal with Tony Warner anymore. Supporting her heavy belly with her hands, she rose to retrieve her camera and steeled herself to face the bereaved parents.

CHAPTER FIFTEEN

"Ill news hath wings, and with the wind doth go ..."
— Michael Drayton, *The Baron's Wars*

In Oxford, Tony Warner received a phone call from his boss, Clive Jenkins, managing director of *People and Places* magazine. Jenkins had just heard the local BBC newscaster announce the death of Keith Clarendon, an employee of the Worth Travel Agency. He told Tony he had no difficulty placing the name of the pompous man who had brought them so much publicity when Nora Tierney won that contest.

"I want you to drop everything and head to the Lake District to get an exclusive interview with Nora," Jenkins told the reporter. "Find out everything you can about the death of the Clarendon heir."

Tony could picture his boss hurrying to retrieve his aluminum Zero Halliburton and pulling out his bulging Filofax to look up Tony's home number. Publicity for the magazine took precedence over even Jenkins' precious daily crossword.

"Absolutely; no problem," Tony told his boss. A few minutes later, Tony was on his laptop, looking up the quickest route to the Lake District. Jenkins' call had stymied Tony's plans to meet later with a lass who had once worked as a maid for Princess Anne, but he accepted this assignment with glee. The maid could be postponed—that story would keep. A good investigative reporter had to be flexible, ready the instant a story broke.

Not only could Tony freelance this story to several papers, he would show that Tierney bitch and her blue pencil he knew how to write.

9:58 AM

In a flat in Nora's old building in Oxford, Val Rogan had stepped out of the shower minutes before, in time to hear the same announcement of Keith Clarendon's death. Val immediately recognized the name of the agency that had sponsored Nora's contest and Keith's name as the chap who had engineered it.

She wrapped herself in a terry robe after carefully drying the tiny gold bar that pierced her left nipple, then blotted her short, dark hair with a towel and ran her fingers through it. Opening the first of a series of tiny boxes set out on a side table, she began searching through each of them successively for the note Nora had given her with the phone number of Ramsey Lodge.

9:59 AM

Nora was in her room, emailing her mother in Connecticut before leaving for the Clarendons. She pointedly left out the news of stumbling across Keith Clarendon's body. It was doubtful that news would reach Ridgefield. When her mobile rang, she saw it was Val Rogan. Either her friend had heard the news of Keith's death and was calling for details, or she had ESP.

Val listened in surprise to Nora's ordeal in finding Keith's body. "I heard on the radio he'd died. I had no idea you were involved."

"I'm not involved, Val," Nora insisted. "I merely stumbled over his body."

Val's nurturing spirit kicked into gear. "That makes you involved. When do you want me? I can get coverage at the cooperative and be there later today."

"Thanks, Val, but I'm absolutely fine. Simon and Kate are taking good care of me, and Kate's fiancé, Ian, is heading up the investigation." Nora knew her friend couldn't help but think about her own recent loss.

Val took a deep breath. "It's so sad. I remember when you won the contest. Keith seemed like a decent bloke. On the other hand, that agency he worked for—what's its motto?"

The two friends chorused: "It's always Worth your while with us!"

"Still," Val said. "There must be something I can do. You want me to start snooping on this end?"

Nora sighed. She didn't want her friend getting into trouble, but Ian had said drugs were involved. What if Val was right, and Keith's death was less than innocent? Still, she was having second thoughts about getting involved herself. "Hmmm. Remember how annoyed Declan was when I interfered in his case? I should let Ian handle this one; he's in charge, after all, and I don't want to get on his nerves."

"Since when did you grow a conscience? I'll be discreet, but I think you need me to do a little sussing out right here in Oxford, Yankee."

10:12 AM

Far out on the Woodstock Road, the same announcement had caused Keith's Oxford associate, Glenn Hackney, to immediately lose his erection, much to the chagrin of his current bed partner, a rather hairy young man Glenn had picked up the night before.

Once he'd thrown the guy out, changed his sheets and showered, Glenn Hackney, as he was known in his current occupation and guise, dressed quickly. He set out for the short drive to the Worth Travel Agency, his office keys in the pocket of his pressed jeans, an empty leather satchel on the seat beside him. Tall and sleek, with longish hair and a haughty manner, he was known to Scotland Yard by an entirely different name.

10:28 AM

At The Scarlet Wench, Daniel Rowley and his best pal, Jack Halsey, were back at their stools along the bar, almost still warm from last evening's session. News of the death of the Clarendon heir dominated last night's conversation and continued into today. The men had been at the door for a special early opening, prepared to drown their sorrows in a succession of real ales and wash down the sad fact that their favorite sport had come to an abrupt end.

"No more noisy town meetings trying to squash KC's development plans," Daniel pronounced.

"Those meetin's won't be the same without Keith to badger," Jack agreed.

The men shook their heads in agreement.

"More time to spend in here, though," Daniel noted.

Jack raised his glass. "I'll drink to that!"

Chapter Sixteen

"What have these lonely mountains worth revealing?
More glory and more grief than I can tell."
— Emily Brontë

10:29 AM

Ian was reviewing reports when his intercom buzzed.

"Dr. Foreman on two for you, guv," the duty sergeant said.

"Hello, Milo," Ian said, picking up. "Have something for me?"

"Sommer Clarendon still have that rare plant collection of his?" Milo was uncharacteristically brusque.

"I expect so. Why do you ask?" Ian heard the pathologist draw heavily on his cigar before he answered.

Milo couldn't hide a tinge of professional pride. "My budget is groaning from the rush on the toxicology, but my instincts paid off. There are definite traces of a plant called Tanghinia in Keith's stomach, not native to England. The only person around who might know of it is Sommer Clarendon. Tough situation."

"Leave it with me, Milo, and I'll get back to you. And thanks," Ian said. He didn't want Milo bumbling over his investigation. The pathologist meant well, but his people skills could use some polishing.

A sense of foreboding stole over the detective as he looked up the number to Clarendon Hall. This was a delicate task, to call the victim's father so soon after his son's death with disturbing news. He framed his questions before dialing.

Minutes later, Sommer Clarendon picked up an extension, and Ian explained what he wanted to know.

"Why yes, Ian, I know of that plant; pretty little thing. It was used in Madagascar centuries ago to ferret out criminals. Highly poisonous, of course, and the blighters never survived." Sommer paused as the reason for Ian's call became obvious. "My God, Ian. This has to do with Keith, doesn't it?"

Ian plowed on. "It's been found in Keith's body. I promise to keep you posted as soon as I know more, Sommer. Right now, I need to know where it can be found."

After a moment's hesitation, the bereaved father replied: "There are only two that I know of in the Lake District, and I own them both. I still have one here; the other I loaned to Simon Ramsey."

10:31 AM

Nora poked her head into Simon's rooms after retrieving her camera. She saw him disappearing into his studio and followed.

"Hi there. I'm going with Kate to Clarendon Hall," she called out. When she reached the doorway, she caught a glimpse of a painting in progress and a plant standing on a table next to the easel. Odd; she'd never known Simon to work from studio specimens. He preferred to sketch en plein air and then develop his paintings in his studio from those drawings, clipped to his easel. She always enjoyed watching Simon at work and was fascinated by his talent. He often took the time to explain his strategies and vision as he worked, conversations they both enjoyed. Her keen interest had cemented their friendship early on.

She stepped into the studio, eager to hear about his new project. Simon saw her and hurried over to the doorway, blocking her view and practically shoving her back into his kitchen as he drew the door shut behind him.

Nora was taken aback. "What's wrong?"

"Nothing," he said, shifting his weight from one foot to the other in that way he had when he was nervous.

Nora had trouble believing him. He was usually open to showing her what he was working on. Today, he didn't meet her eye and was distinctly uncomfortable.

Nora felt his uneasiness and started to speak, then thought better of it. She would have to trust Simon to explain in his own time. "I'm off then," she said brightly and left the room, wondering about Simon's odd behavior.

The quilted bag slung over Nora's shoulder sported a floral William Morris pattern. In addition to her camera, it held her wallet and the various bits and pieces most women accumulate: lipstick, tissues, a compact mirror and a roll of antacids. She'd added a small notebook in which she listed baby names under consideration. After pushing her glasses up her nose, she withdrew it and was consulting her latest entry when Kate found her in the hall.

"Sorry, occupational hazard. Agnes always has a menu question, even though I told her Simon was on duty." Kate carried a covered basket over one arm and pointed to the notebook. "Still name hunting?"

They exited through the lodge's main door, and Nora felt a twinge of relief when Kate guided her away from the scene of yesterday's trauma. "What do you think of Aubrey? It means a visionary leader, someone of moral authority."

Kate wrinkled her nose. "I'm the wrong one to ask. I think it sounds kind of stodgy or abrasive," she said. They crossed the road and walked along the quay in the direction of the ferry dock.

"We'd call that a know-it-all." Nora smiled and drew a line through the name. "When I was looking online at nursery things from the Beatrix Potter shop, I didn't even think of her stories as a resource."

"I don't think you'll find a name there unless it's Peter," Kate laughed. "You can easily walk over to the shop, or I can get Maeve to give you a lift tomorrow."

Nora didn't want Maeve taking her anywhere, as unreasonable as that seemed. "No, Squirrel Nutkin or Hunca Munca won't do, but there's always Benjamin or Jeremiah to think about. I'll get there soon." She stowed her notebook and concentrated on not bumping into anyone with her bulk. The area bustled with travelers navigating the uneven pavement dotted with stretches of cobblestones. It already seemed crowded with tourists, and Nora could see how Keith's plans to increase visitors to the small village of Bowness-on-Windermere would have garnered local detractors in addition to Simon.

"I'm assuming naming the baby after Paul isn't going to fly?" Kate asked, guiding Nora down Rectory Road.

Nora frowned. "If we'd been on a good note when Paul died, it would be a no-brainer. But considering we were hardly speaking and headed for a breakup, it would be tough for me. I've got a list to go through and more pages in my book to browse." Nora stopped to catch her breath and take a few shots of the rising land and the lake behind her, busy with cruising steamers, ferries, private boats and a few canoes. At this distance, it looked picturesque and quaint, like a guidebook picture. Puffy, cotton-candy clouds reflected on the water's surface without any reminder of yesterday's horror.

Nora put her camera away. "It looks so—innocent," she said.

Kate linked her free arm through Nora's and turned her away from the shimmering water. "It usually is," she murmured.

10:45 AM

Simon lingered in the dining room long after breakfast was cleaned up, enjoying a late cup of coffee with the owners of Lindisfarne House in neighboring Windermere. The three compared notes on the uneven tourist season, a result of the slowed economy. Simon was grateful they didn't want to gossip about Keith's death.

He needed this moment's respite from the mess surrounding the death of Keith Clarendon. Yesterday had passed in a blur, and he needed to steady himself. The couple was getting up to leave when Simon glanced at the main hall entrance to the dining room and saw Ian standing in the archway. Simon saw his guests to the door of the lodge and turned back to greet Ian.

"Ian, Kate's not here right now. I don't expect her back for a bit—was she expecting you? Wedding plans to nail down?"

"If that sister of yours would settle on a date for the ceremony, we could actually make some." The lanky detective strode across the dining room, motioning to Simon to follow him. "Could we talk in your rooms, please?" He crossed the hall to Simon's door without waiting for a response.

Once inside the main room, Simon sat down and indicated Ian should do the same. Ian continued to stand.

"Simon, I believe you have in your possession a plant from Sommer Clarendon's collection?"

"Yes, I borrowed it to use in a painting. It's in my studio."

"I'm afraid I'll need to search and secure your studio and take that plant into evidence." Ian sighed. "And you'll need to come to Kendal station and make a formal statement."

"What?" Simon stood abruptly, knocking over his chair. "What's going on, Ian?"

Ian righted Simon's chair. "Sit down, Simon. Milo sent

Keith's gastric contents to be analyzed on high priority. He believes Keith may have ingested a high dose of a glycoside that fits the cardiac failure he found. He found among the gastric contents the seeds of a rare plant—" Ian consulted his notes, "—called Tanghinia that can act as both a respiratory and a cardiac poison." He met Simon's eyes. "It's native to areas like the Seychelles or Madagascar. Around Cumbria, there are only two known specimens: the one still at Clarendon Hall and the one in your studio."

Simon sat down heavily. "This is absurd!"

"Maybe so." Ian shifted his weight and stuffed his notebook back in his jacket. "I've sent a tech to collect the one from Clarendon Hall, too. But unless he committed suicide, and this would be a decidedly unpleasant way to do that, Keith was murdered."

The full impact of Ian's words hit him. "And I'm a suspect."

Chapter Seventeen

*"Thieves respect property. They merely wish the property to
become their property so that they may more perfectly respect it."*
— G. K. Chesterton, *The Man Who Was Thursday*

10:48 AM

Val Rogan followed a shopper leaving the busy Westgate Shopping Centre in Oxford and slid her Escort into the spot as soon as the woman vacated it. She locked up and crossed Norfolk Street, wondering if the threatening sky would unleash a shower. The street was full of Saturday shoppers about their business and many of them carried umbrellas. Her destination was the Worth Travel Agency.

Since Nora's help had cleared her of Bryn's murder, Val would do anything to aid her American friend. Today, she planned to browse the travel agency artlessly and gather as much information as she could about Keith Clarendon from his coworkers. Nice job he'd had, she thought, splitting his time between Oxford and Bowness. There was sure to be gossip as news of his death spread, and Val was very good at chatting up clerks.

Val had dressed in what she called her "Virgin Mary" outfit: a simple blue cardigan that hid the elaborate embroidery she'd done on the back of her white shirt and a long denim skirt. She wore comfortable flats and had removed all but one set of earrings, which today were pearl studs. She wanted to look like a single gal out for a bit of weekend window-shopping and dreaming of a trip to Turkey, the Brits' latest vacation hot spot. Down the block, police lights caught her attention, bringing back with sudden clarity the moment she'd been told her beloved Bryn was dead. Val's heart turned over with the memory; it was a loss she was still getting used to and over which she continued to grieve.

Shaking off the emotional pain, she reached the address she wanted and squared her shoulders. The lights she'd seen bouncing off the buildings belonged to police cars drawn up in front of the office. A cluster of people gathered around the entrance to the Worth Travel Agency. *It's always Worth your while with us!* proclaimed a banner above the storefront's entrance.

Val poked her way to the front of the crowd in time to see a constable taping up a hole in the agency's large glass door, which stood propped open. Peering inside, Val could see an elderly man talking with a note-taking constable.

Suddenly, a slim, well-dressed young man brushed Val roughly aside and strode into the office. Val slid closer to the open doorway so she could hear the conversation inside.

"My God, Edgar, are you all right? What's happened here?" The young man looked distressed as he scanned the overturned racks of brochures, their contents strewn across the floor. Filing cabinets and desk drawers gaped open.

"I found it like this when I responded to the alarm company's call—I'm fine," the older man said, but his face was flushed, and his hands shook.

"And you are?" the constable asked the young man in a nasal voice.

"Glenn Hackney, office manager. What's going on? And please, can't Mr. Worth sit down before he falls over?" He righted a chair and pulled it toward the owner, who gratefully slid into it.

"It would appear to be a robbery of sorts, sir," the constable answered with a smirk. He turned to a clean page in his notebook. "How did you hear about this, Mr. Hackney?"

The office manager delicately picked his way through the debris as he took in the extensive mess. "The alarm company automatically calls me and Mr. Worth whenever it's triggered," he answered with impatience.

The constable scribbled a note, then looked inquiringly at Edgar Worth. "Do you routinely keep large amounts of receipts in the office, Mr. Worth?"

The older man shook his head as Glenn answered for him. "Not really. There's petty cash, but either Mr. Worth or I make a bank drop of the day's cash and checks every night after closing."

The constable nodded and looked up, noticing Val at the front of the eavesdropping crowd. He motioned to the other bobby, who walked over and shut the agency's door firmly in her face.

Chapter Eighteen

*"You are here invited to read the story of an Event which
occurred in an out-of-the-way corner of England, some years since."*
— Wilkie Collins, *Poor Miss Finch*

10:50 AM

Clarendon Hall came into view as the road took a steeper angle
upward. Kate and Nora stopped between two square stone columns at the entrance to the paved drive, lined on each side with
aged horse chestnut trees. Discreet brass plaques read *Clarendon
Hall* on the left and *Estab. 1616* on the right. The notation on the
right caught Nora's attention. "1616—that's the year Shakespeare
died," she noted.

Kate guided Nora through the ornate iron gates. "It's a source
of local pride to announce the Bard of Avon slept here on a visit
before his death, but I suspect someone from Cumbria Tourism
thought of that one years ago."

They stopped halfway up the drive for Nora to take in the view
of the heavily planted grounds. Nora could see the gardens were
dotted with dry fountains and cotoneaster bushes sprinkled with
red berries, but most of the shrubs were asleep for the season.

The stone mansion was impressive, with a large portico shield-
ing the massive entry door. Its wings spread out on either side,
framed by low privet hedges, and its upper story was stepped
back from the front lower-level rooms, giving the ground floor
a soaring, peaked ceiling on the anterior half of the residence.
Heavy drapes at the long windows in the right wing were pulled
open. Sheer panels provided privacy but let light in and allowed
a view of the lake.

"We'll go around back and see Cook first, so I can leave this basket," Kate suggested.

The drive swung around to the back of the mansion. The curtains at the windows were still; a purple bow hung from a plain, green wreath on the front door.

"In Victorian times, hay would be thrown in front of a house in mourning to stifle the sounds from the horses in the road, and all of the blinds would be drawn to shut out the sunlight," Kate said.

"Is that your favorite period?" Nora asked.

"That and Edwardian, probably. In my work, I had to become familiar with all different eras. I love the history behind things. That's why I enjoy refinishing old furniture—it's the sense of what came before that I like." She gave Nora a smile. "Even if running the lodge doesn't always allow me as much time for it as I'd like."

The pair reached a small kitchen garden planted with herbs, zinnias and cosmos. Kate twisted a brass knob set next to the door, and a bell could be heard tinkling inside.

A sturdy woman wearing a spotless apron over her plain house-dress opened the door. The apron matched the white of her hair, which she smoothed in a nervous gesture until she recognized her caller, and then her round face broke into a beaming welcome.

"Well, now, it's Kate come to the back door, just like in the old days. Come in, my dear, it's so good to see you."

"Cook, this is my friend Nora Tierney. She knew Keith from the travel agency."

A shadow passed over Cook's face as she ushered the women into a huge kitchen, complete with a four-oven, green Aga range. Worn but immaculate cabinets were painted white and set with arched, leaded-glass doors. Green tiles lining the countertops continued onto the backsplash, with Arts and Crafts–patterned ceramic tiles scattered here and there, giving the feel of handfuls of wildflowers scattered about. One part of the counter had a huge piece of marble inlaid on one end and a chopping block on the other.

The sweet, floury scent of scones baking filled the room, and a tray set with a tea service stood on a rolling cart near the door to the hallway. Cook led them to ladder-back chairs at the long kitchen table, and Nora sat down, happy to rest after her walk. Kate lifted the towel from her basket and withdrew a shiny plum tart and a smaller version of the same delicacy that she set on the table.

"From Agnes, for the house and for you, with her love," Kate said.

"That Agnes always remembers me, and Mr. Sommer's favorite is plum. Please thank her for me." Cook clucked appreciatively as she sat opposite them. "Miss Antonia asked me to prepare tea and scones for you once you called this morning, so I won't offer you a cuppa right now. But let me see your engagement ring, dear. Very nice for you, Kate."

Kate held out her left hand where a platinum Art Deco ring sparkled, its center diamond graced with sapphire baguettes. "It was Ian's granny's," she explained.

"Lovely, isn't it?" Cook asked Nora.

"Beautiful," Nora agreed, pleased Cook accepted her presence so easily. She was less sure of the reception Keith's parents would give her. As if in response to her anxiety, her stomach hardened into a tight ball. She massaged it gently until it passed.

"How are the Clarendons doing, Cook?" Kate asked.

Cook leaned across the table and lowered her voice. Nora caught a whiff of rose as the woman answered. "My poor nephew Billy had to deliver the news." She shook her head. "I don't know how he does it. Miss Antonia, she didn't believe him at first and ran upstairs to check Keith's bedroom. Mr. Sommer, his face got all white, and I was afraid he was going to pass out—it was just awful. Billy said this American lady staying with you found him by the lake … " Her voice trailed off as she looked to Nora, who nodded.

"That would be me," Nora confirmed, to Cook's grimace.

"Not a nice thing to come across, I'm sure. Then Miss Antonia came running back into the room, and her shouting brought Gillian down, but not before the poor woman had thrown all her Dresden figurines to the floor. They were special to her," she added for Nora's information. "She and poor Miss Julia collected them together. By the time I reached her, she was chucking the very last one, and then she burst into the most heartrending cries you ever heard and threw her arms around my neck." Cook blinked back tears at the memory. "It was a sight, let me tell you." She unfolded a flowered hanky from her apron pocket and mopped her forehead.

Kate reached across the table and patted her hand. "I'm sure it was hard for everyone to absorb."

Cook nodded in agreement. "I finally got her to come in here and made her sit down where you are while I made her tea with a shot of brandy. And Mr. Sommer called in the tour guide and canceled the tours. Gillian sat with her so I could clean up the mess, and then Doc Lattimore arrived—Billy had called him before he even came here. And the doc, he left some pills Mr. Sommer got Miss Antonia to take. She's been in a daze since."

Cook ended her narration and sat back in her chair, exhausted. Nora had the feeling it was a story she would repeat over and over in the coming days to anyone who might ask.

Chapter Nineteen

*"With a little bit of luck, when temptation comes
you'll give right in!"*
— Alan Jay Lerner and Frederick Loewe, *My Fair Lady*

Simon threw down his pencil in frustration after checking the totaled receipts on the long slip of paper that fell from the adding machine. It still didn't match what he had in the cash drawer, but it was off by such a small amount, he thought perhaps Maeve had given the wrong change. He hated to think one of their staff would steal from them. He would speak to Kate about counseling the waitresses again. She had a firm, no-nonsense approach when dealing with the staff. He preferred taking on the nonadversarial roles, as he too often fell for the solemn promises of the young women with their batting eyelashes.

He was distinctly uncomfortable, banished from his own rooms while a forensic tech from Ian's team collected the Tanghinia plant he'd borrowed from Sommer Clarendon. There was no telling if they were being careful with his paintings or with his supplies. He shuddered to think about what was happening to his haven and just hoped there wouldn't be a mess to clean up—let alone the mess there would be if Ian persisted in pursuing him as a suspect.

Ian had suggested he do paperwork, which Simon knew translated to keeping himself out of their way. He still had to give his formal statement about when he'd borrowed the plant and how long it had been in his possession. He didn't care at all for the feeling of being scrutinized in connection with Keith Clarendon's death.

Bloody Keith. Just like him to continue to irritate Simon from his watery grave. Simon mentally pinched himself and stood up behind the desk. What was he thinking? Keith was dead—and probably had died in a horrific manner, from what Ian had said, and here Simon was blaming a dead man for his own discomfort.

He thought back to their disagreements over Keith's plans for expansion. The pub argument that had escalated to a minor fistfight was unusual for Simon; he'd never been in a physical confrontation before. That night, he'd had a few too many pints after the town meeting, not his usual standard at all, and it had been easy to rise to Keith's arrogant baiting, especially once he had started harping on Kate, coming on to her in his stupor.

The fight had been bad enough at the time. He never thought it would have repercussions, but he knew how it now must make him look in the eyes of the police. Simon tried to shake it off. Ian would sort it all out. In the meantime, he would try to be as cooperative in investigating Keith's death as the men had been confrontational in life.

Locking the receipt box in the desk, Simon leaned back in his chair and picked up his sketchbook. He was refining the cover for Nora's next book, and the image would highlight Daria, the head fairy. He had drawn her exhibiting regal grace, with long, red tresses and a crown of bluebells. Nora had not commented on Daria's likeness to herself in the first book's illustrations, but with this larger drawing, it would be difficult for Nora not to notice. If she objected, Simon was prepared to point out that she was the author and was therefore entitled to have the main character resemble her own visage.

Whether Nora would agree to it or not was an entirely different matter. Simon rued the day he'd fallen in love with her. Their relationship now wallowed in uncertainty.

The inn door opened, and a stranger let himself in. The man

imperiously picked up one of the lodge brochures from a holder that stood on a vintage walnut sideboard in the entry hall. Simon watched the man smirk as he leafed through the booklet detailing Ramsey Lodge's mod cons, including free Wi-Fi and wall-mounted plasma televisions that picked up myriad satellite channels, mixed with old-world charm in the themed guest rooms.

Negative emotion grabbed Simon; he instinctively knew this well-dressed young man was destined to be a bloody pain in his arse, and he had a sudden urge to throw him out.

Simon stood as the man approached, and they silently appraised one another. The sandy-haired, slender Simon wore chinos and a button-down shirt with the sleeves rolled up; the shorter, darker man was in an expensive jumper with crisply pressed slacks and blazer. Holding himself in a pugnacious pose, his full cheeks pushed his lips into an unflattering feminine rosebud.

The man withdrew an ornate silver case from his pocket and slapped his card on the desk. He managed a smile, which creased his bulging cheeks, reminding Simon of a small, squealing pig. Simon had to bite back a chuckle. When the man finally spoke, his voice had a false tone and an arched, public-school accent that put Simon immediately on edge.

"Tony Warner, *People and Places* mag. Is Nora Tierney in?"

Simon shifted his weight. "No, I'm afraid she's out. Was she expecting you?"

"Let's say she shouldn't be surprised to see me." The porcine look intensified.

Simon stifled an urge to swat the man across the face. He had never considered Nora's past relationships prior to the one with her late fiancé, but surely this pompous wally—"I have no idea when she'll return. I'll tell her you called." He ended the conversation by tucking Tony's card in the corner of the desk blotter and sitting down, dismissing him.

Tony leaned over the desk, the ingratiating smile on his round face revealing an impressive set of uneven, yellowed teeth. "I'm sure that won't be necessary. I plan to stay here. I assume you have a vacancy?"

Simon's eyes darted to the VACANCY sign posted on the corner of the desk. There was no possibility this fellow hadn't seen it. He reached for the registration book, clearing his throat, a habit he'd developed to help cover personal feeling as he put on his public face. "What kind of accommodation are you interested in? We have—"

"Don't bother with the recital, dear chap. This one's on the boss. Make it the best suite in the house."

Chapter Twenty

"It was a Sunday evening in October, and in common with many other young ladies of her class, Katharine Hilbery was pouring out tea."
— Virginia Woolf, *Night and Day*

11:16 AM

Nora and Kate delicately tried to take their leave of Cook once the scones were out of the oven and Cook had placed them in a linen-lined basket. The kitchen door knocked open. A teenager wearing washed-out jeans and a bright yellow Coldplay T-shirt breezed in. He carried a cloth sack filled with groceries that he dumped on the table.

"Here's the change, Cook. Hello, Kate." The boy smiled engagingly at Nora as he rummaged in his jeans, then dropped a handful of coins in Cook's apron pocket. He pinched her cheek and grabbed a scone from the basket, then tipped an imaginary cap to the ladies. He left as quickly as he'd entered, whistling out of key.

"That boy," chuckled Cook. "He's always in such a good mood." She pushed the door to the hallway open and drew the cart through into the hall. "And devoted to his mum," she added.

Nora raised an eyebrow quizzically at Kate as she hoisted her bag. As they followed Cook, Kate whispered: "That's Robbie, Gillian Cole's son. She's the nurse who takes care of Sommer and Edmunde."

Nora nodded, inspecting the hall as they walked toward the front of the house. The marbled floor echoed their footsteps. The wide, mahogany staircase was carpeted in a rich burgundy.

Huge paintings of earlier generations of Clarendons lined the walls of the lower level, and Cook directed Nora's attention to the artwork as they passed.

"The whole family is here, Miss. And in the upstairs gallery are the newer generations. It's their tradition to have a portrait painted on their thirtieth birthday. Keith had two more years to go." Cook sniffled and stopped before a set of double doors. She knocked, then straightened her back and put a bright smile on her face. She pushed the doors open, and Nora and Kate trailed after her into the library.

"Here's Miss Kate and her friend come to see you. I've got fresh scones with clotted cream and that blackberry jam you like so much, Mr. Sommer. And Agnes has sent a plum tart."

No one rose to greet the newcomers. Sommer Clarendon, confined to his wheelchair, extended his hand in greeting, and Kate crossed the room to shake it. She introduced Nora as a friend of Keith's from Oxford.

Antonia sat on a loveseat, her hollow expression softening at the mention of Keith's name. When she raised her head, the dark shadows under her eyes stood out in contrast to her silky, blonde curls. Her hands trembled. A brief smile passed over her features as she recognized Kate, but it was Nora who held her attention.

Nora shook hands with Sommer, then walked over to Antonia, who grasped Nora's outstretched hand and patted the cushions beside her. As Kate took a chair beside Sommer, Nora sat down next to Antonia. She felt a wave of sadness emanating from the woman beside her. It was as if an entire conversation had passed between them.

"I'll just get tonight's stew started," Cook said and withdrew, leaving the four of them alone.

Antonia turned Nora's hand over and delicately traced the veins on the back, as though she might find a hidden message from Keith inscribed there. The quiet stretched on as everyone's attention was fixed on Antonia. Kate finally broke the silence.

"Nora and I came to see if there was anything we, or perhaps Simon, could possibly do for either of you." She took a deep breath. "We're very sorry about Keith."

"Thank you, dear. I think we have everything under control right now between Cook and Gillian, and even Robbie is pitching in. But perhaps you could pour for us?" Sommer indicated the teacart.

Kate busied herself pouring and handing out scones with dollops of jam and clotted cream on delicate plates painted with violets. When she set Antonia's plate in front of her, the woman started as though snapped out of a trance and dropped Nora's hand. Her haunted eyes searched Nora's face. She lifted her hand and ran it lightly over Nora's belly.

Nora decided Antonia was lost in a memory. A light, floral fragrance accentuated her gentle touch; her hands were soft and smooth. Nora pictured those same hands brushing hair off a feverish child's forehead. Her eyes filled with tears.

"Don't cry, child," Antonia's voice was soft. Nora had to lean in to hear her. "Keith is with Julia now, and my mother and father and Sommer's parents ... " Her voice trailed off, and she sat back into the cushions, hands clasped, lost in her reverie. Nora sipped tea, and Sommer spoke to fill the gap.

"I understand until recently you worked in Oxford, Miss Tierney?" Sommer asked.

"Please call me Nora. Yes, for the magazine *People and Places*, first as a reporter and then as an editor. I met your son when I won the essay contest that Worth's sponsored. I'm here writing children's books now."

Sommer's eyes sparkled. "Keith was quite excited about that scheme. He had a wealth of good ideas, going on about the new

Wordsworth era he wanted." The man rearranged the rug that covered his legs. He continued on in this vein, recounting other plans Keith had brought to fruition during his school years.

Keith obviously had learned how to set a goal and achieve it, Nora thought, filing this information away as she bit into one of Cook's delicious scones, feeling decadent. After yesterday's respite, her usual healthy appetite was returning. Kate topped off teacups as Nora listened politely to Sommer's discourse on Keith, a brief distraction he seemed to welcome until he ran out of steam and changed the subject.

"Simon faring well?" Sommer asked politely.

His wife cut him off by breaking into the conversation. "Keith was writing a book about the Clarendon history. Perhaps as a writer you would like to see where he worked?" Antonia stood, holding her hand out to Nora, who put down her plate and glanced at the others.

"Yes, I'd like that very much," Nora said. "Actually, Keith mentioned sharing his research with me."

"Excellent idea. You go ahead for a tour," Sommer said, consulting his watch. "Gillian will be here shortly for my round of exercises, and I mustn't upset the routine again."

Antonia led the way out of the room. Nora and Kate followed her up the broad staircase. The balusters were intricately carved; the soft carpeting muffled their steps. At the top, a gallery stretched out on either side. Antonia turned to the right, where a standing sign noted part of the wing was private.

They passed Antonia's portrait. She wore a sky-blue gown that shimmered, with a string of creamy pearls that complemented her fair hair and pale skin. She reminded Nora of a young Grace Kelly. Beside her portrait hung one of a younger Sommer, standing proudly extended to his full, lean height. He was handsome in a grey-vested suit, his dark hair slicked back from a noble forehead. A Scottish Deerhound sat at his feet.

The next set of portraits slowed Nora's steps. A man with curly, black hair and a large frame exuded an aura of imperious strength. Nora assumed this to be Edmunde, the older brother. Next to him, his wife, Julia, seemed too delicate for the man she'd married, yet Nora could see the humor in her sweet smile and the fortitude in her firm chin and uplifted, challenging gaze.

Julia Brookes Clarendon wore a strapless dress of lilac satin that glistened in the light and fell in soft folds. A thin piece of black velvet circled her neck, dangling a large, oval amethyst surrounded by a ring of diamonds; it nestled in the hollow of her throat. The artist had captured the highlights in her dramatically upswept chestnut hair that revealed fine shoulders and an erect posture that spoke of her stage training. Julia's eyes seemed full of life and mischief.

Nora paused before the painting. "She's beautiful," she whispered.

"She'll always be lovely, frozen in time," Antonia said. "Julia wanted her portrait to look like a Sargent painting, and I think the artist succeeded, don't you?"

She gazed wistfully at the portrait, and Nora realized this represented another loss of a loved one. There was so much sadness in this house.

Kate spoke up. "I remember a masquerade ball you had here that Mum and Dad attended. Mum fussed for weeks over their costumes until finally Dad told her to relax. 'No one will outshine Antonia or Julia' he said."

Antonia brightened at the memory. "That was right after we'd found out we were pregnant. I think that was the happiest party of my life." She turned abruptly and continued down the hall to the last door on the left, where she hesitated before opening it.

"This was Keith's playroom when he was a boy." Antonia led them inside, walked over to the windows lining the end wall and looked down at the garden outside.

Nora noted the lake view from here, a fitting room for Keith. She inspected the room, outfitted in a hearty male style. Bookshelves lined one wall, with royal-blue drapery complementing the oak linenfold paneling. Window seats that probably used to hold toys and games were covered in a plush, blue-and-gold fabric. A walnut desk with a high-backed leather chair stood in one corner on an angle, facing the windows, complete with the latest computer equipment.

Nora wandered around the space, taking in the feel of the man who'd worked here. A few loose papers on his desk were neatly stacked under a heavy paperweight with the Clarendon crest captured in brass; a small file box of flash drives stood beside the computer, with several new ones, still in their packaging, lying beside it. Research volumes were piled on one corner of the desk, blue index cards with notes used as bookmarks.

"Keith worked on his family history here?" Nora asked.

Antonia nodded. "He had a routine on his days off. He'd walk mornings, work after lunch all afternoon, then scull on the lake after dinner. He'd come down from Oxford on Friday nights and travel back Monday mornings. Mr. Worth was very accommodating about him coming in later on Mondays. Keith would stay later some evenings during the week to make up the time." She seemed anxious to make Kate and Nora understand that her son had not abused his position.

It occurred to Nora that Keith must have had huge detractors. Why else would his mother see the need to defend him to a virtual stranger?

Antonia straightened a few books and turned to Kate, her eyes lit with a feverish glow. "Why, Kate, I believe I know exactly where I have photos of that fancy dress ball you mentioned. Would you like to see them?"

"Of course, Antonia."

"Come with me to my sitting room." Without waiting, Antonia strode out of the room.

"I'd better see to this," Kate whispered.

"No problem," Nora answered. "I'll wait here and look at Keith's books." A sanctioned opportunity to find that research, she thought—and to snoop.

Kate nodded and left, and Nora approached the large desk. She examined the books on the corner, a pile of what appeared to be dry tomes on area history. Nothing much there. Next she sat in Keith's chair, thinking about the young man she'd known briefly. She rocked in the chair for a minute, remembering his pride in his family's contributions to Lakeland history. He'd seemed so connected to the land that it was difficult for her to imagine him committing suicide in the midst of work on his plans and his book about the area.

Nora inspected the computer. It was a MacBook Pro, similar to hers, and its screen saver showed the Clarendon crest in royal blue on a gold ground. Very regal, she thought as she touched the space bar, wondering about the meaning of the crest's four large Cs. The voices of Kate and Antonia receded behind a closed door, and Nora scanned the icons on the desktop imposed over a view of Lake Windermere from the end of a dock.

One indicated a document labeled "SC2MyBk." It didn't take Nora long to decipher it: Shortcut to my book.

Nora sat back. What if Keith had found something she could use in a future book? He had said his research might be of interest to her.

Just a few clicks, and she was quickly scrolling through the pages, wondering if what she was doing were illegal. Nonsense. She wasn't going to plagiarize his work, after all, she was just reading it. And she had his permission, sort of. Phrases slid past her quick scan: "Sixteen sparkling lakes ... mountains, rare in England, all in 750 square miles ... "

Then the words "Belle Isle" caught her eye, and she stopped to read more thoroughly:

> *Belle Isle, just off the shore of Bowness, acts as a natural divider, separating Lake Windermere into two reaches. The history of the island includes an eight-month siege by followers of Cromwell and involved the capture of one Major Philipson, known as 'Robin the Devil' ...*

This was information Nora hadn't seen before. It would give her series a basis in history. Nora's imagination shifted into overdrive. How exciting would it be to have the ghost of Robin the Devil terrorize her fairies? What else had Keith uncovered that she could use?

The whir of the elevator far down the hall caught Nora's attention, and she hesitated only a moment before she grabbed a new flash drive from its packaging and inserted it into Keith's laptop. She clicked on the File menu, scrolled down to the Save As ... command and saved Keith's document to the drive, thrusting it into the pocket of her skirt. In a few clicks, the monitor reverted back to its screen saver.

Nora picked up a worn copy of *The Lake District and the National Trust* by B. L. Thompson and leaned back in Keith's comfortable chair. The door opened, and a scrawny nurse with frizzy, salt-and-pepper hair entered the study, her white uniform and wan complexion blending together.

"What are you doing here?" the nurse asked brusquely.

Nora felt the color rise in her face and knew the tips of her ears were red, even as she recognized this must be Gillian Cole, mother of the cheerful Robbie.

"Hello to you, too," Nora answered, then stood. "I'm Nora Tierney. Mrs. Clarendon left me here. I was an acquaintance of Keith's." She pushed her glasses back up her nose.

The woman's eyebrows rose as she regarded Nora. She nodded once, muttered, "All right, then," and turned to leave the room as briskly as she'd entered it.

Nora's guilty conscience kicked in, and she spoke before she could shovel the words back into her mouth. "Keith's computer was left on. Should I turn it off?"

Gillian stopped on the threshold and turned back to Nora. "I don't touch things that aren't mine, and I suggest you do the same. The police will be back in the morning, and I'm quite certain they know how to turn those off." She managed a thin smile.

Nora understood that Gillian took her role as Clarendon protector quite seriously. The flash drive burned a hole in her pocket. "I'm sure you're right," she answered.

Nodding brusquely, Gillian left the room, leaving Nora to contemplate her new profession as a thief.

Chapter Twenty-One

"There is no such thing as accident. What we call by that name is the effect of some cause which we do not see."
— Voltaire, *Letters de Memmius, III*

Nora left Keith's library and wandered back down the hall, searching for Kate. She couldn't stay in that study another minute; the stolen flash drive weighed heavily in her pocket, and she was anxious to be off with it. She paused in front of the portraits of Julia and Edmunde, Antonia and Sommer and was aware of a stirring familiarity she couldn't identify.

She withdrew her camera from the bag slung over her shoulder and took individual shots of the four portraits. The camera was back in her bag, and she had just realized she should move the flash drive into it, too, when the door directly across from her opened. Kate and a red-eyed Antonia emerged from the chamber and joined her. In the bright daylight, Nora saw how large Antonia's pupils were, the effects of the tranquilizer Cook had mentioned.

"I'm afraid I've monopolized Kate, Nora. I hope you weren't too bored," Antonia said.

"Not at all," Nora assured her, her shame increasing. "Keith had quite a collection of books on this area. I wonder if I might borrow a few in the future?" And legitimize my actions, she added to herself.

"Nora's writing a series of children's book centered on Belle Isle and a troupe of fairies that live there," Kate reminded her.

"Yes, of course." Antonia's expression warmed. "As soon as

Detective Travers says we can release Keith's things, I'd be happy for you to return and borrow anything you'd like."

Antonia's graciousness made the object in Nora's pocket burn even hotter. With a few contrite goodbyes on Nora's part and promises to return for the funeral, she and Kate took their leave of the bereaved mother and walked back down the long driveway.

"Sommer is so polite and reserved, but I think Antonia is mostly in a daze," Kate said as they reached the bottom of the drive and turned onto the road.

Nora was about to answer when a man on a bicycle whirred past them, almost knocking Nora off her feet. Kate grabbed Nora's arm before she went down, but her bag went flying, its contents scattering across the road. Once Nora was righted, her hand patted her stomach and slipped into her pocket. Both items safe.

A strong odor of stale alcohol wafted behind the culprit. He swerved into the bushes near the stone pillars and jumped off it to avoid crashing into one of the large columns. The bike clattered to the ground with a metallic racket, and the drunk staggered over to Nora, who took a step backward as the man's smell preceded him.

"Daniel Rowley, you need to be more careful!" Kate admonished. "And don't you dare show up to work tomorrow without taking a hot bath, or Agnes won't have to complain to me anymore because you'll be on the dole."

She bent to retrieve Nora's camera, checking it for damage. "You all right?" she asked Nora, handing it to her.

Nora nodded as Daniel lifted her notebook. She saw him rifle through the pages before she could snatch it quickly from his grimy hand. "Thank you," she said as she grabbed it from him.

"Let this be a lesson to you, duckie," he growled at Nora and walked back to his bike.

"I think that's everything." Kate retrieved a tube of lipstick and a roll of antacids from across the road. They watched Rowley right the bicycle after prying a few snapped twigs from between the spokes. Reseating himself, he rode away without looking back.

Both women stood looking after him from opposite sides of the road. Kate put her hands on her slim hips and shook her head. "Such a gentleman," she said with heavy sarcasm as she walked to Nora and gave her back her items. "One of the district's finer chaps."

A crime van passed them and turned into the gates, making its way up the driveway.

"Curiouser and curiouser," Kate said.

Nora followed Kate as they walked on, Rowley's warning ringing in her ears. She was convinced he had deliberately run her down—and her baby could have been hurt. Her nose twitched in anger, her mothering instincts kicking in, but with that came a sense of uneasiness at Daniel's comment. "Tell me about Daniel."

Daniel lived in a decrepit shack on Clarendon land, Kate explained. It used to be the gamekeeper's shed when the estate had been fully functioning. He helped Agnes in Ramsey Lodge's kitchen when there was dinner service and did gardening and simple maintenance. "He's not really skilled, but when he hasn't been drinking he can be useful, and he's good with the garden."

"And he works here, too?"

"Cook gives him chores, here and there, so he ekes out a living. He's always hanging around one of the two places."

Nora would need to keep her eyes open for Daniel Rowley from now on. She stopped and pointed to a large building on a hill beside the lake. Through the trees, she could just see Belsfield Hotel in large, white letters. "One of your competitors?" Nora asked.

"Not really," Kate said with a shrug. "They're much bigger than us, and there's enough custom to go around. But see how it overlooks that promenade where the cruise boats sail from?"

At Nora's nod, Kate continued. "It belonged to an industrialist who traveled daily to his businesses in Barrow-in-Furness partly via the lake, then finished his trip by steam train to Barrow." Kate stopped before a bench in the shade, and the two women sat down.

"That might spur a story line for me," Nora said.

"He walked down to the pier every morning, followed by his butler carrying breakfast on a silver tray. Can't you just picture it?"

Nora forgot the run-in with Daniel Rowley as the idea for a story began to grow in her mind. "Do you know his name?"

"Henry William Schneider," Kate answered.

Nora withdrew her camera, intact but for a few minute scratches on the case, and took several shots of the hotel and its view of the lake. Sunlight speckled the water's surface. With the changing autumn colors of the trees, Nora could smell the musty leaves, turning brittle. The whole area resonated with the glow of nature in every season. She felt a sense of rightness that she'd chosen this area, both for her book and for her child. It might be a temporary stop, but it would more than do for a while, and she had to learn to take each day as it arrived on her doorstep.

"Thanks for the great idea, Kate. Maybe the fairies will rescue Mr. Schneider's ghost in a future story."

"Those trays were heavy—maybe they should rescue the butler instead." Kate laughed.

Nora felt a rush of gratitude toward this woman for her generosity and friendship. "Listen, Kate—you know so many local stories. I'd hoped Keith would be a source for that kind of information, and I've got a load of books, but some stories aren't documented. Would you help me from time to time?"

Kate's smile was infectious. "I'd be delighted to, Nora. And you can help me plan my wedding. Ian thinks I'm procrastinating, but I've got a whole folder crammed with ideas. I have a good idea of what I'd like, just not when."

They started walking again.

"You've never told me your wedding date," Nora said.

"That's because Ian and I can't agree on one," Kate explained. "Ian wants to get married in the spring, but I think we should wait until the summer."

"Why wait?" Nora asked. "Not that it's any of my business," she added.

Kate bit her lip. "Once Ian and I are married, things will change at the lodge—they have to. I worry that Simon won't want to carry on, and I know I can't run it without him."

Nora let her surprise show. "You think he's only here temporarily?"

Kate grimaced. "He loved living in France and still has close friends there." She shrugged. "I think he stayed after our dad died so I wouldn't be alone, but that might change when Ian moves in."

"But Ian certainly won't be around much to help at the lodge, no matter when you marry," Nora pointed out. Friends still in France—the phone call she'd overheard made more sense. Just *how* friendly remained to be seen, if she should be caring at all.

"I know," Kate said. She smiled. "I do want to marry Ian. When we started to go out, I had no idea I would fall in love with a detective. He's so conscientious and smart. I love that he doesn't feel black and white about everything. He understands there are shades of grey to most situations and tries to look at every angle. I really admire that he's not judgmental at all."

"And he's quite good-looking," Nora added.

"There is that."

THE GREEN REMAINS

"Then marry the lad before he changes his mind."

"If you agree to help me, I will. And I'll just let Simon decide his own future."

Nora's answering grin felt good as it broke across her face. "It's a deal." Things to look forward to that didn't involve bodies or death.

Chapter Twenty-Two

"'You look familiar,' said the interviewer as he flexed a rubber band between his thumb and forefinger."
— Cindy Packard, *The Mother Load*

11:44 AM

Ian Travers paced the entry hall of Ramsey Lodge, stopping to scrutinize an old oil painting on one wall. It was a scene of Brant Fell, the mountain nearest Bowness, a steep peak but not the highest in the Lake District National Park. Ian remembered climbing it in his youth to impress an outdoorsy date. Despite having been in good shape, he'd still reached the summit ten minutes after her, panting, to her gales of laughter. The memory did not improve his mood.

He waited for Simon to come downstairs from showing a guest to his room. The forensic tech had finished with the studio and had left to pick up Sommer's plant, evidence bags in tow. Ian felt uncomfortable on so many levels. This turn of events would not go down well with Kate, and he would be forced yet again into the position of explaining how important it was that he perform his job without any hint of prejudice. He also knew today's actions might affect the lodge's custom and eventually how the townspeople viewed Simon, with Kate included by extension—especially if reporters, picking up the story, began to hound them.

Simon was a friend; Ian had a tough time seeing him as a murderer. He sighed as he remembered one of his first murder cases, early in his career. The perpetrator had turned out to be the lover of the victim's wife, the same woman who'd gone to pieces when told of her husband's demise. Ian had been convinced she wasn't involved, but he'd been wrong. Her boyfriend had killed his competitor, and she'd been a very good actress. He'd never taken surface appearances as absolute truth again.

The heavy front door opened. "Ian!" Kate gave him a hug. Nora came in behind her and waved hello. "I'm surprised to see you in the middle of the day," Kate added.

"Not as surprised as I was," Simon announced from the stairway.

Kate turned to Ian. "What's happened?" Simon joined them in the hall.

A young couple staying at the lodge came down the stairs and nodded to the four people standing awkwardly in the hall.

Ian said: "Let's go into Simon's rooms, shall we? And I'll explain."

Kate was livid. "You can't be serious! You think Simon is involved in Keith's death?"

Ian was firm. "I'm forced to treat Simon as I would any suspect when the cause of death brings him into the circle of attention, Kate. Having that rare plant in his possession does that. In addition, Simon and Keith argued in public more than once over his expansion plans, and there was that fight at The Scarlet Wench."

Kate's face turned a deep shade of red. "They were both lit, and Keith threw the first punch—Simon just defended himself. I was *there*."

Ian turned to Simon. This wasn't going anywhere. "Let's get this over with. If we go down to the station for your formal statement, I can have it transcribed quickly for you to sign."

Simon nodded. "Kate, this is just procedure. I'm fine. Nora, a friend of yours has checked in and was asking questions about you—Tony Warner?"

Nora scowled. "Tony is not a friend. He's a snob who writes the worst articles I've ever edited. Old Jenks must have sent him to get a scoop from me once he heard about Keith's death—he'd never let an opportunity for publicity pass by."

"I put him in the Sherlock Holmes suite," Simon told Kate.

She nodded absently, still focused on Ian. "I hope handcuffs won't be necessary." She turned on her heel and stomped off.

Ian shook his head. This was only going to get worse.

CHAPTER TWENTY-THREE

"I had taken Mrs. Prest into my confidence; without her in truth
I should have made but little advance, for the fruitful idea in the
whole business dropped from her friendly lips."
— Henry James, *The Aspern Papers*

12:10 PM

Nora sat on her bed and slipped off her shoes. She lay back against the pillows, her mind percolating on poisonous plants and stolen flash drives. Was that why Simon hadn't wanted her in his studio, because that plant was there? What difference could his painting a rare flower make? She felt a ripple of apprehension. No way could he be involved in Keith's death. Not Simon. Her mobile interrupted her reverie, and she saw it was Val.

Nora quickly described the events that led to Simon being taken in for questioning. "I can't believe that Ian will hold him, not right now, but it's still awful, big time," Nora said. Then she remembered their conversation that morning. "Good thing you decided to check out the travel agency. With Ian having to investigate Simon's involvement in Keith's death, he'll need help finding the real killer." Just like Declan Barnes did, solving Bryn Wallace's murder, Nora told herself.

Val explained the scene she'd witnessed at the travel agency, describing the break-in and police in attendance. Nora sat up at Val's description of Glenn Hackney.

"I know who you mean," Nora said. "He was there when I met Keith at Worth's for dinner the night I won the contest." She searched her memory. "No old gent then, but I remember seeing a girl, very mod looking with bleached-out hair and three inches of dark roots showing."

"I don't get that look, do you? I didn't see anyone like that today, although that reminds me—I thought I'd seen this Glenn before and I finally figured out where ... " Val paused dramatically.

"Don't make me beg for it, Val—where?"

"At The Blue Virgin, that club I used to go to with Bryn. I saw him on a Wednesday, enjoying the blue movies shot against the wall. That's the night people go to be checked out—you know, to see who's pierced what, who's alone—get the idea?"

Nora pictured her friend with the odd golden eyes and short pixie haircut. "Got it. You don't have to protect my Victorian sensibilities. Knowing you has shot them all to hell." They shared a laugh until Nora became serious again. She returned to the hot water Simon had found himself in and her intention to clear him. "It makes me twitch to think he'd be involved. Not possible," she said emphatically, tamping down any misgivings. "Let's think about this. Glenn Hackney is probably gay if you saw him at The Blue Virgin. How does that involve Keith beyond the obvious?"

The line was quiet as both women thought this over. Finally, Val spoke up.

"Maybe Hackney's boss doesn't know he's gay—if he's a much older chap, he may have negative ideas about a homosexual employee. Perhaps Keith found out and was blackmailing Hackney?"

Nora considered this. "I don't think Keith was the blackmailing type, but then I haven't met too many blackmailers before. I suppose it's possible Keith was gay, and maybe he and Glenn had a failed relationship?" She warmed quickly to her theory. "Do you plan to go to The Blue Virgin again this Wednesday, Val?"

"I may have a bit of chatting up to do now, won't I? I'll see what dirt I can unearth."

"Thanks." Nora explained her visit to Clarendon Hall and described meeting Keith's parents. She included seeing the gallery paintings and finding the books Keith kept in his study. "And I discovered information on Belle Isle I hadn't seen before—"

The floor creaked outside Nora's door; she paused.

"Yankee, you still there?" Val asked.

"Yeah. Say, at the break-in, was there anyone from the police we ... met before?"

"As in your pal Declan Barnes?"

Nora cleared her throat. "I have no idea what you mean, my friend."

"Busted. But don't worry, your secret's safe with me. No, just the regular plod, no one we met on Bryn's case. I'll call you again after I snoop this week."

"Be careful, Val."

"Cheerio." Ringing off, Nora slipped off her bed and quietly cracked her bedroom door. The hall was empty. She was desperate to hide the flash drive still in her pocket.

She scoured her room, looking for a place that wouldn't be obvious. Then she remembered Poe's classic story *The Purloined Letter*, in which evidence was left in plain view, and went to her desk. Opening a drawer, she selected a label, wrote Belle Isle on it in case someone snooped and slipped the drive into the USB port of her laptop, leaving it on her desk.

Chapter Twenty-Four

*"A great talker—he has the knack of telling you nothing
in a big way."*
— Molière, *Le Misanthrope*

3 PM

Simon realized he should be grateful to Ian for keeping his word about the quick visit to Kendal. He'd never been inside the working part of a police station, but it lived up to his imagination: notices covered the non-descript painted walls; telephones beeped, and copy machines hummed; people, most uniformed but a surprising number in civilian clothes, moved with a sense of purpose. It was a daunting experience to be on the wrong side of the desk.

His almost-brother-in-law had a team member take a succinct statement. Ian kept Simon's appearance low-key, and Simon hoped that news he was helping the police with their enquiries wouldn't spread through the Bowness community. In his statement, he explained clearly about borrowing the rare flower from Sommer for use in a painting. He'd asked for that particular one because of its rareness, not because he knew anything of its poisonous capabilities. "Everyone knows Sommer has rare flowers. That one just caught my fancy—it wouldn't normally be seen in this area, and that fit my concept for the painting." He hadn't been pressed to explain his plans further nor to describe the painting.

Simon was surprised he hadn't been asked about the pub fight he and Keith had had the year before, but Ian indicated this was a preliminary statement until the final lab results were in. When

Simon left Kendal station, he felt sorry for the position Ian found himself in, especially with how it was interfering with his relationship with Kate. Simon decided that at this time there simply wasn't enough evidence to connect him with Keith's death—yet. He knew he would remain a prime suspect until someone else was put in the spotlight. It was an unnerving thought.

When the constable dropped him off, Simon made a beeline for his studio. He was relieved to see his paintings appeared untouched. They stood in stacks around the perimeter, propped against the ledge that ran around three sides of the room and that held supplies. Some paintings were still uncompleted; others waited to be framed. A few were first attempts he'd put aside when he'd been unhappy with his initial results. He'd worked as an artist long enough to know that he might salvage or change his first idea into something usable.

It appeared that only the plant and a few brushes that stood near his easel had been taken. The brushes were easily replaced, and a receipt for everything had been left behind. With a sigh, Simon closed the studio door and sat at his kitchen table with a beer. He didn't want to seek out Kate or Nora just now; they'd be filled with questions or sympathy, and Kate was sure to be angry with Ian. Simon's gaze fell on several sketches he'd laid out on the table, possible cover designs for Nora's books.

For the moment, his creative impulses deserted him, and he viewed the drawings with a jaded eye, although he hoped Nora's reaction to the ideas would be positive. Nora. He worried about her. The fact he was now in the sights of the police for Keith's death was certain to put her inquisitive streak into action. She seemed to forget she didn't have only herself to worry about.

This period in her pregnancy was supposed to be her healthy time, according to *What to Expect When You're Expecting*. Her body was stretching inside and out as the baby grew and gained weight and length. Nora read him passages every week. He knew the boy's lungs were almost fully developed but needed time to mature. What if she stressed herself and brought on an early delivery?

Simon shook his head. Whatever his ultimate relationship with Nora, he'd have to keep a closer eye on her until this business about Keith Clarendon was sorted out. He kept hoping it would all turn out to be a horrible accident. Lurking at the back of his mind was the thought that innocent people had been wrongly convicted of crimes before.

There was a sharp knock at his door, and Simon rose and slid it open to face the cool and annoying polish of Tony Warner.

"Ah, there you are. Sorry to bother, but I wondered if you could spare a moment to clarify some questions regarding the death of the Clarendon lad and his relationship with Nora Tierney."

The reporter had ignored the "Private" sign at the dining room exit to find him. Simon decided Tony must be the first person he'd met who could pretend to be cordial without his face showing a glint of warmth. This wanker had the talk down, all right. Tony's smoothness irritated Simon the way a small pebble in his shoe might worry a blister. As Tony seemed prepared to enter his suite, Simon stood his ground, blocking the entrance. Two could play this game.

"This is a private area, Mr. Warner, and I'm afraid you've caught me working. In any case, I've been officially instructed not to give interviews to the press. They've all been warned off by Detective Inspector Travers, but I guess you missed his report." Simon caught himself before nodding to emphasize what he thought was his own cohesive statement.

Not easily deterred, Tony lounged against the doorjamb, indicating to Simon he would not be so deftly managed. He pressed his point. "I work for the same magazine Nora did. Surely you would want her side of the story presented."

"There are no sides to anything, Mr. Warner," Simon answered coldly. He shuddered to think of this man knowing he was under police suspicion. "There is no discussion, just a set of facts leading to a miserable death, and Miss Tierney had the misfortune to be the first one on the scene. Now if you'll forgive me … " It was with a great deal of pleasure that Simon stepped back and slid his door closed in Tony Warner's face.

Simon closed his door in Tony Warner's face, missing the triumphant smile that spread across it. Tony wanted to rub his hands in glee, but restrained himself as he hurried to the Sherlock Holmes suite. A silhouette of the famed detective's profile was framed over the brass bed, where a herringbone duvet complemented the masculine vintage decor, complete with a wooden hat stand that held a brass-topped cane. Tony had added his own walking stick to the stand when he'd unpacked. He sat at the kneehole desk situated under the window and paused in his typing. The trick, he knew, was to create a sensational, eye-catching headline without also creating a slanderous situation.

He despised Nora Tierney. It wasn't enough that she had the temerity to run her daft blue pencil through his carefully chosen words and phrases, she was a bloody American to boot! He should have been chosen editor in her place, by rights.

He'd been on a slow boil since her promotion. To make things worse, after working for almost two years, she'd had the gall to throw it all away to escape to this sleepy town to write children's books. Some people lacked common sense and didn't know how to get ahead in the world.

Tony knew Old Jenks was primed for and expected a fair article on Nora, and he would complete one in record time. However, there were those eager rag sheets to be considered that paid well without questions, plus the local Cumbrian papers.

Consoling himself with the thought that Nora's blue pencil would never fly through his articles again, Tony sniggered at the thought of getting paid several times over for nearly the same article. He considered just how sensationally he could embellish the facts before dinner.

CHAPTER TWENTY-FIVE

*"Every time a child says 'I don't believe in fairies' there is a little
fairy somewhere that falls down dead."*
—James M. Barrie, *Peter Pan*

3:20 PM

Simon watched Nora walk around his table, inspecting the
sketches laid out before her, Darby at her heels. She paused by
one showing Daria with a regal look, her long auburn tresses
crowned by a coronet of blue flowers. Nora didn't comment on
the fairy's resemblance to herself. Instead, she said, "I like this
one best, showing the base of their tree house. Having Daria up
front implies her dominance. Where would we put the others?"

Simon could feel Nora's restraint in not asking him about his
interview with Ian. It felt like Keith's ghost shared the room.
Was this how it was going to be now, living with the haunting
of a man in death who had not particularly been a friend in life?
"Maybe Cosmo could be up here on a limb, looking down at
her." He pointed to his drawing of the oldest elf, his tiny, gnarled
body eclipsed by an enormous set of dragonfly wings. "Since he
wears a ruby cap, the red hanging tassel will stand out against
the green leaves of the bough."

Nora met his eyes, full of question. "Great," she said, rubbing
her belly. "What about Logan?"

Simon said, "The gnome would be lying adoringly at Daria's feet, maybe reading her a poem." Should he bring it up or
would she?

"With his poet's shirt sleeves rolled up to show off his muscles," Nora suggested.

"You ladies seem to go for the guys with big biceps," Simon said, drawing closer.

"Women want a man who can protect them, even when they don't need protecting," she said, lifting her head to meet his eyes.

Simon ran two fingers along the side of Nora's chin, then bent down and pulled her to him in a gentle hug. "I've been wanting to do that since yesterday." He drew away before she could.

"Simon, was it awful at the police station?"

Finally out in the open. "Nah, it was fine." He ruffled her hair. "Ian was quick and his sergeant professional. I spent most of the time drinking bitter coffee and waiting to sign my statement." He saw the relief on her face. Then her expression changed, and she reached out for his hand.

"Wait for it," she whispered, putting his hand on the crest of her stomach.

Simon felt a ripple run across her and stick out. "Foot, I think." He grinned when the baby pushed back against his hand. "Any closer to his name?"

Nora walked to the sink. "What do you think of Blaine? Sounds relaxed, sort of outgoing." She filled a glass with water and drank.

Simon chewed his cheek. "You want my honest opinion, right?" He had no desire to offend but continued when she nodded. "I think it sounds like someone who'd be a thoughtless know-it-all, intolerant and small-minded." He lifted a shoulder. "Sorry."

Nora laughed. "I do better with fairies. You didn't comment once on Dove, Tess or Sky as names for the sprites."

"That's because they fit. You have to picture your lad as he grows up and think of a name you'd enjoy calling him over and over for years."

Nora wrinkled her nose. "Feels like I'm getting a dog instead of a child."

"What would you name a dog?"

"Chet."

"Chet?"

"For Chet Baker."

"Does that mean the boy could be Chet?"

Nora shook her head. "No, no, Chet is for a dog. A boy's name has to fit certain criteria."

Here we go. Simon asked, "And those would be?" Wait for her list. Humor the pregnant lady.

Nora took her little notebook from her pocket. "It's got to be short, so it's easy to call him when he's out playing. Or if he's in trouble. You don't want to spend too much time yelling for Horatio or Bartholomew when he shouldn't be crossing the street." She said this with all seriousness.

"Bartholomew?"

"Because of the story of the hats, but that's not it. It's too long, which is exactly my point."

"Of course it is." Simon moved a few sketches around the table. "Let's get back to fairies."

4:10 PM

Glenn Hackney smiled at his own initiative as he carefully packed his bags. He covered his dark suit with a garment bag and ran a duster over his black oxfords before slipping them into shoe bags and adding them to the suitcase he would use in Bowness. The rest would stay in the boot of the car. His other personal things were already packed up and would be sent along when the moment was right. It was good to have friends, just a few, that a bloke could trust.

He looked forward to this sojourn in the Lake District. It

meant having to rent a car, but he would charge it to the company, and it would give him independent transport instead of waiting on the stroppy British Rail. A nice ride on a lovely October day, a few days off to check things out and plan for his future—what could be better?

After the break-in and questioning by the plod, Glenn had offered to drive Mr. Worth home. Mrs. Worth fussed over them both and insisted he stay for lunch. He'd fawned over the hag, praised her grotty decorating skills and devoured her chicken salad. She'd been suitably impressed, and he'd enlisted her aid with his plan. It hadn't taken much urging at that point for them to convince the shaken Mr. Worth he should take the rest of the day off at home to relax with his wife.

Glenn would be the one to pack up Keith's desk and bring his things to his family in Bowness-on-Windermere. It sounded idyllic, a small village out of time, like Brigadoon. He'd even offered to represent the agency at Keith's funeral, and a grateful Worth had nodded encouragingly, telling his wife he didn't know how he would ever get along without Glenn.

Glenn knew that at Scotland Yard he was known as Macavity for T. S. Eliot's devious cat, a sobriquet that delighted him. The moniker had been bestowed for his ability to slip right through their fingers, and he intended to do so once again.

130   THE GREEN REMAINS

Chapter Twenty-Six

"John Thomas says good-night to Lady Jane, a little droopingly, but with a hopeful heart."
— D. H. Lawrence, *Lady Chatterley's Lover*

5:40 PM

Ian's ears were still ringing after his meeting with DCI Clarke at Carleton Hall force headquarters.

"I'm pulling you off this case, Travers. There can't be any sense of a conflict of interest seen by outsiders," Clarke had stated.

"No, I can do this, sir. Simon Ramsey is only implicated right now by having the plant in his studio. That's a long way from motive and opportunity." He had to stay on this case. Kate would think he was deserting her and her brother. "I know this village and the people in it, boss, better than anyone else."

"Hmmm ... "

"I would be the first one to remove myself if I thought I couldn't be impartial," Ian had added, trying to keep his face blank.

"Very well. But I don't have to tell you what's at stake here."

Only my bloody career, Ian had thought, hearing "I'll be watching you" between the lines.

"We need a quick resolution to this, Ian," Clarke had stressed as he'd shown Ian to his door.

Don't I know it, Ian thought gloomily as he headed back to his office. Once there, he conferred with Detective Sergeant Stephen Higgins about the team's progress.

"Anything on the house to house?" Ian asked.

Higgins shook his head, his baby face as nonaggressive as

ever. "A few cranks, but we'll check them out." Given Higgins' small nose and receding chin, most people meeting the man for the first time were surprised to learn the nonthreatening, compliant chap was actually a competent detective sergeant. "We're expanding past the Clarendon estate and the lakeside dock. The area's full of people, but most of them don't live here, and passing tourists don't stay in one place long enough to interview."

"Have you been back to the Hall yet?" Ian asked.

"Tomorrow, first thing, to pick up the computer and finish the interviews. DCI Clarke talked to the parents, the cook and the nurse."

"I've seen those notes. Nothing of use there, but you'll have to get formal statements from them all. You'd better see if you're able get anything out of the older brother, Edmunde." DCI Clarke's admonition still rang in Ian's ears. "I hear he doesn't speak much, but it won't do to leave anyone out." Ian sighed. Keith's death wasn't the only case on his desk, just the most pressing. He initialed a few reports and threw them in his outbox. "How about the missing girl?"

Higgins rolled back on his heels. "We had one sighting out at Brantwood we're checking out."

"John Ruskin's old home? What would a young girl be doing out there?" Ian shook his head. "If she had a car, we could at least be using the Automatic Number Plate Recognition system to try to track her."

"The drug squad uses the ANPR mostly, boss, on the M6."

"It may be one of the biggest drug supply lines in the country, but I didn't see any history of drug use with Anne Reed." Ian flipped through his file on the missing girl.

"Her mum insists she was a down-to-earth kid, quite nice by all accounts," Higgins confirmed. "I expect we'll find her in a tarn some day, trussed up and abused before being killed."

"You have such a joyous outlook, Higgins. Just keep the wheels turning. Something will turn up." Ian knew many cases were solved by the tedious connection of seemingly unrelated details.

Higgins left, and Ian rubbed the back of his neck. He glanced at the station clock, wondering if Kate's ire had cooled. Perhaps after she'd had a chance to speak with Simon at dinner, she'd see her brother had been handled quickly and discreetly.

Ian sat back in his chair, remembering Kate in school, always lean and athletic, sure of herself and with the creative Ramsey bent that set her and Simon apart from their classmates. They were both friendly and polite, never condescending. The feeling they gave off was that they saw things with a different eye.

He was not surprised when Kate left Bowness for design school in London and stayed on as a set decorator for some of the West End's top productions. It was when she came home after her mother's sudden stroke to help her father run Ramsey Lodge that he became attracted to her in a way that startled them both. They started dating, and he was increasingly grateful that she stayed in Bowness after her father's subsequent death. For months following the elder Ramsey's death, Ian worried Kate would sell her interest in the lodge and return to her glittery city life. It took him a long time to understand that he was part of the reason she'd stayed.

Ian hit "Save" and emailed his report for his team to review. He printed a copy for the murder book and another for the case manager. He needed to read up on the findings from the rest of the team before going to see Kate. Despite Higgins' pessimism regarding Anne Reed, Ian had to keep his finger on top of it all and keep his team active and involved.

10:30 PM

Ian rose reluctantly from the comfortable chenille sofa that sat in front of the fireplace in Kate's suite. By the time he'd arrived at Ramsey Lodge, Kate had spoken with Simon over dinner, and her anger had dissipated. Ian felt relaxed in her company for the first time since the discovery of Keith's body. Her engagement ring sparkled in the light, and he felt they were back on course.

"If I don't leave now, I'll stay the night," he said.

"You going? I thought—"

"Sorry, Kate, there's nothing I'd like more than to crawl into bed with you." He reached for his jacket on the sofa's arm. "But I have to leave early in the morning to go into Oxford."

Kate raised an eyebrow. "All the way to Oxford? That's what phones and computers are for."

"Don't forget Keith worked there, too." He reached for her waist.

"I should be glad you're not arresting Simon. Don't say it, I know—you're just doing your job." She had been decidedly cool when he arrived but had softened as the evening progressed. "I know Simon is innocent, and that's all that matters. All of this will soon be behind us—I hope." She draped her arms around his neck. She hardly had to tilt her head back to look into his eyes. "Have I told you lately how sometimes I abhor your bloody job?" She pressed her body into him and lightly bit the lobe of his left ear.

He knew she could feel his immediate response against her stomach. "Yes, you have, on numerous occasions." He folded her into his arms, enjoying how they fit together. "Have I told you that you don't play a fair game?" He ran his arms over her back and lightly teased the nape of her neck.

She shivered and leaned into him harder, swaying her hips

across his groin. "You could leave from here. I have your clothes from last time all clean and ready." She kissed his bottom lip, then sucked it into her mouth.

He pushed his mouth against hers in assent as their tongues met in recognition and desire. They broke apart, faces flushed and smiling. Kate led him to her bedroom, turning out lights along the way.

CHAPTER TWENTY-SEVEN

*"Several years ago circumstances thrust me into a position in which
it became possible for the friend who figures in these pages as Godfrey
Loring to do me a favor."*
— David Graham Phillips, *The Husband's Story*

10:45 PM

Simon felt torn between waking Nora or covering her with a
blanket to let her sleep longer in the chair. He studied her, curled
up around a pillow to support her baby bulge, and thought back
to earlier in the evening.

They'd agreed a big meal wasn't what any of them wanted
and raided the lodge kitchen to find leftover chicken stew. After leaving Agnes a note owning up, they ate in Simon's rooms,
avoiding talk of Keith's death or Simon's interview. When they
finished, Kate left to await Ian, and Simon lit the fire. They sat
in companionable silence, watching the flames dance. Nora
paged through her baby name book. Simon turned on the radio;
Handel's "Water Music" became a backdrop to the crackling
fire. Darby settled on the rug in front of the fire and let out a
contented snore.

Nora broke the silence. "I wonder if Keith had a girlfriend?
Kate didn't know. Could he have been gay?"

"I don't know," Simon answered. "When I saw him, it was
usually at a town meeting or out on the lake. Maybe in Oxford
he had a relationship of some sort?"

Nora shifted in her chair. When she spoke, it was almost a
whisper. "Have you ever been a part of something you knew to
be wrong but were unable to stop?"

Where was this going? Simon held his breath. Surely Nora couldn't believe he had anything to do with Keith's death?

Nora didn't wait for his answer. "I never knew Paul properly, I see that now—not who he was inside when he let his hair down or on a deep level, the way I should have if I was going to marry him. That isn't like me at all. I love research, looking into things, exploring them, and that includes people."

Simon nodded and let his breath out. Nora shrugged and settled back into her chair, pulling her glasses off and rubbing the sides of her nose. It was reasonable that death would be on Nora's mind, and this would bring her to the memory of her baby's father. He searched for something to say and settled for honesty. "I think it would've been terrible if you'd married him feeling that way."

"I suppose so, but now that he's dead, I have the distance to see I should've broken off the engagement. When Kate asked if I'd considered naming the baby Paul, I had such a negative feeling, I knew our relationship had died long before he did." Her eyes appealed for understanding.

Simon leaned forward, hiding his relief, a smile playing at the corners of his mouth. "So you think it would have been better for Paul if you'd broken his heart just before he died?"

Nora shrugged. "Neither of us knew that plane would go down. I might have been doing him a favor, something he wanted to do himself and couldn't. But then without him, I wouldn't have little What's-His-Name here. He'll probably be the spitting image of Paul or have his personality as he grows."

Simon sat back. He restrained himself from speaking his thoughts aloud. He doubted any man who had Nora in his life would willingly give her up.

"What will you do about Paul's parents? Will they be a part of the baby's life?"

Nora shook her head. "We only met once, at his memorial service. They blamed me for not seeing Paul when it was his work that kept him away. I didn't know I was pregnant then and haven't contacted them since. They'd made it clear I wasn't their cup of tea. Since it was my decision to raise the baby alone and I'm not asking them for help, I'm leaving them out of it."

Simon considered this. "You can always change your mind on that."

"I suppose." She dozed off soon after asking him what he thought of the name Harold. His expression alone was answer enough but he merely said, "Purple crayons," and she put her book away.

Simon leaned over to scrutinize her relaxed face. The marks her glasses left on either side of her nose had softened but were still visible, two tiny lima bean-shaped depressions. Circles of strain under her eyes looked blue in the firelight. He reached out to wake her but before he could touch her, the night bell clanged.

Straightening up, Simon checked the clock over the kitchen sink. Almost 11. The bell rang in his room and Kate's, but since he'd told her she could have the night off, he'd answer it before it woke Nora. He let himself quietly out of the room and headed down the hall.

When Simon opened the front door, the sleek young man leaning on the doorframe stood up and pushed past him into the wide hall. The scent of vanilla wafted in with him. Simon relocked the door and followed him to the desk. The man put his Gucci leather bag down and retrieved a shiny, black alligator wallet from his breast pocket. Simon took in his narrow, craggy face and his equally narrow mustache.

"Cheerio! Hope I haven't roused you out of bed, but I got a late start. You do have a room?" He smiled and glanced pointedly at the VACANCY sign on the corner of the desk.

For the second time that day, Simon wished he'd flipped the thing over, regardless of the effect this would have on their custom. He cleared his throat and pushed the register toward the young man, his instincts telling him this would be another annoying guest. Simon watched the man carefully write his name in a distinctive script, complete with ornate flourishes. Another poser in the guise of a bright spark.

"Right then, Mr. Hackney. How long will you be staying with us?"

Glenn's wide mouth contained a full complement of capped white teeth, which he hid after changing his smile to what he must have deemed a more appropriate somber frown. "Until after the memorial service for my colleague, the late Keith Clarendon."

Both men turned in the direction of footsteps coming through the dining room. A tousled Nora appeared in the doorway, waved to Simon and turned back toward her room without noticing Glenn, who was fishing out his Platinum card.

CHAPTER TWENTY-EIGHT

*"If you should have a boy do not christen him John ... 'Tis a bad
name and goes against a man. If my name had been
Edmund I should have been more fortunate."*
— John Keats

Sunday, 24th October

7:55 AM

The morning started as usual for Gillian Cole. She rose with the
sun, jotting Robbie a note about his lessons and chores for the
day. Leaving their cottage on the grounds of Clarendon Hall,
she walked the short distance to the main building, breathing in
the fresh morning scents the lake offered as the mist rose: a smell
of oak, birch and conifers mixed with the late-season wild garlic
and the smoke of early-morning fires. An elusive red squirrel
ran across her path, and Gillian took this as a sign that the day
would be a good one.

Her damp hair felt cool against her neck, and she reached
up and spread it with her fingers, fanning it to dry, reflecting
on how the human body could change. Her hair as a teenager
had been thick and full, taking hours to dry naturally. Today, it
would be dry by the time she took breakfast up to Edmunde.

When not in his presence, Gillian thought of Edmunde in
his prime, before the stroke left him to rely on her for his ba-
sic needs. Sommer had been her only patient then, and she'd
been integrated into the small Clarendon household as time had
passed. Edmunde had been the strong one, bold and loud. His
presence in a room had seemed to take up more space than any-

one else's. Gillian knew well, though, the dark rage of loss that had hovered just beneath his lusty exterior and drinking bouts.

Gillian remembered him as a teen, when she'd glimpsed him in town, home for the holidays from the exclusive school he and Sommer had attended. With his swarthy good looks and brazen nature, he had been difficult to miss. While she had a vague recollection of the brothers' elderly parents, they'd been dead for many years before Sommer's accident provided her with continuous employment. Later, Edmunde's stroke guaranteed it.

She stopped to admire the view from the path and pulled in a deep breath of the crisp air as she drew her sweater closer around her thin shoulders. She'd always been grateful that she'd listened to her mother about following the nursing path. "You'll always find a job, dear, and never worry about putting food in your stomach," her mother had told her only child, advice borne from her own experience struggling to provide for the scrawny girl she'd raised after the baby's father was long gone.

Gillian reached the kitchen door. Rosemary grew on one side of the stoop in a lush bush. A handful of tiny winter pansies survived the coolness, and she reached down and tore off a clutch of the delicate stems, adding a small, fragrant branch of the rosemary. It was a pity people didn't stop more often to enjoy what was right before their eyes. She carried the tiny blooms inside to decorate Edmunde's breakfast tray.

8:30 AM

Detective Sergeant Stephen Higgins dismantled Keith Clarendon's computer, carefully packing the flash drives and tower. His detective inspector had filled him in on the poisonous plant, and he knew the only fingerprints found on the container with the confiscated plant from Clarendon Hall belonged to Sommer Clarendon. Those on its twin, retrieved from Simon Ramsey's studio, were smudged with overlays, but Simon's and Sommer's were both identified. He'd never heard of this plant and would have to look it up online when he got a chance. Of all the damn things to use for a murder weapon.

After he'd checked the desk drawers and written out a receipt, Higgins walked down the hall and knocked on the door Cook had described after she'd signed her statement.

When Travers had instructed him to determine if Keith Clarendon's uncle was competent enough to make a statement, Higgins had wanted to balk. It had been bad enough taking statements from Cook, whom he knew slightly, and the nurse, whom he knew only from village gossip. But he had firsthand knowledge of Edmunde Clarendon's heated temper from the past, and Higgins didn't know the man's current state, only what was rumored.

He also felt uncomfortable entering what he considered a sickroom. Although he knew he couldn't catch anything from the man, the idea of seeing someone as proud as Edmunde Clarendon in the throes of his affliction was distasteful.

A female voice called out: "Come in."

Higgins entered to find Gillian Cole adjusting a tray on the over-bed table set across Edmunde Clarendon's lap. The head of his bed was raised, and a large linen napkin spread out across his chest. Higgins set his jaw so his reaction to the man's loss of function wouldn't show. Good God. When Higgins had been a constable, this was the same man he'd helped wrestle out of The Scarlet Wench on numerous occasions. Leave it to Travers to have him deal with the sick man.

Higgins nodded to Gillian and moved closer to the bed,

withdrawing his warrant card. "Mr. Clarendon, I'm Detective Sergeant Higgins. I'm very sorry about the loss of your nephew. I have a few questions for you today, sir."

There was no reaction from the man. Gillian cleared her throat and stood back from the bed. Higgins knew she'd been Sommer Clarendon's nurse for many years. He tried again. "When was the last time you saw Keith, Mr. Clarendon?"

Edmunde stared ahead, the drooping lid over his right eye almost closed. Higgins' frustration escalated.

"Did Keith visit you here, Mr. Clarendon?" He spoke louder and waited respectfully for some sign the man had heard him. He knew a stroke might affect the man's speech but surely not his hearing? Finally he burst out: "Blink an eye, move a finger, do something, Mr. Clarendon."

Higgins kept himself from flinching as Edmunde moved his head slightly to face him, staring at the detective with his good eye, and slowly raised his tremulous left hand. At last, some kind of reaction. Was Edmunde trying to shake his hand?

With a vicious shove, Edmunde sent his breakfast flying down the front of Higgins' best suit.

"I think he got that, sir," Gillian pronounced.

CHAPTER TWENTY-NINE

"A few weeks ago, at a dinner, a discussion arose as to the unfinished dramas recorded in the daily press. The argument was, if I remember correctly, that they give us the beginning of many stories, and the endings of many more."
— Mary Roberts Rinehart, *The Red Lamp*

8:35 AM

The morning's tea was English Breakfast, and Nora gulped the sweet brew down with relish, enjoying the toasty warmth of her bed. She could stay here all day, reading her name book, but an overriding sense of purpose fueled her out of bed when she remembered Keith's work. She was curious to see what Keith had unearthed that she could use; more importantly, there could be a clue as to why he was poisoned.

It was obvious that whether Ian wanted Kate to believe it or not, Simon was viewed as a potential perpetrator in Keith's death. The idea that this might be ridiculous didn't enter the equation, as she'd learned from Declan Barnes during Bryn Wallace's murder investigation. Declan's job had been to follow the evidence. That damned rare flower would force Ian to shine his spotlight on Simon.

After a hot shower, Nora knotted her fluffy, blue robe around her. The chenille barely covered her huge belly, and Nora said hello and talked to her son as she rubbed Vitamin E on her taut skin. "I'm still working on your name," she told him as she turned on her laptop and toweled her wet hair. "I'll know it as soon as I hear it," she promised.

Nora's compulsion for order led her to copy the contents of

Keith's flash drive onto her hard drive. She didn't consider herself computer literate and harbored the nagging feeling that one day she would hit the wrong button, and all of her work would be floating in the ozone.

Scrolling down through the opening pages of his manuscript, Nora read attentively. First was his dedication: "To Antonia and Sommer Clarendon, with love for the charmed life I've led on Lake Windermere."

Next was a list of acknowledgments, what appeared to be a compilation of authors and academics he'd read or consulted. Then, an opening epigraph to be used as a frontispiece:

> *At the little town of Vevey, in Switzerland, there is a particularly comfortable hotel; there are indeed many hotels, since the entertainment of tourists is the business of the place, which, as many travelers will remember, is seated upon the edge of a remarkable blue lake—a lake that it behoves every tourist to visit.*
> Henry James, *Daisy Miller*, 1878

This was Keith's thesis, and an ambitious model to be sure, with its old-fashioned use of the word "behoove," Nora thought, then kept reading. Keith's copious research notes followed a tentative outline for proposed chapters. He indicated at the beginning of each new section the chapter into which he saw that bit fitting. There were quotations, blocks of text and reference notations punctuated by the staccato appearance of research still to be done, as in: "Wansell—Hundred Year Stone—Galava Fort."

Nora had no idea what that meant, but the work that seemed most complete concerned the history of the area and of the Clarendon family in particular. That made sense. Clarendon Hall library was probably filled with useful texts on that score. The ones she'd seen piled on the end of Keith's desk were more about the entire area.

She sat back and reflected on her impressions of the town. Bowness seemed to bustle with traffic and tourists already. She wondered just how many people had been keen on Keith's idea to embellish the area with an artist's colony that would make the town a place that would "behove every tourist to visit." She might have to pencil in a visit to the tourism office.

Nora's stomach growled. With a glance at her watch, she put her laptop to sleep. As she dressed, she thought about her fireside chat with Simon and her revelation about her relationship with Paul. She knew what she had said was the truth, as the gauzy layer of disbelief that followed Paul's sudden death lifted with the passage of time and she finally confronted her true feelings. It wasn't comfortable, but it rang true, just as she thought it would when she came across her son's name.

Her khaki jumper would do for today, with a clean, green blouse that the jumper's front hid. No one would know she couldn't button it all the way down. As she tied her sneakers, she pondered what it was about Simon that allowed her to get to the heart of her thoughts. She admired his creativity, of course, but she responded to his quiet air of assurance and subtle humor.

Val had told her Simon's dark-blue eyes held the soul of an old man. They were so different from Declan Barnes' grey eyes, which studied her and seemed to bore inside her, then lit up when he smiled, the corners crinkling with laughter.

She was ridiculous, behaving like an emotional adolescent. The last thing she needed right now was a relationship, no matter how much the security of Simon or the allure of Declan appealed to her. She hurried out of her room, taking the time to lock the door behind her, a habit she was determined to develop now that she had Keith's flash drive in her possession.

The tantalizing odors of a breakfast fry-up reached her as she entered the dining room. "Morning," she said to an athletic couple who passed her as she strode across the room to her usual table. She stopped midstride as a familiar figure entered from the hallway. Nora saw with dismay that it was Tony Warner, dressed for a hike with a walking stick carefully arranged over one arm.

"Tony—what are you doing here?" Even as she spoke, the knowledge of what he was doing there struck home.

"Hello, old girl. Chuffed to see me? Some kind of mess you've stepped in, I see." Tony augmented his malicious smile by turning his walking stick so Nora couldn't fail to notice the colorful travel badges arranged like prize trophies along the shaft.

Nora pointedly ignored the stick and walked him toward the main door, out of the way of guests trying to enter and leave the dining room. She tamped down her rising fury and spoke softly.

"I'm not allowed to give any interviews, so you might as well pack your bags and head right back to your titled friends and their playmates."

"Oh, I don't think so, Nora dear," Tony replied, kneeling to retie one of his hiking boots. "You've been scooped without ever opening your mouth. I dare say no editor will run a blue pencil through any of these articles."

Leaving Nora without a fast comeback, he sauntered out the door.

9:20 AM

Nora tucked into scrambled eggs and bacon with whole-wheat toast. Sunday breakfasts were always later than usual. She was determined not to let Tony Warner and his threats spoil her meal, and she poured another cup of tea. Kate waved to her from the kitchen, but Simon was nowhere to be seen.

A tall, well-dressed young man rose from the table next to Nora's, the local *Cumbrian Chatter* in hand, and stopped by her table. Nora looked up at him; she knew he was familiar but couldn't place his face. The man studied the paper and then stuck his well-manicured hand in her face.

"Glenn Hackney here. I believe you are Nora Tierney?" He grinned broadly.

Recognition set in. Glenn's mouthful of white teeth reminded Nora of Alice's Cheshire Cat, and she was immediately suspicious of anyone who buffed his nails to that kind of high gloss. Still, she shook the proffered hand, knowing Glenn was a link to Keith's background. "Yes. What can I do for you, Mr. Hackney?"

"I wanted to extend my sympathies. Keith Clarendon was my colleague. Actually, I'm the manager at Worth's Travel." He put his hand on the back of the empty chair next to Nora and leaned in confidentially when she didn't issue an invitation to sit down. "I'm here to comfort Keith's family and to represent the agency at his funeral." He rocked the chair back on its heels.

Simon suddenly appeared at the table. "Morning, Mr. Hackney. Nora, thank you for waiting for me." Simon placed his hand on the chair in question and pulled it out, sitting down next to her. "I see you've started without me." He looked back up at Hackney. "I hope you enjoy your day, Mr. Hackney." Simon picked up the menu, studying it as though he'd never seen it before, dismissing Glenn.

Hackney righted himself. "I intend to, Mr. Ramsey," came his reply. "Perhaps more than you or Miss Tierney." He turned his attention back to Nora. "I've finished with the local paper. Would you care for it?" He handed the folded paper to Nora, turned on his heel and left the dining room.

"Thanks for rescuing me, Simon," Nora said. "I think you managed to annoy him."

"Then my job is done. He did seem pissed, didn't he?" Simon agreed with a smile. "I have taken an instant dislike to our two most recent arrivals." Simon rose and busied himself at the serving board, giving his order to a waitress and filling up his coffee mug.

Nora turned to the paper that had been thrust at her. The *Cumbrian Chatter* chronicled fetes, social announcements and local news. Along the right side of the front page, the issue listed the times of various events associated with the St. James Anglican Fete in Support of Distressed Mothers and Infants to be held in Ambleside. The left-hand column discussed the wedding of Miss Cynthia Hepplethwaite to Mr. Dylan Crumbley. But it was the article and pictures in the center column that captured Nora's attention. A large headline proclaimed: **Suspicion Surrounds Death of Clarendon Heir**.

The accompanying photographs included one of Keith Clarendon handing Nora her prize certificate the day she'd won the essay contest.

Simon returned with a full plate and his coffee. He looked at the photo Nora scrutinized and frowned. "Sorry, Nora; there goes your privacy, I fear."

Nora noted the byline of the article with dismay. "Tony Warner! The sleaze himself!" She pushed her glasses up her nose and looked at Simon. "I say that with confidence based on personal experience." She read the article out loud to Simon. "The glories of nature to be found in the Lake District were ruined recently by the grim discovery of a body floating at the edge of Lake Windermere."

Nora paused and looked at Simon over the paper. "What a maudlin beginning. Edits needed right there." She continued:

"No discussion is needed, noted Ramsey Lodge proprietor Simon Ramsey, on what he characterized as 'a miserable death' that involves both himself and writer Nora Tierney."

Nora sat back, stunned. Why would Simon say they were involved? He'd made it sound like they were somehow responsible for Keith's death. Simon saw her face and picked up the paper, skimming the front page.

"What a bloody ass!" Simon threw the paper down.

Nora pushed her chair back. "I'm taking a walk."

"Nora, wait—"

She ignored Simon and left the dining room before she said something she'd regret.

CHAPTER THIRTY

"'Matrimony was ordained, thirdly,' said Jane Studdock to herself,
'for the mutual society, help, and comfort that the one ought to have
of the other.'"
— C. S. Lewis, *That Hideous Strength*

9:30 AM

Gillian watched Sommer Clarendon wheel himself over to the mahogany table and carefully replace the portable phone in its charger. She tried to allow him as much independence as possible. For the life of her, she didn't know how he managed to stay in such a pleasant mood during his dreary daily routine, confined to a motorized contraption with no end in sight; his only outings were to garden shows. Despite what Gillian knew must be his crippling grief over losing Keith, Sommer had completed his morning exercises as he always did, with the concentration of someone preparing for a marathon. But perhaps staying alive *was* a kind of marathon for Sommer.

Gillian wondered what it would be like to be the wife of an invalid. She tried to imagine going through life knowing your husband would never improve from his disability and pondered how that would affect wanting to get up each morning. With the entire physical aspect of the relationship removed, what held Antonia and Sommer together? Quiet conversations and decent meals didn't seem like much of an exciting daily routine.

Gillian wasn't unhappy she didn't share her life with a man. Her son and her work were enough to keep her busy and satisfied. Her evenings at home were sometimes too filled with television and books, but she was physically tired at the day's end and had the knowledge she'd been useful and worked hard.

Sommer swiveled his carriage to face his wife, ignoring his precious plants. Gillian didn't know if he could ever regain the sense of joy they used to provide him. Today they seemed to mock his loss.

Antonia stood before the windows of the library, looking down the fell at the shimmering surface of the lake and at Belle Isle beyond.

Sommer cleared his throat. "That was Mr. Hackney from Worth's, dear. He has Keith's belongings from the Oxford office and has come to Bowness to deliver them."

"Sometimes I think I can see the Round House on Belle Isle from up here," Antonia said.

Sommer caught Gillian's eye and frowned. "I've told him to come by later."

Antonia turned to Sommer. "Wordsworth felt it was the first Lake District house built solely to beautify the country—did you know that?"

Gillian saw the way the light behind Antonia lit her hair, making her fair curls appear translucent. Her pupils were huge dark spots against her wan skin.

"Keith told me that," Antonia continued. "He said the house always reminded him of a large tea canister." She started to laugh, a high, unnatural tinkle.

Sommer grimaced and motioned to Gillian. "Antonia, please—"

"Antonia, please," she mimicked him cruelly. "Please what, Sommer? Please don't tell you stories about Keith? Please don't laugh anymore now that our boy is gone forever?" Tears ran down her face, and she threw herself onto a worn brocade chair, grabbing a gold velvet pillow that matched the fading drapes and pressing it into her eyes.

Gillian padded over to the sobbing woman. "Time for a lie-down, Mrs. C," she said. Her firm voice brooked no argument. She tugged gently on the woman's shoulder.

Antonia's sobs petered out. She sniffled and stood, allowing Gillian to lead her from the room. Pausing beside Sommer, Antonia lifted a hand to caress his shoulder. "I was good yesterday when the women came, and today when the police were here I held it together. I'm trying, Sommer, really I am ... " Her voice wound down to a whisper.

"I know you are, dear." Sommer reached for her hand and brought it to his face. He turned it over and kissed her palm, folding her fingers over the kiss to enclose it as a talisman.

As she guided Antonia out of the room, Gillian glanced back at Sommer. He'd wheeled himself over to the window where Antonia had stood. Gillian decided he was searching for signs of the Round House and the beauty Wordsworth knew dwelled in their community. It was a beauty lost to him now.

CHAPTER THIRTY-ONE

"Across the most vital precincts of the mind a flippant sprite of memory will sometimes skip, to the dismay of all philosophy."
— Booth Tarkington, *Cherry*

10:20 AM

Agnes sat with Kate in the lodge kitchen, going over the schedule for the upcoming week. They had to iron out staff assignments, days off and deliveries as well as complete draft menus that would be subject to last-minute changes if one of their suppliers let them down due to availability or the lack thereof; flexibility was the name of the game from Thursday evenings through Sunday lunches, when the Ramsey Lodge dining room was open to the public. Maeve was proving to be an asset, Agnes grudgingly acknowledged, and Kate was inclined to use her more and more to encourage her to learn the business. That was fine with Agnes. The kitchen was the only domain she wanted.

"I have enough to do to keep my kitchen clean and get the food out on time," she told Kate over and over.

That chore finished, Kate sat back and recounted Nora's run-in with Daniel Rowley the day before as they'd left Clarendon Hall.

Agnes nodded after Kate's recitation. "Be just like Daniel to run her over and not apologize."

Kate agreed and added: "What bothers me more—and I didn't say this to Nora, so don't go winding her up—was that I had the feeling he'd deliberately run her down. I didn't raise it with her because I didn't want to upset her, but I wonder if she had the same feeling."

Agnes raised an eyebrow. "Who knows what goes on in that

head of Daniel's? I swear, sometimes I get so angry I want to throw him out that back door. Then I feel sorry for him, no family left, living all alone in that hut up there, and I think: Agnes, the good Lord wants you to be nice to him, to show him some Christian charity."

She watched Kate sigh and shift in her seat. The poor girl must feel the weight of business ownership and all the responsibility that goes along with it, too, although her brother shared it; and her supposed to be planning her wedding, although Agnes hadn't seen much planning going on yet.

"You're right, Agnes," Kate said. "But I don't trust him, and it bothers me not to have trust in one of my employees." She ran her fingers through her cropped hair. "I have the feeling Daniel is capable of a lot more than we give him credit for." She stood, thanking Agnes as she always did after their weekly meeting. "I'd better get a jump on that refinishing project if I'm to get it done." She winked at Agnes and left the kitchen.

Agnes smiled at Kate's retreating back. Kate and Simon watched over her, especially after her own son emigrated to Canada. Her motherly demeanor toward the siblings became more profound every year. Their mum and dad would be so proud to see how they carried on. She'd happily added Nora to their little family and couldn't wait for that bairn to be born.

After checking a sauce recipe, Agnes had the rest of Sunday and all of Monday off to rest at home. She didn't like to leave anything undone, and once she'd checked the pantry for the sauce's ingredients, she shrugged into her cardigan and prepared to leave. You've become a creature of habit, Agnes girl.

She looked around the spotless kitchen with satisfaction. Maeve would see to Monday's breakfast and make certain the kitchen looked the same when Agnes returned to work Tuesday morning. The Barnum sisters, two dailies in their early twenties who did up the rooms, knew better than to invade Agnes' kitchen when she was off. They delighted in shocking her with blue streaks in their hair and green or yellow nail polish, but both were diligent workers who tidied the rooms and changed linens industriously.

Agnes smacked her forehead. She'd forgotten to tell Kate that the Barnum girls had called, citing car trouble. They would be more than an hour late by the time their older brother came home to give them a ride. She shook her head. Such forgetfulness at times.

She looked out the window and saw Kate just outside the door to her studio, hands already gloved, hard at work sanding a dresser. Robbie Cole stood talking to her as she worked, his thick hair trapped by an orange baseball cap. Gillian's son seemed interested in Kate's project. She wouldn't bother them; the girls would be here soon enough. She'd take a few clean towels into Nora's room and head home, where she looked forward to leafing through that new cookbook her sister had sent from Edinburgh.

CHAPTER THIRTY-TWO

"It was to be the consultant physician's last visit and Dalgliesh suspected that neither of them regretted it, arrogance and patronage on one side and weakness, gratitude and dependence on the other being no foundation for a satisfactory adult relationship however transitory."
— P. D. James, *The Black Tower*

10:28 AM

Nora had left Simon gaping at Tony Warner's article and had taken herself to the lakeside to blow off some steam. She dutifully completed her walk, arms pumping, although she noted it was taking longer and longer each day to complete the circuit she'd chosen for herself early in her pregnancy and had shortened twice as her pregnancy advanced.

She tried to clear her mind of heavy thoughts and concentrated on her breathing and on noticing the people and the world around her. A crowd of Asian students chattered happily as they passed her. Three older black women strolled with their arms linked and stopped to pat her belly for good luck when she paused to catch her breath. It was a glorious day with scudding clouds and the sun peeking out to shine across the lake.

She found her favorite bench just across from the lodge and slumped on it, tired and suddenly disheartened. Tony Warner was a jerk, but he'd still managed to get under her skin. Looking out over the sparkling lake, she wondered why she'd ever thought this was a peaceful place. Maybe she was just the kind of person who could never expect to find contentment. As soon as the maudlin thought crossed her mind, Nora smirked at her melodramatic musings and gave herself a mental shove. She was usually upbeat and positive. Must be the hormones.

The rising fells around her met the skyline in this land loved by Wordsworth, Potter, Coleridge and Ruskin. Her eyes searched the opposite shore, marveling at the craggy mountains that surrounded her as she thought of the different ways each writer had paid homage to the area. In some small way, her children's books were a part of that. She understood the authors' affinity for this place, where the majesty of nature was so powerfully displayed.

The lake's surface was already filling up with boats, canoes and kayaks. They reminded Nora of Keith's last moments. She pictured his arms getting too heavy to guide the scull back to shore. With a catch in her breath, she wondered if he had had any knowledge in his final moments that they were his last, and she trembled at the awful idea.

An older couple shared a laugh in a paddleboat; they crossed in front of her and waved. They reminded Nora of her mother and Roger, and she waved back. Her mother had had a great love for her father, and when he'd died, she'd been alone for many years, but she hadn't hesitated to nurture a new life and a new love with her second husband. Would Nora find that rare combination of partner, lover and friend that were the hallmark of the only kind of marriage she wanted?

Nora pulled a strand of hair forward and played with it, rolling and unrolling it around her finger while her son danced inside her. She definitely would not be naming him Tony. As she considered Tony Warner's article again, she knew it was precisely the type of tabloid coverage he excelled at; she shouldn't have been surprised at all.

In fact, she should have been anticipating it, once she knew he was there in Bowness. She really was slower on the uptake these days. Knowing Tony as she did, she should have known he'd twist Simon's comments for shock value and to ensure a catchy headline.

Nora started back across the road to the lodge, anxious for Simon to understand she didn't blame him for that ridiculous article. Simon met her on the path, and they both started talking at once.

"Simon, I wasn't angry with you—"

"Nora, I never said those things, not like that—"

They stopped together. Nora shaded her eyes from the sun with the back of one hand and looked up at him. "I should have considered the source. Tony's specialty is sensationalism." She watched Simon's shoulders relax.

"I'm glad you know I wouldn't say anything negative about you. I think you've been an absolute brick, the way you've handled yourself."

"Thanks." She smiled and grabbed his elbow. "But I think we may have a murderer to catch. Let's get to work." She directed him back toward the lodge before he could protest.

CHAPTER THIRTY-THREE

"It occurred to Min that thinking about your family is like gardening. The mood hits you, the sun is beaming down, the smell of wet black earth coming in strong through an open window, and you say to yourself, Why not? I've got a few minutes.
So you go out that door."
— Karen Lawrence, *Springs of Living Water*

11:15 AM

Glenn Hackney sipped tea, careful not to let his pinky finger get caught in the delicate handle of the bone china cup. His Auntie Maude who'd raised him had made tea in cups like these, ones his father had thrown in the rubbish after her death. "None of that chintzy stuff for us men," his father had insisted, as though removing those cups would make all the difference in Glenn's sexual persuasion. He could still remember the tinkling crash the porcelain had made as it hit the bottom of the wheelie bin. In the end, all the ales his father had quaffed had not made a whit of difference to Glenn.

He looked around the library with its tall windows and shelves lined with plants. The room was showing its age, and some of the upholstery looked downright shabby, but there was no mistaking the grand lines of a well-built house. "Shabby chic" had come from somewhere, and this place had it in spades. His expert eye told him that despite the wear, the tables were all antiques. Too bad they would be missed if he were to return after dark. He wondered what kind of security system had been installed.

"Delightful tea," he commented. "Such a wonderful fragrance. I don't believe I know the blend."

"We have it sent in from a London store," Sommer explained. "It's called Buckingham Palace Tea Party blend."

Of course it is, Glenn thought, smiling broadly without a hint of a sneer.

Keith's mother sat across from Glenn on a loveseat. She had blue circles under her eyes. When he'd arrived, she'd looked like she'd just awoken. She sorted through the contents of the carton he'd brought, as though a careful perusal of notepads, pens and the collected jumble people accumulate in their desks might give her a clue to Keith's demise.

"I was hoping to find that lovely fountain pen with the gold nib we gave him for his twenty-fifth birthday," she explained with a shoulder raised in apology.

Glenn could have told her it was a fruitless search. He helped himself to another piece of buttery shortbread. "Your cook is an extraordinary baker."

"I'll tell her you appreciate her efforts," Sommer said.

"Cook has been with us for years and years," Antonia said. "I don't know what we'd do without her." The mother put the carton down on the floor. "It was very kind of you to bring this to us, Mr. Hackney."

"Don't give it another thought, Mrs. Clarendon." He'd combed the contents of Keith's desk as he'd packed the box, and neither the information he'd been looking for, nor the knowledge Antonia craved had been in Keith's desk.

11:30 AM

Robbie Cole waited on the corner by Ramsey Lodge for his mother, his attention on the fells that rose beyond the lake. He'd spent time talking with Kate Ramsey, gaining pointers from her as she refinished an old dresser.

"It's a surprise, Robbie, so keep it under your hat," she'd said. "You have to always sand in the direction of the grain," she'd explained. "After it's done and I've cleaned the dust off, I'll be painting it and then add a poly finish and let it cure."

Kate was so generous with her information. He liked that in people, being willing to share. Looking across the lake, Robbie enjoyed the way the dry-stone walls wriggled through the land, creating a living patchwork when seen from a distance. Up close, he knew there were grass tracks, stiles and cattle grids. He loved this place. He had the true good fortune to live in an area where one day could bring the weather of all four seasons.

Robbie hadn't traveled far yet, and he looked forward to that, too, but he also knew he would always return here. The peace and grandeur of this spot were so much a part of him that he felt a twinge of uneasiness as he'd pretended to be a fan of Keith's promotional ideas. He hadn't had a choice: Clarendon House was his mother's livelihood, after all, and the family had always been very kind to him and his mum. But he brightened at the idea that now the whole subject would likely be dropped.

There was a slight tug on his sleeve, and he turned to see his mother, out of uniform and dressed in a shapeless dress and sneakers. Her cheeks were flushed, and she was out of breath.

"Mum! I was beginning to think you weren't coming." Robbie's look was fond. His mum was really his best friend.

"And not spend my half-day with you?" Gillian linked her arm through his. "They have company up at the Hall anyway. Cook can handle that. Did you finish your assignment?"

Robbie nodded. "Sent it off this morning as a PDF. Really easy. I checked the spelling before I sent it."

His mother was pleased. "I knew that online course would

be good for you. It's a great way to build up credits. You always did like to work at your own pace. Now, where do you want to eat lunch?"

From the bottom of the garden, Kate watched the animated exchange between Robbie and his mother. Gillian had always been a devoted mother. Kate wondered how she'd managed after being widowed while still pregnant and left alone to raise a child. Nora would soon be facing that same challenge. Kate didn't envy her the role.

She fully recognized how fortunate she and Simon were to have had a stable family life, although she knew there was no such thing as normal family. Her mother, a social worker, had taught her it was just a matter of the level of dysfunction.

All families had eccentricities or secrets or skeletons hiding in closets. Her own Grandpa Ramsey had liked to sleep in the nude, right until the day he died. She had a childhood memory of her parents hastily struggling to put pajamas on his stiff body before the doctor arrived the morning he was found dead. In the end, they pulled a nightshirt over his head, pinning his arms to his sides, covering him up respectfully but not fooling anyone, "I expect the undertaker has seen worse," her practical mum had pronounced. She and Simon had laughed over it as teens, and the memory still brought a smile to her face.

A pang of sorrow ran through Kate. She missed her parents fiercely, especially in the evenings after their guests were settled. She and Simon used to do their homework around the oak table that stood in the public drawing room now. It was the first piece of furniture she'd helped Dad refinish, peeling away layers of grime and old paint to reveal the inner beauty that lived in the wood. Mum enjoyed her sherry and Dad his single malt while they talked about improvements to the lodge and her mother paged through magazines, searching for new recipes.

Kate bent to her task, guiding the sander carefully in the direction of the grain. Helping their parents at the end of their lives was a gift she knew she and Simon would never regret. She felt she and Ian might form the same kind of competent team. This business of him questioning Simon unsettled her, but she put it aside because she knew Ian took his job seriously, and she wouldn't have it any other way. She sometimes came down hard on him about his job because she wanted to be certain he found joy in his work. There had to be joy of some sort, not just dogged determination, to make it all worthwhile.

Kate straightened up. Just how dysfunctional was she, she thought, to expect Ian to find joy in murder?

CHAPTER THIRTY-FOUR

"'There's been an accident,' they said,
'Your servant's cut in half; he's dead!'
'Indeed!' said Mr. Jones, 'and please
Give me the half that's got my keys.'"
— Harry Graham, *Mr. Jones*

11:40 AM

Nora sat at Simon's table. She'd tried to convince Simon they had to take his position seriously, but when she'd taken out her notebook, he'd stubbornly refused to help her make a list of anyone who could have a motive for wanting Keith dead.

"Not enough information, Nora. We weren't close enough to him." He'd tapped the tip of her nose. "You are supposed to be resting and working, not on a murder case. Leave the detecting to Ian."

Like that's going to happen, she'd silently retorted as he escaped to his studio to expand upon the book cover sketch he'd started the day before. She could hear the Mozart sonata he'd put on.

Nora tried to make a list, but Simon was right. She could write down the people who were at Clarendon Hall, and then what? She wavered at the thought of adding Simon's name and felt instantly disloyal. She could add any townspeople who didn't approve of Keith's plans, but how would she know who they were? There had to be a way to narrow the focus, but she didn't see how she could do that at this point.

She brought her water glass to the kitchen sink and refilled it. Her doctor had stressed the need to keep fluids circulating through her system, important for the baby and for her circulation. Looking out the window, she saw Robbie and Gillian Cole talking on the corner. As she watched, they moved off toward the town center, and Daniel Rowley crossed their path, hurrying somewhere. They stopped to talk briefly, causing Nora to wonder what the older man's relationship was with the younger. Another thing she needed to figure out.

She should be working on a story idea. She'd made some notes about Kate's industrialist, then jotted down ideas for calamity at the church, but when she tried to flesh out either story, her band of fairies started to whine. She couldn't concentrate when there were more important things on which her brain could focus, like Keith's death. Nora drained her glass and put it in the sink. She was thinking of stealing back to her room to inspect more of Keith's work on the flash drive when Simon came out of his rooms, carrying an empty water jug. "I admire your dedication to your work."

Simon put his jug in the sink. "Not going so well on your end?

"Terribly." Nora stretched her arms over her head, arching her back to loosen it up. "I need to get away from it for a while. Right now I hate them all."

Simon laughed. "I know that feeling, when a painting isn't going right," he assured her. "I was going to take a break anyway. How about a pub lunch today—The Scarlet Wench?"

"Lovely." A chance to listen to gossip and grow her list of suspects. "What about Kate?"

"She's working." In two long strides, Simon reached the kitchen door and opened it, calling out across the garden. "Kate—leave for lunch in five at the pub?"

Nora watched Kate appear around the corner of the lodge, stripping off her gloves. Simon joined Nora at the sink as she washed her hands. Before he had turned off the water, Kate came in and added her hands to the running water, then started flicking droplets at Simon. Nora thought the silliness was just what they needed, with Simon under a cloud of suspicion and Kate on edge with Ian. She joined in, wetting her hands and slinging water at Simon's face.

Simon flicked back, and a serious water fight erupted, with all three of them laughing and flinging water at each other. Kate grabbed a cup lying in the sink and tossed the accumulated water at Simon, who ducked just in time. The water hit Nora smack in the chest, soaking her blouse and the front of her jumper and running down her belly.

Kate sucked in her breath, her mouth forming a silent O, but when Nora exploded with raucous laughter, Kate joined in, and soon the three of them were wiping tears from their faces.
"Simon, you owe Nora a dry shirt," Kate said. "That cupful was meant for you."

Simon pulled paper towels from the roll and handed them around. "Yes, but I had the good fortune to dodge it. I'd say *you* owe Nora a pint at lunch, but since she's not able to drink, I'll have hers and she can have a shandy." He grinned broadly, mopping his face.

"You're on," Nora said, swiping droplets from her hair. "Let me just change these wet clothes." She opened the kitchen pocket doors and walked down the hall. Reaching into her pocket for her key, she stopped when she saw the door was ajar.

Nora was certain she'd locked her door that morning. She pushed the door open, then sharply drew in her breath, stifling a scream.

Every drawer and door stood open; clothing lay in heaps on the bed and on the floor in a riot of mixed colors and textures. The file box holding her flash drives was overturned. Then a low moan issued from the bathroom.

CHAPTER THIRTY-FIVE

"Elgar Enders patted the four new, crisp rent books in his pocket
with tender satisfaction. At last he had a business ... "
— Kristin Hunter, *The Landlord*

11:45 AM

The streets of Oxford were busy with weekend traffic. Ian Travers drove past Inspector Morse's Randolph Hotel to St. Aldate's police station to check in with the local force as a courtesy. Speaking to Detective Sergeant McAfee, he explained his reasons for visiting Oxford. McAfee told him about the break-in at Worth's and made him a copy of the report. It was unlikely the event was related to Keith Clarendon's death, but both detectives agreed the report could contain information he needed.

Ian decided to walk the few blocks to Worth's and left his car safely in the police station yard. Walking up St. Aldate's past the magnificence of Christ Church Cathedral and College, he noticed an advert for a new production of *A Midsummer Night's Dream* that Magdalen College was mounting next month, complete with pyrotechnics and acrobats.

Just the sort of event Kate would enjoy, he knew, navigating the busy, narrow streets crowded with a mix of travelers and locals, students and dons, the latter often attired in the dark coats of academic sub fusc. He paused at the corner of the Covered Market before turning left on Queen Street, resisting the impulse to stop in, though a medley of scents from foods, baked goods and flowers reached him. The unique shops inside offered the promise of a far more enjoyable afternoon than did pursuing a murderer. There was an air about Oxford's centuries-old architecture and academia mingled with a sophisticated cultural life that provided a compromise to the rat race of London. He resolved to bring Kate here for a few days' getaway amongst the golden spires as soon as this case was solved.

"This case!" He could hear Kate's remonstration clearly, accompanied by a snort of annoyance. "All right, Keith's murder," he replied in his mind, for that was the firm pronouncement from Milo Foreman that he'd received on the drive here. Once Tanghinia poisoning had been confirmed as the respiratory and cardiac toxin producing the results Milo had seen in the autopsy, the pathologist insisted it was an unlikely way to commit suicide. Ian wondered if they would ever be certain.

He would have to re-interview Simon, a task he was reluctant to pursue. He couldn't imagine Simon had anything to do with Keith's death, but duty forced him to follow every lead. Kate would be upset with him again. He'd also need to investigate more closely the inhabitants of Clarendon Hall, where Sommer's plant collection stood readily available to anyone coming in and out. He needed something more, a lead that would tip this investigation into an area to follow, and maybe this break-in would give him that link.

The mess inside Worth's had been cleaned up, but the glass had yet to be replaced in the door. When Ian entered, a girl looked up from the stack of brochures she was sorting from a pile on her desk. She stood, sniffing into a crumpled tissue and showing off a clingy knit blouse that outlined small breasts and an equally tight knit skirt that covered an area no larger than a dishtowel.

Ian couldn't decide if the dark roots of her otherwise white hair were evidence of the need for a touch-up or were an integral part of her fashion statement. Silver rings gleamed from every finger, including her thumbs, making her stubby fingers appear even smaller. With unexpected delicacy, she removed a blob of purple gum from her mouth and rested it on the edge of her blotter for future use.

"Can I help you?" she asked.

Ian showed her his warrant card. "Is Mr. Edgar Worth available?"

The girl looked at his card and then at her watch. "He should be here shortly."

Ian's raised eyebrow indicated she should continue.

"He called and said he'd be in today, as our manager is away, but he's running late."

Ian nodded in encouragement. This one wasn't a talker. How did she get this job?

"After what's happened this weekend, he was awfully upset, you know?"

"Yes, the police at St. Aldate's explained you'd had a break-in. I'll just wait for him then. I'm here from Bowness to ask a few questions about Keith Clarendon."

The girl's eyes misted over at the mention of Keith. She motioned Ian into a chair and slumped back into her own. "I can't believe he's really dead. I keep expecting it to be a mistake or something." She dabbed at her eyes.

Ian nodded sympathetically.

"He was bursting with happiness lately," she continued, tearing at her soggy tissue.

Ian's instincts perked up. "And why was that, Miss, er—?" Ian reached into his pocket with a practiced gesture and withdrew his notebook.

"Franks, Amy Franks. Mr. Worth was talking of opening a satellite office in Bowness. It had been a dream of Keith's for a long time. It was to be headquartered right in Clarendon Hall. Can you imagine that?"

Ian could think of too many people, including his almost-brother-in-law, who could imagine that and wouldn't like it at all.

Chapter Thirty-Six

"We dance round in a ring and suppose,
But the Secret sits in the middle and knows."
— Robert Frost, *The Secret Sits*

11:55 AM

"Simon! Kate!" The urgency in Nora's voice had the brother and sister sprinting down the hall. Nora heard them stop at the threshold of her disheveled room. "In the bathroom—" she called out.

Nora knelt awkwardly on the tiled floor beside Agnes, wiping her face with a damp cloth. Semi-conscious, Agnes moaned and muttered as Nora tried to calm her. "It's all right, Agnes. Kate and Simon are here now." She looked up and saw their anxious faces. "Call an ambulance and get some ice." They hurried out, and she continued to croon to Agnes, whose eyelids finally fluttered and stayed open. She looked at Nora with a panicked expression, then winced in pain.

"Don't talk," Nora told her. "You're in my bathroom, and we're getting an ambulance. You'll be just fine."

Kate returned with a plastic bag of ice wrapped in a towel. She helped Nora turn Agnes slightly, and Nora pressed the pack against the back of the woman's skull. The skin had split, and blood lay in a small puddle on the floor and was caked in her hair.

Kate helped Nora stand and took her place, talking quietly to Agnes in the same unflappable tone. Simon returned to report that the ambulance and the police were on the way. It was crowded in the bathroom, and he pulled Nora into her bedroom.

"Don't touch anything, Nora," he instructed. "We shouldn't disturb things until the police get here."

Nora surveyed the mess. "Poor Agnes—who would do this? She could have been killed!"

Simon pushed his hair off his forehead. "Nora, it's your room that was ransacked. Somebody was looking for something. There's every reason to think it wasn't Agnes they were after—it was you."

2 PM

Agnes was at the hospital, and Nora's room swarmed with a video cameraman and other crime scene techs. Ian had been notified, but until he could make his way back from Oxford, DS Higgins was on site to cover the case.

Higgins took brief statements from Nora, Kate and Simon, and the whereabouts of the other lodge guests were quickly established. Tony Warner was supposedly on a hike and missed all the commotion. Glenn Hackney had asked directions for Clarendon Hall and had not yet returned. The other four guests were out on a tour north to Keswick; they'd had Simon trace the route on their map at breakfast, as they were huge Walpole fans and wanted to see Watendlath, the hamlet he used as the setting for his *Herries Chronicles* novels.

In the lodge kitchen, Simon sat with Nora and Kate around an old drafting table that Kate had outfitted with a marble top and that Agnes used for prep work and baking. They picked at a plate of sandwiches Simon had thrown together.

"This is where Agnes rolls her pastry," Kate noted, tracing her finger in a pattern of the marble. "I wish they'd release me so I could go to see her."

"She'll be all right," Simon reassured his sister. "The hospital called. They're doing a scan to rule out a skull fracture. She needed stitches, but with luck, she'll just have a nasty headache for a few days."

Nora had been uncharacteristically quiet, brooding in silence. She sat up straighter, as though she'd reached a decision.

"Look, I'd like to take you both into my confidence about something, but I don't want to mention it to the police right now, nor compromise your relationship with Ian. Any suggestions?"

Kate spoke up. "I appreciate your tact, Nora, so it's probably in all of our best interests that I don't know anything Ian might try to pry out of me, and on some level I'm still annoyed with him." She slipped off her stool and carried their plates to the sink. "It's time for me to call Agnes' sister in Scotland."

Left alone with Nora, Simon watched her look down at her entwined hands, resting on her belly, and then as the quiet stretched, she picked at a cuticle on her right thumb.

Finally she cleared her throat. "I don't know how to explain this unless I can get you to see it from my point of view."

Nora paused, and Simon met her eyes, nodding in encouragement. With the light coursing through the windows, he could pick out gold flecks in her green eyes.

"When I found Keith's body, I felt thrust back into the story of someone else's life, the one that started the day a man arrived at my office from the Ministry of Defense and told me Paul's plane was missing. There was never a crash site nor debris found; the plane simply disappeared." She paused and swallowed. "It makes it harder to accept someone's dead when there's no body to mourn. That was followed by the horror of Bryn's death. And then, just when I shook off that fog by moving here, I found Keith's body."

Simon saw her distress and covered her hand with his own for a moment as she continued. "I was still in that surreal place when Kate and I visited the Clarendons the next day. I was left in Keith's study, and he had some interesting research on his computer about Belle Isle. At one point, he'd promised to share it with me, and I reacted without thinking it through." She hesitated and dropped her gaze. "I guess maybe I thought there might be a clue to his death there."

Simon nodded and hoped he kept his expression from being judgmental as Nora described how she'd impulsively taken a flash drive and copied Keith's file.

"So you see," she finished in a rush, "I feel responsible for what happened to Agnes, because what if someone was looking for that drive?"

Simon took a moment to digest what Nora told him. He watched the pink blotches that appeared on her neck extend to a rosy flush that gave her a feverish look. He knew he'd been taken into her confidence after careful consideration, and he needed to calm her down. "No matter what you did, no one had the right to ransack your room—or to assault Agnes. It isn't your fault."

Nora's frown deepened. Oh-oh, wrong tack to take. Simon tried again.

"When she was on the stretcher, Agnes told me she thought you'd left your door open for the Barnum girls. They were late, and she was bringing you clean towels and went right into the bathroom. Just as she heard a movement behind her, she said 'the lights went out' before she could see anything more."

Nora's hand shook as she sipped her glass of water, watching Simon intently.

He sat forward on his stool, his thoughts racing, resting his chin in a hand. He needed more information. What if Nora was right? This could be the very thing that could clear him, too. "Do you know if anyone saw you make that copy?"

Nora shook her head. "I didn't think so at the time, but Antonia might have guessed, and Gillian Cole came in just after I'd finished. Then Daniel Rowley almost ran me down with his bicycle a bit later as we were leaving the Hall, but the drive was in my skirt pocket so it wasn't among the things that fell out of my bag."

"And where is it now?" he asked. What the hell was he going to do?

"Zipped in my laptop case, in your kitchen. And I made a copy on my hard drive. I've only just started to look at it."

"I see." Simon hid his surprise. He was a possible murder suspect and knew Ian would see this very differently. Then he looked at Nora, expectant and worried, and chose his words carefully. "I think I know how hungry you can be for knowledge when you're deeply committed to a project. Part of you was snooping about Keith's death, but more of your motive was to gain information for your use, is that it?"

Nora nodded eagerly and sat up, hanging on his every word.

He couldn't believe he was going along with her. Every instinct told him Ian needed to know about this. "Why don't we keep this between us for now and let Ian in on a need-to-know basis?" But wouldn't it be nice to turn Ian on his head? And he didn't want to do anything else that might rile up Kate and jeopardize the wedding. Despite everything, Simon still trusted Ian and knew he was the right match for his sister. Beside him, Nora let out a breath. One day, he thought with a rueful smile, they would all laugh about this—or at least dismiss it. Chances are there was nothing on that flash drive worth killing for, anyway.

"Thanks for not judging me. I know I'm impulsive at times." Nora lightly touched his arm.

"We'll blame it on the fairies, but promise me if you find anything suspicious, we'll both take it to Ian."

Nora nodded solemnly. Simon wanted fervently to believe her.

CHAPTER THIRTY-SEVEN

*"I will begin the story of my adventures with a certain morning
early in the month of June, the year of grace 1751, when I took the key
for the last time out of the door of my father's house."*
— Robert Louis Stevenson, *Kidnapped*

2:15 PM

Daniel Rowley blended in with the small crowd that gathered
outside Ramsey Lodge. People were so involved in everyone's
business. It drove him crazy, but sometimes it was useful. The
place teemed with police and crime lab techs. A tourist stepped
on his foot trying to get a better view. Daniel yelped and pushed
the burly man back, then crossed the street before a confrontation broke out. He had better things to do with his time than get
involved in a fistfight, deserved or not. In broken English, the
German traveler shouted out an apology that Daniel ignored.

He recrossed the street near the back of Ramsey Lodge,
walking past Kate's studio and through the garden to the lodge
kitchen. A quick glance inside revealed it to be empty; he used
his key to let himself in. He saw a few plates in the sink and
knew Agnes would raise a stink about them if she saw the mess.
He walked briskly to the far wall and hung the master key on
its hook after remembering to wipe it clean. Daniel heard voices
coming from the dining room and heading in his direction. In a
few steps, he was back at the kitchen door; it clicked shut as he
hurried away.

Kate showed Higgins through the dining room and into the lodge kitchen. She thought she heard the click of the kitchen door shutting, and she felt Ian's colleague inspect her from the back. He must be aware of her engagement to his superior, even though they hadn't formally announced it in the papers. With Simon under scrutiny, their discretion had proven to be a good thing, as Kate believed it had helped avoid Ian being removed from the case. At least, Kate hoped it was a good thing Ian was still on the case.

The kitchen was empty, and Kate led Higgins to the back stairs leading to the second level, explaining, "Simon, Agnes and I have our own master keys. We keep the spare here for the Barnum girls … " Her voice trailed off as she reached the hook at the bottom of the staircase where the key swung on its peg.

Higgins raised an eyebrow at the key in motion, and Kate watched him spring into action. "Sit there." He pointed to a stool at the table, and Kate sat down. Summoning a constable from outside, Higgins had the perimeter of the house closed down and instructed a canvas of the crowd outside. "I want to know who was seen in the area recently." The constable hurried out.

"Who was on the premises during the critical period?" Higgins asked Kate.

"I already told you: me, Simon and Nora Tierney were here when we found poor Agnes. I thought she'd gone home." Kate's clipped tone showed her frustration.

"What about those girls giving tea to my staff in the dining room?" he asked.

"The Barnum sisters arrived with the ambulance; they had car trouble this morning, which their brother can verify." A thought struck Kate. "They would have seen anyone who entered by the front door to return the key."

Higgins waved her statement away. "I've had a constable on that door since we arrived."

Kate shrugged. What more did he want? She wasn't a mind reader, and it was obvious they'd just missed seeing who had taken the key.

The constable stood in the door. "Sir—" he consulted his notebook. "Locals seen in the area in the last hour are Jack Halsey, Daniel Rowley, Robbie and Gillian Cole, and the butcher's delivery boy."

"Who arrived just after the ambulance; I watched him leave after I stowed the order," Kate clarified.

"Stay here," Higgins instructed and left the room.

2:25 PM

Higgins separated Nora from Simon. Nora waited for the SOCO to finish in her plundered bedroom, where Higgins questioned her.

"Simon was in my company all morning," she insisted.

Was that the truth or an alibi? Higgins had been surprised when Ian Travers had brought in his fiancée's brother for his statement but not when he'd read the report that indicated the presence of the plant implicated in poisoning their victim. There was that time that Ramsey and Keith Clarendon had had a dust-up at the pub with a few punches thrown, although neither had pressed charges. Could Ramsey have held a grudge all this time and gotten his own back in a horrific way? Wouldn't that be a kicker if Ramsey were involved in Clarendon's murder?

Higgins called Clarendon Hall next and spoke with Cook, an acquaintance of his mum's.

"Mr. Hackney arrived just after 11 and stayed to lunch," she reported. "And of course, none of the Clarendons have left the Hall."

"What about the Coles?" he asked.

"They're still out," Cook explained. "On her day off, Gillian gets the men ready in the morning, and the rest of the day and the putting to bed are down to the district nurse. Gillian and Robbie were to eat out and go to the cinema today, but I don't know where."

Higgins left a message on the Coles' phone, asking them to call when they returned. Everyone seemed covered, then, but of course, Higgins reasoned, it was just as likely it was someone who had not been seen who was the culprit.

Higgins thought of himself as a methodical policeman. Slow and steady gets the job done, he reasoned. He dispatched a constable to scour the pubs for Rowley and Halsey, starting with The Scarlet Wench. He enjoyed being in charge in Travers' absence and decided this was nothing to bother the bereaved parents with; a call at the back door of Clarendon Hall would be appropriate to cross the Ts. After all, no one could be certain there was a link between the assault and ransacking and Keith Clarendon's death.

And if he timed his visit right, Cook would give him a tasty pudding.

2:45 PM

Tony Warner lingered at Ye Olde Sandwiche Shoppe, hoping to overhear a snippet of local conversation that would allow him to insert himself in a genteel way. Most small towns had their own coterie of rampant gossips.

He'd enjoyed a brief but easy hike. Not one to overly exert himself, Tony had driven south from Bowness-on-Windermere

on the A592 toward Ulverston. The walk he'd found in *Cumbria* magazine had taken him over good paths and tracks for
just more than two hours, following a pretty walled lane at one
point. He'd had a coffee in one of the many cafes and had bought
a new badge for his walking stick before returning to Bowness.

The sandwich shop was the third place he'd visited after returning, studying the people eating and drinking and those
waiting on them. He fancied he could distinguish between visitors and locals—and not just due to the absence of trainers and
a backpack. The locals knew the name of their waitress, for in-
stance. And there was the Scots influence in their dialect. So far,
the few locals he'd exchanged pleasantries with had been polite
but distant.

Tony decided he gave off too much of a cosmopolitan air to be
taken quickly into anyone's confidence and returned to Ramsey
Lodge to rest and meditate.

As he parked, he saw people walking away from the building,
leaving a small pack at the front entrance. There were several
police cars nearby, and Tony hurried to the front door only to be
told by a dour constable on duty that he could not enter until his
credentials were checked and one of the Ramseys verified that
he was a guest.

"What's happened?" Tony asked.

"An incident on the premises," the close-mouthed policeman replied. He spoke into his radio, asking for an identification of a guest.

An attractive woman caught Tony's eye, and he stepped down
closer to her. She happily told him that he'd missed an apparent assault, and someone had been taken away in an ambulance.
When Simon Ramsey appeared in the doorway, he nodded to
the constable, who admitted Tony.

Lingering in the hallway, Tony tried not to grind his teeth. Simon stood at the door, talking quietly to the constable, and from what Tony could overhear, he was waiting for other lodgers to appear. Tony thought hard. His next installment on the Clarendon murder for the local papers would have to come from information gleaned from others when he could have been an on-the-spot correspondent—or even have been interviewed by the police himself. If only he'd been on the grounds at the height of the excitement. He wondered how he could quote himself while worrying how he would explain to Old Jenks that he'd missed this scoop. His irritation was high, and he blamed Nora Tierney.

The tall man he'd seen this morning appeared and was cleared to enter. Tony corralled him with an outstretched arm and a wide smile, introducing himself as another patron who'd found himself caught up in "this mess" that had occurred at the lodge that day.

Glenn Hackney accepted the hand and the introduction. "Tough to be on-site with all of what's been going on in this little corner of the world," Tony speculated, hoping vagueness would cover real information.

He saw Glenn draw himself up. "Actually, Keith Clarendon was a co-worker. I'm here on business for the Worth Travel Agency, representing the owner at the funeral. Just came from visiting the bereaved parents."

"You don't say?" Tony leaned in and lowered his voice. "Don't let this get around, but I'm here on business, too. I'm a journalist. Nora Tierney is a former—colleague." He couldn't bring himself to say "boss."

Glenn nodded. The two men appraised each other.

"The administrative centre at Oxford is called the Clarendon Building," Tony ventured. "Wonder if Keith's family is related?"

"Quite," Glenn replied ambiguously. "How long have you known Nora Tierney?" he parried.

CHAPTER THIRTY-SEVEN

"Long enough," Tony answered.

They exchanged broad smiles of kindred spirits

"How about a nice lakeside stroll before dinner?" Glenn suggested.

"You're on," Tony replied.

Chapter Thirty-Eight

*"Night is the time to escape from the past, for then all illusions of
safety are most easily created, most easily believed, and a secure
future beckons as it does not in the harsh light of day."*
— Albert Halper, *The Fourth Horseman of Miami Beach*

4 PM

A rosy glow lit the afternoon by the time Nora was allowed back
into her room to sort her belongings. She surveyed the damage. Silver fingerprint powder coated surfaces. Agnes' blood had
dried on the bathroom floor in a mahogany splatter.

A heavy brass vase that had stood on a side table had been
found on the floor in one of the heaps of Nora's clothing that
had been pulled from her armoire. As the suspected implement
of the cook's injury, it had been bagged carefully and taken away
by the forensic tech.

Simon appeared in the doorway with a few baskets. "Higgins says material doesn't hold prints, so we can wash all your
clothes, Nora."

"Sounds good to me. The whole world has seen my under-
wear today, anyway." At least she'd resisted maternity baggies
with the elastic panel and wore bikini panties under the rise of
her belly. She took a basket and started to sort darks and lights
into piles. Simon followed her lead. They were halfway through
when Kate arrived, back from the hospital.

"Agnes has a concussion. They're keeping her overnight for
observation," she told them. "She's also sporting a row of stitches
in her scalp, and they gave her medication for her headache and
nausea. Her sister is coming down from Scotland tomorrow to

stay for a few days. I left her asleep." Kate approached the dark walnut armoire, its warm patina glowing with age and use. The doors were flung open; hanging clothing inside was half on and half off hangers. "I'll tidy these. At least whoever did this had the good grace not to damage the furniture."

The laundry baskets filled quickly. Kate offered to get the first load started and left for the machines that they all used under the stairs from the kitchen. Nora rubbed her back and walked over to her set of French doors to gaze out to the flower garden she had sat in this weekend.

She turned at the sound of dragging to see Simon moving the large trunk from the foot of her bed over in front of the doors. "I'm not taking any chances," he said. "I want you to feel safe in here at night."

A chill came over Nora. It hadn't occurred to her that whoever had attacked Agnes might return. Whom had she hurt or offended that made this attack personal? Or did someone know she'd copied Keith's work and was desperate to get it back? What could Keith possibly have unearthed that couldn't be known?

4:30 PM

Higgins sat at Cook's table, waiting for Gillian and Robbie Cole to return. The cottage they inhabited was just at the end of the kitchen garden; they would have to pass the kitchen door on the lane to get home. It didn't seem that they'd been involved in the assault, but he wanted to check on whom they'd seen at Ramsey Lodge before leaving the area.

"How's your mum, Stephen?" Cook asked as she poured him a second cup of tea. Higgins' mother and Cook met often in the library's romance section.

"Good, quite good. Doting on my sister's kids up in Penrith this week," he replied. He watched Cook slice a thick wedge of almond pound cake and pile on a hearty scoop of berries before setting the plate before her admiring audience of one. If the expectant detective thought Cook was on edge, who wouldn't be with the death of the house's heir?

CHAPTER THIRTY-NINE

*"My regret
Becomes an April violet,
And buds and blossoms like the rest."*
— Lord Alfred Tennyson, *In Memoriam*

7 PM

It was with a deep sense of misgiving that Jodie Halsey watched her father-in-law, Jack, walk down the hill, clutching the hand of her young son. Jack constantly complained the boy was too attached to her and needed toughening up.

"He's not a mot, he's a boyo," Jack had explained in his Cumbrian dialect. "An hour at the most."

"But no pubs!" she'd admonished. She could just picture Jack and his pal Daniel Rowley having a few too many whilst they forgot her boy altogether.

"On me t'ol lass's grave, I'd never drag a bairn into the pub."

After Jack swore on his mum's grave, Jodie had relented. Her husband traveled frequently for work and wasn't around tonight. The child seemed so anxious to go with his grandfather, too, clearly sensing an adventure, that it was hard to turn him down.

Jodie decided it wouldn't hurt for her to have an hour or two for herself. Maybe she'd take a hot bath and shave her legs for a change.

She wanted to believe Jack's promise, but as she ran the bath water, Jodie wondered how long it would take her father-in-law to find a way around his oath.

8:20 PM

Sommer Clarendon put his book down on the night table. He supposed it was too early to go to sleep, but he seemed to lack any stamina these last few days. Leaning heavily on his hands, he tried unsuccessfully to lift his hips enough to shift his weight. He reached for the bedside call button before remembering the district nurse had signed off and he was on his own for the night.

It wasn't usually a problem. The bag attached to the catheter that drained his bladder had been emptied; it meant his sleep was never disturbed. No, he thought wearily, his problem wasn't sleeping through the night. His problem was fighting down the swarming images that kept him from falling into that blessed state of unawareness when white space surrounded him. He still remembered the time immediately after his accident, when he fought sleep for fear he wouldn't waken. Now the sense of oblivion he equated with death would be most welcome.

He heard Antonia in their bathroom, running water and closing drawers, and he called out to her. "Darling—could you help a minute, please?"

The taps shut, and a moment later Antonia came to his bedside. Her face seemed composed, her hair brushed out around her face. The tie to her robe had come undone; the ends dangled at her sides. Just like my legs, Sommer thought. Aloud, he said: "Would you rearrange my legs for the night?"

"Of course." Antonia brought his covers down to the foot of the bed and raised each leg by the heel, slipping on sheepskin heel cups to prevent bedsores. She smoothed the crumpled linen beneath him while Sommer flattened the bed using the control clipped to his pillow. She lowered the rail at the side of the bed while Sommer used his trapeze to lift his weight. She untucked the draw sheet and pulled it tightly to eliminate creases, the bane of skin care. Sommer tugged the large reading wedge from behind his shoulders and slid it onto the floor, adjusting the pillow at his head. Antonia covered him and competently tucked in the sheet.

"Thank you, my dear. You are my angel of mercy tonight." His lips brushed Antonia's forehead in their usual goodnight ritual when she leaned over him. Instead of raising the railing, Antonia climbed into bed next to him and rested against his chest as she had done in the wheelchair the day they'd been told Keith was gone. He could smell the jasmine shampoo she always used.

Sommer closed his eyes, remembering when her hair fell to her waist, blonde and shimmering. He knew that if he were capable of achieving an erection at will, the memory of that scented hair would be all he needed. He longed for the intimacy they'd shared before her pregnancy and his accident. It had been so long, yet on occasion he could still summon the sweetness of those moments together when he woke up early.

Sommer caressed his wife's back, running his hand up and over her shoulders in soothing circles. Her silent tears wet his nightshirt.

"I love holding you in my arms like this," he murmured. She nodded and clung harder to him. "I'm so sorry this has happened," he continued. "This is so very difficult for us, but we have to get through it, darling, and we will if we stick together. We've gotten through rotten times before, and we'll do it again."

Antonia lifted her head from his chest, her wet eyes seeking his. "Children aren't supposed to die before their parents. It's unnatural."

He ached for her then more than ever, recalling the other tragedies they'd shared. "You have had to endure too many losses, my love." He couldn't ignore the pangs of guilt he'd felt since realizing the poison for Keith's death might have come from one of his plants. Had the hobby he loved resulted in the death of his beloved child?

He brushed his lips against Antonia's hair. Her breathing slowed, and she fell asleep in the narrow hospital bed, clinging to Sommer, curled up under his arm.

CHAPTER FORTY

"On an April night almost midpoint in the Eighteenth Century, in the county of Orange and the colony of Virginia, Jacob Pollroot tasted his death a moment before swallowing it."
— Steve Erickson, *Arc d'X*

8:40 PM

At The Scarlet Wench, Nora stared in awe at the manifestation of Simon's ravenous appetite. Some people ate less when under tension; Simon was clearly one of those who ate more. She enjoyed her fish and chips but couldn't finish the large serving. Simon ate his and the rest of hers. He eyed Kate's remaining chips before paying the check and returning to the lodge to relieve Maeve, on desk duty.

Nora and Kate stayed on at the pub, the cheerful noisiness a distraction, and watched a boisterous dart tournament to its end. Nora moved around the pub, straining to overhear any conversation regarding Keith. The dart game proved to be more popular.

"Any movement on the name game?" Kate asked. "I've always liked the name Miles."

"Oh, dear," Nora replied. "I remember a Disney cartoon I watched growing up, and I'm afraid I'd keep seeing Elmer Fudd!" The two women laughed.

Kate took a call on her cell phone from Ian. He would be back in the area shortly and would stop at the station before dropping by the lodge. Nora saw Kate's face tighten; her voice grew tense as she spoke to Ian. She shook her head.

Nora hoped Kate and Ian would find a way past all of this.

She knew how much they loved each other. It gave her more resolve to do something to unravel the mystery surrounding Keith's death and release Simon from suspicions. Her mind went into overdrive. Surely there was something she could do to crack the case?

They left the pub, and once outside, Nora groaned. Her legs felt cramped from sitting, and her son was particularly active.

"You go ahead, Kate. I'll walk slower and don't want to hold you up. I need to get some of these leg cramps out." Kate hesitated. "There are street lamps all the way to the lodge and tourists everywhere. I'll be fine. Go." She shooed Kate away and watched her disappear down the road.

When she was certain Kate was out of sight, Nora took off her earrings, pocketed one, and stole back inside the pub. She approached the bar away from the tournament action and snagged an empty stool while she waited to catch the barman's attention.

"Yes, miss?" He looked pointedly at her bulge of pregnancy.

"I don't want a drink," Nora hastened to assure him. "I wondered if anyone turned in a hoop earring like this?" She held out one of her braided gold hoops.

"Let me ask the missus." He turned toward the kitchen and bellowed, "Daisy."

Nora perched on the edge of the stool. The barman wandered back to watch the darts, checking the fill of the glasses he passed. A minute later, the kitchen door knocked open and a cheery-looking woman backed out, holding a tray in front of her. While she unloaded fish and chips in front of two patrons, the barman paused to speak to her and flicked his glance to Nora, who gave the woman a little wave. She nodded and, wiping her hands on a towel, came down the length of bar to where Nora waited.

"Sorry luv, no one's turned in anything tonight. But I'll keep my eyes open when we sweep up at closing."

"That would be wonderful," Nora gushed. "I'm Nora." She held out her hand. "I'm staying at Ramsey Lodge for a while."

The woman looked uncertainly at Nora's hand and finally gave it a vapid shake. "Daisy." Then she tilted her head to one side and took in Nora's full stomach. "You the lass found the Clarendon boy?"

Nora encouraged her with a mournful smile. "Unfortunately, yes."

The woman grimaced. "How about a ginger ale? I'm having one myself."

"Maybe a small one," Nora agreed. She watched Daisy pour their drinks.

The woman put them both in front of Nora and crouched down to slide out from under the bar. "Move along down, John. Let me set a bit." She hit the man sitting next to Nora on the shoulder, and he obligingly moved off down the bar.

"Thank you," Nora said, sipping her soda. She didn't have much room for more but wanted to be polite. More importantly, she wanted to mine Daisy for information.

Daisy, it turned out, spent most of her time in the kitchen. Yes, she knew Daniel Rowley, Jack Halsey and a few of their cohorts liked to talk down Keith Clarendon's expansion plans, but Daisy suspected that was just to make noise at the town meetings. Half the town hadn't taken Keith seriously, to her mind, and the other half would have had a long wait before any of Keith's plans were finalized and approved.

When Nora brought up Simon's name in connection with their work, Daisy beamed.

"Such a nice lad and a good eater, too."

Nora nodded. That wasn't quite the kind of information she needed. She put her head to one side. "Someone told me Simon and Keith had a fight here?"

Daisy brushed the idea aside. "A small dustup, to be sure. I've seen worse in my years here. Now if you were talking about Edmunde Clarendon, that man could swing his fists at the slightest provocation once he'd had a drink in him." The woman shook her head. "I kind of miss him. Quite a swagger he had. I hear there's not much left of him now."

"I wouldn't know," Nora admitted.

Five minutes later, soda finished, she thanked Daisy and left the pub, her frustration level ratcheted up. That was a waste of time. She tried to shrug it off and headed toward Ramsey Lodge.

Nora needed periods of time alone, intervals of not having to think hard or to carry on a conversation. She thought of it as rest time for her brain. Stepping carefully over the uneven pavement, looking in shop windows along the way, she admired the gay profusion of souvenirs: Kendal Mint Cakes, caps and tweed hats, china and crafts. Some of the shops were housed in buildings that still bore the mullioned windows and beamed exteriors of past centuries. She took a few deep breaths and emptied her mind. Window-shopping therapy.

She was warm now, the bulk of pregnancy a thermal heater. She stopped to appreciate the display of soft leather jackets and coats at one shop and unbuttoned her sweater. A mewing sound caught her ear, and Nora cocked her head. It sounded like a lost kitten meowing for its mother.

For the moment, she was alone on this part of the street. Nora listened intently. The crying was accompanied by sniffling, definitely of the human species. Following the noise up the narrow alley that ran beside Lakeland Leather, she came upon its source. A young boy with unruly brown hair sat on the loading dock, leaning disconsolately against a pole. His small face was streaked with tears. His sniffles stopped when he spied Nora, and he shoved a thumb into his mouth.

"You poor thing," she said, keeping her distance to avoid frightening him. "Are you lost?"

The child frowned and considered this as he sucked harder. Nora noted he was shivering. She took off her cardigan and, stepping closer, held it out within the boy's reach. "My name's Nora. What's yours? Would you like to borrow my sweater?"

The boy hesitated, then grabbed the sweater and stood up. He found his voice as he wrapped himself in it. "It's a jumper, and m'name's Andrew but I'm called Andy 'cus Daddy is Andrew, too. I'm not supposed to talk to strangers, 'specially one wot talks funny like you." He looked at the jumper and frowned again.

Nora sidled closer. "I think your mum would want you to be warm, Andy." He allowed her to roll up the sleeves until his fists poked through. "How old are you?"

"This many." Andy thrust three stubby fingers into the air.

Nora nodded solemnly. "And you're really not lost?" She looked around the empty lot for signs of adult supervision.

Andy's eyes filled up again. "See, Grampa Jack told me to wait right here, and I did. I'm not lost, I'm here. An' I been waitin', but he's not come back—" Andy's coherence deteriorated into a full rush of tears.

Nora felt in her pocket for her mobile. "I think we should call a nice constable to take you home—"

Andy leaned toward her. "I gotta pee, I want Mummy, I wanna go home!"

She hugged him and helped him off the platform. "First things first, then." She helped Andy unzip his tiny jeans and held the ends of her sweater back, then turned pointedly away as his stream of urine hit the pavement. The last thing she needed was to be seen anywhere near a child's genitals in a dark alley. She heard him closing the zipper and turned back.

"Right then," she said brightly, adjusting the sweater, which fell to his ankles like a topcoat. "Let's go to the road and see if your home is near here. We'll call a policeman under a light where I can see my phone better." She held out her hand, and the boy took it. Walking him back to the road, she paused under a streetlight.

"Look around, Andy. Do you know where we are?" Nora asked.

"Town," he answered proudly.

"Very good, yes. Let's try this, shall we?" She punched in 999, the United Kingdom's emergency number, as another angle occurred to her. "Andy, what's your family name?"

"Halsey," the boy answered.

Nora had a sinking feeling "Grampa Jack" was Daniel Rowley's drinking pal. One call, and a few minutes later, a patrol car pulled up to Nora and Andy, waiting under the streetlight as instructed.

"Andy Halsey, your mum is worried sick," the young constable said through his open window. A woman with wet hair and wearing jeans and a "Full Monty" T-shirt jumped out before the car was fully stopped.

"Mummy!" Andy cried, running from Nora's side and leaping into his mother's arms.

"Thank God." His mother buried her face in Andy's hair, then raised it to meet Nora's eyes. "Thank you."

Nora nodded.

The constable was the same one who had answered Simon's

call when Nora found Keith. "You seem to have a knack for finding lost people, Miss Tierney," he said, reaching into his pocket for his notebook.

Nora launched into another statement to the police. "He said his grandfather left him earlier this evening at the loading dock behind the leather store and never came back."

"I've had years of experience with Jack," the constable said. He spoke briefly to Andy's mother, sitting in the back of the patrol car with the boy on her lap. Then he radioed in to have The Scarlet Wench checked out by a colleague. "Let's see where you found the boy," he said to Nora and followed her up the alley to the loading dock, his flashlight sweeping from side to side.

"He was sitting right here," she said and pointed.

The constable continued his sweep, picking out a large commercial rubbish bin. He walked over to it, with Nora a few steps behind. Icy sweat broke out between her shoulder blades. The constable lifted the metal lid and played his light over the contents.

It must have been emptied earlier in the day; little remained except for a few slimy carrier bags stuck to the bottom and the heavy scent of decay. He led the lid drop, and the resounding thunk startled Nora, calling the policeman's attention to her presence.

"Please don't follow me, Miss Tierney." He pointed his flashlight back at the loading dock and played the beam underneath it.

Nora walked away, her eyes getting used to the darkness. Hulking shapes appeared, casting menacing shadows. She looked toward the end of the alley and saw a gate in a fence for delivery lorries and bin removal that let out onto a back road running behind the shops.

Nora watched the constable search the fence's perimeter. She heard another patrol car pull up out front on the main road to help in the search, radio squawking its arrival. Before she was ordered back to the main road, she walked hastily toward the gate, letting herself out onto the back road.

The air seemed fresher here, and she leaned back against the gate, postponing Simon's inevitable grilling, her own fault because she'd stopped to help a little boy—but she knew Simon would say it was because she couldn't keep her nose out of other people's business.

A sign on the guesthouse across this back road identified it as the Rose Cottage B&B for the rose vines that wrapped lazily up and over an arbor at the entrance to its tiny front garden, Nora assumed. The vines were now past blooming except for a few browned tips. Her eyes swept admiringly over the pretty trellis as she pictured it in full bloom but stopped abruptly on a dirty white trainer.

Someone had lost a sneaker. She started to cross the road toward the arbor when she heard the gate opening behind her, then stopped midway when she saw the sneaker was still firmly attached to its owner's leg.

The smell of vomit and alcohol reached her. Surely this was the irresponsible Jack Halsey, lying slumped on the garden bench in an alcoholic stupor. Nora felt a surge of anger at the grandparent who'd abandoned his little grandson.

Looking back toward the fence, Nora recognized the female constable from Saturday who'd guarded Simon's door. Fervently hoping Jack was stinking drunk, Nora pointed wordlessly to the extended foot.

The constable's beam swept the inside of the trellis, revealing the ghostly face of a small man slumped into the corner, ignorant of the heavy thorns that pierced his scalp and neck. A crushed wafer cone in a paper sleeve lay by his knees. Leaving a trail down into his lap, dried vomit stood out against his denim shirt, arriving in a white pool of melted ice cream.

Nora held her breath as the constable moved closer, directing the beam of light onto his face. Jack Halsey's eyes stared back at them, filmed in a milky coating of death. The peace of the evening was shattered when the constable hit the emergency button on her radio.

CHAPTER FORTY-ONE

"'You've got to get him, boys—get him or bust!' said a tired police chief, pounding a heavy fist on a table."
— Mary Roberts Rinehart, *The Bat*

11:55 PM

It was near midnight when Ian swept up the back steps to Simon's kitchen door. His stop at the station had taken longer than he'd planned due to Jack Halsey's death. There was still no sign of Anne Reed, the missing girl, and he'd had a mountain of paperwork to wade through. When he'd finished reading Milo Foreman's formal report, he'd realized what he had to do, and the knowledge made his heart heavy.

On the ride over, he'd worried Ramsey Lodge would be shut for the night, but the lights were still on in Simon's rooms, and he could see Nora slumped in a chair by the fireplace. Across from her, Simon spoke earnestly. In pantomime, he appeared to be reassuring her. Darby lay by her feet, sleeping. He noticed Kate's head was barely visible on the arm of the sofa, but she leapt up at his knock, smoothing her ruffled hair as she opened the door.

"Back from beating the bushes in Oxford?" She ushered him into the room. He leaned forward for a kiss, but Kate stepped pointedly back, leaving him to stand awkwardly outside the warmth of their circle. She sat back down.

Ian pretended not to notice and plopped beside her. "I've been going over the initial reports on Jack Halsey's death. Sorry you had to find him, Nora. Can't have been fun," Ian said.

"Not how I expected to end the weekend, after Agnes' assault," Nora agreed, sitting forward on her chair.

"At least Halsey's grandson was returned to his mother before he saw his granddad like that," Simon said.

Ian balled his fists and girded himself. "I'm afraid you'll have to come back down to the station, Simon," he said, bracing for the reaction.

"Whatever for?" Kate's eyes narrowed, her anger palpable.

"Keith's tox reports confirmed the Tanghinia poisoning," he explained. "I need a list of anyone you can think of who had access to your studio while the plant was in there."

Simon's face darkened. "That could be almost anyone, Ian, even you."

"Then you'll just have to make a long list, won't you, Simon? Or would you rather I just arrest you?" the weary detective replied.

Kate exploded. "You're carrying this too far, Ian!"

"No, Kate, I'm actually being considerate of Simon because he's your brother, and by rights I should be putting him in handcuffs."

"If that's what you call consideration, I have some considering of my own to do," she said coldly, twisting her left ring finger. She threw her engagement ring at Ian and stomped out, banging the sliding door to the hall behind her as Nora stood up and rushed after her.

Chapter Forty-two

"It is no time for mirth and laughter,
The cold, grey dawn of the morning after."
— George Ade, *The Sultan of Sulu*

Monday, 25th October

7:10 AM

Antonia Clarendon stood on the small balcony outside her bedroom. The early morning haze had yet to burn off. She could see the peaks of the nearest fells through a layer of lavender mist, and she shivered, wrapping her dressing gown tightly around her thin frame.

She had slipped out of Sommer's bed before he woke and before Gillian came to do his morning routine.

So many wasted years, she thought, watching the haze swirl and waver in the weak light. So very many years of the same routine, the same dull chores to be attended to if Sommer's life was to be preserved. But she couldn't imagine her life without him in it. At least he had his mind and his speech. If she had been Edmunde's wife—she shuddered at the thought.

Antonia rubbed her temples to ease the tightness that hadn't left her since absorbing Keith's death. She knew from the expression on DCI Clarke's face when he came to the house that he carried devastating news. That sober man had the gravest task of all, having to tell families their loved ones had perished.

After she'd run up to Keith's room and seen the undisturbed bed, a cold fear had gripped her head and had tightened over the next hours. Shock, she'd imagined. What could she be afraid of now that the worst had happened? Those pills Doc Lattimore had given her lessened the tautness a bit but left her feeling like a sleepwalker. Even so, they did lighten the heavy feeling of dread, a hollowness surrounding the knowledge that she had nothing left in her life to look forward to, no purpose to sustain her.

No, she decided, it was better to face the facts instead of dulling the pain; better to steel herself for the phone calls and flowers and gestures of sympathy she'd pretended not to notice all weekend. She'd save the pills for the next day's funeral service, which she knew she'd have trouble getting through, and then she'd hoard them for a day down the road when she couldn't face getting up anymore.

Antonia remembered another funeral she had wept through steadily but quietly, supported by her mother and father, her body weak and in pain to match that in her heart. Her husband lay in critical condition, his future uncertain. Her brother-in-law remained locked in his rooms, refusing to leave for the service as though he could delay facing the death of his wife if he stayed away from the chapel and from those coffins, one miniature and white next to the large one of oak.

She thought of the baby who'd waited for her that day, the lone impetus that allowed her to make it through that day and the next and the next, the sole reason she'd retained her lucidity while her world collapsed around her.

Now that child was gone, and no other would ever take his place. And she wondered if this time she would be able to hold onto her sanity.

8:45 AM

Kate rose late after crying herself into a fitful sleep. Had she overreacted last night? She had sat with Nora for more than an hour, hashing out the entire situation. The only thing she'd decided firmly was that if Ian wanted to go after Simon, he'd have to do it without her help. She'd sent Nora to bed and fallen into her own, exhausted.

At this moment, she didn't think she could tolerate being a police officer's wife, if suspecting their closest relatives was part of the job. How could she be loyal to both men in this situation? If she sided with Ian, she was being disloyal to her brother; she had no choice but to defend Simon. Underscoring it all was the fact that she knew Simon's history with Keith.

As she dressed, she wondered how Simon was doing today. Last night, she'd left an urgent message with their family solicitor, who should be working on Simon's case at this moment. She'd check with him once she got herself sorted. She had so much to do today.

Yesterday, she'd called Sally Kincaid, who substituted for Agnes when she was on vacation or out sick and who agreed to work for the next week, and today Maeve was to bring around the planned menus for Sally to review. At least it was Monday, and they had no dinner service until Thursday. They would see how Agnes felt after that.

Once she knew about Simon, she would pick Agnes up from Saint Margaret's Hospital and get the patient settled at home. Then she would retrieve Agnes' sister Hazel from the train in Windermere. Hazel had insisted on coming down when Kate had spoken to her, but had asked for her visit to be a surprise for Agnes.

Half an hour later, Kate stopped in her workshop to inspect

the drying of a painted piece she was working on. The creamy yellow was drying well, and she was trying to decide whether to add a pale green glaze to pick out its features. This was her therapy, a way to distract and calm herself after last night. A movement at the end of the garden caught her attention, and she walked over to the studio door and looked out.

Simon knelt, weeding. Nora stood over him, talking and leaning on a hoe. The morning soil was damp and made pulling weeds easier. It all looked so normal, but shocked to see her brother, Kate hurried out. Seeing her excitement, Darby ran up to greet her. She fondled the dog's ears as she resisted the impulse to grab Simon and hug him.

"Hey, you two."

"Hello yourself," Simon answered, getting up and slapping his gloves on his dirty jeans before pulling them off. "Get my note?"

"What note?"

"The one I left on your door when I got home after talking with Ian. He didn't arrest me, Kate." Simon's face was drawn. "But I'm to have legal guidance, whatever that means."

"Oh." She stepped forward and hugged him anyway. "I came out through my studio, so I didn't see any note. I thought you were locked up."

Simon draped his arm over her shoulder. "Not quite yet. How's my sister holding up?"

Nora looked tired but smiled at Kate. "I heard him coming in, and we had tea together early. I made him toast and eggs, and he wolfed them down."

Simon kept his arm around his sister but looked away. "We had a few cancellations. The news must have hit about Agnes being hurt on the premises."

Kate noted Simon didn't include the cloud of suspicion that hovered over *him* as a reason for the guests' change of mind.

Nothing horrible like this had ever happened when their parents were in charge, and it seemed like a betrayal of their good work. Kate felt like her entire world was falling apart. Had she and Simon made a mistake keeping the lodge running?

Nora stepped over to them and broke her reverie. "Hey, you two. My mom always says, 'This too shall pass.' Just give it time."

Simon squeezed her shoulder before dropping his arm. "Let's change the subject. Too nice a day to dwell on last night. It will all work out, you'll see."

Kate wished she shared his confidence, but she acceded to his wishes. "I'm glad you're home and working hard."

"Want to help? My helper here pleads pregnancy for weeding; lousy excuse, I think." Simon held out his gloves.

Kate held up her hands in defense. "No, thanks, I've got my own chores today, and most of them revolve around Agnes." She looked around. "What happened to Daniel? He was supposed to weed today."

Simon put his gloves back on. "Didn't show, and since I was up, I thought I'd get a jump on it."

Kate frowned. "I'll bet Daniel slept in. I could use him to pick up some things to help Sally out. I'll give him a call and roust him out of bed." She moved to head back to the lodge.

"Can't," Simon called after her.

She turned around. "Can't what?"

"Can't call Rowley—phone's been disconnected over a week. Hasn't paid his bill again. Didn't Agnes or Maeve tell you?"

"Neither one mentioned it." Kate chewed the inside of her lip. "And no mobile. Maybe I can get Robbie Cole to rally him. His cottage is closest to Daniel's hut."

9:30 AM

Robbie Cole put aside his online reading to carry out Kate's request, leaving behind the technical world of environmental science to climb the path to Daniel's hut. The track from Clarendon Hall's kitchen to the small cottage he and his mother shared branched off into the woods, and he paused as a butterfly distracted him.

Looking up at the puffy clouds, edged in pink and purple, he closed one eye, making them seem near enough to push away with his fingertip. Across the lake, the steep fells became the rugged mass known as Pillar, rising almost three thousand feet above sea level, but with one eye closed, it appeared no taller than his pinkie. Amazing.

The view was more than picturesque to Robbie. The rough tracks and hiking paths had attracted travelers since the early 1800s, the peace and stillness of the nature-filled area sought by many. It was busy enough already, he ruminated; all this area offered could be worn away by those unable to take vigilant care of the primordial beauty he called home. He was comfortable here and liked his life just as it stood.

Robbie tackled his coursework in the mornings and did chores Cook listed for him some afternoons. When he had free time, he hiked and consulted his trail logs. He'd started a birding journal, too, after joining a group in Windermere, and he was saving for a really good pair of binoculars. Six days a week, he helped his mother get Edmunde or Sommer in and out of the large stainless whirlpool bath with the aid of a mechanical lift. His small paycheck from Sommer gave him spending money and a small modicum of independence.

He thought of his mum with pride as he resumed his walk. She'd made a decent life for them both with her career. He hoped to take care of her one day, when he finished this course and could earn his way. Interested in the land and the environment, he thought his future would lie in its preservation. Now that Keith was gone, there would be no conflict between his mother and the Clarendons on that score when he followed his plans. The pretense of supporting Keith's development ideas could just fall away, and he would be free to follow his dreams. Robbie pictured himself in a crisply pressed uniform, patrolling the lakeside and the fells.

The air shifted, and he frowned, smelling the hut before it came into view. Animals had knocked down Daniel's garbage bins and torn open the bags inside. It had taken Robbie months to get Daniel to stop burning his garbage. Now several weeks' accumulation had spoiled in the sun, spread out over a large area behind the hut, fouling the air.

Robbie considered picking up some of the larger stuff, but he'd need to re-bag it all to tote down the road, and he hadn't come prepared. At least he'd offer to give Daniel a hand with it. He knew most of the town avoided the man, but he'd seen him talking to his mother, and Robbie knew many people who never took the time to do that.

Daniel liked his ale too much, Robbie mused. He knocked on the back door to the grey wooden building several times. No response. A pane in the window over the sink was missing; a loud buzzing made him squint to look inside.

Flies hummed noisily amongst the stacks of piled dishes, feeding greedily on leftovers and dregs of takeout food. Robbie thought every dish Daniel owned must be thrown in that sink. He rattled the doorknob.

"Daniel! Daniel Rowley! Open up in there."

He decided to walk around to the front. Robbie stood for a moment enjoying the view of the lake, breathing in air warmed by the autumn sun, crisp with dried leaves—land getting ready to slumber for the winter. He had a good view of Belle Isle and even Ramsey Lodge across the bay from up here. The boats were out in full force already. A steamer headed toward Ambleside, its decks filled with colored sprinkles like on ice cream, the mixed colors of tourists and brightly clad hikers exploring the area where he lived.

Robbie mounted the two rickety steps to the porch, avoiding the broken chair set outside the front door. After pounding on the door and calling for Daniel again, he peered through the one window in the front room. He could see through to the tiny kitchen and the door to the water closet off of it. Dirty clothing lay in heaps on the floor. A worn cot sagged in the right front corner of the main room; a rough, wool blanket had landed on the floor in a heap. Lying amongst the tattered, grey sheets was the hairy bulk of Daniel Rowley, face down, one leg hanging off the bed.

Robbie banged hard on the door, calling for Daniel in a voice so loud he was certain it echoed across the lake. He felt in his pockets and realized he'd left his mobile at home.

Bloody sod, he thought, and started back down the hill. He'd have to call Kate Ramsey back and let her know that once again, Daniel Rowley had had one too many and wouldn't be coming in to work today.

CHAPTER FORTY-THREE

*"The manner of Hercules Flood's death made a scandal which
eclipsed every other scandal that, during the long, candlelit evenings
of Bristol winter, disturbed drawing-rooms
and kept business lively in taverns."*
— Marguerite Steen, *The Sun Is My Undoing*

II AM

Ian sat at his desk and rubbed his eyes. They burned from lack of
sleep. He'd put Kate's ring in his sock drawer when he'd rolled
in for a few hours of snatched sleep. He had stopped thinking of
it as his grandmother's ring because now it belonged to Kate. He
hated that Kate thought he was being cold and officious.

Despite the intense tension between them, he refused to do
less than his best on this or any other murder investigation.
When Kate had time to realize this, she would see she couldn't
possibly marry a person who would do less, and he was certain
they would forge a reunion. She needed time to sort out her
thoughts, a gift of love he was willing to give her when their
future together was at stake. One day, they would look back on
this and laugh over the night she'd thrown his ring back at him.
At least, he hoped they would.

He should be reviewing the reports on his pending cases,
and he forced himself to dive in, paying special attention to the
meager results on the missing Anne Reed. There were a few potential sightings in Windermere, and one caller was sure she'd
seen her with a young man at Sizergh Castle, south of Kendal.
All would be investigated. After making team assignments, Ian
initialed the files and tossed them in his out box.

He pulled the file containing his copies of everything to date on the Clarendon case to the center of his blotter. Last night, he'd called Higgins in to take Simon's statement, despite his awareness of budget constraints regarding officers accruing overtime. His need to be seen as objective so as not to be thrown off the case loomed larger.

Higgins had arrived yawning but eager to work. After instructing the sergeant on the salient points he had wanted covered, Ian had watched the interview from the next room, taking notes as Simon had described to Higgins how his kitchen door, never locked, opened right near his studio door, also never locked. Ian already knew this but had needed it documented.

After some resistance and insisting on their innocence, Simon had finally given Higgins a list of the lodge's employees. Afterwards, Higgins had hit Simon with allegations that he and Keith had been enemies, at which Simon had scoffed.

"We didn't agree. People don't always, but I didn't hate the man. I'll readily admit I would have continued to fight this planned arts centre he wanted to bring to town. But I'm certainly not the only one who feels that way."

"You don't have to continue that fight, now, do you, Mr. Ramsey?"

Ian had admired how Simon had kept his temper in check.

"Who knows how his family will feel now? They may forge ahead—trying to pay just the heating bills on that monstrous place must cost a small fortune."

Ian had to concede that Simon had a point, although he felt the defeated and ill family wouldn't pursue this aggressive plan.

"What about this fistfight you and the victim had at a pub in town?" Higgins had consulted his notes and had read out the date.

Simon had sighed, and Ian had heard the tiredness creep into his voice.

"Look, that was a silly mistake on both our parts. It was after a particularly contentious town meeting. Keith and I both had had too much to drink, and when he hit on my sister, I told him off. He got angry and threw a wild punch that connected. If he'd missed, I'd never have hit him back, but it was a protective instinct. We got pulled apart right away."

Ian had groaned. It was the first he'd heard that Simon had been protecting Kate. No wonder she was certain Simon hadn't been the instigator.

After having conferred with Higgins, they'd agreed the evidence to arrest Simon wouldn't pass the sniff test, and Ian wasn't about to arrest a man to make his superiors look good. He was also aware that the longer Simon was a suspect with no resolution to the investigation, the more his reputation would be affected.

Ian decided it would be best for everyone if he kept out of Simon's way today and left Kate alone to settle. He could hardly expect the man to be happy with him right now, but he hoped Simon would feel he'd been treated fairly and would pass that on to his sister.

Ian's report from Oxford had been filed. No real leads had panned out in his visit there, and he was disappointed. Edgar Worth hadn't been able to contribute much to the case. Yes, Keith had big plans, which he supported. An extension office in Clarendon Hall would connect the two areas nicely, and with Keith's planned increase in tourism, this had seemed a good plan. No, with Keith no longer working on the project, he didn't think he would go forward at this time with an extension office in Bowness. Without the Clarendon name and the use of an office at the Hall, it seemed it would require too much effort for the older man to manage it on his own. None of Keith's co-workers had added anything of substance to the interview. After hearing of Jack Halsey's death back in Bowness, Ian felt it had been a huge waste of time.

"You asked for this, guv." A civilian handed Ian a copy of an article Sommer Clarendon had mentioned during his interview. The family rooms, while off limits to the tour, were never locked, and anyone could have slipped away and found their way to the plant. When asked how a member of the general public would have knowledge of the particular plants he raised, Sommer had mentioned that he'd given an interview in which the Tanghinia plant had been highlighted for its rareness. That article had appeared in the spring issue of *Lake District Review*.

Ian read through the transcript, zeroing in on Sommer's description of the plant's history: "Tanghinia venenifera has lovely, glossy leaves and pretty white, star-shaped flowers with a pink base when it blooms, but it's known as the 'Ordeal Bean of Madagascar' because kings in Madagascar used it to have criminals confess. They thought ingesting it would reveal guilt or innocence. Since most of their subjects died, it was probably a moot point, but the name stuck."

It was as Simon had indicated: Anyone with a burning desire to murder Keith Clarendon would find the means at hand. Now Ian had to find out who had had the best opportunity and what his or her motive could have been. Thinking of Simon brought Kate back to mind. He thought of her slender neck and how she shivered when he kissed her there.

With effort, he tried to put Kate to the back of his mind and to concentrate on the tasks at hand. The inquest on Keith Clarendon was tomorrow morning and would be adjourned until further information came to light. In the afternoon, Keith's funeral would tie up the rest of his day. He'd be busy testifying at the first and observing who attended the second.

Ian opened his bottom desk drawer and withdrew a much-used briar pipe. He inhaled the scent of his grandfather's black cherry tobacco, a fortifying aroma that never failed to steady him. He stuck it in the corner of his mouth. He'd never developed the habit of smoking, and there was a ban on smoking inside the station, but the smell and the familiar feel of the stem clamped in his mouth braced him as he drew the Clarendon file toward him and began to review the entire case, starting with the report of the constable who'd responded to the summons to Ramsey Lodge early Saturday morning. There was more than just a mysterious death to compel him—his marriage and his whole future were at stake.

CHAPTER FORTY-FOUR

*"I am the last man to be suspicious of a colleague, but on thinking it
over I have the distinct feeling that the Vice-Chancellor's motives, in
button-holing me as he did this afternoon,
were at least partly feigned."*
— John Wain, *Strike the Father Dead*

2 PM

Nora opened her laptop. The two lodging couples had checked
out this morning, and the whole place felt strangely quiet. She
suspected they were fleeing after the assault on Agnes.

She clicked on Keith's manuscript and continued to read it,
notebook and pencil ready to jot down anything of interest that
she could use or, more to the point, which would allude to a
reason that someone could want Keith out of the way. Chunks
of script flew past her:

> *The extensive gardens at Holehird in Windermere be-
> long to the Lakeland Horticultural Society. Rocker-
> ies and scree beds capture in miniature the essence of
> the Cumbrian landscape that surrounds them. Think
> of these gardens as counterpoints to the majesty of the
> mountains surrounding them.*

Nora saw Sommer's influence on his son here. Keith noted the
gardens at John Ruskin's Brantwood as his personal favorites.
He described Ruskin as a "troubled genius" and recounted his
influence on Proust, Gandhi and even Tolstoy. Interesting,
Nora thought, but hardly the stuff of murderers. No mention of

Ruskin's penchant for poisonous plants, although she knew the Pre-Raphaelite era included a fascination with arsenic.

Munching on an oatmeal cookie, Nora read on.

3:15 PM

Simon returned from visiting the family solicitor, who advised truth and patience. He told Simon about his conversation with Ian Travers that morning, during which he had stressed that his client had assisted the police to the limit of his abilities, and further questioning would be seen as harassment. He also told Simon he doubted the strength of the case against him since he hadn't been arrested last night. Nora had seen Simon's drawn look, and she realized that despite his faith in Ian, this was having its effect on him.

He and Nora settled into work mode and spent the afternoon together, Nora outlining a story and Simon suggesting illustration layouts for their second book. She wrote some potential copy, trying to stay focused on fairies instead of poisons, while Simon sketched. She had her fairies arguing about who slept where inside their tree house, a veiled attempt to educate young readers about compromise. Nora made minor changes as they talked, their collaboration helping her polish the action.

"Let me find that book on Arthur Rackham's illustrations," Simon said and disappeared into his studio, unlocking it.

Nora could understand why he was locking the studio, although it seemed a bit late for that, but it didn't explain why he'd kept her out it. Come to think of it, he'd never fully explained why he'd borrowed that plant from Sommer. Nora cleaned her glasses, reflecting on these last few days. She was upset with

Kate's decision to return Ian's ring but felt certain they'd reconcile as soon as Keith's murderer was found. That would take the spotlight off Simon and allow Kate and Ian to find their way back to each other.

What was she missing in the situation? She couldn't think of anyone who had been near either Simon's studio or Clarendon Hall who had a motive to kill Keith. Be unhappy with him, yes, but kill him?

Nora cradled her belly and turned to a back page in her notebook. She listed all the people with direct access to Simon's studio:

Simon, Kate, Agnes, Maeve, Daniel

She discounted all but Daniel, based on his behavior toward her, and Maeve, based on personal prejudice. Although how did she know Maeve hadn't had a personal relationship with Keith? Maybe he'd thrown her over for someone else, and she was pissed. Nora warmed to the thought and put a star by Maeve's name. She refused to believe Simon could have had anything to do with Keith's death, despite his weird behavior concerning the studio.

She couldn't think of anyone else to add. She knew the Barnum girls didn't go into the family rooms. They cleaned hers as her pregnancy progressed and left her fresh towels, but both Kate and Simon took theirs from the linen closet. Everyone did their own wash in the laundry area under the back stairs. Kate ran the vacuum and duster over Simon's rooms, and he cleaned his own bathroom and changed his sheets, tasks Nora had seen him do in her time living here. They made him seem more like a Renaissance man than ever in her mind—a man who cleaned up after himself! But she was digressing. She hurriedly wrote her list for Clarendon Hall before Simon returned:

Antonia, Sommer, Cook, Gillian, Robbie, Daniel

Nora scrutinized this list. Daniel made both lists. She knew the docents from the National Trust didn't enter the family rooms, but someone could have slipped away, although that seemed like a big chance when he or she wouldn't know where the family was at any given moment. And how did that get the poison into Keith? Of course, the Hall must have daily or weekly cleaning help from the village. She made a note to ask Kate and sat back, massaging the hard ball her uterus formed. Who was she missing?

What about Glenn Hackney? They didn't really know when he'd come to Bowness, only when he'd checked in at Ramsey Lodge. Nora pictured him leaving the lodge this morning with Tony Warner.

She'd been putting Darby's leash on to take him on a walk when the two men came downstairs.

"Morning, Nora," Tony said. Today's costume was tweeds with an argyle jumper. "Going walkies?"

Nora thought only Tony could sound like the Queen Mum and not think a thing of it. She nodded to both men and refused to share her itinerary.

"Hello, Miss Tierney." Glenn took a brochure from the rack in the hall. "Here we are, Dove Cottage."

"There's a map on the back," Tony noted. Both men perused it.

"I think we can jolly well find our way there," Glenn pronounced, leading the way to the car park.

"Do have a good day, Nora, whatever that entails," Tony smirked as he left.

Sitting at Simon's table, Nora wondered what they had up their mutual sleeves in this unlikely alliance. They'd been the only ones not to flee after the attack on Agnes. Perhaps it was nothing more than two reprobates recognizing each other. Still, she added Glenn's name to her list but left Tony's off. Not liking someone was not a good enough reason to appear on her suspect list, although it hadn't stopped her in Maeve's case. As far as Tony was concerned, she'd add him, too, if evidence arose to support her doing so.

From the studio came the sound of cabinets banging shut. Quickly, Nora moved on to motive, and here her thoughts whirled with imagination. Had Keith been gay and hid it from his co-workers? Or maybe he'd dodged the advances of Glenn Hackney and set off a murderous bout of revenge? But what about her room being tossed? Had she been less discreet than she'd thought, and someone knew of the stolen thumb drive? Could Keith have uncovered something that meant he had to die?

Nora warmed to this theme. His death certainly was premeditated. Someone needed to have access to that plant and then had to add it to whatever drink Keith had imbibed just before going out on the lake. It couldn't have been at the meal he had had with his parents, or they would have been poisoned, too. Unless someone in his family was involved.

She couldn't see any reason for Sommer wanting to murder his only child, and while his arms worked fine, being confined to a wheelchair, even a mechanical one, did pose logistical problems. Ditto for Edmunde. She'd never seen the man, but it seemed he was in worse shape then his brother. Antonia couldn't be a suspect to Nora's mind; her grief seemed too real and too raw, although on consideration, she supposed the woman's fragile mental status could have led to a psychotic break.

The Coles were an enigma in terms of motive. Murdering Keith wouldn't further Gillian's career; as far as Nora could tell, she had her hands full caring for the two disabled brothers and had had no responsibilities toward Keith. Robbie just seemed like a nice kid. But then nice kids were known to be murderers.

"Here it is. Check this out," Simon said as he returned to her side, turning pages of Rackham's illustrations for J. M. Barrie's *Peter Pan in Kensington Gardens*.

Nora closed her notebook with a snap. She didn't want to embarrass Simon by reminding him of the fix he was in. Nor did she wish to annoy him. Renaissance man or not, Simon was vocal in his disapproval of her snooping and especially sensitive when he was the reason for it. Where could she turn for help?

Nora reached her favorite bench facing Bowness Bay and brought out her mobile. Simon had accepted her explanation of needing a break and had gone back to his studio to pack up the proof pages to mail to their printer. He insisted on carrying on meeting their deadlines. "I won't have your work jeopardized, Nora," he'd said when she'd suggested leaving it for another day.

She looked in her contacts at the number she'd stored there but never used, weighing the pros and cons of making this call. Taking a deep breath, she hit "call." Her pulse increased with every ring, and just as she decided he wasn't in the office, he answered.

"Barnes."

"Declan, it's Nora." If he said "Nora who?" she would hang up and wobble back to the lodge in humiliation.

"Hallo!" Declan Barnes voice was deeper than she remembered, but just as warm. "How are you?"

She ignored the thrill that shot through her and tried to focus on the reason for her call. "Really well, although I'm as big as a house." Nora mentally kicked herself for the image contained in that response.

"Any luck deciding on his name yet? I know you have your lists made. Declan is very nice."

"Very funny." What was it with everyone and this baby's name? Still, he made her smile. "Still whittling down my favorites," she said. She'd forgotten Declan knew from their time in

Oxford that she made lists. She had to resist her impulse to ask him personal questions just to hear his warm voice. "That's not why I called, though. I need to ask your advice."

"Of course." He sounded pleased. "Fire away."

Maybe he wouldn't be so pleased when he learned she wanted to help Simon. Nora succinctly explained how Simon had become a suspect in the death of Keith Clarendon due to the presence of the poisonous plant in his studio. "He's been brought in for questioning twice now, and he's given statements."

"He's obtained legal counsel?" Declan asked.

"Yes. And his solicitor has spoken to the senior investigating officer, too, and will be present at any future questionings." She added that the officer was Kate's fiancé, Detective Inspector Ian Travers.

"I remember speaking with Travers this summer. But Nora, if he had concrete and overwhelming evidence against Simon, he'd have arrested him by now. Is that what you wanted to hear?"

Was she imagining a touch of fancy in his voice? "I suppose so. I just feel so helpless, when it's obvious Simon wasn't involved."

There was a pause, and she thought at first that Declan had hung up.

"Maybe it's obvious to you, Nora, but it might not be to Ian Travers or to his superiors."

"I suppose you're right." She bit her lip. She decided not to tell him about the assault on Agnes in her room. "Isn't there anything I can do?"

This time, Declan's answer was swift and firm. "No. And I don't want to hear you're involving yourself in this investigation, Nora. I thought after what happened in Oxford you'd given up meddling with the professionals. This is *not* something you should be doing."

She tamped down her annoyance. He could get to her quicker

than anyone she knew. "I'm just asking if there's anything else you can think of that I could do to clear Simon's name." She tried to appear reasonable and already regretted calling him. "I'm not about to put myself or this baby in jeopardy."

Declan's answer chilled her. "That's what you thought the last time."

6:30 PM

Nora had hurried back to the lodge after her less-than-satisfactory call to Declan Barnes. The increasing menace she'd felt around her since the assault on Agnes seemed almost palpable. Before Kate arrived home, Nora and Simon agreed not to bring up Ian's name or the broken engagement.

"Let's have a quiet evening," Simon urged. "She defended me and got carried away. If she needs to talk about it, she'll bring it up. This will blow over and make their relationship even stronger."

"I hope so," Nora agreed. "I like Ian—usually."

"Leave Ian alone on all fronts for now." Simon had a warning finger in the air when the door opened to admit Kate.

They put on smiling faces for her. She carried Chinese takeaway, obviously a Darby favorite from the fuss he made over her bags. The pungent odors of moo shu pork and curried chicken quickly filled Simon's kitchen.

"Enough work, peasants!" Kate pronounced. "I've had too much tea and not enough protein today." She unpacked cardboard and foil containers while Simon put out plates and utensils.

Nora knew Kate well enough to see through her forced gaiety. Her stomach growled in response to the tantalizing aromas. "I think little Sylvester needs food, too," she said, stacking the books they'd been using and clearing the table. "It means 'of the forest.'" She saw the startled look on the siblings' faces and flapped her hand. "Just kidding."

"How's Agnes?" Simon asked, opening a waxed paper bag and crunching on a crisply fried wonton.

"Thrilled to have Hazel down and to be waited on for a change by her younger sister. Her headache's gone, although the lump where the stitches are is quite sore." Kate opened a small dish of orange sauce and offered it to her brother.

Nora slathered hoisin sauce on a pancake and wrapped it around the shredded pork and vegetable filling. Her thoughts strayed back to her lists and the questions she had. "Kate, you said Keith didn't have a girlfriend?"

Kate looked up from twirling lo mein noodles onto her chopsticks. "Not that I know, but with him away in Oxford so much, who knows?" She chewed her noodles, pointing her chopstick at Nora. "He could have a honey there we don't know about."

Nora chewed a huge bite of her pancake and swallowed. "Delicious." She sipped her water, running down her mental list of questions. "Who does the cleaning at Clarendon Hall?"

"The Trust takes care of the public areas. Cook does the kitchen, but I think someone in town does the family rooms about twice a week. Don't know who it is right now." Kate slurped up her lo mein. "Why do you ask?"

Handing Darby a crunchy noodle, Simon answered for her. "Because Nora has an insatiable need to poke her nose into other people's business."

CHAPTER FORTY-FIVE

"A man's dying is more the survivors' affair than his own."
— Thomas Mann, *The Magic Mountain*

Tuesday, 26th October

10 AM

"Time of death is estimated between 7 PM Friday night and 2 AM Saturday morning."

Nora watched Dr. Milo Foreman give his testimony at the inquest into Keith Clarendon's death. Dressing this morning, she'd felt flutters of anxiety about testifying.

Kate and Simon flanked her on chairs set up in Kendal's County Hall. Nora noted Kate kept her eyes forward, not looking around for Ian, who sat at the back of the room near Sommer Clarendon and Gillian Cole.

Nora remembered the first inquest she'd attended, last summer in Oxford. She wasn't a witness then and had had the luxury of watching the proceedings with interest, remembering Declan Barnes giving evidence. She'd admired his composure and appearance. She wondered where he was today and what he'd thought after they'd hung up the day before. It had been impulsive to call him and expect him to be supportive of her efforts. She had no business calling him for any reason. At that moment, Simon reached out to squeeze her hand, and she felt a twinge of guilt that brought her attention back to Dr. Foreman.

"The body was clothed in green shorts and white Reebok T-shirt, worn under a black windcheater. Black sweat pants were found in a rucksack clipped to an inside rib of the scull. The pack also contained the wrapper from a tuna salad sandwich and the dregs of tea in an insulated bottle. There were no visible signs of external premortem violence or wounds. Toxicology reports show no controlled drugs but a high level of a respiratory and cardiac toxin also found in the tea bottle, identified as belonging to the Tanghinia family."

There was a gasp from the audience as Milo interrupted his recitation to sip from the water bottle at his elbow. Nora realized the information she'd been privy to had not been common knowledge.

The coroner asked a question. "Have you identified where this poison would have been obtainable, and also, what would the deceased have experienced after this ingestion?"

"The poison comes from a rare Tanghinia venenifera plant, which has been found in two locations in Bowness." Milo wiped his forehead with a bright white handkerchief.

Nora realized this next part was painful for him to recite in court in front of the boy's father. She liked him for that.

"The poison affects the cardiac and respiratory system. There would have been initial nausea and dizziness with trembling and muscle weakness, which would account for him being unable to row closer to shore. As his breathing became more difficult and his heartbeat irregular, he would either have had convulsions or lapsed into a coma. From the lack of bruising, I feel it more likely he fell into a comatose state before succumbing to full cardiac arrest."

The coroner made a note. "Ingested poison, then, leading to the consideration of homicide if suicide can be ruled out?"

"Precisely." Milo clasped his large hands over his larger abdomen, while a murmur of speculation spread through the crowded town hall.

The pathologist was excused, and the court officer called

the next witness. "Elsie Ewart" was revealed to be Cook. She'd dressed in her Sunday suit and heels and carried a matching purse.

After being sworn in, Cook tearfully confirmed the clothing Keith was found in as the outfit she'd last seen him wearing before retiring to her rooms after cooking a hot meal in the early afternoon. She explained that on most days, the Clarendons ate their large meal in the afternoon with a light snack in the evening, as this worked better for Mr. Sommer's disposition and therapy schedule. Keith often took a sandwich out with him on the lake.

The coroner continued his questions. "Did you see Mr. Clarendon preparing his snack?"

Cook shook her head. "I'd made tuna salad earlier for the evening meal, and it was in the fridge in a bowl. The tea was what he always took this time of year. I keep a kettle on low, and he'd fix it himself and poured it into his thermos." She withdrew a lace-edged hankie and paused to dab her tears. "By the time he left that evening, I was in my room at the end of the hall. I had the telly on." She blushed. "I need to keep it up high these days—my hearing isn't what it used to be. I never heard him in the kitchen or leaving at all." There was a pause before she admitted: "I might have dozed off after cleaning up."

"Of course," the coroner said. He thanked Cook for her time and dismissed her.

It seemed to Nora that the audience turned en masse toward her when her name was called. Simon stood to allow her an easy exit, and she made her way to the front table, swaying uncomfortably. She felt huge and had the same feeling of being watched as in third grade at Ridgefield School, going to the blackboard to solve a difficult math problem. Arithmetic had never been her forte, and today she felt the same anxiety to "get it right." As she was sworn in, she reminded herself she only had to tell the truth.

Settling her hands on the arms of her chair, she crossed her ankles in what she hoped was a composed manner. Nora explained how she'd known Keith from the contest and from her subsequent move to Cumbria.

In response to the coroner's succinct questioning, she described coming across the overturned scull on her morning walk. "I pulled on it until it was anchored up on the beach, and as it fell over to one side, I, um, found the body." Nora's stomach turned as Keith's hideous face loomed before her. Sweat broke out on her palms, and she tried to focus on a friendly face in the sea of curious onlookers in front of her. Kate smiled encouragingly; Simon nodded in support. Across the aisle, Tony Warner scribbled furiously while Glenn Hackney whispered in his ear. She saw Tony balance a voice-activated recorder on his lap. The coroner consulted his paperwork, then excused her.

As she made her way back to her seat, the court officer called out: "Sommer Clarendon." A hush ran through the assembly as Sommer came up the aisle from the back of the hall, his wheelchair humming. He was dressed in a white shirt and subtle tie with a navy blazer. The lap robe covering his withered legs was heathery beige cashmere. Sommer's expression was rigid and directed to the front of the room. The man's upper-body strength was apparent as he steered up the aisle, accompanied by Gillian Cole.

Nora saw the faint smile on Gillian's face reflecting the pride she felt that her patient looked so well cared for after eighteen years of disability. Whispers spread through the crowd.

Having seen Gillian at Clarendon Hall, Nora noted that the nurse had taken pains with her own appearance. Her thin hair was clean and pinned back in a sleek bun. Her white uniform was starched and pressed; she appeared professional and competent. Nora rested a hand on her pregnancy, appreciating

CHAPTER FORTY-FIVE

Gillian's efforts to hold down a demanding job while she raised Robbie alone.

Sommer reached the head of the walkway, and Gillian sank into the front row like a parent escorting a bride down the aisle. He wheeled himself in front of the improvised witness chair and deftly twirled the wheelchair around to face the gathering.

"Thank you for attending today at this most difficult time," the coroner addressed Sommer. "I would like to establish your son's recent frame of mind."

Sommer spoke in a clear voice. "Keith's mood was extremely buoyant. He had development plans for the area that included the expansion of the travel agency where he worked in Oxford with a satellite office in Bowness. He'd also launched a book project, a local history to educate tourists about the stories and beauty of our region."

This statement was accompanied by a snort from the row representing the worst of The Scarlet Wench regulars whose most vocal compatriots were noticeably absent: the unfortunate Jack Halsey and Daniel Rowley. The outburst was quelled by a stern look from the coroner, who asked: "There were no signs of depression or moodiness, I take it?"

"Absolutely none. He was entering the prime of his life and had much to look forward to, including robust health." Sommer's tone indicated he wanted to put the idea of suicide to rest.

The coroner asked him to describe Keith's last day at home.

"Friday we had a hot lunch. He retired to his study to work on his manuscript. I stopped in to see him when Mrs. Cole took me up for a nap." Sommer shifted in his chair. "He was on his computer then. About 3 o'clock, I'd say. He told me he planned a row on the lake later; he enjoyed watching the sunset from the water."

Sommer paused to look down at his hands, lying gracefully in his lap. Nora imagined he was thinking that was the last time he'd seen Keith or heard his voice.

"So you don't know the exact time he left the house?" the coroner asked.

"No, only that it was after 3. On Fridays after napping, his mother and I have been watching a serial of BBC classics, *Jane Eyre* this week, so we had sandwiches on trays in our room around 6 and didn't go down again."

"And you didn't notice that he hadn't returned?"

Sommer smiled sadly. "We tried not to interfere with his life when he was home. He was an adult, after all."

The coroner thanked Sommer for appearing at such an unfortunate time and excused him after formally expressing his sympathies to the Clarendon family. A few minutes later, he handed down his decision to adjourn his verdict, pending further investigation.

The mass of people rose as instructed by the court officer and streamed out into the sunlight. Nora approached Cook and complimented her on her turn on the stand. "Such a difficult experience," she commiserated.

Red tipped Cook's ears. "You're very kind, I'm sure. Are you going to the service today?"

Nora nodded. "With Kate and Simon." She knew Kate had promised to go to the Hall early to help Cook with the preparations.

"Stop in the kitchen once you've made the rounds. I'll keep some special goodies set aside to thank Kate for her help, and there's plenty to go around."

Nora thanked Cook profusely for the invitation. She had been handed an opportunity to poke around and intended to take full advantage of it.

CHAPTER FORTY-SIX

"After the funeral they came back to the house, now indisputably
Mrs. Halloran's."
— Shirley Jackson, *The Sundial*

I PM

Gillian insisted Sommer have his usual nap to prepare for the
afternoon ahead. He acquiesced when Antonia said she would
lie with him for a brief rest. When they were settled, Gillian left
them to tend to Edmunde.

She found Edmunde sitting up on the side of the bed. "Good
for you! Used the trapeze? I told you those exercises would pay
off." She walked around to face him. "Are you planning on coming down for any part of the service or reception?"

Edmunde shook his head emphatically "NO," making a small,
brusque motion with his left hand, dismissing her suggestion.

She regarded him thoughtfully and nodded. "Very well. But
I can't control visitors up here, so we'd better make you present-
able, just in case." She opened his closet and scanned the row
of dressing gowns and sweat suits. The pants had Velcro strips
sewn down the outside of each leg up to the waistband. Gillian
would place the bottoms in his chair, then use the mechanical
lift to lower Edmunde into it. Once settled, she would fit the
top of the pants on and press the sides together. This was her
own design, one she'd made up soon after it became apparent
Edmunde would never wear his well-cut tweeds and suits again.
It was never an issue with Sommer, who preferred the use of a
lap rug without too much weight, which bothered his legs. Edmunde insisted on his pants.

"I'm not sure your usual jogging outfit is appropriate," she mused.

Edmunde banged his left foot noisily on the metal rung of his chair.

"Pissed, are you? Don't like having your routine upset? Still a spark of the old Edmunde in there." Her voice soothed him as she displayed a silk smoking jacket. "A compromise, then. We'll leave your comfy pants on but cover them with a lap rug, like Sommer, and you'll be dressed nicely from the waist up." She leaned down to his eye level, ignoring his sour breath, searching for warmth in his left eye. "It'll be our little secret," she whispered, brushing the thick hair off his forehead.

His left eye blinked once.

2 PM

Kate lifted a heavy platter of sliced meats and waited for Cook to wrap plastic wrap around it. They were almost finished setting up for the reception after the funeral, and Kate's thoughts strayed to this morning.

It had been difficult to see Ian at the inquest without catching his eye or having a conversation. She pretended she didn't see him, but she could feel his eyes boring into her back. Conscious of her posture, she sat up straighter. He probably thought she was coldhearted to avoid him, but she didn't see how to get herself out the difficult situation she'd put them in. Part of her felt it was impetuous to break their engagement. But she couldn't reconcile the man she loved, that sweet, gentle yet confident fellow, with anyone who would treat her brother as a serious murder suspect. Could they find their way back to each other once this case was settled and Simon was off the hook?

Kate sighed and handed the platter over to Robbie Cole. He used his hip to push open the door into the hallway to bring the platter to the formal dining room.

"That one's an angel, no mistaking it," Cook told Kate. "Thanks for your help, dear. Daniel never showed up as he was supposed to, and Robbie had to set up the tables alone. I want to get done to go to the chapel service."

"I'm glad to help, Cook, and I'm sure Robbie is, too." Kate arranged tiny iced cookies on a tiered silver salver. "I wish I knew what's happened to Daniel. He was to work in the garden for me yesterday and didn't show up then, either. I sent Robbie up to his hut, and Daniel was flat out on his cot."

"Probably mourning the passing of his buddy, Jack," Cook said. "But that's no excuse. By today, the worst drink should've worn off."

Robbie re-entered the kitchen and heard the last of their conversation. He contributed his own cheerful outlook. "That's assuming Daniel didn't wake last night and go out and get snookered all over again!"

2:15 PM

Ian watched with interest as his friend, the vicar Basil Northrup, fussed over the Altar Guild ladies, who prepared the cloths and hangings on the chapel altar. Decorated with the Clarendon crest, these would drape the altar on either side of the ornate cross that had been in the family for generations. Ian had befriended Basil when the young cleric arrived four years ago, and he knew the priest considered himself a director of sorts. Some people directed plays, but Basil directed Life Events, as he referred to weddings, christenings and funerals. The two men had struck up a friendship after a silver Eucharist chalice had been stolen from St. Martin's. Ian had recovered it a week after the ruffian had pawned it, and he'd caught the thief soon after, thanks to the hidden cameras mounted in the pawnshop. Today, Ian stopped by to offer Basil his regards.

"I think my somber face is one of my best," Basil said, practicing this expression as he drew on his robes, giving Ian a wink. "I've already run through the litany of phrases I keep handy for funerals."

Ian knew Basil's dry humor helped him cope with the awkward moments he faced, much like some policemen he knew. "You look fine, very sincere and very priestly."

"I worried about handling these things when in seminary, you know. I kept trying to locate a book for new priests that conveniently listed the top ten appropriate comments for difficult situations." Basil kissed the cross on the neck of his skillfully embroidered stole and adjusted it around his neck. "Someone would make a bundle in seminaries if they'd publish that."

Ian thought Basil had grown into his office through his succession of parishes, and with maturity had come the words that calmed and soothed. He had a gift for sincerity belied by the humor he showed to Ian. Basil was scheduled to marry Ian and Kate—that is, if they ever got married. He supposed he should tell Basil the engagement was off. If he were interrogating himself, Ian would call this a lie of omission. He shifted his weight onto his other foot and kept silent.

A few minutes later, Ian stood outside his car, parked under a rowan tree near the Clarendon Chapel. This spot allowed him full view of the mourners as they arrived. Townspeople walked through the family graveyard before the service, inspecting the headstones. More stood in clusters, talking quietly. The funeral, a social event in the middle of the usual business day, gave the villagers a reason to take a half-day from work or to close up shop out of respect.

Ian searched the faces, many familiar to him, from the farmers to the herders to the innkeepers. He'd already sent for copies of the town meeting minutes to determine what local opposition there had been to Keith's plans besides those of Simon and The Scarlet Wench hecklers.

Pretending he was not looking for Kate, he saw two men he'd seen this morning sitting together at the inquest. He'd found out one was Keith's associate; the other was from Nora's former workplace in Oxford. They were too chummy for his liking, and he added them to his mental list for background checks. People weren't always what they represented themselves to be.

A flash of red hair caught his eye, and he saw Nora inspecting the headstones, while Simon stood nearby talking to Cook and Kate. As he watched, Simon detached himself and strode purposefully toward him. Popping a mint in his mouth to stave off hunger pains, Ian shook hands with Simon.

"Careful—fraternizing with the enemy, Simon."

Simon smiled and came right to the point. "It seems Daniel Rowley didn't show up to help Cook today."

Ian was unimpressed. "I don't get the impression that's so unusual for Rowley, is it, Simon?"

"He didn't show up yesterday at the lodge when Kate expected him, either. She sent Robbie Cole up to his hut. He said he could see Rowley through the front window, flat out on his cot. If he's still there, he might be ill or have had a stroke." Simon thrust his hands in his pockets. "The ladies are worried."

"Ah, the plot thickens," Ian chided him. "It's me now who's the bad egg if I don't check up on him and something's happened." He saw Kate watching him. "Tell 'the ladies' I'll have Higgins run up and have a look. I need something to get me back in your sister's good graces." Reconciling with Kate would take more than a grand gesture. It would require solving the mystery of Keith's death.

Ian watched Simon head back to the three women. The vicar appeared at the chapel door, greeting the first mourners. It occurred to him that there was a good likelihood that inside this sacred place, a murderer prayed.

2:50 PM

After thanking Simon for speaking to Ian, Kate took Cook by the arm to save seats inside the chapel. Nora remained in the graveyard with Simon, her attention caught by an elaborate stone next to the gaping hole dug that morning for Keith. A marble angel spread its wings protectively over the carving of a tiny lamb. The inscription read:

Rose Julia Clarendon
Only One Day New
Gone to Live with the Angels

Next to the angel and lamb stood a second marker, a carved open book watched over by a second angel. That inscription read:

Julia Catherine Brookes Clarendon
Her Gifts to Us Manifold

CHAPTER FORTY-SIX

Her Glory Knows No Bounds
Her Story Left Untold

"How sad." Nora pointed to the carvings as Simon took her elbow and they walked away. "Little Rose, 'only one day new.' What a difficult time that must have been."

"One that continues," Simon said, directing Nora's attention to the paved pathway to the chapel that ran from the back of Clarendon Hall. Gillian Cole guided Sommer's wheelchair over the stones toward the chapel. Antonia held his hand and walked slowly alongside him, her black suit and hat in acute contrast to her pale face and curls. She cradled a large cluster of white roses in her free arm.

At the chapel door, Antonia fell away and walked into the graveyard, not seeing Nora or Simon, seeking out Rose's grave. With a bow of her head, she laid several of the roses at the foot of the carved marble lamb. Nora could see her lips moving silently. Antonia placed several more at Julia's grave, retaining a few. She closed her eyes briefly and disappeared inside the chapel.

CHAPTER FORTY-SEVEN

"My heart aches, and a drowsy numbness pains
My senses."
— John Keats, *Ode to a Nightingale*

Simon admired the stained glass window high over the chapel's altar as the choir sang the opening hymn. The sun was at the right angle to cast a purple-and-gold beam onto the brass plaque that adorned Keith's coffin. The oak and bronze casket at the head of the main aisle rested on a catafalque covered in royal blue with gold bullion edging and the Clarendon crest embroidered in gold. As he followed the service in the prayer book, Simon's eyes started to close. He hadn't been sleeping well since Keith died, which was no surprise, and trying to keep some semblance of normality in his life was proving harder than he'd thought it would be. He'd assumed working with Nora while he kept painting would be enough to distract him from the looming thought that he was a suspect in Keith Clarendon's murder. He worried about the effect this was having on the lodge business, too, even though he was the first to admit he wasn't as good at business as Kate.

Dear Kate. He hated that this had spread to her relationship with Ian. He wanted fiercely to believe that their broken engagement was a momentary glitch. When he'd assured Nora of that thought, he realized he'd been reassuring himself.

Nora presented her own complicated line of thinking for him. He needed to support her as best he could while she finished this pregnancy and launched the book series, her new career. He worried, too, about her impulsive streak, but he'd tried to stop thinking about the nature of their personal life. They didn't have one, beyond being close, caring friends. Months ago, he'd promised to act as a father to her baby—if she would let him. That idea seemed far-fetched to him now, between her firm independence and her inability to focus on a relationship. He understood the reason, but he also knew feelings were fluid. He hoped hers might change once the baby was born and he could play an active role with the child. That's assuming he wasn't locked away for Keith Clarendon's murder.

Basil was in high form, Simon decided, focusing on the vicar's oratory on the important points of Keith's brief life, including his scholastic and sports achievements. Simon stole a glance at Nora, who listened intently, a slight frown between her eyebrows. She remained a remarkable person to him. Twice now, she'd been brushed by death in the form of murder, and both times she'd handled herself with strength and grace. Another person wouldn't have visited the family at home nor attended the funeral of a casual acquaintance, especially when both events had to remind her of the ghastly way she'd stumbled upon Keith's body. And all while she was heavily pregnant.

No, Nora was one tough cookie. If he could keep her from intruding into Keith's investigation to clear his own name, he could worry less. On his side was the knowledge he had nothing to do with Keith's death. He believed Ian would eventually clear him and find the real culprit. It was sit-and-wait time, but one thing Nora didn't do well was sit and wait.

3:45 PM

Nora realized the vicar had stopped speaking. She brought her attention back to the service. The shuffling and coughs that accompanied the vicar as he sat down ceased when Sommer Clarendon wheeled away from the family pew. Pausing in front of Keith's coffin, Sommer raised one hand and patted the polished wood, his fingers lingering, tracing an unknown pattern. Nora felt her throat constrict with emotion.

Sommer spun his chair to face the crowd, withdrawing a paper from his jacket pocket. He drew a deep breath and cleared his throat.

"One of Keith's favorite poets was John Dryden. I've chosen his words, written in memory of a lost friend, to honor Keith." In a voice that trembled slightly, he began to read:

> *Farewell, too little and too lately known,*
> *Whom I began to think and call my own;*
> *For sure our Souls were near ally'd; and thine*
> *Cast in the same Poetick mould with mine.*

Sommer continued the poem in a stronger voice. Nora closed her eyes as she pictured Keith, smiling to the reporters that day in the lobby at *People and Places* and being carried into the chapel today. Too young to die, she thought, thinking of Paul and of Bryn Wallace.

Behind her closed lids, fresh tears stung her eyes. The air felt close in the small, crowded space, and she started to fan herself with the program she'd been handed as she'd entered.

Her midsection hardened into a firm ball, and she took a few deep breaths. Braxton Hicks contractions, her obstetrician had explained, in which the uterus practices for labor and delivery. The spasm passed, and the hardness relaxed. She felt her control returning and opened her eyes.

Nora scrutinized the gathering. She knew some faces, but

most of them were strangers to her. She checked her mental list of suspects. Who amongst them might be a murderer? Who had needed Keith to die for his own survival?

Maeve Addams slipped into the row in front of them. Her short, leather skirt was black, set off with a tight, black lace top and matching tights that, except for their color, were unlike any funeral attire Nora had ever seen. She looked down at the navy maternity dress she wore; not exactly a fashion model.

Maeve turned to catch Simon's eye and flashed him a smile, ignoring everyone else. The woman had been verbal in her support of Simon, as if she were the only one who truly believed his innocence. Or was she covering something up for herself by deflecting attention to Simon? Nora pretended not to notice her, then seconds later leaned over and whispered to Simon: "Is she always fashionably late?"

He whispered back, "Only when she wants to be the center of attention."

Nora thought he tried awfully hard to keep the smile off his face.

3:50 PM

Near the back of the chapel, Glenn Hackney shifted on the hard pew and crossed his legs. He admired the checkered pattern of the trousers Tony Warner wore but refrained from mentioning it. It was obvious Tony wasn't gay, and Glenn felt certain by now that Tony Warner didn't have any particular information he needed. Still, you could never be too careful in his profession; he didn't want to discourage the reporter from any confidence. He'd picked up on Tony's royal hankering on their first walk.

"My uncle by marriage is Duke of Arbuthnot," Tony managed to work into their conversation. "Twice removed" was almost whispered.

Glenn recognized a fellow con man, although of a different sort. Tony coveted societal position, whereas Glenn was an acquirer, mostly of other people's possessions.

"Very nice," Glenn had replied. "We've done the cruise work for the Ogilvies for the last few years. Such sporting fellows, these titled people." He had never met an Ogilvy, titled or otherwise, but much of a con was down to sounding convincing.

"I quite agree," Tony had replied, a glint in his eye.

Glenn still hoped their carefully contrived "friendship" would come in useful down the road. But his goal for today was to find a way to get into Keith's work files to know just how much Keith had unearthed about him.

3:55 PM

Ian sat in the last row of the chapel. The constable he'd assigned to make a list of attendees was a local Windermere lass who knew the majority of the mourners by sight. He glanced at his watch and wondered how long it would take Higgins to check on Daniel Rowley and get back to the Hall.

Keith's father finished reading and made a few remarks, inviting the congregation back to the Hall for a reception, then motored back to the end of the first stall. His wife took Sommer's hand as everyone stood for a closing hymn. Ian took the opportunity to slip outside. Squinting in the brighter light, he examined the imposing Hall that rose on the other side of the graveyard. No wonder the family was forced to give public tours.

The utility bills alone must be enormous, to say nothing of the upkeep. His eyes roamed over the stone edifice, and he noted a movement at one of the upstairs windows. The curtain moved, he was certain, and yet the family was still in the chapel.

Then it occurred to Ian that Keith's uncle had not made an appearance; in fact, had not been seen outside Clarendon Hall since his debilitating stroke. It must be Edmunde at that window, Ian surmised, watching for activity from that huge, cold house. How much mobility the man retained had not been clearly established in Higgins' interview, other than a strong left arm that moved enough to throw his breakfast and stop the questioning.

3:55 PM

Edmunde enjoyed being alone. He leaned forward, brushing the curtain aside with his good hand.

After Gillian had settled him near his bedroom window, she had left to assist Sommer to the chapel. He'd heard Robbie volunteer to stay behind in case Edmunde used the call bell in her absence. The boy had entered the room once for a few minutes to check on him. Edmunde had pointedly ignored him. Robbie had told him he would be in the kitchen loading the dishwasher and had left.

Edmunde continued studying the scene in front of him and saw a tall, blonde man exit and look up at his window. Finally, the vicar emerged from the chapel, followed by Keith's casket, hoisted onto the shoulders of six sturdy pallbearers. Antonia followed with Sommer, guided by Gillian, and then he saw Cook and the rest of the crowd file out.

They walked slowly toward the gravesite and the garish hole.

Heads bowed as the vicar raised his arm, and the coffin was lowered into the ground. He read from his prayer book for a few minutes and then took a clod of earth and dropped it on the coffin.

Antonia detached herself from Sommer's side long enough to throw on top of Keith's casket the spray of white roses she carried. Edmunde shifted restively in his chair, annoyed that his vision blurred even further as one large tear rolled from his good eye.

Chapter Forty-Eight

*"I have just buried my boy, my handsome boy of whom I was so
proud, and my heart is broken."*
— H. Rider Haggard, *Allan Quatermain*

4:10 PM

Glenn Hackney and Tony Warner joined the throng that walked
respectfully a few paces behind the family to Clarendon Hall.

"Classy touch, those white roses instead of dropping clumps
of dirt on that lovely oak," Tony commented.

"Very nice," Glenn agreed. "So much of these rituals are antiquated, but then tradition is what England is all about."

"Oh, I agree, totally," Tony assured him. He pasted a smile
on his full face, anxious to agree with Glenn, his ticket into the
reception. "Shall we?" He gestured for Glenn to precede him as
they reached the wide doorway.

Glenn nodded and led the way. Tony slipped his hand into
his jacket pocket and felt for his recorder. He fervently hoped
someone would drop Nora Tierney's name into conversation in a
disparaging way.

Inside the Hall, the men found silver trays and laden platters
placed on long tables running down one side of the formal dining room. White damask cloths that covered the tables were embroidered with the royal blue Clarendon crest in a border along
their edges. Large pieces of furniture had been pushed back into
corners, and chairs from other rooms added to the seating capacity in here and in the drawing room.

The two men spent half an hour on line, filling their plates, and ate with relish. After polishing off his food, Glenn decided the time had come for a bit of exploration. The majority of people wandered about the room, gawking at the displayed antiques and oil paintings. More adventuresome souls climbed the staircase and examined the family portraits in the gallery.

Mumbling an excuse to Tony about finding the loo, Glenn left his new acquaintance mingling at the fringe of a group, ear tuned to local gossip. Once in the hallway, Glenn joined a handful of villagers headed up the broad stairway, noting no one had the nerve to walk down the hall toward the private rooms. He stood with them as though he belonged there, reading the plaques under each portrait. Antonia Clarendon's beauty had faded, but Julia Clarendon's was preserved in a time warp.

Glenn looked around the hall, trying to figure out which doorway would lead him to Keith's study. He realized his greatest source of information stood close at hand and attached himself to a stout woman he'd seen running one of the tourist shops in Bowness. She admired the portrait of young Sommer Clarendon.

"Beautiful dogs, and quite some heritage," he said to her.

The woman turned to him with a suspicious expression on her face but nodded in agreement.

He met her look head on with his most charming smile, thrusting his hand at her. "I don't believe I've had the pleasure—Glenn Hackney. I'm an associate of Keith's from Oxford. And you must be related to the Clarendons?" His insouciant manner was spot on.

The woman blushed, thrilled to be mistaken for a relative of the most prominent family in town, and shook his hand. A few more well-placed questions and compliments, and Glenn had won her confidence. He pointed down the east wing and leaned into her, asking modestly, "Dear lady, do you suppose the facilities are down that way?"

"Oh, no," she answered, happy to impart the correct information. "That's the way to the Clarendon family rooms. There's a loo down that short hall."

"You have been a frequent guest here," he gushed, confirming Keith's study lay in the east wing.

"You do go on, Mr. Hackney," she giggled, her ample bosom jiggling. "You can see the layout in the tour brochure."

He thanked her and walked toward the guest wing, reflecting how easily people could be duped by a few choice words.

5:05 PM

Antonia moved restlessly through the throng of people who'd invaded her home. She'd tolerated these last hours in a medicated fog. After acknowledging everyone and receiving their sympathies, she felt she'd done her duty and longed to be left alone. Yet the crowd only thinned slightly as people wolfed down Cook's offerings and admired what was left of the Clarendon trappings.

She was aware that Sommer sat in the middle of a group involved in a discussion, and even as she thought she should rescue him, a ripple of fatigue swept over her. She slipped out of the room, nodding to a few people standing near the kitchen door talking with Cook, and took the elevator upstairs, too hollow inside to plow through the eager guests coming down the main staircase.

Those who had ventured upstairs satisfied their curiosity in the gallery. Antonia walked alone down the hall of the family wing, the thick runner muffling her footsteps. She turned the handle to her bedroom door and stopped, drawn irresistibly to her son's room.

Standing on the threshold to his bedroom, Antonia took in his collected belongings. Shelves held pieces of driftwood or stones Keith had collected by the lake. A telescope stood by the largest window, pointing to the heavens. She fancied she could see Keith making a minor adjustment. If she were to bend down in the dark of night and look through the eyepiece, would she see him waving to her, the way he'd once waved to the shore?

Antonia quivered and crossed the bedroom to the dressing room and bath that joined his room with his library.

After the police had finished with his rooms, she'd let the village helpers change the sheets and remake the bed. No one knew she had stolen into the room and taken the pillowcases from the hamper. Opening the mirrored closet door, she reached up and took the wrinkled cases off the top shelf, burying her face in them, breathing in the scent she was afraid she would forget. She inhaled deeply, trying to commit to memory the combination of musky cologne and perspiration that she recognized as Keith.

The door to Keith's library opened, the sound startling her, and Antonia threw open the connecting door in time to see the back of someone tall and slim slip out of the room. The scent of vanilla lingered as she hurried through the room to the door, but when she opened it and looked out, the hall stood empty.

5:12 PM

Tony looked around for Glenn and noticed him return to the drawing room, a sullen look on his face. Tony waved him over before Glenn could melt into a grouping; he needed the man as his introduction to the thin nurse who hovered near Sommer Clarendon.

"Took you long enough," Tony grumbled. "Everything come out okay?"

Glenn's distaste was evident. "I never discuss bodily functions. I was admiring the Clarendon portrait gallery," he announced.

"Of course. Let's go visit the nurse, shall we?" He nodded in the direction of Gillian Cole.

"Why the interest?" Glenn whispered.

Tony leaned into him. "Because she leaves here after both of the gimps are in bed. She may have seen someone on the grounds last Friday night." Tony rubbed his hands together. "And I'd love if it was Nora Tierney."

Glenn considered this. "Warner, you are a true charlatan."

But Tony noted he said it with a smile.

CHAPTER FORTY-NINE

"Major Malcolm Barcroft was sixty-seven when he died,
the last male of his line."
— Shelby Foote, *Love in a Dry Season*

5:15 PM

Nora moved around the drawing room, noticing Maeve had attached herself to the circle of people, including several other inn owners, with whom Simon and Kate were engaged in a discussion. This was a woman determined to ram her point home. Nora didn't think she'd like to be on Maeve's bad side.

She lingered at the edge of several groupings, ears alert to anything negative said about Keith, picking up stray comments.

"I feel so awful for the poor Clarendons."

"Can't complain about the rise in custom with all this press around."

"The plod really think murder, then?"

Nora smiled at everyone; several gave her appraising glances of recognition. It wasn't too difficult to figure out she was the pregnant gal who had found Keith's body. She was treated to a discourse on the National Park Authority at one group and the Right to Roam Bill at another. Raised voices in one corner caught her attention, but when she made her way over to investigate, the argument turned out to be about the best hiking shoe for the rigorous fell paths.

Nora was impatient. Despite her innate nosiness, Simon had saved her from certain death in Oxford, and she longed to repay the favor by clearing him of any suspicion in Keith's death. To do that, she needed information.

Passing her eyes over the buffet tables, Nora spotted an empty platter. She scooped it up and carried it into the kitchen, where Cook was refilling a silver server with iced cookies, held by Robbie.

"This one's broke, Cook." Robbie grinned and popped the cookie into his mouth. "But it still tastes delicious."

"Go on now, and check the other platters for empties like Nora did," Cook admonished him.

Robbie saluted Cook and pushed through the swinging door.

"Here you go, Cook." Nora handed over the empty platter. "Everyone is enjoying your efforts."

Cook thanked her and inspected the tray. "This one doesn't need to go out again. Things should start to wind down. I think this is the perfect time for that cuppa I promised you. I could use one, too, some of that nice blend I got for my birthday." She moved to the pantry and left the door open as she rummaged around the shelves. "The police confiscated all of my opened tea, but I had this in my room, unopened, so they let me keep it. I've had to replace everything for the house."

Nora sat at one end of the long table and looked in at the full shelves. Canisters of sugar and flour stood alongside flavorings, baking soda and powder on one shelf. A second shelf held a row of pint bottles of a Scotch she'd never heard of, followed by Marsala wine and cooking sherry. Lower shelves held bins with root vegetables, potatoes and onions. She ruminated on the open tea. But if the poison had been in that open tea, everyone in the house would have taken ill. Nora still had no clear idea how the poison made its way into Keith's tea.

Nora took a deep breath and tried to relax. She felt tense, her shoulders tight. Her baby was quiet, but the Braxton Hicks contractions had continued all day. It was a not-so-subtle reminder that in a few weeks, she would be a parent. Part of her couldn't wait to hold her baby in her arms; part of her was scared to death of life as a single parent. The responsibility for another life seemed overwhelming. She sucked in a breath. Too late to change her mind. Maybe her determination to clear Simon was serving as more than a little distraction.

Cook emerged, tin triumphantly in hand, and moved the kettle from the simmering plate onto the boiling plate of the Aga cooker. Nora inspected the stove with its four ovens, a standard fixture in most English kitchens. Time to get on Cook's good side. "How do you cook on that without any knobs or dials?" Her curiosity was genuine.

While she busied herself getting out cups and the teapot, Cook explained the design of the stove, which was always on with the ovens set for different temperatures, and described how she moved food among the oven's racks to adjust the heat. "These top plates work the same way," she said, pouring boiling water into the teapot. She swished it around to heat the pot and tossed it out. Measuring loose tea into a strainer, she added it along with hot water to fill the pot. "You control the heat on top by the amount of contact the pots have with the plate. So, when you see an Aga on telly sitting with its lids open, you know it's not really turned on." She winked at Nora, setting the teapot between them to steep, adding a china plate filled with her cookies and a small assortment of little cakes.

"Cook, were many villagers opposed to Keith's plans for the area?" Nora asked.

"I suppose. We seem to be crowded enough around here, but then, anything new had to pass the Development and Planning Committee, and it was early days. It would have been a great financial help to the Hall. No one was anxious yet, except maybe Daniel and his crowd, but they're always complaining about something. I think they just look for a chance to rile things up.

These were Keith's favorites," she said, as she picked up one of the almond-scented cookies and popped it in her mouth.

Nora ate one and agreed they were delicious. Cook poured their tea, and Nora stirred in sugar and let it cool. A scent of heavy Assam tea reached her. She tried to think of a gambit to encourage Cook to open up on a more personal level.

Cook added sugar and cream to her tea and polished off two more cookies. "My grandmother's recipe, even the icing. There's nothing like a good cuppa and a morsel of sweet to give comfort, don't you agree?"

"Unquestionably." Nora plunged ahead. "Especially at a time like this. Keith's death must have turned this house upside down."

"My, yes, and him such a young lad and so full of promise. It's hard to take in." Cook shook her head as her eyes misted over.

Nora nodded sympathetically and sipped her tea. "The police feel he died that evening on the water because the poison was in the tea bottle he had with him." She restated the facts to see Cook's reaction.

Cook refilled her cup. "It's just horrible, that's what it is."

Nora noted Cook avoided making eye contact. "I suppose a big house like this still has lots of activity going on at times."

"I couldn't say, and that's what I told the coroner and the police. After the dinner things are washed up and the kitchen tidied, I head to my room to put my feet up." Another cookie disappeared.

Nora helped herself to a cookie and nibbled. She was approaching delicate ground. "You must be glad to sit down after being on your feet, especially at the end of a long week. Do you visit friends?"

"Only on Sundays. I'm too tired on a work night. I watch telly or call or write my daughter. She's a schoolteacher in Australia," she told Nora.

"That's wonderful." Nora glanced down the hall to Cook's

sitting room at the far end of the kitchen as she drained her cup. "But you would know if someone came into the kitchen?"

"Only if I'm listening, which I wasn't, or maybe if I didn't have the telly on." Cook shifted in her chair.

"So you didn't hear Keith leave?" Nora persisted. "Or anyone else?"

Cook took their cups and carried them over to the sink. She turned on the taps and sloshed water into them, her back to Nora.

Nora realized Cook had no intention of answering her. "You heard what happened to Agnes, Cook. I don't mean to frighten you, but your life could be in jeopardy if you know something you've not told the police."

There was the sound of china clinking hard against the soapstone sink as Cook dropped one of the teacups and it shattered.

5:40 PM

Kate entered the kitchen with a tray filled with empty teacups to find Nora helping Cook clean up broken cup shards in the sink. "Playing with your food again, Nora?" she asked impishly.

Nora shook her head. "I'm afraid Cook and I were trying to figure out how Keith was poisoned, and it upset her." She ran water in the sink and washed away the last slivers. "I didn't mean to distress you, Cook. Come and sit down."

Kate helped her settle Cook in a chair. The kitchen door banged open, and Ian entered without knocking. Her heart thudded at his handsomeness. What a fool I am, she thought, then took a clear look at him; something was drastically wrong.

"Doc Lattimore still here?" he asked. His face was taut and flushed.

"In the drawing room a moment ago," Kate answered. "What's wrong?"

Ian drew in a deep breath and let out a sigh. "You'll hear soon enough. Daniel Rowley's dead."

CHAPTER FIFTY

"If everyone hadn't died at the same time,
none of this would have happened."
— Paul Monette, *Afterlife*

5:42 PM

At Ian's pronouncement, Cook gasped. Kate stared in disbelief, one hand clapped over her mouth, forming an unuttered "oh." There was a soft thump, and Ian turned to see Nora lying in a heap on the kitchen floor.

The women helped Nora sit up as she came to. "Why don't you help Nora into Cook's room? I'll have Doc Lattimore come in and check her out," Ian said. "Having any pain?" he asked her.

When she shook her head, still wearing a dazed expression, he made his way into the drawing room, scanning the thinning crowd. The doctor was talking with Sommer and Simon. Ian hurried over.

"Doc Lattimore, I've got a pregnant woman who's fainted. Can you take a look at her?"

"Nora?" Simon asked, instantly on alert. "Is she in labor?"

"I'll just get my bag from the car." The doctor hurried off.

"I don't think so," Ian answered. "I'm afraid I shocked her. Sommer, Daniel Rowley's been found dead in his hut."

Sommer briefly closed his eyes. Simon told them he would check on Nora. "Bring the sherry with you," Sommer instructed as Simon hurried off.

"The pathologist's been notified," Ian continued.

Both men knew the only path to Rowley's hut ran past the Hall's kitchen. "You do know Daniel was best mates with Jack Halsey?" Sommer said.

Ian felt eyes on him and looked up to see Glenn Hackney and Tony Warner listening in on their conversation. He moved around, turning his back on the men, and lowered his voice. "I knew that. Since he's been found on your grounds, I'm afraid I'll need to take the names of everyone here, and then we'll send them home."

"Of course, Ian." He shook his head. "I didn't think this day could be anymore beyond belief, but I was wrong."

Ian squeezed Sommer's shoulder as Higgins came into the room and zeroed in on him.

"Constable's keeping guard, guv," Higgins pronounced. "Dr. Foreman's radioed in; he's only ten minutes out, no need for Doc Lattimore to pronounce. Oh, and Milo said to say you've managed to ruin a spectacular booya base."

Gillian checked on Edmunde. She hated men like those two downstairs who tried to pump her for information—a reporter and a co-worker of Keith's. Did they really think she couldn't see through their pretenses?

She'd never trusted men, never had a father who stayed around more than a few months at a time. She'd watch the last piker charm his way into their meager household only to break her mother's heart when wanderlust or a better offer came up. Her mum seemed to attract the same sodding kind. Not wanting to depend on anyone, she'd taken her nursing course at the first possible chance. She'd been home visiting her mum right after graduation when Sommer Clarendon had been terribly injured in the motor accident.

Edmunde had hired her whilst Sommer was in rehabilitation; Edmunde, mourning the sudden death of his young wife and that poor little infant; Edmunde who frightened everyone with his erratic moods—everyone but Gillian.

At her interview, she had trembled inside but had hid her fears beneath a façade of maturity she didn't possess. She had been the only applicant who asked to be sent to the rehab institute a week before Sommer came home to develop a relationship with him and to learn his particular needs and care from the nurses there. Edmunde had roused himself from his depression long enough to be impressed by her initiative. And so she had started her long entanglement with the Clarendons, broken only by her year away in Scotland.

Gillian smiled as she approached Edmunde's room, remembering the way she'd ignored him in the those early days, refusing to let him see that any unkind remark hit home. Antonia had been overwhelmed, trying to care for the premature baby and get her own strength back while she dealt with the reality of Sommer's disabilities. That was when the elevator had been added and an upstairs sewing room turned into a therapy area. The young mother had welcomed Gillian's assistance and had told her to ignore Edmunde when he'd been drinking.

What Antonia hadn't known was that after Edmunde's drunken rages had subsided, he'd noticed the quiet, competent girl with the thick, dark hair and solemn face.

5:44 PM

Sommer watched the remaining company line up in two neat rows to leave their information with either Ian or his sergeant.

A cloud of misery engulfed him at the thought of another murder. He doubted Daniel Rowley would have given in to any normal illness, but there was always the hope the dead man had succumbed to a heart attack. He could just see tomorrow's headlines: **Third Death in Sleepy Bowness-On-Windermere**.

How would Antonia cope with the news? She hadn't reacted much to the death of Jack Halsey, but Daniel did chores in the Hall and lived on their property. He would never say it aloud, but three deaths in the town might affect the house tours, too— income they needed to survive.

Sommer scrubbed a hand over his face. What the hell was he doing, thinking of finances when they'd just buried Keith?

At least he'd thought to send Simon to the kitchen with the sherry on the heels of Doc Lattimore. If Edmunde were well and downstairs, the entire afternoon would have included wine, brandy, sherry and anything else his brother could lay his hands on.

He wondered how Edmunde would take this latest news, if he would show even a flicker of emotion for the dead man who had lived near them and had helped around the Hall for years. The brother he had known and loved had been lost to him and grew further removed as time passed.

Glenn Hackney appeared before him, breaking him out of his reverie.

"Quite a commotion, Mr. Clarendon. And the police here again, such a shame."

Sommer looked up, taking in the man's false smile. He'd reached the end of his patience and good manners today. "Did you have a point, Mr. Hackney?"

"Please, call me Glenn. After all, your son and I were best mates at work."

"Really?" Sommer arched one eyebrow. "At home he never spoke of you at all." It was the high point of Sommer's grief-stricken day that for once, the smooth-talking Glenn Hackney had nothing to say.

5:45 PM

Edmunde was pleased to see Gillian. He knew he'd only lived this long because of her. Earlier, she'd sent Robbie up with a tray that he'd picked at with his good hand while his eyes continued to stray to the fresh grave.

She smiled and helped him motor from the window to his bed.

There was a tap at the door, and Robbie stuck his head inside. "Daniel Rowley's been found dead at his hut. Doc Lattimore wants you to find Miss Antonia and break the news, maybe get her to lie down."

"I'll be right there." Gillian patted Edmunde's arm and hurried out.

Blast those silly women, both of them. If Daniel Rowley was already dead, it seemed to Edmunde there was no earthly need for anyone to hurry anywhere.

He sighed. He was tired, and his back hurt. He wanted to nap. He looked longingly at the bed with its cool sheets and wondered what Gillian would think if he put himself to bed. Wouldn't she be surprised?

CHAPTER FIFTY-ONE

"Don't believe everything you hear."
— Marcy Heidish, *Witnesses*

5:57 PM

Nora rested on Cook's sitting-room loveseat, a warm afghan spread over her, watched over by Kate who was perched by her feet. She held her hands out in front of her, seeing her swollen fingers but feeling they belonged to someone else. Cook's lair was small but cozy; family photos covered the wall over the television. Through a doorway, Nora could see a neatly made iron bed. Simon appeared in the door from the kitchen, holding glasses and a bottle of sherry, and Kate waved him in.

Nora rose up on one elbow. "I'm so embarrassed. I've never fainted in my life."

Kate sat on the edge of the cushion. Simon moved into the small room and stood next to them.

"I turn my back on you for ten minutes, Red, and look at the fine mess you've got yourself into," he said in his best Cary Grant imitation.

Nora laughed. "*The Philadelphia Story,*" she said appreciatively, swinging her legs over to sit up. "I'm fine." She inspected her thick ankles and puffy feet. "But it appears from my size and the baby's weight that the count might have been off. Doc Lattimore thinks I'm due sooner than we'd calculated."

Kate raised an eyebrow. "How much sooner?"

"Instead of the third week in November, more like the first or second."

Simon frowned. "Shouldn't your OB in Windermere have caught that?"

Nora blushed. "Don't blame Dr. Ling. She already raised the idea."

"Which you didn't share with us," Kate threw in.

"Not knowing when I got pregnant made the due date a guesstimate from the beginning," Nora protested. "She told me last week I was larger than expected but said that could also be down to my being so short—there's no room for the baby to go but out." She gestured in front of her. "I'm to see her at the end of this week for measurements."

"An appointment one of us will take you to," Simon said firmly.

"Absolutely," Nora agreed. "I know better than to argue with you, Simon. I want to keep this baby healthy, and I need to know how much time I have left. I don't even have his name." She shook her head. "Some mother I'm going to be."

"No other problems?" Simon asked.

"No, the doctor checked my blood sugar and blood pressure, and both are fine. He thinks I've been on my feet too long today after the strain of the last week, and the added news of Daniel pushed me over the edge." She shrugged. "Any news on how Daniel died?"

Kate looked away. "Ian won't be trading confidences with me now."

Nora looked up at Simon. "I bet when Robbie Cole checked on Daniel he was already dead. And there's his friendship with Jack Halsey—their deaths are connected."

Simon blew out an exasperated sigh. "Can't you confine yourself to worrying about things like what to name your baby and when he's due?"

Nora struggled to her feet. "Did you know Doc Lattimore's first name is Mungo?"

She saw the look that passed between Simon and Kate. "What? It's Celtic for 'beloved.' And didn't Eliot use it for one of his cats? I think it's rather sweet."

Kate said, "Now I know she needs to see her doctor."

6:15 PM

Nora sat at the table watching Cook rinse a platter, which Kate dried. She'd been forbidden to help, but Doc Lattimore had allowed her to partake in a sherry, and she'd protested at the thimbleful Simon poured her. He sat at the table with her. The green baize door swung open, and Sommer motored into the room.

"The guests have gone, and Robbie's giving a statement about going to Daniel's hut yesterday," he announced. "And I am very ready for my sherry."

Simon obliged and handed him a glassful, which he sipped gratefully. "Doc Lattimore saw Antonia, and she's lying down. I see you're up and about, Nora. Hope you're feeling better."

Nora felt a surge of empathy for the man. After all he'd been through this day, he still had the grace to inquire after her. "Just a momentary glitch," she assured him.

"Robbie said Daniel's garbage is all over the place up there," Simon said.

"Yes, I'll get someone to clean that mess up eventually, but for now Ian says it's a crime scene." Sommer blew out a long breath. "What a bloody hellish day."

6:16 PM

Gillian assisted Edmunde into bed and was leaving his room when Robbie found her in the upstairs hall.

"Ian Travers wants a word, Mum. I've finished my statement."
The young man was subdued. "I wonder if Daniel was still alive
when I saw him yesterday. I should have broken in."

Gillian rubbed his arm. "Nonsense. Don't bother yourself
over that sod, Robbie." She inclined her head toward Edmunde's
closed bedroom door. "I've just settled him. Plain knackered out."

They started down the main stairs side by side. Robbie
grabbed his mother's elbow, stalling her. He whispered, "I didn't
say anything about you and Rowley being friendly."

There was a long pause. Gillian looked down the staircase
toward the entry hall. The front door stood ajar, and she could
see the legs of a constable who paced the hallway. When Gillian
spoke, she addressed Robbie's left ear, her face devoid of emotion. "I have no idea what you're talking about."

CHAPTER FIFTY-TWO

*"I returned from the City about 3 o'clock on that May afternoon
pretty well disgusted with life."*
— John Buchan, *The Thirty-nine Steps*

6:30 PM

Ian climbed the track to Daniel Rowley's hut. On top of Keith's
murder and the death of Jack Halsey, now Daniel had been
thrown into the mix. His quiet corner of the world was suddenly
a hotbed of dead bodies, and it didn't bear thinking about how
this would go down with his superiors. Then there was the attack on Agnes, and Ian had the feeling they were all connected.
DCI Clarke was pretty reasonable, but the higher-ups often be-
haved as though a really good copper could stop anything negative from happening on his patch.

When he arrived, the area had already been sealed off around
its perimeter. He nodded to the constable logging people in and
out of the crime scene and ducked under the blue-and-white
tape. The stench of rotten garbage and dead body mingled in an
odiferous, rank foulness that seemed to seep into his clothing.

Milo Foreman came out onto the small porch, and Ian
stepped up to meet him. The pathologist removed his second
glove with a snap that tore the thin latex; he threw it into the
SOCO's garbage bin.

"Better out here, Travers. Too crowded in there, and the smell
is—unpleasant."

"I can tell that from here." Ian had his pen out and his notebook open. "Anything you can tell me?"

"Dead several days. Unfortunately, I need to get him on the

table to even hazard a guess when. Something's been at him—rodents, I imagine. I'm waiting for toxicology on Halsey, too, but based on his appearance, I won't be surprised if it shows the same poison as with the Clarendon boy. Could be the same here, too. You're keeping me busy these days." He stopped a masked SOCO carrying video equipment out of the hut. "Nesbitt, please radio in and ask my office to call the house and tell my wife to take the bouillabaisse off the heat. I can't get any bloody mobile reception up here."

Ian shook his head and wrinkled his nose. "How can you even consider food after seeing what's left of Rowley in there? It's enough to put me off my dinner, I can tell you."

The pathologist uncapped a small bottle of antibacterial gel and squirted a dollop into his palm. Rubbing his hands together briskly, he told the detective: "With the amount of death that surrounds me, I'd say the question should be, 'How can I not?' Life's short, Travers—get every pleasure whilst you can." He added, "Would you and the lovely Kate care to join us tonight? Always room for a few more around the table."

"No, thanks, I couldn't really," Ian answered, wishing to do just that, especially with Kate. "I'll take a rain check, though."

"Splendid. I'll come up with something really special. You're not Scottish, by any chance?" The gleam in the doctor's eye was unmistakable.

"My grandfather, but no haggis for me, thank you, Milo. A nice joint of beef goes down well or a bit of fish?"

Milo was disappointed. "Too mundane. Leave it to me to suss out something wonderful. After we clear this mess up, of course." He started down the hill.

"When can I expect some details?" Ian called out after him.

"No idea, but I'll keep in touch," the pathologist called back, waving as he disappeared.

Ian watched his back retreat. He wished he were going to Milo's home tonight with Kate. For that matter, he wished he were going anywhere but back into this hovel. He straightened his back and marched into the hut.

Chapter Fifty-Three

*"Lord Melamine is right about one thing, at least.
I was never a spy."*
— R. V. Cassill, *Doctor Cobb's Game*

6:45 PM

Kate entered Ramsey Lodge by the front door. Its sense of history and her pride in maintaining the place gave her a moment of comfort. At least she could do *something* right. Then she thought of her small emergency fund and wondered how long it would hold out if she had to spend it defending Simon. She hadn't realized how much she'd been counting on Ian being a part of her vision for the future. If he was truly out of the picture, could she carry on alone?

She checked the registration log. Maeve hadn't signed in anyone new, which meant they were down to Tony Warner and Glenn Hackney. On one hand, she was glad not to have to deal with new guests; on the other, continued cancellations were going to be difficult to overcome. News of the attack on Agnes would fade, but if Simon were detained, that might be insurmountable, even if—no, she corrected herself, *when*—Keith's death was solved. Not to mention Jack Halsey and now Daniel Rowley.

Agnes had left a message saying she felt much better, and she was making noises about coming back to work Thursday. Maybe this newest death would gain national attention and bring a round of reporters. She hated to be gruesome, but they needed the income. She flipped through the weekend dinner reservation book. Simon appeared from the lodge kitchen, drying his hands on a towel.

"There are individual frozen shepherd's pies in the oven for the three of us." He glanced at his watch. "Where's Nora?"

"She said she was feeling better, so I dropped her at the drug-store on the quay. She had to get some heartburn tablets." Kate closed the book. "I'm actually relieved our census is low. Too much going on for business as usual."

Simon nodded in agreement. "Kate, I know it's hard for you to communicate with Ian right now, but I wish you would see that I'm fine with how he's handled things. You have to admit he would have been less than professional if he hadn't questioned me. I did have access to that plant."

"So did tons of other people, Simon," Kate said curtly. "But you're missing one important thing." She ran her fingers through the curls at the nape of her neck.

Simon lounged against the wall, ankles crossed, and tossed the towel over his shoulder. "What's that, then?"

"You didn't do it."

6:50 PM

Nora left the chemist with fresh antacids in her shoulder bag. She walked along the quay in the direction of Ramsey Lodge, feeling fat and ungainly, her thoughts swirling. The lights were on in the various shops and strung along the quayside, but their cheeriness did little to improve her mood. A third dead body, Simon still under suspicion, Kate's engagement broken—and her baby coming sooner than she'd expected rounded things off nicely. The thought of a third body struck a new thought: could there be a serial killer at work? She hoped that the two newer deaths at least would take the focus off of Simon.

The fresh air felt good. She slowed her stride when she recognized Glenn Hackney ahead of her on the promenade. Allowing a group of Asian students to fill the gap between them, she discreetly followed him until he stopped at a carousel of telephones. As he lifted the receiver, Nora ducked into the entrance of a postcard shop opposite, maneuvering through the store until she was opposite him at its exit. She stationed herself at a rack of colorful scenes of the Lake District, pretending to compare the merits of the first two she grabbed off the rack.

Why use a public phone when she was certain he had a mobile? Nora could see him from the side and shifted her eyes to catch the movement of his lips, studying them closely. After a few seconds of careful scrutiny she decided lip reading was definitely not in her bag of tricks. She rotated her position so her back was to Glenn and edged closer to the door, hoping to overhear his conversation.

Nora closed her eyes as she strained to pick out Glenn's voice above the tourist chatter. A gentle tap on her shoulder startled her. She opened her eyes to find the shopkeeper pointing to her cards.

The broad man with a tired face said, "You gonna buy those, miss, or just memorize them?"

Nora whirled around to the open door. A woman walking her black Scottie, a tartan bow tied jauntily around his neck, had taken Glenn Hackney's place.

7 PM

Nora closed the lodge door, her parcel from the chemist's crackling in her shoulder bag. Only a few more weeks of indigestion, swollen hands and feet, and pressure on her diaphragm and back, and she would be free again.

Cancel that. Only her body would be free. She would be tied forever to the baby who kicked inside her, already fighting his way out.

She trudged down the hall. Her failure to overhear Glenn Hackney's conversation still stung. Darby came prancing up to greet her. "Some detective I'd make," she told the dog, bending down to scratch his rough ears.

Kate appeared at the end of the hall. "There you are. Come into the lodge kitchen. Simon's heated up some dinner for us."

Nora decided Kate looked as defeated and tired as she herself felt.

Dinner was a quiet affair, and the three friends digested their food while discussing the news of the day. Talk moved from the death of Daniel Rowley to Nora's new due date. Simon put out cookies with berries and ice cream; he was the only one of the three whose appetite seemed unimpaired.

"We need to get that alcove painted for the baby," Kate said. "I should have time tomorrow with the census so low. You can work or rest in my room so you're not around the paint, although it's not supposed to have fumes."

"I'll give you a hand," Simon offered. "It's a small space and won't take a tick."

"You two are so good to me." Nora crumbled a cookie and added it to a small scoop of ice cream and berries, eating it all together. "Thank goodness you've both been to childbirth classes with me. I need all the support I can get."

"Wouldn't miss it for the world," Simon said. "The camera's all ready."

"I'm excited," Kate admitted. "I've never seen a birth before."

"Me, neither," Nora said dryly, and all three of them laughed. "No turning back now."

Simon patted her hand. "It will be fine. You're going to be a spectacular mum." He cleared their bowls, and they sat nursing mugs of tea.

"I spoke to Agnes," Kate said. "She's definitely coming back Thursday. She already heard about Daniel's death, and I think she's brave to come back under the circumstances."

"She can't handle missing all the action," Simon said.

"A third dead man; that surely must be the end of it," Nora said. "My grandmother McAllister always said deaths come in threes."

"Let's hope so," Simon said. "By the way, Mr. Hackney is checking out in the morning."

"I wonder if he's accomplished his mission," Nora said. "Whatever his true mission has been."

"Hackney hasn't been able to score with Tony Warner, who should be leaving soon himself," Simon said.

"Somehow I doubt we'll be that lucky," Nora said. "I wager tomorrow's headline will make it seem he was almost an eyewitness to Daniel's death."

8:15 PM

After cleaning up, the three friends retired to their respective rooms. The day had been long and exhausting, and Nora was finally alone with her thoughts. She should turn to Keith's work, but she couldn't handle the thought of concentrating. Instead, she brought out her notebook, turning to an earlier list she'd made of things to do before the baby came, and crossed off "paint alcove." She could count on Kate getting that done with Simon's help tomorrow. She still needed a dresser and a changing table. The wing chair she'd brought from Oxford that would be perfect for nursing was already situated in the room, as was the crib, still in its box. She'd have liked a bassinet to keep the baby next to her bed for the first months to make nursing easier, but she was on a budget. She'd just have to get up more often.

Her mother had sent a box of layette clothes, and Nora felt drawn to the alcove and sat in her chair. She opened the cover of the carton and lifted out the tiny garments, onesies and blanket sleepers that looked incredibly small. Receiving blankets in soft pastels were at the bottom along with a pack of cloth diapers—"for burp pads" her mother had noted on a sticky note attached to the outside.

Amelia, Nora's mother, planned to visit with her stepfather, Roger, for a few weeks after the baby was born. Should she have them change their travel plans? Were their tickets even subject to changing?

Nora bit her lip. Maybe she should let her mother keep her travel arrangements as planned and be surprised if the baby came early. That would give Nora a little time to get used to taking care of the baby herself. She wouldn't seem too bumbling in her mother's eyes. Amelia was such a capable person, all efficiency and good cheer. Sometimes, she was overwhelming.

Nora's hormones would settle a bit, too. The more Nora thought about it, the more she thought she wouldn't say anything to her mother right now. Besides, first babies were notoriously late, which is why Amelia had thought she might be there for the birth. Maybe Nora was getting her knickers in a twist for nothing.

She walked back to her bed, picking up her baby name book and turning on her CD player. Ella Fitzgerald sang about being "Bewitched, Bothered and Bewildered," and *she* had Oscar Peterson to accompany her. Nora knew exactly how the singer felt. Too early to climb into bed, Nora sat instead in a chair near the French doors, propping her puffy feet up on the trunk Simon had moved over.

Mentioning her Grandmother McAllister had given Nora the glimmer of an idea. What was this baby about, after all? Making a family of her own, husband or not. Nora valued the importance of family, so she started making a list of all the names of relatives she could remember. Movement at the front of the lodge distracted her. Thanks to the light over the front door, she could see someone walking up the front path.

Instinctively, Nora looked at the French doors. Still firmly locked. She got up from her chair and leaned over the trunk just in time to see Maeve Addams entering.

On her way to visit Simon. That woman just didn't give up. Nora didn't know whether to admire or hate her persistence.

8:45 PM

Simon stood at the hall desk, putting stamps on bills to be sent out in tomorrow's post. The door opened, and he was happy to see Maeve walk in rather than Hackney or Warner.

Maeve approached, and Simon caught the scent of her perfume, sweet and strong. The hall light bounced off her glossy hair. He remembered how alluring she could be when they'd dated. A wave of desire swelled him.

Maeve held up a set of keys. "I found these in the pocket of my skirt when I got home." She handed the desk keys over and smiled warmly.

Simon didn't see how she fit her hand into the tight leather skirt. "Thanks. You could have waited until tomorrow."

"No problem. Fancy a quick one at the pub?"

Simon hesitated. That tight skirt emphasized her curves. "Thanks, Maeve, but after today I'm beat, and I have a lot on my mind. Maybe another time."

"Right then, I'm off. See you tomorrow." She left as gracefully as she'd arrived, and if she was disappointed, she hid it well.

Simon watched the roll of her hips as she sauntered down the hall. It was only when he'd settled on his sofa, feet up and the latest issue of *ARTnews* in hand, that he wondered exactly what Maeve had been offering—and if he was a fool for having refused.

CHAPTER FIFTY-FOUR

"The police came and found arsenic in the glass,
but I was gone by then."
— Gayl Jones, *Eva's Man*

Wednesday, 27th October

II AM

Ian finished typing up his interview notes from the day before and ran the spell-checker before saving the documents. He printed them and added a copy to the main file and made one for the case manager.

No one present at Clarendon Hall had pertinent information about Daniel Rowley or Jack Halsey. Several had tales of drunken brawls or rude behavior to report from past brushes with the men, but there was no indication as to why either of them would be murdered. Their vocal dislike of Keith's development plans had been mentioned, but Ian acknowledged this was unlikely to be the cause of all three deaths. The schemes were a long way from being accomplished, and the victims were on opposite sides of the equation.

Ian could see why Rowley would be intensely against expansion. Never one to work hard for a decent living, Daniel managed to drink away the wages he eked out between Ramsey Lodge and Clarendon Hall. Rowley would have been afraid he'd be forced out of his hut and his jobs if Keith's plans to turn the Hall into a grand retreat were realized. It was common knowledge that Daniel felt he had a right to stay in the shack because it was the only home he'd ever known.

While Ian could rationalize that as a motive for Daniel wanting to murder Keith, it didn't explain someone wanting Daniel or his good friend Halsey out of the way. He could understand if Daniel had killed Keith and then taken his own life in remorse, but why take his friend with him? And was Daniel even capable of remorse? None of it made sense—yet.

Ian left the station to attend the autopsy on Daniel, hoping Milo Foreman would have some answers for him.

NOON

Tony Warner sat alone in The Scarlet Wench with a ploughman's and a pint. He picked up the paper again, noting the byline with great pride under the bold headline:

Third Body Found in Serene Bowness
By Anthony L. Warner

Tony took a bite of his sandwich. Glenn Hackney had settled his bill and left right after an early breakfast, leaving Tony feeling oddly unsettled. The man had been useful, and Tony felt alone.

"Can I get you anything else?" The waitress appeared suddenly at his elbow.

Christ, he hated being startled like that. He shook his head, and after she'd gone, he re-read his article, scanning for typos. His mum kept a scrapbook of anything he published. He'd stroll down to one of the shops and pick up a few more copies once he finished his lunch.

First things first, he decided, and withdrew a faux ostrich-covered notepad. Flicking to a clean page, he thought for a moment and then wrote:

People and Places Former Editor Nora Tierney and

Illustrator Simon Ramsey Questioned in Multiple Lakeland Murders.

It wasn't sensational, and he would have to be certain he explained they weren't the only ones interviewed. He wanted to stay in Bowness to cover the story but had to dangle a carrot to get Old Jenks to foot the bill a little longer. He wasn't worried about Jenks finding out about his moonlighting for the locals, but he didn't know how long he could justify scouting Nora and her friends when he hadn't yet come up with anything concrete. How many times could he rehash the same suppositions? Especially when one of Nora's frequent remarks, with her bloody blue pencil deleting large paragraphs he'd labored over, had been "unsubstantiated rumor."

With a sigh, Tony drained his glass and decided he'd better call in to encourage Jenks that it was reasonable for him to stay on a bit longer. After all, a second and now a third body in a matter of days? Perhaps he should hint at the threat of a serial killer on the loose? That might make Old Jenks cave in.

What Tony couldn't shake was the feeling he'd let the real story escape when Glenn Hackney had roared back to Oxford.

12:15 PM

Arriving in the outskirts of Oxford, Glenn Hackney planned to go directly to the travel agency office. Worth usually took Wednesdays off. He would call the old man at home so he'd know Glenn had come in to check on things and had everything under control. He would also be sure he mentioned how thrilled Keith's parents had been that Worth's had been represented.

Glenn was confident the Clarendons were unaware of their

THE GREEN REMAINS

son's foray into homosexuality. The man's parents had been too polite to him for them to have known, and he'd already forgiven Keith's bereaved father for being testy with him yesterday at the Hall; it was certainly understandable, given his grief.

Glenn grinned when he recalled the few times he'd bedded Keith. He'd thought for a few weeks he was onto something there, maybe an end to this nomadic lifestyle of his, having found a good partner in the heir. He'd even started creating his own history for Keith's benefit, one that left him an orphan without relatives to visit or entangle. Too bad that after a few really bright moments, Keith had abruptly decided he was remaining heterosexual in his relationship pursuits after all and had just been experimenting.

Thankfully, Glenn's search of Keith's desk contents and a quick scout of his rooms hadn't turned up any evidence pointing to Glenn's current scheme. Keith's laptop was missing, with the police no doubt, but Glenn didn't believe the young man would have documented anything on his computer. If he'd truly become aware of Glenn's embezzling, he would have gone directly to Edgar Worth.

Glenn spent a tremendous amount of time on what he termed "research and development" for his maneuvers. This was serious business he did, even though Scotland Yard and the Criminal Investigation Department preferred to call them scams.

Glenn "Macavity" Hackney settled back to enjoy the rest of the ride to Oxford. He'd stopped once along the way to stretch his back and admire the offerings in a jewelry shop along the way, and he was in an expansive mood. Maybe he'd even offer to let Amy go home early tonight. He considered this as he sped along the motorway. By now, she would have organized the files he'd strewn around the office, and it would be all neat and tidy.

Oh yes, he thought, a thin smile sliding across his face. Poor

Amy worked too hard over the last few days, and when she leaves, I'll have the latest bank record all to myself.

CHAPTER FIFTY-FIVE

"People know when you are trying to be something you are not."
— John O'Hara, *The Big Laugh*

1 PM

It drizzled all day, off and on, the droplets tapping on leaves and plants outside Ramsey Lodge. True to her word, Kate bundled Nora off to her own rooms to work after lunch. Over the next few hours, she and Simon would paint the alcove with the low-fume, pale green paint Nora had selected.

Nora obediently waited until she heard Simon moving a ladder into her room and then he and Kate talking together. She slid her feet back into her shoes after leaving a note, saying she was out taking her walk, on Kate's coffee table in case either Ramsey came looking for her. On impulse, she lifted Kate's cloak off a peg near the door. The voluminous, green, boiled-wool cape covered Nora's bulk, reaching her ankles. She hid her hair with a plaid scarf stuffed in its pocket. Closing the front door quietly, she hurried in the direction of the Lake District Touring Company's office.

A few minutes later, Nora arrived at the kiosk on the quay that offered half- and full-day sightseeing tours of Lake District highlights. A poster urging "Tour Historic Clarendon Hall!" had a notice pasted over its particulars: **Tours cancelled until further notice.**

Nora withdrew her notebook and waited for the woman on duty to deal with a family of four. After she'd pointed out the van stop where they could be picked up for Kendal's film festival, the family moved off and Nora approached. She felt thrilled to be on the snoop again.

"Yes, how can I help?" The woman was tall and seemed too large for the small kiosk she occupied. Her knitted, cream hat was pulled low over short, black hair.

Nora hoped the cloak would hide her pregnancy and her identity. She put on her most pleasant smile. "Hello, I work for *People and Places* magazine." She neglected to add: *But not for the last eight months.* "I suspect you know our coverage is national."

"Oh, yes, my neighbor gets that and hands it over when she's read it." The woman stood taller. "Were you wanting to do a feature on us?"

Nora leaned in confidentially as far as the counter would allow. "Actually, I was hoping for a good quote from someone in the know on the cancellation of the tours at Clarendon Hall."

The woman's eyes narrowed, and she pursed her lips. "That is a true tragedy. We could hardly intrude on the family's bereavement at this sad time."

"Of course not. That is absolutely the right thing to do," Nora agreed. This wasn't quite what she'd hoped to get. "I've heard the dead man wasn't very popular in the village with his development plans."

"That's a distortion if I ever heard one." Her nostrils flared. "The Clarendons are one of the oldest and most respected families in the area. You can quote me on that," she said loudly. She looked around and leaned forward, lowering her voice. "You didn't hear it from me, but if Daniel Rowley and Jack Halsey were involved, there was criminal activity in the mix, count on it." She sniffed and consulted her watch. "Time for my break."

She reached up to pull down a metal security gate, leaving Nora to wonder if she'd imagined the woman muttering, "Ballsy American."

Nora tried to think of another way to gather information. She spent the rest of the afternoon with her feet up on Kate's comfortable couch, alternating between notebooks: the one in which she worked on storylines for her book series and the one in which she jotted ideas and notes to herself about baby names and about possible identities of the murderer going around Bowness. Kate's cloak was back on its peg, the scarf in its pocket. Nora felt the frustration of not being mobile and quick on her feet. Her brain must be off. Couldn't she have thought of a better gambit to get that woman at the tour company to talk more? She was losing her touch.

The weight of pregnancy on her small body was making her fatigued. It must be interfering with her brain cells. Those Braxton-Hicks contractions were becoming more and more frequent, and Nora was glad the baby's room would soon be ready.

Now that dinner was over, Simon and Kate escorted Nora to her room to show off their handiwork.

"The green you chose is perfect, Nora," Kate said as they entered the suite. "Just a hint of color of the outdoors."

Nora's chair was moved into a corner of the room next to the alcove window. Except for the chair, the crib box and the clothing cartons from Nora's mother, the space was empty and waiting.

"It's lovely," Nora said. "The crown molding and trim stand out in that crisp white. Thank you both so much." She followed Simon's eyes and looked up at the ceiling, drawing in a breath. Simon had painted it pale blue and added wispy clouds. It was the perfect nursery for her son. Tears filled her eyes. "I don't know what I did to deserve such good friends. It's wonderful!"

"Teary again? You rest," Kate said. "I've got a few things to do before Agnes gets back."

"Me, too." Simon ruffled her hair. "See you tomorrow."

Nora didn't miss the look that passed between the siblings—they were up to something. Darby scratched outside her door and padded in as the others left. He stretched out at her feet when she sat at her desk and turned on her laptop to continue reading Keith's work. She put aside her workbook and leafed through her personal notebook as it booted up, looking at her jottings from today.

She remembered she had no idea when Glenn Hackney had really arrived in Bowness, only when he'd checked into Ramsey Lodge. He was a good suspect to think about. She wrote several motives next to his name: Blackmail—maybe Keith had some goods on Glenn and he wanted to stop payments? But Keith didn't strike her as a blackmailer. What if she turned it around? Glenn could have been blackmailing Keith, who tired of it and threatened to go to the authorities. But over what? Keith's sexual orientation, or an affair with Glenn? Surely that wasn't grounds for blackmail in today's day and age. But with the expectation of carrying on the Clarendon name, might it be? Nora was impatient to hear from Val. Next to Cook's, Gillian's and Robbie's names, Nora left question marks; not enough to go on there, despite her sense that Cook was holding back information. Nora added a second question mark next to Cook's name. There was more under the surface to be explored.

Then the parents. She simply couldn't fathom a parent killing his or her own child, but she knew others had. Still, Sommer was clearly incapacitated, and Antonia's grief seemed too real to be faked. As for Edmunde, why would he want to murder his nephew?

And then what about Jack Halsey and Daniel Rowley, if Keith's murder did indeed have a family motive? Nora couldn't abandon the feeling that the key to all three deaths lay in something Keith had unearthed.

Barefoot, she lightly ran her feet over the dog's wiry coat and continued reading Keith's file where she'd left off, her frustration growing as her eyes got heavy. She felt she was missing the significance of some small detail, but she couldn't see how Lake District chronicles or history could help her.

8:45 PM

Tony Warner turned off his phone, and a satisfied smile spread across his face. He'd convinced Old Jenks he should wait around Bowness for another two days while the investigation continued into the additional deaths of Jack Halsey and Daniel Rowley.

"Yes, Mr. Jenkins, I have a direct pipeline, what with our Miss Tierney here. Clear access to the investigation team, too. The way these bodies keep piling up—" He lowered his voice and spoke directly into his mobile. "I've heard rumors of a serial killer—who can say what will happen next? But I can guarantee *People and Places* will have an exclusive article from my unique, on-the-spot perspective."

Tony was confident any news would reach his ears before it reached Old Jenks, and he was bored without Glenn Hackney to impress. He took out his Lake District guidebook and paged through it. There were so many attractions in the area, and he hovered over the pages on Beatrix Potters' Hill Top cottage as a spot to visit the next day. In the afternoon, he might give the Windermere Steamboat Museum a shout. A few pictures and notes, and he'd have a feature article waiting to be written down the road. While he awaited new developments, he might as well enjoy himself.

10:30 PM

Nora woke with a jerk. She'd dozed off, this time on her bed with her list of names open beside her. Checking the clock on her nightstand, she thought Val would be in from her evening snooping. Nora decided to call before she fell asleep again.

To her relief, Val answered on the third ring. "Just got in, and I have one word for you, Yankee: smar-r-r-my."

It was good to hear her friend's voice. She missed Val. "I agree, Val. I thought he might show up, since he left here this morning."

"I hung around The Blue Virgin right after the cooperative closed. The club's just not the same, I don't mind telling you that."

"I know you miss Bryn, Valentine."

There was a pause, and Val continued. "I was actually thinking of leaving and letting you down when in he walks, very full of himself. Just the way I remembered from the travel agency, smug and too much vanilla, like a bloody ice cream soda. But I know the lad he started to chat up, so it made going over easy."

She described the conversation, which consisted mainly of Glenn trying to lure the fellow home for the night. "He can't dress in those expensive clothes and have that kind of a watch on his salary, unless I have seriously underrated the income of a travel agent. He's an arrogant wanker, isn't he?"

Nora agreed. "Then where does his money come from? Family? Or ill-gotten gains?"

"He comes across all mysterious, as though he has this big secret. And another thing: No one there knew Keith Clarendon when I dropped his name into conversations, so I think it's unlikely he was a part of that scene."

"So you don't feel it was his homosexuality that Keith held over his head or vice versa?"

"This cheeky one?" Val snorted. "No, Yankee, some wear their sexual orientation on their sleeve, and this one's a queen through and through. I don't suspect he's ever tried to hide it. He revels in it."

Nora sighed. "I still don't know where the other two deaths fit in."

"Other *two*?" Val shrieked. "Are you safe there, Nora?"

Nora ignored her and explained about Jack Halsey and Daniel Rowley. "So if Glenn's involved, it must revolve around something else." She described the tour guide admitting Daniel and Jack were likely to be up to no good. "But I couldn't get much else out of her. She seemed to think I was an ugly American."

"You're a pussycat. But it sounds to me like Keith was the kind of guy who'd have no problem telling someone to piss off, whether it was Daniel, Jack or Glenn. Glenn's not nice, but I think you need another angle for murder, Nora."

They talked for a few more minutes, with Val describing an art installation she was getting ready to mount in Manchester. "I was thinking I'd drive to you tomorrow and spend the night. I want to see you in all your glory before you deliver."

"I'd love that, Val. When would you get here?"

"Late afternoon. I have to sort out a few things at the cooperative first."

"Perfect." Nora looked forward to seeing her friend. And Val's late arrival would leave her plenty of time for the interview she wanted to cram in.

CHAPTER FIFTY-SIX

"Everybody agreed with Mrs. Baskett that her baby was a most remarkable child."
— Joyce Cary, *A Fearful Joy*

Thursday, 28th October

9 AM

Simon helped Agnes perch on a stool, back in control of her kitchen once more.

"Welcome back!" Kate and Nora chorused a fanfare of good wishes. Darby leapt up to be petted. Sally Kincaid, who had been substituting for Agnes, beamed. A good-natured woman with a large mole just under her chin, she'd offered to drive Agnes in.

Simon noted Agnes wore more makeup than usual and had combed her hair over her stitches, but her smile was wider than ever.

She gave the room a searching look. "Very neat and clean, Sally, thank you very much."

"Agnes, you're only here to supervise, remember," Kate warned. "Sally will stay through next Monday, and you're to let her do the real work."

Agnes nodded, and Sally smiled sweetly. Simon guessed Sally was eager to hear Agnes' firsthand account of the attack. He had his own business to get in order before Nora's surprise, and he left the women chatting in the kitchen.

Going to the desk, he set about making up a bank deposit, noting the money in the cash drawer was correct. He wondered how much of this was due to the absence of Daniel Rowley. Consulting the registration book, he saw a large party was set to arrive Sunday. Thank goodness. That would help increase the deposits. Either they hadn't heard about events in Bowness or didn't care.

Alone for the moment, Simon sat back and reflected on Nora and her baby. Last summer in Oxford, when he'd told Nora he loved her and the baby as well, he'd never imagined they wouldn't have cemented their relationship by now. But she continued to hold him at arm's length, giving in to small shows of affection here and there. He knew this wasn't the time to press her, but he was frustrated. Bloody awful to be in love with a pregnant woman when the child wasn't his.

He thought about the classes he and Kate had gone to with Nora at the health centre. The majority of the other women had husbands or partners with them; Nora was the only one with two attendants. She'd introduced them as her good friends, and while he hadn't really cared, he'd seen the looks from other couples and had understood what several must have been thinking: If he's the father, where does the other gal fit in? He'd enjoyed learning about the physical side of the delivery process, though. Practicing the breathing techniques had made them all laugh more than once.

"Babies always look so charming in other women's arms, but they're really helpless, aren't they?" Nora had mused on the way home from their last class. "What if I don't take to mothering?"

Simon had jumped in to calm her. "You'll figure it out, Nora. Babies have a magnetic appeal, like puppies—even the funny-looking ones are endearing."

Nora had laughed. "Are you saying my baby will be ugly, Mr. Ramsey?"

"Not at all," he had hastened to assure her.

"I'd think babies who are endearing to outsiders are absolutely gorgeous to their mothers," Kate had stated. "They seduce us with their vulnerability. Don't new mums call their little ones the prettiest, cutest, most clever babies ever born?"

"Well—" Nora hadn't been convinced.

"Surely a woman is built for this kind of thing," Simon had insisted. "They have breasts to feed their young and the equipment to have carried them in the first place." An image of his one coupling with Nora, with her small but full breasts dotted with freckles, had risen before him and he'd felt a jolt of desire.

"That sounds terribly sexist, Simon. Reducing us to incubators," Kate had chided.

"What about mothers who move cars off their children, do almost anything to save them?" Nora had asked. "Do you suppose that's something that grows inside of you, too?"

Simon had raised a hand in mock resignation. "As my sister has pointed out, you are obviously asking the wrong person."

Kate had gracefully ended the conversation. "Maybe that's why pregnancy takes nine months—time for you to get used to the whole idea."

Nora had become introspective, and then they'd arrived home.

Simon could only imagine Nora's thoughts today. The day after finishing the prep classes, Nora had found Keith's body, unraveling into this string of deaths that had startled their peaceful corner of the world. He could only hope it was all about to be over.

1:15 PM

This time, Nora wore her own clothes. After all, she'd already met the object of today's inquiry. Consulting the address she'd looked up, she walked a few streets past The Scarlet Wench and turned up a side road. She hoped her timing would work out as she stopped before a cottage, the front yard littered with children's toys. This must be the place.

Opening the gate, Nora strode to the yellow front door and knocked briskly; a wreath of fall leaves adorned it. A moment later, Jodie Halsey opened it. Nora saw the look of recognition cross her face.

"Hello." Jodie Halsey turned and looked over her shoulder into her home.

Gauging if the inside was neat enough for company, Nora decided. "Hi, Mrs. Halsey. I was out walking and wanted to see how Andy was doing." She put one hand on her stomach, drawing emphasis to her bulk. "Boy, that last hill was a killer."

Jodie stepped aside. "Would you like to come in for a drink? Andy's napping. And call me Jodie."

Bingo. "That's very kind of you. I'm Nora." She stepped over the sill and into the bright room that ran the entire side of the house and ended in a small kitchen. "I'd love a glass of water."

"Come on through." Jodie led the way to a round table. She opened the refrigerator door. "I have apple juice if you'd rather."

"Water's fine, really," Nora said, sitting down. "I'm sorry about your father-in-law." She flashed on the image of the dead Jack Halsey and shook it off.

Jodie bit her lip. "Sorry you had to see him like that, but I'm glad you found Andy." She brought two glasses of ice water to the table and put one in front of Nora, then sat down. "The boy's having a hard time understanding he won't see Grampa Jack anymore."

"I can't imagine explaining death to a child," Nora agreed. Another situation she had no idea how to handle.

"Honestly, Jack could drive me crazy, but I hate the way he

died. My husband's taking it pretty bad. Jack wasn't a bad person; he just liked his drink too much."

Nora nodded. "The police any closer to finding out what happened?"

Jodie sipped her water. "Not that they've told me, that's for sure. All I know is that he got some kind of poison into him. And then Daniel, too—" She shuddered.

"I knew Daniel from Ramsey Lodge," Nora said. That was sort of true. "Who would have wanted them both to die?"

Jodie looked at the stairs to be certain Andy wasn't lurking. "I don't like to speak ill of the dead, but I'll tell you one thing: If Daniel Rowley was involved, it can't have been a good thing."

4 PM

Nora worked in her room before Val arrived. Jodie Halsey seemed like a nice woman, but she had added little to Nora's knowledge that would help her uncover the murderer. She knew from personal experience that Daniel Rowley's presence was never very appreciated. What she needed was more local knowledge to investigate "the mystery of the three deaths," which she thought sounded like the title of a Nancy Drew book, and to finish Keith's manuscript.

She decided to see if the *Cumbrian Chatter* was online, and was pleasantly surprised to find she could access its archives for the past six months. She spent almost an hour reading past issues, learning more than she'd ever wanted about daily life in the Bowness-Windermere area.

Daniel Rowley had been warned off twice in the last six months for disturbing the peace by singing loudly in the streets after closing down The Scarlet Wench. That was a disappointment. She'd hoped to find a tie to more significant illegal activity.

She found her own name in a March issue, when she had been mentioned as the winner of the essay contest that was "the creation of Bowness' own Keith Clarendon." There was no mention of Jack Halsey at all.

Nora decided it was time to go back to Keith's manuscript. She'd left off at his description of the Lake District National Park.

> *The Lake District National Park actually encompasses more than 885 square miles and receives more than 14 million visitors a year. A large amount of acreage is privately owned. Landowners assist the National Park staff to keep more than 1,800 miles of footpaths in use.*

Nora rubbed her lower back. Perhaps this was where the connection to Keith and Rowley lay, she thought: in a dispute over keeping the Clarendon estate in the National Park, which would affect Rowley's hut. Maybe Jack Halsey was just a man who got in the way. But she kept coming back to the same circular thought: If Daniel was her prime suspect for Keith's murder, he seemed to have put himself out of the running.

She thought of the plant that produced such a terrible poison. Despite its rarity, there were many people who could have had access to it. Keith may have been the first victim, but it seemed increasingly likely that Jack Halsey and Daniel Rowley had been given the same poison.

Daniel had worked at Clarendon Hall, enhancing his opportunity to poison Keith's tea. Daniel had also worked at Ramsey Lodge, the link to the assault on Agnes, which might have been intended for Nora. When she recalled the day he'd deliberately run her down with his bicycle, a tremor ran through Nora's body.

She sat back as a new thought occurred to her: What if there had been two murderers at work? Daniel might have murdered Keith, and someone who'd known about it might have then seen fit to get rid of Daniel; Jack's death was simply a tragic result of being Daniel's friend. Nora was certain all the men knew their murderer. Nora felt a new determination to clear Simon's name and extinguish any hypotheses of Ramsey Lodge's involvement. No one would be safe while a murderer walked free.

There was a tap at the door, and Val Rogan burst into Nora's room.

"Yankee, I can barely get my arms around you," Val squealed as the two friends embraced.

"I'm so glad to see you." Nora felt her eyes well with tears. She'd missed her friend and ally.

7:20 PM

At dinner, Val was quickly drawn into their lighthearted conversation, and Nora thought they all needed the diversion. Val and Simon had met last summer in Oxford and had gotten on well; now Kate was warming quickly to Nora's friend. It was Kate's suggestion to head to Nora's room to look at the crib that needed to be put together.

"We might as well do something constructive," she said. "Agnes will get off early tonight."

They trouped down the hall and into Nora's room. Val admired Simon's cloud painting and Nora's choice of wall color.

Simon inspected the box containing the crib and opened it. He pulled out the instructions and started to read. "I think this will go up in a jiffy."

Kate said, "We'll do it now. I'll get the tools."

"I think it's a great idea," Val said.

"We really don't have to do this now," Nora protested.

Val poked Nora's stomach. "Your mum is stubborn, baby."

"Nonsense," Kate proclaimed. "Simon and I are old hands at this. Go show Val the lake. She didn't drive all this way not to have you to herself for a few minutes."

Nora had her mouth open to argue when Simon said, "Nora, there's hardly room in this alcove for four and a half people and an assembly project. Take Val across the road to see the quay at night, and we'll get this sorted."

"But you've already done so much," Nora said.

"Come on, Yankee, follow orders," Val said, picking up Nora's jumper and dragging her out of the room and back through the dining room. The dining room was deserted but for Darby, asleep under a table. "We'll take Darby with us."

At the sound of his name, the terrier woke and was at Nora's side in an instant. Val put on her jacket and secured him to the leash Nora pointed out, hanging by the desk.

Nora directed them down the path and across the road. The sun had gone down, and the quay was lit up for the evening. A handful of tourists wandered about. Nora pointed out the bench she liked to sit on and pulled her sweater around her. There was a light breeze off the lake, and the two friends sat down and watched the water rippling.

Nora squeezed Val's hand. "Thanks for coming. I know it's out of your way.

Val rubbed her hand over Nora's stomach. "I had to see you—it's an image to torment you with after you give birth. How are you feeling?"

Nora described her fainting spell and explained the baby might be due sooner rather than later. "On one hand, I'm ready for it to be over. I want to see my feet again and have my body back." She patted her stomach.

"I can't imagine not being able to see my feet," Val said. "And on the other hand?"

Nora turned to her friend. "On the other hand, my life will be changed, and there's no going back. I'm scared to bits, Val. I've been trying to find out about the murders here to help clear Simon and keep myself from thinking too much, but I'm not doing a good job at either." Her voice dropped, and she stared across the lake.

"Ssh, stop that," Val said, leaning into Nora. "It will all work out." Darby jumped up on the bench between them, and Val drew the dog onto her lap, stroking his neck. "Kate is just as lovely as you'd described. And Simon? He's still the same Simon I met in Oxford: very kind and very in love with you."

"I know," Nora said. "He's disgustingly wonderful. I've only seen a flash of temper here and there, and who doesn't have one? He's been so good about not forcing the issue about our relationship, too."

"Is Declan Barnes in the way?" Val asked.

Nora's head jerked up, and she looked at her friend.

"It doesn't take much to see there's terrific chemistry between the two of you."

Nora leaned into Val and put her head on her friend's shoulder. "I don't know what to do, Val. I'm supposed to stay at least a year in Bowness while we work on the books and I get used to being a mom. Part of me wants to commit to Simon and a permanent life right here." She sat up and looked around her. "Who wouldn't want to live in this beauty and raise a child here?"

"But?" Val asked. "There's a huge 'but' for you, isn't there, named Declan?"

"I don't really know Declan Barnes. I thought I knew Paul,

and that wasn't the relationship I'd hoped for. What if I gave all of this up, including a man I know loves me—a good, decent man—and it didn't work out between Declan and me? How do I even know he wants a woman with someone else's child? That's who I am now—a package deal."

Val stroked Nora's arm. "First off, Declan knew you were pregnant when he met you. Second, Simon is aware you have misgivings about getting involved right now."

"And third?" Nora asked. "Help me decide what to do."

"Third? You don't need to make any of these decisions now. That's a decision in itself. If it's meant to be Declan, he'll find his way to you. In the meantime, you accept Kate and Simon's love and support and stick to Plan A for the next year."

Nora bit her lip. "And after that?"

Val laughed. "After that comes Plan B, and you'll know what it is when you need to make it."

8:30 PM

Simon was right, Kate thought. The crib had come together quickly. Simon was tightening the Peter Rabbit mobile Nora had bought onto the railing when they heard Nora and Val coming down the hall.

Darby ran in, followed by the two women and then Ian. Kate felt her face grow warm. She watched the man she loved come into Nora's room, look around him and then notice her in the alcove.

His face lit up at the sight of her, and her heart skipped a beat. Then she watched as the warmth she'd seen fell away, replaced with a professional expression.

Nora chattered to cover the uneasy atmosphere in the room. "Ian, look what Simon and Kate have been doing. Isn't it a great crib?" It was English walnut in a sleigh bed design.

"It turns into a junior bed down the road—" Kate's voice trailed off as she looked at her brother. Simon's eyes were locked on Ian's face. Neither man said anything, but it was obvious to Kate that Ian had not come to see her.

Simon broke the silence. "I have the feeling Ian is here for me."

Ian cleared his throat. "Dr. Foreman has completed the posts on Rowley and Halsey. He feels both men died from the same poison as Keith did."

Kate stepped forward. "That's horrible, Ian," she said stiffly, "but how does that affect us?"

"Simon needs to come down to the station. I must have him add to his statement about his whereabouts at different times." He met Kate's scrutiny. "I'm sorry, Kate, it's procedure, and I must—"

"Don't say it, Ian," Kate broke in tersely. "You must treat Simon with professional regard, the same as any bloody suspect." She turned to her brother. "This time we'll call your counsel. And *I'll* drive you to the station."

Simon reached out to touch his sister's arm. "That's not necessary, Kate."

She stood up to her full height. "I'm afraid it is."

8:45 PM

Ian, Kate and Simon left without speaking. A minute later, Nora heard the sound of car doors slamming. All was quiet except for Darby scratching at the front door. Nora whistled, and the dog

THE GREEN REMAINS

bounded back into her room. She explained to Val about Kate and Ian's broken engagement.

"I could feel the ice the moment he walked in," Val admitted. "Poor Kate."

"Poor Ian, too," Nora added. "He really is doing his job. It's not his fault Simon had clear access to the poison that was used in three deaths." She caught the odd look Val gave her. "What?"

"You really would make a good detective's wife," Val stated. "So damned accommodating to the needs of a policeman. Personally, I can see why Kate would be upset with him."

"I do, too," Nora said. "But he has no choice. If anything, he needs to stay on the case to find the real murderer, and he can't do that if he seems partial to Simon and gets thrown off the investigation."

"I thought *you* were going to find the murderer and clear Simon," Val said mischievously.

"I've snooped, I've asked impertinent questions and I'm almost finished going through Keith's work. I did get Cook rattled once, but I'm not convinced she knows anything except the Clarendon secrets, and she's not sharing."

"Every family has secrets," Val pointed out.

"Yes, and I need to get to the heart of the ones at Clarendon Hall."

Chapter Fifty-Seven

"It was the Bad Godesberg incident that gave the proof, though the German authorities had no earthly means of knowing this."
— John Le Carré, *The Little Drummer Girl*

Friday, 29th October

9:15 AM

Nora waved goodbye as Val drove off on her way to Manchester, tooting her horn. The two friends had shared tea and toast this morning at Nora's desk. Val always had a calming influence on her. Nora walked back into the quiet lodge. She loved that she could always count on Val to make her feel better in an honest way.

Neither Kate nor Simon had surfaced yet, but with only one lodger, they were probably having a well-deserved lie-in. Last night, she worried Simon had been arrested at the Kendal station when he and Kate hadn't arrived home before she and Val had turned in. She had pictured Kate calling their solicitor and Simon locked up in a cell.

But after 2 AM, she had thought she heard Simon's kitchen door open and close, corroborated when Darby had raised his head, ears twitching, from the rug next to her bed. She'd quieted him down, and had heard whispers from Simon and Kate. Finally, Simon's door had slid closed, and Kate had returned to her own room. The fact that Simon hadn't been detained made Nora hopeful that Ian was able to take the spotlight off him. She'd left a note on Simon's table, explaining that she'd fed Darby and had walked him with Val before turning in. No doubt she'd get the full report later today.

Determination to finish Keith's manuscript drove Nora. She felt a tug of fear that if the clues she searched for weren't present, she had no place left to look. Once she finished, at least, she could throw out the drive and erase the document from her laptop. She preferred to think of it as borrowed but knew Ian might see it differently.

Facing the glow of her laptop, she reviewed the last few pages of the main document and read through the two pages at the end, Keith's notes to himself. A question mark caught her eye. She scrolled back up to it and read:

TO DO: Crest origin? birth record.

It was the first question mark Nora had come across. She leaned back in her chair and pondered its meaning. Did Keith have a question about the family crest or about a birth record. If it was a birth record, then whose? And why?

Nora stood and stretched her back, swinging her arms to loosen them up. She paced her room, mulling over options in her mind. What was the link between someone needing Keith, Jack and Daniel to die? Who had hurt Agnes? Had the attack been meant for her instead?

If Rowley had seen something suspicious, and Nora had no doubt the man had often turned up without notice, perhaps the murderer hadn't been able to leave him be. Or maybe he had assisted the murderer and then had become a liability. If so, had Jack been a cohort, an accomplice or an innocent bystander?

Nora spied her bag and took out her camera. She removed the memory card and downloaded the pictures she'd taken at Clarendon Hall. Concentrating on the gallery portraits, she felt she was looking at an answer to a question not yet formed.

She thought of her father and knew he would have told her to follow her instincts. Grabbing her bag, she left the room before she could change her mind.

Nora made her way to the Clarendon chapel, slowing as she managed the incline of the steep driveway, stopping twice to catch her breath. Doves cooed in a nearby bush. No Daniel to worry about today. She rounded the house. Three glossy-black crows were eating the remains of a small animal near the doorway. Nora shivered and turned from the sight.

The vicar would be at Saint Martin's, but the chapel door was unlocked, and Nora tugged it open. The chapel felt smaller empty, its stone walls reeking of dampness. She noticed a moldy odor that the funeral attendees' mixed perfumes had masked.

Nora walked up the aisle and opened the door to one side of the undressed altar that led to a small sacristy. Once inside, she couldn't shake the feeling she was being watched. Probably her conscience kicking into high gear. Leaving the door ajar a few inches, she ignored two tall closets and the drawers between them. She turned her attention to a cupboard of weathered walnut that hung over a small table and chair.

It was locked. Of course, she thought in exasperation—the Clarendons might leave the chapel unlocked for the tour but wouldn't leave their family records open for an intruder such as herself to examine. She pulled out the ancient chair, sat down and forced herself to think calmly. The key must be in here somewhere.

She took a visual inventory, starting at the sacristy door. Next was the wall with the cupboard before which she sat, then came the wall that held the vestments and drawers. The last, narrow wall was bare, a high, leaded-glass window letting in gilded blades of golden sunlight that hit the vestment wall. Pointing to a starting place, Nora decided, rising and opening the left closet.

Black cassocks in different sizes hung from a single rod. She pushed them aside, looking for keys hanging on a nail at the back. Nothing. She closed that door and tried the other side, where she found crisp, white surplices and heavily embroidered albs. All were clean and pressed for the vicar, thanks to the dedicated Altar Guild ladies from Saint Martin's who were happy to fuss over the bachelor vicar no matter which church he visited.

She tried the drawers next. The first two slid open easily to reveal altar linens, starched and ironed, waiting for the next time they would be called into service. She had to crouch down to try the third, her large belly getting in the way. The drawer offered resistance but slid open a few inches. Elated, Nora tried to jiggle it open only to have it jam on an angle.

A portion of the drawer was open, but the damp wood was swollen, and when Nora tried to close the drawer and reopen it, it wouldn't budge. She hammered it with her fists on either side until she managed to close it a little, then tried to ease it open straighter.

This time, she succeeded in getting the drawer halfway open, enough to see it contained worn and patched linens, probably no longer used but kept for historical value, she reasoned. She thrust her hand inside and rifled the pile—nothing. She worked her left hand to the back of the drawer, sweeping it along the back panel of wood. Her hand brushed the hard edge of something, and she knelt down and tried to look inside.

Where was a flashlight when you needed it? Nora thought. Suddenly, her fingers hit the hardness she'd felt before and closed on a bent nail holding a key.

Chapter Fifty-Eight

"Bright reason will mock thee,
Like the sun from a wintry sky."
— Percy Bysshe Shelley, *When the Lamp is Shattered*

10:05 AM

Once Nora had opened it with the found key, the cupboard on the wall revealed a few outdated prayer books and a small stack of even older registers, all with leather covers in varied stages of deterioration, most with page ends foxed or darkened from age—except the one at the end of the row.

She drew out the slim, royal blue volume. Stamped in gold on the front cover were the four interlocking C's of the Clarendon family crest. A loud creak issued from the front of the chapel and startled Nora, who dropped the register onto the table with a disturbingly loud thunk.

She crept to the sacristy door and peered out. The hair on the back of her neck rose as she squinted into the dim interior. She couldn't see anyone and didn't sense any movement.

Turning back to the register, she sat down and opened it. The frontispiece held a second rendition of the crest; this time the motto was indicated underneath the entwined initials:

Clarendon   Courage   Civility   Character

Pretty standard stuff, Nora thought; no mystery there that she could see. She skipped to the last page that had writing on it and immediately saw what had caught Keith's eye.

The last two entries were from twenty-eight years ago, documenting the birth of a female, Rose Julia, and a male, Keith Edmunde. Beside the entry for baby Rose, an additional date recorded her death under a column headed by a black cross. A different handwriting, which Nora supposed belonged to the current vicar, documented Keith's death date.

What drew Nora's attention was that the two birth entries had been written over previous entries. The correction fluid, although carefully applied, could easily be noted, especially in the death column next to Keith's name. Yet he had just died—why should that have needed a correction?

Nora shifted in the rickety chair, contemplating what this meant. If an error had been made in a date, or in spelling, it would not have involved both birth entries nor the new death date, years apart. Only one possible explanation occurred to Nora.

She reshelved the register, locked the cupboard, returned the key to its nail and used her foot to slam the drawer closed. Retracing her steps to the front of the chapel, she looked around, then hurried along the path behind the house that would bring her to the kitchen door.

10:30 AM

Cook was sweeping the back steps when Nora appeared on the walkway, holding one hand under her huge midsection. Slightly out of breath, her bag slung across her shoulder, she slowed her pace and tried to appear relaxed while her mind worked out her best approach. She waved cheerfully as she drew closer.

Cook stopped her broom and, after a slight hesitation, gave a brief wave back.

"Hi, Cook. Time for a quick tea break?" Nora saw Cook's

frown as she reached the steps. She looked up at the older woman with what she thought was her most pleasant smile. "I was hoping you had some of those iced cookies stashed away."

The comment must have softened Cook's resistance. She smiled back at Nora and invited her in.

Cook set the tea things out. Nora grabbed a cookie and inquired about Antonia's health. She discussed the reading Sommer had given at the funeral service. All the while, she struggled mentally, conflicted over the deceits she had recently committed. She decided to be honest with the woman, hoping she wasn't contributing to a killer's scheme.

"Cook, I know you are very loyal to the Clarendons, but I also know you'd like nothing better than to help unearth Keith's killer." Nora paused to gauge the woman's reaction as Cook poured their tea. "I want to see Simon totally cleared with his reputation intact."

Cook nodded and chimed in. "I don't care a whit who did Daniel or Jack in, God forgive me, but the boy … " Her eyes swam with tears, and she took a deep gulp of hot tea.

Nora got to the heart of the matter, choosing a succinct compression of the facts. "Because of a question Keith had, I went to the chapel and saw the changes in the family register." This was merely good editing.

Cook remained silent, paying rapt attention to the rose design on her china cup.

Nora took a deep breath. "I believe Keith was really Julia and Edmunde's child, and Rose was born to Antonia and Sommer. It's right there if you're looking for it."

Across the table, Cook visibly stiffened. Silence. Nora sipped her tea and watched dust motes dance in the light over the kitchen sink. When she looked back at Cook, the woman's tears splashed on the table in front of her.

Cook noisily used a hankie she withdrew from her apron pocket. She met Nora's eyes and gave her a brief nod. "Twenty-eight years I've kept the secret. She was the sweetest little angel, a beautiful tiny babe, not a mark on her." Cook's resistance collapsed, and she poured out the story between sniffing and dabbing at her nose and eyes.

"Miss Antonia went into labor after news came of Sommer's accident. Her sweet little girl was perfect but had underdeveloped lungs, they said, and only lived a few hours. The whole thing threw Miss Julia into labor that night, and she delivered a healthy boy by Caesarean, but something went terribly wrong, a bleeding complication, and she died hours later."

Nora drew in a breath and touched Cook's hand, encouraging her to continue.

"Mr. Edmunde was out of his mind with grief. He wouldn't go to the nursery; he refused to hold the baby and said he wouldn't take him home. Miss Antonia, she was filled with her own heartbreak over losing Rose and hadn't left the hospital yet when Sommer was stabilized enough to transfer him down here. She divided her time those first few days between nursing the boy and staying at Mr. Sommer's bedside until he was out of danger. Mr. Edmunde finally went to see his brother, and Mr. Sommer begged him to let them raise the boy as their own. He worried for Antonia's sanity and could see Edmunde didn't want anything to do with the babe."

Cook shifted in her chair and paused to sip her cooled tea. She swallowed. "In for a penny, in for a pound," she said, more in control now. "Mr. Edmunde agreed and used money and favors to 'correct' the birth certificates. I'm the only one who knew, besides the last vicar, who's dead now."

"What about the hospital staff, the nurses and such?" Nora asked.

"They knew Miss Antonia was the baby's aunt, but he was only there for three days, and Saint Margaret's isn't around the corner. Then Gillian was hired for Mr. Sommer, and between us we managed pretty well. 'Cepting at the beginning when Miss Antonia hovered over him and the baby day and night. At one point, we had to get in a night nurse because she wasn't sleeping; she was afraid Keith would die from that no-reason thing—"

"Crib death, or Sudden Infant Death Syndrome," Nora supplied.

"That's it." Cook's tears had dried, and she stuffed the damp hankie back into her apron pocket. "We'd bring her the baby to nurse between resting or sitting with Mr. Sommer, and she gradually got her strength back. I think after a while, we all forgot he wasn't theirs. That lad, he was such a blessing to them both … " Cook ran out of steam.

"That explains the register change," Nora said. "But how would the real facts have altered anything? Edmunde never remarried, so Sommer and then Keith would eventually inherit the estate after Edmunde's death, instead of it going directly to Keith, right?"

Cook agreed as a bell rang in the kitchen. "That'll be Miss Antonia, wanting her elevenses. She and Mr. Sommer always have their tea together. I'll get theirs up to them."

She rose to take the kettle from the warming plate of the Aga and prepared the teapot, resting it on a prepared tray on the counter.

Nora sprang up from her seat as quickly as her bulk would allow. "Let me take that up, Cook."

"Don't upset Miss Antonia with your snooping. Promise?" Cook pointed a finger at Nora.

"I don't see how there's a motive there for Keith's murder, no matter who his parents are. It was more a matter of emotion at the time," Nora said.

Cook handed her the tray. "You give me your word you won't say anything? " Cook admonished. "She's too fragile."

"I promise." Nora raised her hand in a solemn Girl Scout salute.

Cook appeared satisfied and showed Nora how to use the elevator. "They're upstairs today."

Nora took the lift upstairs, and as she turned the corner, she wondered how she could get around her promise.

The door to Antonia and Sommer's suite stood open, and Nora could see the parents sitting together on the small balcony off their bedroom, holding hands. The balcony overlooked the back lawn and gardens, and the view revealed the autumnal reds and golds of the birch, rowan and horse chestnut trees that lined the way to the purple fells in the distance. Blackbird calls competed with periodic fits of a singing thrush; thin trees in the garden bent to the breeze that was bringing in a low mist.

Nora thought it was a scene evocative of what Dorothy Wordsworth, William's devoted sister, had called "a glorious wild solitude." This harmonious connection to nature hit her squarely as she entered the room with the tray; it was a feeling she remembered from hiking in the hills of Connecticut. She collected herself and spoke quickly to ward off questions as she broke into the couple's reverie.

"Hello, sorry to interrupt. I dropped in to see how you were doing and volunteered to bring this up for Cook. I hope you don't mind." This was reasonably close to the truth, Nora decided, hoping her color wouldn't rise. Her son chose that moment to give her a hearty kick.

"Please, bring a chair and join us, Nora." Sommer recovered first, ever the gentleman. He looked down at his legs.

Nora understood he would have carried her chair out if that were possible. She set the tray on the small table between them and took a chair from in front of Antonia's dressing table onto the balcony.

"I've just had tea with Cook, so have yours while it's hot. Would you like me to pour?" She turned to include Antonia in the conversation.

Antonia's subdued manner, as though she were seeing the world through a layer of dulling gauze that had descended over her, was instantly recognizable to Nora. Grief was a series of stages, and Nora had been surprised to discover she had traversed those stages in the wake of Paul's death; perhaps insisting she would have been unhappy with him was actually a coping mechanism. She would never really know.

Intense empathy spilled over Nora, and with it came melancholy shame at ever having suspected these dignified people of murder. Quelling her guilt, she told herself they would be the first ones to want to identify Keith's murderer.

Sommer asked about her book. She explained about sending the proof off as a step toward its impending publication. This was safe ground. "I'm always on the lookout for a story idea for coming books," she noted. "Keith was so supportive of my books being set here on Lake Windermere."

Antonia stirred at Keith's name and made eye contact. The two women smiled at each other. "He loved books, our Keith. We read to him every night when he was little, both of us," she explained.

Sommer added his own thoughts. "I couldn't do a lot of things other fathers did with their sons, but I could read to him. He read on his own very early, you know," he said, clear pride in his voice.

"I do know," Nora said with warmth. "Keith was very proud of that. We talked about it one night in Oxford. He felt it gave him an edge over other boys when he went to school."

Antonia brightened. "Thank you very much for telling us that. It's something to hold onto."

A comfortable silence descended over the balcony. Nora knew she couldn't introduce the baby switching without compromising her promise to Cook.

Antonia broke the stillness. Her comment made Nora aware she had become a silent partner to their secret. "Do you know my most happy memory of Keith?" Antonia didn't appear to expect either of her companions to guess. "It was the first time he called me Mummy."

CHAPTER FIFTY-NINE

"In the end Jack Burdette came back to Holt after all."
— Kent Haruf, *Where You Once Belonged*

10:50 AM

Ian felt exhausted. Things with Kate were pure crap, as his Gran used to say, and there appeared to be no joy to be had in any of his cases. As he reviewed the rest of the background checks that he'd asked for, one note caught his eye. Nothing else seemed to be of much use toward the three murders, but one item bore checking out. He asked the civilian at the computer terminal to track down a birth record in Scotland. "All routes of inquiry should be pursued," he'd learned in training, justifying the request to himself as the door to the incident room banged open and Higgins rushed in.

"Sir, there's been a reliable sighting of the missing girl in Windermere," he said.

"Grab the keys and ride with me," Ian instructed.

The young detective kept to the speed limit, just, as he drove them north of Kendal to the town of Windermere, filling Ian in on their destination.

"We had a call from the hostel with a description match on Anne Reed," he said, pointing up the High Street. "That distinctive teal anorak gave her away."

Ian hoped he was right. It would be nice to close this case with a positive result. They pulled in front of the Lake District Backpackers Lodge and entered the orange-painted haven of dorm beds ("laundry on premises"), used largely by international travelers and students on a strict budget. Ian knew the place, near the train station, had a good reputation and thought it was remarkably clean for this kind of housing.

Flashing his warrant card to the ponytailed man at the desk, Ian established he was the person who had called in to head-quarters. The man pointed and said quietly, "Laundry," motioning to the back room, anxious to remain uninvolved. Still, Ian acknowledged, he'd done his civic duty.

The sound of whirring machines, augmented by the smell of hot air, bleach and detergents, led the men to the laundry. At their entrance, a scrawny young man with too many earrings in his left ear nudged a slender, chestnut-haired girl, who folded clothes to the beat of the music in her ear buds. The wire led to an open black-suede backpack. Pulling the ear buds from her ears, the girl looked furtively toward the back door. Ian motioned to Higgins, who covered the exit.

"Excuse me, a word please," Ian said pleasantly, his stiff smile indicating he would brook no argument. He flashed his card, introduced himself and Higgins, and pointed to a row of plastic chairs.

"We haven't done a thing, not a bloody thing," the girl said, but they sat, the young man draping his arm protectively around her shoulder.

"It's fine, Peach," he assured her. "We've nothing to hide. Always glad to assist the police with their enquiries," he added cheerfully.

He's a polite charmer, Ian thought, but then she was supposed to be a bright girl. "Do you have any identification?" Both nodded and produced driving licenses. "Peter Morris, age twenty, of Sawrey; Anne Reed, age seventeen, from Windermere." He thanked them and returned their cards, wondering where the two young people had met. Some athletic event, he decided, noting the pile of folded clothes contained several brightly striped rugby shirts.

"Miss Reed, your mother has filed a missing person report in Windermere and is extremely worried about you." In fairness, he didn't know if the girl's stepfather shared this sentiment.

The girl colored but set a determined line about her mouth as she answered. "I'm seventeen, almost eighteen, and old enough to make my own decisions. She's got the little ones to fuss over, him to take care of and I don't need to be their babysitter any more. I'm allowed to have some fun and have my own life, you know."

She glanced at her companion and blushed harder. "Besides, they didn't understand how much Peter and I really love each other and want to be together the right way. He takes care of me."

Ian sat back and rubbed his hand over his face. Legally, he could do nothing to force Anne Reed to return home, nor would he be able to convince these youths they were making a huge mistake running away together. At least he could tell her mother she was alive and looked well. "What are your plans?"

Peter pulled Anne against him. "We're getting ready to head down to Weston-super-Mare, got a lead on jobs at the SeaQuarium there, right, Peach?"

"Down to North Somerset?" Ian asked. "You haven't traveled very far in a week," he noted.

This time it was Peter who blushed. "What kind of a blighter do you take me for? We were married last Friday, been having a proper honeymoon for a few days in Bowness, Peach and me, at Rose Cottage."

Rose Cottage? It turned out there might be some joy to be had after all.

Ian directed Higgins to speak with Anne Reed's mother and reassure her that her daughter was safe and acting of her own accord. The newlywed reluctantly promised to call home that evening, probably in search of funding. He could imagine the teary reunion call.

He had his sergeant drop him back at the station and went directly to the incident room to check on his earlier request. He read the information that confirmed what he'd suspected, while one part of his mind replayed the unexpected information his careful questioning of the couple had elicited. It all came together now.

Yes, they'd admitted, they'd been at Rose Cottage when all of that fuss had occurred in the front arbor. They remembered having come in after dinner, close to 8. The arbor had been empty then.

"Did either of you know the dead man?" he had asked, a matter of form.

"No, sir," Peter Morris had replied, eager to be taken as a compliant adult. "It really upset Peach here when we heard the sirens, didn't it, luv?"

Anne's pretty face had lost its color. "It was so sad," she'd agreed. "Especially when he'd seemed so happy when we passed him."

Ian's pulse had quickened. It had been the connection he'd hoped for when he'd heard the couple had stayed at Rose Cottage. "Where was that, Miss—uh—Mrs. Morris?"

The girl had beamed at the use of her married name. "At the ice cream stand right near The Scarlet Wench. He and a bloke were sharing a nip from a grotty old flask."

Ian had felt a surge of excitement. Simon had been nowhere

in this vicinity; he would be able to clear him shortly. His copper's instincts had told him this case would soon be solved. He had resolved to visit Kate at his first opportunity to plead his case. The conflict that had dogged him about doing his duty versus loving her had melted away. He was on firm ground now, thanks to the young couple.

CHAPTER SIXTY

*"... watch with glittering eyes the whole world around you because
the greatest secrets are always hidden in the most unlikely places. ... "*
— Roald Dahl

11:15 AM

Simon was pleased with how his painting was progressing. He'd
had to paint in a different flower when the rare one he'd borrowed from Sommer had been taken into evidence, but since it
had turned out to be an instrument of death, its presence would
have been disconcerting. The art was a surprise for Nora. He
hoped she would be pleased and not view his gift as interference
or worse, as possessiveness. He meant it as an assurance of her
strength and his support of her decision to raise her child alone.
He hoped Nora would see it the same way.

He felt better now after getting real sleep. With only Tony
Warner at the lodge to have breakfast, Sally and Agnes had
coped and he and Kate had both slept in. Last night had been
surreal. The stark interior of Kendal station was starting to become too familiar and had looked far more menacing at night.
He'd felt a tremor of dread pass over him when he stepped inside. Kate had gripped his hand tightly. She'd remained at his
side until Ian had showed her to a small side room, allowing her
to watch as Sergeant Higgins conducted the interview in the
presence of his solicitor.

All of Simon's fear had dissipated. If he were a serious suspect
in Ian's eyes, someone Ian really felt was capable of murder, Ian
never would have allowed the woman he loved to watch while he
took her brother down.

Simon had decided this was calculated to keep Ian on the right side of procedure as he tried to win back Kate's love. Simon had answered the sergeant's questions comfortably and felt relaxed as he recounted his movements over the last week, none of which had taken him in the vicinity of Clarendon Hall. As they had waited for Ian to excuse them, Kate had hugged him.

"See, that wasn't so bad, Katy-did." His use of her childhood nickname had made her beam.

"I was so afraid for you," she had admitted. "I had the solicitor promise me you wouldn't have to spend the night in a cell."

"What? You thought I had something to worry about?" Simon had stood away in mock horror.

"Never," Kate had grinned. "I just hate to see you caught up in this. Nora feels the same way. Let's get some sleep."

Thinking of Nora had him checking his watch. He decided to see how her morning had gone. When he got to her door, it stood open. The bed was neatly made, and Darby was stretched out on the soft duvet right in its middle. There was no sign of Nora.

"Down," he told the dog and turned to leave with Darby slinking at his heels when he noticed the screen saver on Nora's laptop, a montage of Connecticut: the hills and shore views from her hometown's Main Street, a meadow in flower, a tall white flagpole with a huge American flag undulating in the breeze.

Simon advanced into the room; she must be in the alcove, admiring the baby gear, if her door was unlocked. The side room stood ready for its little occupant. The crib and cradle had been made up with the new linens, the clothes and tiny outfits stored away. Nora had placed a worn volume of Mother Goose nursery rhymes on the small table next to the lamp.

Simon picked up the book and flipped through. It was a 1917 edition of the original 1881 book with illustrations by Kate Greenaway. He flipped to the first page and saw written in pencil in a childish scrawl:

Nora Alicia Tierney
Bought with my allowance, 1987

How Simon wished he'd known her then! Still small, she had probably been teased for looking younger than her age with those freckles across her nose. He wondered when she had started wearing glasses, remembering she'd said she'd tried and hated contact lenses. He wished he knew more of her childhood. She had no sibling to share those days and had told Simon that books were her constant friends. Her love of travel had been born in her books, as had been her desire to write.

Where was Nora, anyway? Since the assault on Agnes, she'd been locking the door if she left the lodge. Putting the book down, Simon walked to her desk and touched the space bar to bring up her screen. The document that appeared before him was labeled KCman.doc. As he examined it, he saw the question mark Nora had seen and instantly knew where to find her. He left the lodge, Darby at his side, and didn't stop to make the dog go back.

11:25 PM

At first, Simon thought he'd been mistaken. There was no sign of Nora, but he was certain she'd been there. The chapel stood empty and silent, already regaining its musty odor but with a hint of the lemony scent Nora used. Darby picked up on his tension and ran around him in circles, barking.

His anxiety propelled him along the path toward the Hall, but he faltered when he approached the kitchen door. This kind of pursuing behavior had gotten him into trouble with Nora before. But she had been on the trail of something; her scent in the chapel confirmed that. Plus, she'd left her computer on and her door unlocked. This was not the same as wanting to shadow her every movement. With a determined set to his jaw, Simon raised his hand and knocked.

11:26 AM

Ian took the corners fast, causing Higgins to put a steadying hand on the dashboard. The background check from Scotland had had a surprising result. He checked his watch. Things were falling into place, but his instincts told him to hurry.

He gave Higgins the number for Ramsey Lodge and took the phone from him when Kate answered. He thought he heard a softening in her tone, but he didn't have time to make up with her at that moment.

"Keep everyone in your household away from Clarendon Hall, Kate."

"I don't know where Simon or Nora are—Ian, you're frightening me."

"I don't mean to." He covered the phone and directed Higgins to make a call. "But if you see either of them, don't let them go up to Clarendon Hall."

CHAPTER SIXTY-ONE

"A mother's love for her child is like nothing else in the world. It knows no law, no pity, it dates all things and crushes down remorselessly all that stands in its path."
— Agatha Christie, *The Last Seance*

11:27 AM

Nora thanked Sommer and Antonia for the visit and let herself out of their room. Her son had kicked hard for the last few minutes, so she pushed his foot in and was rewarded with an answering shove, a game she never tired of. Doc Lattimore had said his head was down, in position; those kicks under her ribs were his strong feet. She would know more when she saw her OB in the morning.

She walked down the hall, deep in thought, evaluating her actions. She felt justified getting involved in this murder investigation to clear Simon, but she knew others would have a different perspective.

"Snooping," Cook had termed it, and with a pang of regret, Nora wondered if she would ever stop being a busybody. Maybe motherhood would cure her. She stopped in the gallery to the right of the stairs, searching the portraits of the four handsome, young people whom fate had seen fit to injure, each in a different but permanent way.

Nora studied the two women: Julia, the chestnut-haired beauty who had never known she was a mother; then Antonia, the fairer one who needed above all to be one. Next she studied the two men, wondering what childhood had been like for the muscular Edmunde, with his luxurious dark hair, and his thinner brother, Sommer, hair straight and slicked back. Each must have the major genetic makeup of the opposite parent for the brothers to look so different.

Nora leaned on the gallery railing as a memory came back to her. She was about nine and had traveled to Manhattan with her parents for a long weekend. It started with the Thanksgiving parade, which they watched from their hotel room high above the crowded street, warm inside on the cold November day. She refused to leave the window during the entire spectacle, the huge balloons floating past the glass and stunning her with their nearness. She thought it had to be the most fantastic sight she'd ever seen.

But she'd been wrong. The most fantastic sight for her that weekend turned out to be a billboard her father pointed out as they walked through Times Square while her mother shopped. Above the jostling throngs and the yellow taxis with their cacophony of horns, above the earthy smells of roasting chestnuts and hot, soft pretzels, the billboard had captured her attention and her imagination.

It wasn't what the board displayed; it was that every fifteen seconds the image split into vertical panels and rotated a quarter turn to the right, emerging with a completely different ad. This switch fascinated Nora, and she stood rooted to the spot through numerous revolutions until her father tired of watching it and dragged her off.

Nora stared at the portraits in front of her. She pictured Robbie Cole without his baseball cap. If she stood back and combined all of the information she had on the Clarendons, everything shifted into place.

Thoughtfully, she left the gallery, negotiated the wide central staircase and unlocked the front door. She didn't want to face Cook again, so she stood on the broad front step, looking out at the shimmering lake in the distance. A huge cloud passing overhead was reflected in its surface, and she thought distractedly that they were in for more rain. Nora turned toward the dock and the stone gazebo that sat at the end of it. She would sit there, examine her idea and ruminate on what was reality and what was her imagination in overdrive.

11:32 AM

When Simon asked for Nora, Cook sent him upstairs. He left Darby outside and ran through the kitchen into the hallway and up the main staircase, trying to contain his agitation.

He found Antonia and Sommer on their balcony, watching the heavy fog roll down the fell. They turned at his knock.

"Sorry to bother you, but Cook said Nora was here." Simon thought he heard footsteps coming up the staircase.

Sommer answered, "She left us just minutes ago."

They were all startled by the appearance of Ian Travers in the doorway. "Where's Gillian Cole?"

11:33 AM

Nora stepped out onto the Clarendons' stone dock. The cloud bank had stalled overhead, turning the day grey. She walked toward the octagon-shaped stone gazebo at the dock's head. Mist swirling around the dock held the promise of a shower, and she knew she should get back to the lodge before she got wet.

This was the other face of the Lake District, the rapidly

changing weather, but Nora still appreciated a different kind of beauty intrinsic in the murky fog. She felt damp and shivered, looking into the water lapping the pilings, surprised at its depth. Like people, she thought, pulling her sweater closer around her chest: unimagined depths, swirling emotions, hidden motives.

Concentrating on her insight, unraveling the puzzle that had her in its grip, she abruptly sensed movement at the foot of the dock and looked up. The brume had already covered the dock's junction with the land, and Nora had the odd sensation of standing inside a cloud as the mist whirled around her ankles. She listened intently. Just as she convinced herself she was being ridiculous, she heard a definite footstep on the stone dock.

"Who's there?" she called in a voice much stronger than she felt. The only immediate response was a dog yapping nearby. Out of the mist Gillian Cole appeared, her right hand hidden deep in the pocket of her navy cardigan. Her white uniform accentuated her ghostly appearance, and she advanced slowly toward Nora.

"You think you have it all figured out, don't you?" Gillian's voice was menacing in its quiet tone. "I watched you leave the chapel."

Nora swallowed hard. Her uterus tightened, and she felt a surge of pain grip her lower abdomen, causing her to clutch at her stomach.

"Tell me!" Gillian commanded.

Nora took a step away from Gillian's advance, talking earnestly, wondering if anyone would hear her should she scream. "I know that Keith was really Edmunde's son. And I think Robbie is Edmunde's, too. Your dead husband never existed. You murdered Keith so your son would inherit the Clarendon estate."

Gillian's laugh was a loud bark. "You're only half right. Robbie *is* our son. But Keith's own biological father killed him. Edmunde owed me that. I never asked him to do it—I wouldn't—but he did it for me and for Robbie."

Nora didn't understand. Edmunde had murdered Keith? "How is that possible?" The wave of pain had passed but had left her nauseated.

Gillian's mouth curved into an unattractive sneer. "He can do more than he lets on. He took the elevator to the kitchen weeks ago when Antonia and Sommer were napping and Cook was asleep. It was a simple matter of crushing a few seeds from that plant and putting them into the first bottle of scotch in the pantry. Keith sometimes added a dollop to his flask before going out. It was only a matter of time before he did it again and died. It could have happened any time he decided to fortify his tea."

"But why would Edmunde kill his own son?" Nora stalled for time as she remembered she'd told Simon this family was like a Greek tragedy. She put a tentative foot behind her and shifted herself away from Gillian. Was that a knife in Gillian's pocket? Nora's legs cramped from coiled tension. She could barely hear her own voice over the noise of her heart pounding in her ears. Short of jumping off the dock into the deep water, she couldn't see a way out.

Nora tried to keep the woman talking. "Surely blood testing would prove paternity, and Sommer would have to provide support for Robbie."

"I'm dying," Gillian said. "Pancreatic cancer. There was no time for a court battle against Keith. I needed to know my son would be taken care of, and Edmunde *owed* me! He promised me Robbie would inherit if I continued to take care of Sommer." The woman's eyes had taken on a fierce light. "And then he had his stroke, and Sommer had to take over his affairs legally." She gave a sharp nod. "My son deserves it! All the years I've been the village gossip and taken care of this family down to wiping their bums. Edmunde *hated* Keith. He blamed him for Julia's death. This was a gift of love to *me*!"

"When you realized what he'd done you were glad?" Nora couldn't keep the incredulous tone out of her voice. "What about Rowley?" She raised her voice, hoping in vain that someone would overhear their voices carried on the fog, willing her legs to support her.

Gillian snorted at her question. "He became a liability. I knew you'd been at Keith's computer. I told Rowley to watch you, and I'd pay him well, but he wanted to be paid for knocking you down and finding nothing. Then he saw me leaving the lodge after tossing your room—yes, I knocked Agnes out. She came into the room and almost found me. After that, he had to go. A truly worthless piece of humanity." She shrugged. "It got rid of the scotch bottle from the pantry, and he took if from me very willingly."

So Daniel *had* been looking for something in my bag, Nora thought sadly, knowing it didn't do her any good to be right on that point. She tightened her knees to stay upright as a wave of weakness washed over her. All at once, a warm gush ran down her legs and into her shoes, followed by the hardest contraction yet.

Nora gasped and stumbled closer to the end of the dock. "What did Jack Halsey have to do with it?" Was that her name being called?

Gillian's eyes blazed. "Another useless man, but then most of them are. Wasn't my fault Rowley shared his flask with him."

This time they both heard a dog barking. Gillian sneered, turning the expression into a grotesque grin. "There's no one to save you. I'll tell the others I heard you scream as you fell in. A shame I got here just a moment too late."

Gillian advanced. Nora fantasized the barking was getting louder and closer. She was aware of the moist air on her scalp and the clinging dampness between her legs. The treated wood gave off a scent that reminded her of Martha's Vineyard, and for a moment she saw her father's face smiling at her over Gillian's shoulder. It gave her courage. She appealed to the nurse's instincts. "My water broke—I'm in labor. Please, help me save my baby."

Gillian was so close Nora could smell her fetid breath. "Jump, or I'll push you," she hissed, one hand in her sweater pocket, the other held out in front of her, ready to shove Nora into the lake.

Nora crossed her arms protectively over her stomach just as a voice shouted from the top of the dock, stopping Gillian's advance toward Nora.

"Gillian! This is Ian Travers. Simon and I have heard everything. Put your hands up."

Barking furiously, Darby rushed onto the dock. A siren whined in the background. "Put your hands up, for God's sake!" Simon shouted.

Gillian wheeled around from the running dog and back to Nora in a panic. "Not for God's sake, for Robbie's sake!" With a cry of frustration as Darby snarled and leapt at her, Gillian hurled herself into Nora, pushing them both off the dock and into the depths of the lake.

"No!" Nora heard Simon's shout, saw the edge of Gillian's sweater in Darby's mouth and took in a huge breath as they hit the water with a tremendous splash.

Hitting the frigid water with the scrawny woman on top of her, Nora gasped at the cold but held her breath, feeling them sink. She struggled to free herself—she had to save her son! She kicked upward toward the surface. Gillian slid down her body, hanging on to Nora's legs to keep them under water, dragging them down toward the icy depths of the lake.

CHAPTER SIXTY-TWO

"First you are very small and the color is old-rose and pink,
and you are kept very warm."
— Stephen Longstreet, *God and Sarah Pedlock*

8:10 PM

A kitten mewed near her left ear. Put it outside. She needed
sleep. A shushing voice sounded like Val. Someone held her
right hand. Finally, she felt warm. She had a terrible backache.
She tried to turn on her side. Severe pain across her lower abdomen encouraged Nora's eyes to flicker open.

Val. Standing by a window, rocking a bundle wrapped in a
blue blanket. Nora's eyes jerked wide. Kate squeezed her hand.
"I think she's awake."

Val beamed and walked over. Simon appeared at the door
holding three cups; the tantalizing smell of fresh coffee woke
Nora completely. Kate used a control to elevate the head of the
bed, and Val held out the blue bundle.

Nora reached for the baby, struggling to clear her fuzzy brain.
"Didn't bring one for me?" she asked Simon. Everyone in the
room laughed. Nora felt the warmth of her son and peeled back
the corner of the blanket to gaze at the sleeping infant.

Small pursed mouth with pink lips. Translucent skin. Tiny
fingers with minute nails. Perfect. Her son was just perfect. She
pressed her lips to his forehead and inhaled his baby scent. She
started to unwrap the blanket.

"Relax, they're all there, ten and ten," Val said, wiping her
eyes. She brushed hair off of Nora's forehead.

"What are you crying for? I'm the one who apparently

has a huge gash in my stomach. And I thought you were in Manchester?"

Another round of laughs. "I'm crying because he's such a lovely baby," Val sniffed. "Kate called me, and I came back as soon as I could."

Gillian and the dock came rushing back to Nora's memory. "Gillian?"

Simon shook his head. "Divers are looking for her. Probably for the best."

Nora hugged her baby. "She died the same way Keith did, giving herself up to the lake." She looked at her baby again. "He's sleeping so peacefully, but I want to take off all of these coverings and inspect every inch of his body." She noticed his lips were shaped just like hers and that his eyebrows were definitely shaped like Paul's.

"Plenty of time for that," Kate said. "And I think you have to start with water, or I'd share my coffee with you."

The baby chose that moment to yawn, and everyone gathered around to watch him open his tiny mouth and squint his eyes as he arched his back. Nora had to laugh. "You'd think he was the first baby to do that."

"He's beautiful, Nora," Kate said.

"Too bad he doesn't have a name," Simon teased.

"But he does," Nora assured him. "I decided to honor my roots, so his middle name is my mom's maiden name, McAllister. And for my father, John, the same first name in Gaelic, Sean."

"Sean McAllister Tierney. Flows well," Val announced.

"He'll fit in just fine," Kate agreed.

"Brilliant! Very manly," Simon added.

A tall man appeared in the doorway. "Thanks for the compliment, Simon." Ian Travers entered, and Kate immediately stood. "Just came to see how you and the little man were doing." He stood at the foot of the bed with his hands clasped behind his back.

"I guess I have you to thank for saving my life?" Nora asked.

"No, no," Ian shook his head. "That's down to Simon—he jumped in before I could, damn him. I stayed on the dock to haul you both out."

Nora smirked as she looked to Simon. "So I have to be eternally grateful to you twice."

"Don't worry, I'll find a way for you to repay me," Simon said. Ian touched his arm, and the two men spoke quietly in a corner of the room.

The baby sighed, and Nora laughed. "I think he's tired of me already." She saw Kate trying not to look at Ian. "Would you like to hold him, Kate?"

Kate stepped forward and took the baby in her arms. Ian and Simon broke apart, and Ian walked over to Kate, looking over her shoulder at the baby.

"Sweet lad, Nora," Ian said, resting one hand on Kate's shoulder. She leaned into him. "We need to talk." They moved over to two chairs by the window. Ian held the baby while Kate sat, then handed him back. He sat in the chair next to her, their heads together, talking quietly.

Val and Simon opened their coffees.

"Smells so good," Nora said, moving gingerly in the bed. "When can I get up?"

Val handed her a water jug with a straw. "Drink up. I'll go ask the sister." She left, and Simon sat down next to her.

Nora took Simon's hand and squeezed it before letting it go. "Seriously, thank you for rescuing me and the baby." She thought Simon blushed, and she lowered her voice. "What was Ian telling you?"

Simon hesitated. "They brought up Gillian's body, trapped

under the dock. Ian said her face was relaxed and calm. In her pocket was a candle, no knife. Just a bluff to frighten you."

Nora nodded. "She was convinced it was the right thing to do for her child." She shivered. "It still leaves Robbie without his mother and the Clarendons without the child they loved as their own. Plus two others dead—it's awful. At least you're cleared."

"Ian's job is just what you were doing—trying to juggle puzzle pieces to see which ones go where," Simon noted. "I stopped being upset with him days ago."

Nora jutted her chin in the direction of Kate and Ian, still admiring the baby. "I think Kate's forgiven him, too."

Simon nodded. "She saw how he treated me last night at the station. They'll be fine." He turned back to her. "How about you?"

"After all of this waiting, I missed Sean's birth. And the classes you took—" Nora shook her head. "Mostly, I'm grateful he's healthy and that I'm still around to care for him."

"You might have been out of it, but Dr. Ling let us watch the Caesarean. Kate held your hand, and I got some great pictures on my phone."

"You're quite pleased with yourself," Nora said.

"It's not every day I get to rescue a woman in distress and watch a baby being born."

"You really are a Renaissance man. Maybe the next fairy book should feature you!"

CHAPTER SIXTY-THREE

"But tell of days in goodness spent,
A mind at peace with all below."
— George Gordon Byron, *She Walks in Beauty*

Monday, 1st November

11:30 AM

Nora had never seen Val drive so slowly or so carefully. They were on their way home to Ramsey Lodge. She was still sore, but she hardly noticed her discomfort when she held Sean.

The weekend had been filled with visitors, and she'd had to give Ian a formal statement at one point, all while learning to breast-feed. There had been several calls from Connecticut, and she'd reassured her mother that she and the baby were fine. Amelia and Roger were to keep their plane tickets as planned. "Don't even think of christening that baby until I get there," her mother had threatened.

At night, when she had finally had time alone, Nora had reflected on all that had happened in the past days. She had still been able to feel the icy cold of the lake and knew how close she and her child had come to dying. Every time she had held the baby, she had felt grateful for his presence.

Val's car pulled up in front of Ramsey Lodge with its precious cargo. Nora was certain that with Simon totally cleared, business would begin to pick up again. The public had a short attention span, and people would be looking for the next scandal. She glanced over her shoulder at her son, sleeping peacefully in his car seat in the back. He wore a hand-knitted, blue-and-white sweater and hat that Agnes had brought to the hospital during the weekend.

"It won't itch or scratch his skin," Agnes had purred, holding the infant. "He's a lovely bairn, Nora."

"I'll bring him home from the hospital in it," Nora had promised, and she'd kept her word.

Val undid her seat belt. "You get yourself out; I'll take Sean. We'll get you both settled, and Simon can help me unload your stuff."

"Yes, Auntie Val," Nora beamed. She hauled herself out of the front seat and stood for a moment, taking in the comforting sight of the lodge. The day was crisp and cool, the leaves almost gone from the trees. She still wore maternity clothes—no comfy jeans yet—but that would change. Already, the swelling in her hands and feet had gone down. Slowly, Nora was getting back to normal. Then she looked at her sleeping child in the carrier in Val's hand and knew she had to redefine what normal meant.

She followed Val into the hallway. Val turned to go through the dining room.

"Surprise!" Simon yelled the loudest, accompanied by Agnes, Sally and the Barnum girls. Maeve stood by the doorway. Blue streamers and balloons hung in one corner of the dining room over a table piled with presents in baby paper.

Nora was startled by the noise, but it didn't faze the baby, who slept on. Val deposited the carrier on top of an empty table, and the women rushed over to coo over the infant.

"A baby shower? You didn't warn me," Nora chided Val.

"It's called a surprise, Yankee." Val laughed and pointed to the chair by the laden table. "Your throne, madam."

"We planned to do this ages ago," Kate explained. "But it seemed the timing kept going wrong with Simon being hauled into the police station. That's in the past. This is about the future." She motioned to Simon.

He and Maeve carried in a dresser, a vintage piece painted a creamy yellow with a pale green glaze over it, sporting new hardware. A thick, covered pad with sloped sides was attached to its top, transforming it into a changing table.

"Did you do this?" Nora asked Kate, who nodded, eyes shining. "No wonder you've been disappearing into your workshop. It's beautiful." She admired the way the drawers slid out easily and knew the time and effort Kate had put into restoring the piece.

"The cover can be changed and thrown in the wash," Kate explained. "There are two more in a drawer." She pulled open a drawer, her engagement ring twinkling. "And the pad itself is waterproof, so you can wipe it clean."

"More presents!" Val declared, pushing a carton in front of Nora. The women pulled their chairs closer and sat down.

Simon lounged in the doorway. "Don't mind me, I'm the token male."

"Apparently my mother was in on this," Nora said, opening a carton that had been shipped from Connecticut and contained several wrapped boxes. She opened the first and gasped as she pulled out an ivory christening dress, her smile broadening. "This has been in the McAllister family for decades. My mother and her brother wore it, and I did, too."

Everyone admired the pin-tucked batiste gown, carefully wrapped in acid-free tissue paper, complete with matching hat and booties. Nora's mother had threaded thin, blue satin ribbons through the hat and had tied blue bows on the booties and on the shoulders of the gown. A note pinned to it read:

Not to be used until Grandma arrives

A smaller box in the same carton proved to be a baby book from Nora's stepsister, Claire. Roger's daughter was finishing up grad school in Connecticut. "She's a lovely girl, lost her mother when she was twelve," Nora explained. "Roger did a great job raising her. She's going to teach English and poetry."

The Barnum girls passed around a tray of punch and platters of warm scones and finger sandwiches. Darby sniffed every box and carton and settled down next to Nora to await tidbits. Nora continued to open her gifts, feeling swaddled in a warm and friendly cocoon as her baby slept on.

Maeve and the Barnum girls had chipped in for a clock for the baby's room from the Beatrix Potter shop. It featured Peter Rabbit stuck in a green watering can. Agnes and Sally had bought a set of Peter Rabbit books from the same source. A tiny box revealed a silver teething ring, sent by Janet Wallace, Bryn's mother. Nora looked to Val.

"She wanted to," Val said. "She's been bugging me for yonks to let her know when you were going to have a shower."

Nora opened Val's gift next. A textile artist, Val had made a blanket and matching wall hanging. Strips of pale-blue and green velvet and chenille were interwoven with bits of material containing the Potter characters. The blanket was lined in a warm fleece; the wall art had loops across the top for hanging and pockets for toys and accessories. "Just wonderful, Val," Nora told her friend.

"Not every baby has two Val Rogan originals," Val said.

Just as Nora reached for the last small box, Simon and Kate disappeared. "Back in a jiff," Simon promised.

Nora opened a small box and was delighted to find a silver infant spoon and fork set. A ripple of surprise went through her when she read the card:

Best wishes for a healthy boy, Declan Barnes

CHAPTER SIXTY-THREE

Nora looked at Val, one eyebrow raised.

Val shrugged. "He came into the cooperative to ask how you were doing, and I was working on your blanket. I mentioned getting it done for the shower and coming to see you. The next week he dropped this off and asked me to bring it to you."

Nora sat back and sipped her punch as the women admired her gifts. She wondered what Simon would make of this last gift. She felt sheepish but also ridiculously pleased.

When Simon and Kate reappeared, they carried a large object between them, covered in an old sheet he obviously used as a drop cloth, splattered with different colors of paint. They set it in front of Nora.

"Goodness, what's all this?" Nora asked.

"This is my contribution, on loan," Simon said. With a flourish he pulled the sheet off a vintage oak cradle, large enough to hold her baby for months at her bedside. The bottom was caned and had a thick mattress and bumpers, both covered in the Potter pattern.

"It's been in the Ramsey family for years," Kate explained. "Simon and I both used it."

"Hard to picture you fitting in that, Simon," Val remarked, sparking a round of laughter.

"Just so you know, it was a bugger to re-cane that," Simon said with good humor.

Another round of laughter. Nora's eyes filled with tears. "You're so good to me. Thank you all, for everything. I'm so very grateful."

11:40 AM

Somehow, and he wasn't quite certain how, Nora Tierney had

managed again to come out on top of things and in the spotlight, Tony Warner mused, turning on his computer at *People and Places.*

He wasn't too unhappy. He'd gone back to Oxford with Nora's exclusive interview on his laptop. The story of her confronting a murderer, her close call with death and the subsequent emergency delivery were all documented, along with a nice choice of photographs. He could see it winning a few awards. When he'd returned to Oxford, Old Jenks had talked about moving him to a larger office.

His boss had certainly been thrilled, but not as thrilled as Tony had been on meeting Nora's replacement. A slim woman who wore pearls to work every day, she turned out to be a delightful lass whose grandmother had been a close friend of Princess Margaret's. Best of all, she admired his prose.

11:50 AM

Cook was settling into a new routine, one she shared more and more with Antonia as the entire household became more casual. She was glad Sommer insisted Robbie stay at the Hall for a while as they thought things through. She and Antonia fussed over the distraught youth, who struggled to comprehend his mother's actions and to accept that Edmunde was his father.

Sommer had donated his entire rare plant collection to the Kendal Museum, a gesture of which Cook had very much approved. Two new nurses had been hired to alternate days to care for the brothers. Both seemed capable, although they complained to Cook that Edmunde gave them a difficult time.

The police had come to interview Edmunde, but he had been

his usual recalcitrant self, grunting and refusing to answer questions. Antonia confided to Cook that the superintendent had said the Crown Prosecution Service was still deciding whether to press charges against Edmunde. No one had ever seen him in the kitchen, and there was no evidence against him other than Gillian's accusation that he was the instrument in Keith's death.

"I refuse to believe any parent could willfully murder his or her own child," Antonia declared over tea to Cook right after the accusation came out.

"Course, that must have been what Gillian wished had happened," Cook agreed. Privately, Cook felt Edmunde was exactly the kind of person who could kill, even if it was with the misguided notion that he was fulfilling a promise to Gillian while eliminating the person he blamed for Julia's death. Rowley's flask had tested positive for the poison, as had the whiskey bottle found in his garbage pile, but the only fingerprints clear enough to decipher on either belonged to Daniel.

Cook still carried guilt. If Edmunde had been able to manage the elevator to the kitchen—and why wouldn't he have been, with a toggle switch to help him maneuver in that mechanical chair—if only she'd heard him, she might have been able to prevent Keith's death.

One of the first chores she'd given Robbie to keep him busy was to install a device on the elevator that rang in her bedroom when someone used it. Now she jumped up several times a day at the sound of the bell to find one of the nurses in the kitchen, but Cook felt it was a small price to pay for being on guard.

11:55 AM

The nurse settled Edmunde in his chair by the window, arranged a lap robe over his legs and opened the curtains. She believed in independence, and to that end she left his water jug on his nightstand next to an old-fashioned school bell.

"If you get thirsty, Mr. Edmunde, just toggle over here and help yourself," she said, checking the time on her watch. "I'll be with Mr. S next. Ring the bell if you really need me."

She closed the door behind her, and Edmunde looked at the bell. As if. He'd not rung it yet and had no plans to, ever. She could rot in hell, treating him like an imbecile.

With his left hand, he used the toggle to wheel closer to the window, giving him a clearer view of the chapel and the graveyard. He stared at Julia's headstone, ignoring the fresh plot next to it. He remembered his dark hand moving over her creamy skin and the way her laughter sounded like a hundred tinkling bells.

And then there had been Gillian, with her quiet reserve. He had been the one to kindle the passion in her dark eyes. She had given him moments when he'd been able to forget Julia was dead.

He looked down at his hands. One gripped the arm of his chair; the other lay idle, curled in his lap. How many more years of this solitude could he take, alone with his raging thoughts and broken body, while the two women he'd loved were both lost to him?

Edmunde mumbled "No!" and smacked his good hand on the armrest. He turned from the window. His bed looked inviting; the clean, cool sheets beckoned. He rolled over to his bed and, opening the nightstand drawer, took out a bottle of paracetamol. It took him four attempts to snap off the cap with one hand. Pouring the contents into his lap, he picked out the smaller sleeping pills mixed in with the mild painkiller. He'd been hoarding these for months, setting them aside on the nights he felt exhausted enough not to need them to sleep. A few stuck together from being in his mouth until the nurse left, but most of them had dried out nicely.

There were at least thirty of them, and he judged that would be enough. Scooping them up, he popped the handful into his mouth, and when some fell out, he picked them up and stuffed them back in. He leaned forward to drink from the straw. At least this bitch kept his water iced, the way he liked it.

Edmunde choked from drinking too fast, gagging as some of the pills stuck in his throat. He forced himself to drink more, swallowing and swallowing until the last tiny pill went into his stomach.

Looking up, he saw his reflection in the mirror that hung over his bureau across the room. He loathed the distorted face that looked back at him, hated the shriveled man he'd become. He wanted to throw the jug into the mirror, make it break into a million little pieces to match his shattered life.

Wheeling back over to the window, Edmunde stared once again at Julia's grave. He'd never been religious, and he did not believe in an afterlife, which he perceived as the pathetic grasping of humanity to soften the blow of facing nonexistence. But now, waiting for the pills to make his head heavy with sleep, he prayed that somewhere, Julia waited for him.

2 PM

Simon knocked softly on Nora's door.

"Come in. He's awake and guzzling," she called.

Nora sat in her chair in the alcove, feeding Sean. Simon took

THE GREEN REMAINS

in the maternal picture as she threw a receiving blanket over her exposed breast and shoulder. "He's gotten the hang of this all right, but I swear I feel like a human filling station," she said. Her eyes looked heavy from lack of sleep, but otherwise she looked like her old self.

Simon looked at the furniture set in place, the stack of gifts waiting to be put away. He had had no idea that babies needed so much gear.

"Val said she picked up what you needed from your storage unit," Simon explained. "Want me to bring it in here? It's tiny. She and Kate have gone to Kendal to pick up the pram your mother ordered."

"They've become fast friends. I may get jealous." Nora picked up the corner of the blanket. "No, he's on his second side and falling asleep. I'll come out in a minute." Her smile was broad. "I have a feeling I'll need to remind myself that life exists outside of this room."

"I'll see you in my kitchen, then," Simon said and withdrew, making his way across the hall to his rooms.

He was nervous. He couldn't wait to give Nora his gift, but he wanted to relish the moment. Simon stood by his kitchen window, looking out across the fallow garden to the lake. So much had happened, and he had no idea where he stood with Nora. Deep down inside where he didn't want to examine it too closely lay the suspicion that they would always be good friends but nothing more. The thought depressed him.

Simon entered his studio, where the painting stood on its easel, covered with a drop cloth. It was based on a Carl Larsson domestic scene, showing the back of a woman wearing a long blue-and-white dress, hair pinned up, holding a watering can over a bright-red rose. The rose sat on a stand in front of a large paned window with ornately painted cabinets below it. Behind the woman stood a young boy, waiting to be noticed, holding his offering of a handful of little purple flowers. On the windowsill, a puppet dressed in a suit and top hat watched the scene.

Simon had painted over the poisonous plant he had originally included with an image similar to the rose in Larsson's work. He didn't intend to tell Nora that the people depicted were the artist's wife and son. He wanted her to enjoy it purely for the image, a representation of things to come and of a son's love for his mother. Looking at it now, he wondered why he'd chosen this particular scene. If the painting represented Nora and Sean, did that make him the puppet?

No, that was unfair. Nora had always been honest about not being ready for a committed relationship. Still, he'd much prefer to be the rose, waiting to bloom in their lives.

2:15 PM

Nora thought she might get a snack while her baby slept. Her eating for two certainly hadn't stopped, although her stomach had deflated quite a bit. She shook her hair out of its ponytail and ran a brush through it.

When she reached Simon's door, it was open. So was his refrigerator, as he perused the contents.

"Come in. Want some juice?" At Nora's nod he added, "Cran-apple or orange?"

"Cran-apple, please. Any cheese to go with that?"

"Hungry again?" Simon laughed. "I've got white cheddar and grapes, or I could go into the kitchen and poke around."

"No, cheese and grapes are fine." While Simon set out their snack, she looked out at the lake. It had stopped raining, and the afternoon promised to be sunny, though cool.

"I think I'll take Sean for a walk when the girls get back with the new pram. I've heard fresh air tires babies out."

Simon sliced cheese. "I know you're sleep deprived."

"All part of the game. I'm fortunate not to have a day job right now. I can't wait to see the bound book, though." She watched a sunbeam light up the water; sparse clouds reflected on the surface. "It's hard to believe everything that's gone on this past month, and I'm sitting here looking at the same lake Arthur Ransome rowed. It's still beautiful to me," she said.

"His boat is on display at the Windermere Steamboat Museum. Would you like to see it?" Simon asked. "Here, come and eat."

Nora moved to the table and sat down. "Thanks, I'm ravenous." She chewed a grape and reached for a chunk of cheese. "That sounds like fun. Maybe when my mother and Roger are here, I can leave the baby for an afternoon." She didn't mention she'd need to pump breast milk to do this. Simon seemed a bit squeamish about the intimate details of life with an infant.

"Here's your package." Simon handed her a small box wrapped in brown paper.

"Actually, this is for you," Nora said, her eyes lighting up as she tore off the brown paper. Val had tied a gold ribbon around the rectangular box inside. She handed the box to Simon. "It's a small thank you for saving us. And don't tell me I didn't have to—" she added as he opened his mouth to protest. "I wanted to."

She watched him open the box. Carefully nestled in tissue paper lay a well-preserved book, elegantly bound in green leather, its pages with gilt paper edgings.

Simon opened the book and read the title aloud: "*The Poetic Works of William Wordsworth.*" He looked at the publication date. "1832."

Nora took the book from him and closed it, then directed

his attention to the long edge and carefully fanned the pages. A painting of Wordsworth's Dove Cottage sprang into view.

Simon leaned forward. "A fore-edge painting! Brilliant! Wherever did you find this?"

Nora was pleased at Simon's delight. "My father had a small collection that's now mine. This one belongs with you."

Simon came around the table and wrapped Nora in a huge hug. They drew apart, and he pressed his lips to her forehead. "I will always treasure this."

Nora hugged him again. She broke the embrace before it could be something more.

Simon fanned the pages once more, and the painting came into view again. He put it carefully in its box and held out his hands to her. "Turnaround's fair play. Come with me, Mother Goose."

Nora frowned as she rose. "Makes me sound like a brood hen, Simon." He laughed, and Nora followed him into his studio.

With a flourish, Simon drew the sheet off his easel. Standing on it was a painting that reminded Nora of Carl Larsson's technique and style. It was an indoor scene of a woman watering a rose, while a small, blond boy behind her held a bunch of violets, waiting for her to turn around and notice him. "It's beautiful, Simon." She inspected it carefully and saw his signature in the lower corner. "I love that you did this for me."

Simon looked happy. "There's plenty of wall space in your room."

Nora stood on tiptoe and threw her arms around his neck to kiss his cheek. She rested her head on his shoulder a moment. "It's absolutely wonderful. Thank you."

The buzzer sounded at Simon's door, and Nora broke away. Likely Maeve with her impeccable timing. Or Kate and Val, wanting help with the pram.

Nora stayed to examine the painting and heard Simon slide his door open. Then a man's voice spoke.

"Hallo! The gal out front, Maeve, directed me here."

Surely not? A thrill shot through her as she moved out of the studio and into the kitchen where Declan Barnes stood talking with Simon.

"Hi there, Mum," he greeted Nora. "You look wonderful. I was just telling Simon I came to clear up that embezzlement business with Glenn Hackney."

"What business?" Nora was puzzled. Declan looked taller than she recalled, and his smile was wider. She despaired that she wore her navy maternity dress.

"When he got back to Oxford, there was a full audit of the travel agency books slated for the following week. Apparently, the befuddled Edgar Worth had a moment of common sense and ordered the audit himself. Glenn didn't come to work the next morning and seems to have disappeared."

"You're kidding," Simon said.

"Val always said he was smarmy," Nora added. "Any leads?"

"There was a sighting at the Barcelona airport," Declan explained.

Nora ignored Simon's frown. "Nothing else?"

"We think he's a con man and embezzler known as Macavity."

Nora nodded. "The mystery cat—never know where they'll find him."

Declan said, "I'm going to see if he gave the Clarendons any hint of his plans."

It sounded plausible enough, but Nora wondered why he hadn't just called the Clarendons from Oxford.

"So where's the baby, Nora?" Declan asked. His smile lit up his eyes.

Nora led the way to her room and into the alcove. The baby lay on his back, his tiny arms thrust out on either side of his head. He made sucking motions with his mouth. In just a few days, his face had filled out, and there was more of his downy red-blonde hair.

Declan looked from the baby to Nora and back. "Don't see much of the biological dad here. This baby's all Tierney," he pronounced.

Nora was ridiculously pleased. "He does have Paul's eyebrows," she pointed out. "Would you like to hold him?"

"Later. My gran always said to never wake a sleeping babe," Declan explained. "I'll be here for a few days, and I'd love to hold him when he's awake."

"Wonderful," Nora proclaimed. "Where are you staying?"

"Right here," Declan said. He turned to Simon. "Maeve said you had vacancies."

Simon cleared his throat. "Of course," he said.

Simon managed to sound gracious without meaning it. Only someone who knew Simon as well as Nora did would know he was not terribly pleased that Declan Barnes would be around for several days.

But Nora was delighted.

ACKNOWLEDGMENTS

England's Lake District is special to me. It comprises almost nine hundred square miles of national park, the largest such area in England and Wales, all lying within the county of Cumbria. It is the most picturesque area I've seen in England, with the bluest skies and fluffiest clouds, and it contains England's highest mountain, Scafell Pike, and its largest lake, Windermere. There are shallow tarns, rising fells, sparkling ghylls and every species of tree found in Britain in its woodlands. The area's unparalleled beauty beckons lovers of nature: hikers and campers, fisherman and boaters, artists and writers.

Ramsey Lodge and Clarendon Hall and all of my characters are fictional, yet they inhabit a very real area. Having spent time in the village of Bowness-on-Windermere and its neighboring town of Windermere, I have tried my best to describe the area accurately; any errors are my own.

I am grateful for the kind assistance of Steve Sharpe, Cumbrian South Lakes police officer (retired), who patiently answered my questions about everything from policing to the weather, and his help has been invaluable, as has that of Evelyn Blatchley. I hope to thank them in person one day.

My sincere thanks extend to so many others, especially: Sgt. John Stephens, Lakes Neighbourhood Policing Team, Windermere; the Screw Iowa gals: Mariana Damon, Nina Romano, Lauren Small and Melissa Westemeier; readers Maggie Mendus, Marianne Haycock and Pat Gulley; fellow writers and colleagues at Coastal Carolina Mystery Writers, Sisters in Crime and Writers Read. Special thanks to Lauren Small at Bridle Path Press for her vision and support.

I can't offer enough gratitude to friends and family for their love and encouragement: Barb and Mike Jancovic; the Minnesota Graffs; my two favorite librarians, Matthew and Kimberly Graff; and the newly minted Burk family: Sean, Robin, Mara, Austin and Kaylyn.

To Giordana Segneri: Your talents shape and define my vision. It is a continued pleasure to work with you—grazie mille!

Love to my mother, Kathleen Travia; and always, looking outward together in the same direction, my heart to Arthur.

About the Author

M. K. Graff is the author of poetry, fiction and nonfiction. She wrote throughout a successful nursing career, including feature articles for New York's edition of *Nursing Spectrum*; her background includes working in television and motion pictures on scripts and on set for medical scenes. For seven years, Graff conducted interviews and wrote feature articles for *Mystery Review* magazine before studying literature at Oxford University, which inspired the setting for the first Nora Tierney mystery, *The Blue Virgin*. She has taught creative writing and memoir and heads the North Carolina Writers Read workshop for adults and young authors. A founding member of the Screw Iowa! Writers Group, Graff is co-author of the group's guide for writers, *Writing in a Changing World*. She also started the Coastal Carolina Mystery Writers group and is a member of Sisters in Crime. Her creative nonfiction has most recently appeared in *Southern Women's Review*. *The Green Remains* is Graff's second novel in the Nora Tierney mystery series.

CPSIA information can be obtained at www.ICGtesting.com
Printed in the USA
BVOW070032160113

310673BV00001B/2/P